CW01425622

LIGHTS OUT

Book 1: After The Silence

DEVON C. FORD

Copyright © 2021 by Devon C. Ford

All rights reserved.

No part of this book may be reproduced in any form or by any electronic or mechanical means, including information storage and retrieval systems, without written permission from the author, except for the use of brief quotations in a book review.

Any unauthorised use of the material or artwork contained within this publication is prohibited unless express written authority is obtained from the author.

Any scanning, uploading, or distribution of this book without permission is theft of the author's intellectual property.

www.devoncford.com

Cover design by Claire @spurwingcreative

Dedicated to procrastination on other projects with deadlines, without whom this book would not exist.

AFTER THE SILENCE
BOOK 1

LIGHTS OUT

DEVON C FORD

PROLOGUE

I t wasn't like the whistling of falling bombs that television had mentally prepared her for. No gathering scream of ordnance falling from a darkening sky warned them of their impending doom. Absent were the air raid sirens or the shouts of warning, and even if those cautionary sounds had played, there would have been nowhere to go that was safe. No underground shelters existed there, at least not ones for the regular people housed in their tiny boxes and tents above ground, and only distance from the target could hope to offer any form of salvation.

The first impact rocked them all. She didn't know what it was, but it could have been anything from a rocket to a falling satellite as far as her knowledge of such things went.

The man with them would know, she thought, but he was frantic. Frantically trying to get her to move. Yelling in her face and shaking her shoulders as behind him a massive, blossoming display of fire and death grew upwards like the lighting of the biggest Christmas tree she had ever seen.

She stared in shock, mesmerised by the hideous beauty of the destruction, but such introspective moments can only last so long.

With a particularly hard shake of her shoulder – strong enough to yank her head around atop her neck like a car accident would – she focused on his face and with the return to the moment came the sounds around her.

The dull bass of the rolling boom from the explosion was felt more than heard, but the screams were far too audible for her liking. She winced, trying to shut out the sounds and concentrate on anything else.

Still, she couldn't make out the words he was yelling. She only saw his lips moving on his dirt-streaked face, while at her left leg a dog was barking in fear and confusion suggesting aggression.

She looked down at the dog. Her dog. She knew he wasn't aggressive, at least he never had been unless he had to be, but he was barking so loudly that she couldn't think.

He shook her again, hard this time with both hands so that the gun strapped to him bashed her painfully in the leg with the dangerous end.

"Where is she?" he screamed.

She couldn't understand why he was angry with her, but she complied and pointed a shaky hand in the direction of a low building.

He grabbed that hand, dragging her along behind him and by process the dog after her, so they formed a chain of three very different living creatures.

Another impact, this time flashing so brightly that the dark evening was temporarily turned into daytime for the briefest of moments. The dark returned, like a dimmer switch being wound down fast, and the darkness seemed that little bit darker afterwards. She didn't know why, something about the cones in her eyes, her brain tried to tell her, as if irrelevant facts could help her understand what was going on.

She faltered, but his iron grip on her hand and the speed at which he was dragging them all made her stumble and scrape her knee on the rough ground through the dirty jeans she wore. She gave a yelp of pain, fighting back a sob that had more to do with fear than injury, but he dragged her up and onwards relentlessly.

The dog offered no such audible protest, but he followed as dutifully and loyally as he always did.

He released her hand when they reached the row of tiny buildings that had appeared to be just one building then braced his feet and stamped out to splinter the door off weak, flimsy hinges. It bounced back at him, wobbling violently and sending a message to her brain to imagine the noise it made over the insane cacophony assaulting her ears.

She was inside, face down on the bed but alive. She was trying to get up, but she seemed dazed like she was drunk or had suffered a blow to the head. Shock and confusion. The paralysis of fear.

He yelled again, the words still not translating in her mind, as he dragged the prone form to her feet and gave instructions for them to link hands and not let go.

She had her own hand placed firmly on the belt or straps of the equipment he was wearing. The tough material holding ammunition and bandages. That material chafed her skin as he set off, dragging two females and a dog behind him as he kept the frightening weapon tucked into his shoulder as if ready to use it on the people they had been living alongside.

"Wait!" she yelled, not hearing her own words but he clearly had, because he stopped and spun back to her. She turned herself, looking back to another shed opposite the one they had just forced open, to see a woman in long skirts struggling out of the door gripping a bag in one hand and the forearm of a child in the other.

The woman saw them, stumbled and dragged herself and the child over to join the line, and they linked up to set off in search of safety.

"Come on!" he bawled. "Stay with me! Don't let go!"

She complied, but it sounded to her more like he was saying those things to hype himself up rather than to inform them.

All around them were flames and screaming, but their objective ahead was devoid of destruction. She saw the neat lines of dark green trucks under an expanse of camouflage netting erected on metal poles, all parked exactly where they were supposed to be because scary men and women yelled at others if it wasn't done properly. She didn't see the difference or even the point in lines being almost straight or perfectly straight, but right then she wasn't even sure she was still alive or not.

A man blocked their path, yelling and babbling with his hands held together in front of him. The leader of their multi-organism caterpillar snaked to go around him, but the pleading man turned to lift a child no older than five or six.

It was his only shot, she thought, to use a child as a passport to safety, and it worked. The man and child joined their escape, running alongside her as the man cried aloud, although the child was oddly silent and calm, as if it was waiting to see what would happen before it could know how to react to it.

A hundred paces from the dark silhouettes of the trucks,

the world beyond them erupted into yet more artificial daylight.

The silhouettes were emblazoned on her eyeballs with such clarity it was almost as beautiful as the fireball she had watched climb into the sky. The sharp lines of the uncomfortable trucks were shown to her in crystal clarity in the moments before the wave of boiling air thumped into them.

"Down!" the man leading them yelled, only his words were swallowed by the rolling thunder that followed the bright explosion as if the two events were locked in a close game of chase.

Her breath was taken away by the punch of heat, so when she tried to speak, she only choked on what felt like exhaust gases.

He was already up, grabbing each of them in turn and looking at them before shoving and yelling until they were all back in a line which he then led uphill away from the burning vehicle yard and into the darkness that now surrounded the camp.

She couldn't breathe. She was so stunned and exhausted by what she had just witnessed, by what she had lived through, as though some violent video game had immersed her too deeply in the make-believe world in which she was playing a part. He legs didn't want to work, and every laboured step she took away from the burning carnage put her one step closer to passing out.

She didn't drop first. That medal went to the man who still carried the child clinging to him like an infant monkey would grip the fur of its mother during perilous tree climbs.

"Please... I can't... I can't..." he sobbed, landing on his backside and rocking back and forth as though he were comforting the child and not the other way around.

"We can't stay here. We're too exposed."

She looked at the man who spoke, resplendent and intimidating in his full battle gear, minus the bulky helmet. She knew he was right. Whatever had befallen their unhappy colony was far from over, as more explosions shook the ground under their boots.

She stood, not realising she had even sunk to her knees when they had been forced to halt their escape. She dusted unseen dirt from her knees as if the gesture would make any real difference, but she knew a reflex when it happened. She ignored it. She stood tall and nodded at their unelected leader to signify that she was ready.

They moved, climbing the low hill into total darkness with only their backs illuminated by the orange glow of the burning camp. More had joined them, seeing their escape from the bombs and flames, so they now led a drawn-out snake of human detritus over the hill and far away from danger.

From that specific danger, at least.

CHAPTER ONE

Two weeks earlier
Four days before the collapse
Shaun

His flight landed at Edinburgh airport in just enough time for him to make it to the small service that culminated in his father's cremation. It was attended by precisely nobody who would admit to being the man's friend. After a rushed, uncomfortable flight and an argument over the availability of an appropriate hire car, Shaun Taylor had arrived at the crematorium blanketed in fog to bid farewell to a man he hadn't seen in years.

It was duty more than love that summoned him. A legal duty to exercise the man's last will and testament.

After shoehorning himself behind the wheel of a Ford Fiesta, he had made the journey east from the airport to arrive late. Making an angry but impassioned plea for them to hold proceedings all of five minutes, he changed into the black suit that had grown just a little snug since the last funeral he had attended.

He listened to a man of God he didn't know say things about a man that none of them really knew, heard a few passages from the bible that bore no real relevance to the man he hadn't seen in close to two decades, then watched as the cheap, pine box moved along squeaking rollers to go beyond the purple velvet curtain.

And that was that.

He was asked if he wanted his father's remains to spread his ashes somewhere important, but he explained that he'd already made the arrangements with the local authority over the telephone.

His father's remains were to be buried in a public plot at minimal expense, and they had kindly agreed to defer the payment for it all until such time as the man's estate had been settled.

Job done, Shaun thanked the strangers for their kindness and squeezed back into the tiny car to find where his father had been living.

———

"Your destination is on the left," the mapping on his phone told him. He slowed, looking left at a low, stone wall and miles of misty fields rolling beyond.

"Well, it bloody isn't," he muttered to himself in complaint. With a sigh of tired annoyance he stopped, looking up to check his mirrors in case he was blocking the road for any other motorist, then remembered that he hadn't seen another car for miles.

Tipping out the brown envelope onto the passenger seat,

he saw the house keys fall first. He saw the faded, battered, leather key fob with the Ford logo barely visible on it, and paused. He'd seen that key fob when it was brand new, when it came with the shiny, green Cortina as a complimentary gift from the dealership, and he still recalled the smell of the fresh leather as a young boy when he was permitted to stand on the rear seats and look out of the windows as they drove.

Disregarding the keys and the memories they brought back, Shaun pulled out the estate agent's information pack on the drab cottage to see if he could recognise the surrounding and place where he was in relation to it.

Going one step further, he found directions written on the pack and took a few moments to figure out how they could help him.

With a better idea of where he had to be, Shaun turned on the radio for company while he drove.

"More from your regional stations later," the voice on the radio said. Something in his tone made Shaun think that either the preceding story or the one to come had been grave news. "The International Space Station programme is facing further criticisms, this time from Russia for the continued sanctions against China by the United States and parts of Europe. This follows recent difficulties that saw Russia's involvement put at risk last year over similar issues concerning political tensions between themselves and the United States. Now, if you want to know more about the ISS and who is currently there, you can go to our website and see live images of the—"

He hit the off button, already bored of even the radio becoming host to yet more clickbait.

"Enough bloody problems down here," he grumbled as he drove.

Intermittent data signal reaching his phone made the job

harder, but eventually he turned down the correct unmarked track off the main road – such as it was without paint markings or even a second carriageway – and bumped the little car over the rutted tracks as the overgrown bushes scraped along the dark paintwork.

Shaun Taylor's father's house was the epitome of the man himself.

It stood alone; grey and uninviting, and everything about it was miserable. Shaun was so put off, so daunted by the prospect of entering, that he killed the engine and just looked at the place through the windscreen that slowly grew obscured with the permanent raindrops filling the Scottish air.

When the automated wipers kicked in, he jumped, jolted from his trance by the outside stimulus, and shook his head to clear the fog inside his mind.

Snatching up the keys and paperwork, he retrieved his carry-on from the back seat and walked up to the closed wooden gate hanging limply from rusted hinges.

The bottom of the wood scraped on the uneven flagstone of the path, forcing him to lift it and squeeze past. The stones beneath his feet were slick with a layer of wet grime as if nature had already begun the process of reclaiming the abandoned cottage, which made him have to take short, careful steps towards the front door, like walking on a layer of ice.

Slotting the heavy deadlock key into the hole, he turned it, wiggling the handle to convince the lock to turn. The front door, made of oak panels much older than he was, yielded eventually. The wood had swollen in the damp through not being used, and he had to apply some pressure from his shoulder to force it wide enough to get inside.

The door admitted him directly into the front room. Dark carpet showed signs of wear in two directions: one to the chair beside the fire and the ancient television set, and one towards the kitchen beyond.

It seemed smaller somehow on the inside than it appeared externally, being basically a two-up two-down with low ceilings and very little natural light through the tiny windows.

The place was dusty and smelled of damp, and another smell permeated the room that he could place immediately. His eyes were drawn to the old armchair, with the right armrest threadbare and the seat heavily stained. Shaun knew what that stain meant. He had been told the circumstances of his father's death and closed his eyes at the thought of the man, once so strong and stubborn, sitting dead in that chair for days before someone discovered him.

The open fireplace, scorch marks spreading out over the tattered, old hearth rug, smelled of wet wood and charcoal. Standing in the doorway, he assessed the sorry state of his father's existence, and behind him the ominous roll of distant thunder served as a reminder to shut the front door and spoke of further horrors he might discover there.

The kitchen was worse. The man seemed to own a pathetic collection of assorted crockery, cutlery and glassware, and the only uniform items were the empty bottles of unbranded dark rum that lined the worktops. He let out an involuntary huff of amusement at the sight, knowing that the suspension of alcohol purchases from the nearest small supermarket had been the very reason he'd even been discovered.

He almost cleaned up, feeling the urge to remove his jacket and roll up his sleeves to begin washing up, but he didn't feel the need given how far gone the place was. He didn't even think he'd be able to make a dent in it.

The two rooms upstairs were no better, with boxes and newspapers stacked high just inside the door to leave only enough room to make it to the one side of the bed that was accessible.

Shaun grimaced at that sight, knowing that he would have to either get back in the tiny hire car and drive for miles or else brave sleeping in the filthy sheets. The bathroom was the deciding factor. The stench of ammonia was so strong that he couldn't even bring himself to peer into the bowl.

Walking back down the narrow, creaking stairs, he pulled up the collar of his jacket and shot one last forlorn look at the stained armchair.

"How the hell did you end up like this, old man?" he asked the chair sadly, knowing the answer but wishing it had been the responsibility of someone else to prevent what had happened from happening the way it had.

Not even bothering to lock the door, he pulled it closed behind him and threw his carry-on onto the back seat again. Heading back towards civilisation, he was forced to open the driver's side window and admit some flowing fresh air in spite of the rain that was beginning to fall heavily, because that smell just wouldn't leave him alone.

Had he been anywhere else, he would have been able to stop and book a hotel from a choice of venues, all from the safety and comfort of his phone. He wouldn't even have needed to pull his debit card from his wallet to complete the transactions, because all of his payment details were stored and ready to authorise with just his face as the required proof.

He didn't really like that, not even for all the ease it provided. He was one of those people who used to recall telephone numbers like a rolodex. He remembered every account number, every PIN, every password, right up until the moment his fingerprint or his face took over and freed up all that brain space for useless information to take over,

Because he was now in what was effectively the 1970s, he was forced to drive miles west towards the juxtaposition of modern metropolis and ancient history that was Edinburgh.

Eventually finding a chain hotel offering a room at a barely affordable price, he bit the bullet and paid online before heading towards it.

———

"And it's just for three nights, Mister Taylor?" the very pretty but very young receptionist asked. Shaun smiled politely and nodded. He hoped by that time the cottage should be at least habitable.

"Are you here to watch the match?" she asked, forcing a frown to appear on his face.

"The Scotland versus England match at Murrayfield tomorrow?"

Shaun almost slapped a hand to his forehead, finally realising why the flights had been so expensive and hard to get, and why every hotel within a fifty-mile radius of the city was filled to capacity.

"No, I… I'm actually here because I buried my father today."

Her face dropped so much, showing abject horror for her unwitting callousness that he felt instantly sorry for her.

"It's not your fault, you weren't to know… it's just been a long day…"

The girl smiled at him sadly, holding up one finger and

reaching under the counter to come back up with three slips of paper.

"We give these out to customers who complain about things, but I think you need them more than anyone else," she said, handing over the complimentary slips entitling him to a set amount in the hotel's small bar-cum-restaurant.

Shaun smiled back at her, genuinely happy to receive a small token that told him someone recognised that he was having a shitty time.

Thanking her and taking the cheap, plastic key card in the awkward fold of cardboard, he listened to her instructions for how to get to his room before forgetting them instantly.

"Oh, does the room have a Yellow Pages?" he asked as an afterthought. She smiled at him, unsure if he was joking or not.

"Sorry, a what?"

"A Yellow Pages? Or any local directory?"

In answer she only gave an apologetic grimace and waved her phone in the air weakly.

As much as Shaun had been ready to adopt the new ways to pay for things, he hadn't realised that such a stable of his life was no longer a thing.

In an online, digital world, he'd still been analogue in so many ways. Just not as much as his father had been.

Taking advantage of the generosity, or the guilt, he used up two of the vouchers, ordering three beers and a burger. Given the option of waiting or having it brought to his room, he opted for laziness. It was only fair, he thought, seeing as how he'd been forced to spend over a hundred pounds on a thirty-five quid bed and breakfast just because thirty men wanted to run into each other at speed for over an hour.

His room was the same generic, bland attempt at classy he

found everywhere, but at least the mattress was large and firm.

Dropping his carry-on case on the weird little rack they provided in the room he opened it and pulled out his charger in anticipation of the twenty percent battery warning showing up on his phone.

Sitting at the desk or dressing table, he wasn't sure which it was supposed to be, he started googling what he needed.

"Skip... hire... near... me..." he mumbled out loud, peering down his nose at the screen as his thumbs tapped out the letters.

The top five results to come back were all paid advertisements, so he scrolled down until he found the first local company and hit the screen with his thumb to call them directly.

He explained his needs, explained the timeframe, and thanked the first person before hanging up and trying the next on the list.

On his fourth call he fell on better luck, finding someone who could provide what he needed the very next morning. Only, as always, there was a hiccup.

"Except I've only got the next size up from what you wanted available, unless you wanted to wait until Saturday."

Shaun fought the urge to groan or sigh or give any other indication that he knew he was being played for a fool. He needed it, and when it all worked out, in the end it was his father who was technically paying from the sale of the house.

"How much extra will th—"

"It's another eighty pounds before VAT," he was told, confirming to him that the desperation he gave off in his request had been met by opportunism. Supply and demand; the way of the world.

"That's fine. What time can you deliver it?"

"Early as you like. Seven okay?"

Shaun agreed, giving his card details over the phone the old fashioned way and paying the extortionate amount of cash requested in order to get somewhere to dump the disgusting contents of his father's house.

He hung up, checking his watch even though the time was displayed on the screen in front of his face, and wondered if they were killing the cow personally before making his burger.

"Cold food and warm bloody beer," he grumbled to himself, just as a knock at the door startled him.

Accepting the food and enjoying the warm smile he gave the awkward young man who hovered expecting extra money for taking his time in delivering the room service, Shaun returned to the desk and found that he was, in fact, correct.

The bottles of beer, each costing two hundred percent of what he would expect to pay in a supermarket, were covered in condensation. The burger, which looked nothing like it did on the menu picture, was cold and just looked depressed.

He ate it, washing it down with a cool beer, and brought up the map on his phone to check for the nearest supermarket where he could buy the cleaning products required to restore the cottage to something resembling habitable.

On his second beer by then, he went started to Google local cleaning companies and sent a few web forms requesting a quote for what he needed.

"I clear everything out first," he told himself out loud. "See how bad it is after that."

He knew he'd pay instead of scrubbing the filthy cottage himself, but he convinced himself he'd at least consider doing the hard work as a kind of penance.

With the third beer starting to flow, he considered a shower and an attempt to get some sleep, only the thirst was threatening him by then and he opted to go back down himself to collect more.

Handing over the last token and topping up with a contactless payment on his debit card, he took another three beers back to the room, drinking one in the lift on the way back up while it was still cold.

Back in the room he stripped off, considered the odd vestigial appliance in the room that was a fitted trouser press, and threw his suit over the back of the chair with the promise to himself that he'd fold it back neatly into the case the next morning.

Too mentally exhausted, and with the beers making his head swim, he lay on top of the covers and looked at his phone screen, opening up the calls list and hovering over a name as if in two minds whether to call.

The beers eventually made up his mind for him, and he tapped the screen before holding it to his ear and clearing his throat.

It was answered on the fifth ring, and the tone on the other end sounded tired and wary.

"Hello?"

"Hi…"

Silence hung between them, filled eventually by her voice so far away.

"Shaun, it's late. What do you need?"

"I… I just wanted to hear a friendly voice. One that wasn't Scottish at least," he said, chuckling his way through the weak jest.

She sighed, annoyed like she was sick of going over old ground.

"Shaun, you know you aren't supposed to contact me—"

"I buried him today. Well, cremated him…"

"Shaun… I'm sorry, I really am. Look, it's late and Lydia's just gone to bed and—"

"I was… I was hoping I could talk to her."

"Shaun, it's not a good idea… I'm sorry, you shouldn't have called. You can pick her up on the fifteenth like we'd arranged. Goodbye, Shaun."

The phone clicked, leaving him staring at it until it went black.

CHAPTER TWO

Four days before the collapse
Abbie

"Mum, have you seen my headphones?"

Abbie slammed the butter knife she was using to the worktop and looked up, eyes closed at the ceiling in her kitchen as she tried to remain calm.

"Do you mean your new headphones that you've had for less than a week?" she yelled back, grinding her teeth as she resumed the sandwich-making progress so aggressively that she tore the soft bread with the hard lump of butter. Growling in frustration, she threw the lump of torn bread and butter at the dog's bowl and started again with a new slice.

"*Have you seen them or not?*" Lydia yelled back, snapping at her mother with the savagery of a young girl not yet accustomed to the influx of hormonal anger. Abbie bit back her response for a few seconds and let out a breath before she spoke.

"No, I have not seen *your* headphones that cost two hundred pounds that are *your* responsibility to look after."

"No need to be like that," Lydia grumbled as she walked through the kitchen at a fast stomp to check the pockets of her jacket hung up by the front door. She let out a noise that, to Abbie at least, sounded a cross between utter relief and frustrated annoyance that she had been forced to fix an issue personally.

"Great. They're dead," she complained, throwing up her hands as if the world had ended at an inconvenient time. Abbie kept her eyes on the task of making a packed lunch she knew wouldn't be eaten anyway, but pointed with her left hand at her phone charging on the worktop.

"Plug them in there, you should have enough juice to get you to school and back."

Lydia did, huffing as she removed the plug from the phone.

"You've only got twelve percent battery," she informed her mother, as if she was unaware of the fact, despite plugging it in herself.

"I know. My charger upstairs isn't working. I'll charge it when I get to work."

She'd been lucky that there had been enough power left in it to make her alarm go off after she'd been up too late scrolling through the junk her social media was filled with. Truth was that the cause of her current insomnia was also to blame for her daughter's insufferable behaviour.

They both missed him, but only one of them understood why he couldn't be there with them. The phone call had broken her heart and angered her at the same time. She wanted him back, but she mourned for the man she knew and not the one that had called.

She finished the sandwich, spinning it on the chopping

board to cut the diagonal line across before sliding both halves onto a piece of tinfoil.

"Pick yourself some crisps," she instructed Lydia, already drained from the retort she hadn't even heard yet.

"Ugh, would it kill you to buy food that isn't just carbs?"

Abbie slammed her hands onto the worktop and snatched up the chopping board, throwing it into the sink and smashing the wine glass she'd left in there the night before.

"I dunno, would it kill you to be civil? How about *you* do the food shopping, hey? Seeing as you know everything and I know nothing, how about that? Why don't *you* plan the meals this week and work fifty hours? That way you can buy *me* organic fucking hummus and artisanal fucking carrot sticks."

Lydia had stood rooted to the spot as she exploded, eyes wide in shock and fear at the response she'd forced out of her mother. That look broke Abbie's heart, because although each of them was suffering and struggling to adapt to their new life, she was the parent, and she had the responsibility for both of them.

"Sorry," Lydia muttered, her eyes cast down to her feet on the tiled kitchen floor. Abbie said nothing but walked over and wrapped her daughter up in a hug she tried to resist at first but relented and melted into.

They stood there for a time, locked in a hug that conveyed how they felt about each other when words couldn't accurately convey it. Lydia tapped her back twice, speaking from the muffled confines of her mother's chest.

"Enough now, don't make me cry before school."

Abbie released her, sliding the plastic tub and sandwiches down the worktop towards her charging headphones.

"Don't want to mess up that makeup you aren't supposed to be wearing to school?" she added, lightening the tone, and changing the subject away from what they were both thinking.

"What's it to you, copper?" Lydia asked, smiling but fading into sadness at inadvertently using one of her father's favourite lines. Abbie smiled too, looking away so the emotion of the reminder didn't show too much.

Her husband had been the one who had made the sandwiches in the morning. He had been the one who made bad jokes and got all of them fired up for the day.

Only he had stopped doing that, and when he could barely drag himself out of bed in the mornings, the whole dynamic of their small family had moved on and moved apart.

He hadn't been getting up early because he'd been staying up late. That went hand in hand with the drinking, and while it had always been recreationally heavy at the weekends, it had never crept in during the week. When he started drinking spirits on school nights, when he'd still been drunk in the mornings and driving to work without breakfast, Abbie had taken enough of it.

She tried to help him help himself, but she had been leading that particular horse to water for too many years only to watch it deny that it was thirsty. No intervention she ever tried had been enough, so one day she took control and made a decision that hurt all of them. That was the only way she could think of to break the cycle.

Lydia took herself to school, her new headphones charged sufficiently to play the awful noise she believed to be music, and Abbie got in her car juggling her keys, large travel mug of coffee and handbag ready for another long day of answering questions that she believed to have painfully obvious answers.

Head of regional marketing strategy was a grandiose term, and when she had taken the promotion, it had come with a healthy increase in salary, but over the years the workload had increased alongside the explosion in social media platforms. She had to manage twenty-two-year-olds with fresh degrees in digital marketing and media studies, and while all of them knew how to boomerang reel a Tik-Tok story streak or whatever the hell they did, she understood the science behind targeted demographics.

She felt like a sheepdog trying to keep a bunch of semi-literate lambs in one spot most days, and the pressures from her bosses came so far from the other end of the spectrum that she spent more time explaining to clients why they weren't putting more ads in the local papers than actually doing her job.

She was sick of explaining that it was the twenty-first century, that times had moved on rapidly, like social media had been the next industrial revolution, all the while babysitting her entitled workforce through their various requirements; to take a mental health day because some obscure South American village had suffered a flood, and the images on Instagram had upset them.

Adding to her own stress of a divorce and a moody daughter wasn't high on Abbie's list of things to do, but that day was even harder for her because she had to find enough time in her day to get to a meeting with her solicitor.

Driving past the gym she used to go to three times a week, she allowed herself a small moment to feel sorry for herself. She'd given up the gym to free up time and save the significant membership fees to be able to pay for the mortgage herself, but right now the positives of being able to stop off on the way home from work and relieve the stress far outweighed the negatives.

She missed being able to spar with a friendly rival or work a bag until she couldn't lift her arms any longer, and she worried that she was snapping more and more at people because those pent-up feelings had nowhere to go.

She knew the real reason she couldn't go back there was because her husband would doubtless pick himself up and start training again, and she didn't want to be there when he walked back in looking to lose the stone of comfort the alcohol had put on him.

An angry blast of a horn behind her startled her, threatening to spill her coffee down her white blouse, and she waved a hurried apology in her rear-view mirror as she selected first and moved her car the whole fifteen feet she was delaying the car behind from achieving.

"Do it again, I fucking dare you," she muttered angrily, more annoyed at herself for apologising than the impatient driver behind her who probably had their own stresses piling up just as she did.

The traffic was bad because she was ten minutes late leaving the house, and that knock-on effect meant that she had finished her coffee, sipping anxiously as she sat in the stop-start traffic, so that by the time she arrived at work she was already fighting the urge to pee.

Faking wide smiles as she walked through the office, waving off questions with obvious answers and postponing people as best she could, she dumped her bag and pushed open the door of the ladies'.

Eyes closed, head in her hands even though it was only ten past nine in the morning, she sat there long after she had finished just to try and gain some focus.

The door banged open and rapid squeaks followed as someone walked fast for the sinks.

"Fine, dad, I'm alone now. What's so important? I am at work, you know?"

Abbie frowned, holding her breath to listen to one side of a conversation that she hoped would be juicy. No matter who you were or what you had going on, overhearing someone else's business was always a hidden treasure.

"What? What are you talking about? I can't just leave! And go where?"

Silence followed and Abbie's frown deepened.

"What do you mean, it isn't *safe* near the city? What are you t—"

The girl said nothing for a good thirty seconds before her tone dropped to a frightened whisper.

"Oh my God. *Seriously?*"

More silence, before she started to interrupt.

"No, I get it, *okay*! Okay, I'll call you when I'm on my way... Bye."

The tap ran for a few seconds where Abbie imagined that person taking a cinematically long, hard look at themselves in the mirror, before the squeaking footsteps announced her departure.

Abbie washed her hands, heading back to her office to find a young woman nervously waiting for her. She bounced her right foot fast on the ground as she sat there with eyes focused on nothing in the foreground.

"Morning," Abbie said as she walked in. She wasn't one of those 'my door is always open' people because she liked to see those working for her making their own decisions. As soon as she started giving out minor advice to one person, they'd all be in there asking her what they should do, and when that happened, she might as well let all of them go and start again.

"Oh, hi, look, I need to go home…?"

Abbie recognised the voice immediately, but she forced her features to remain unchanged, other than to adopt an appropriately corporate caring look.

"Is everything okay? Is it something we can help with?"

"No, it's, err, it's a family thing. Plus, I don't think I… I mean, I feel a bit sick. Might be a bug or something, you know?"

Abbie smiled, dismissing the claim of feeling sick because it was utter fiction, and tried to pry as to the other reason without sounding too obvious.

"If there's anything we can do to help with the family issue, just speak to HR and—"

"No! No, there isn't anything anyone can do about that, apparently… I… I'll get a note from the doctor or whatever, I just need to go home."

Abbie smiled sympathetically again, saying all the right words to be supportive and not believing a word the girl was saying to her.

She watched her leave in a hurry, ignoring the phone on her desk that was already ringing, and logging in to the computer to access the personnel database so she could record the sickness.

There had once been a department who did this, but as with everything it was all automated, user-friendly, browser-based blah-blah. She selected the correct employee from her dropdown menu of dozens, activating the protocol to mark her as absent and kickstart all the appropriate algorithms that sent automated emails to the relevant people and departments.

She ignored the pinging sounds of emails arriving, one of them informing her that a member of staff was absent through sickness as though she didn't already know. Glancing down at the envelope icon and the three figures of emails waiting for her to disregard almost all of them, she clicked on the girl's employee profile on a whim.

"Oh, hey," a male voice from the doorway said. It carried the artificial attempt to sound smooth and casual, but Abbie was by no means an insecure, inexperienced young woman.

She knew when she was being hunted.

She turned to see one of the oldest people in her department, positively a grandfather at thirty-one, leaning awkwardly around the doorframe and leaving greasy fingerprints on the glass.

"Morning, Ed. How can I help—"

"Just wanted to get your thoughts on the big plant proposal for next month. How about dinner?" He straightened up, still lingering in her doorway like a bad smell.

"Thanks, but no. I do want something on my desk by Friday though. If not, I'll have to shift it to Erin's team to get something worked up," she said, returning the smile with the hidden subtitles that he should stop trying to hunt the cougar and do his job.

"Gotcha. Friday it is," he said, walking backwards and firing his imaginary finger guns at her as he walked directly in the path of someone stepping fast with their attention glued to their phone screen.

Abbie turned away to save adding humiliation to his embarrassment, focusing on the HR details of the employee who had been so eager to escape work following the odd phone call.

She was halfway to convincing herself that there had been a death in the family and that the girl was too shocked to talk about it, only the comment she had made about the city not being safe nagged at her consciousness.

Clicking on the next-of-kin tab, she found contact details for the person listed as her father, providing a 'care of' address listed as an RAF base in Bedfordshire. She minimised the tab and brought up a browser, tapping in the information and clicking the wiki link.

He found herself staring at an image of three flags, none of which made any sense to her, but she wasn't naive enough to ignore that the girl's father was somehow connected to the joint military intelligence services.

Another bang on the door startled her again, but the offer of coffee that followed it was accepted gratefully from her secretary.

"And don't forget you've got that ten o'clock about the health authority teeth-brushing campaign," she was told. Abbie smiled, pretending that she hadn't forgotten about the meeting, and forgot all about the issue she had been looking into because she was simply too busy.

Lunchtime came and went with half a sandwich being inhaled at her desk as she worked, and only when the alarm on her charged phone reminded her of her other meeting did she snap out of work mode and leave the office with her handbag.

"I'll be an hour. Unless it's urgent, like life or death urgent, it can wait for me until I get back," she instructed her secretary, leaving the office and taking the stairs so she didn't get caught in a mundane conversation with a colleague.

It wasn't that she didn't like her job, it was more that nobody else she worked with seemed to have much of a life outside of it. She tried to balance life and work too much, and she was already considering relocating the eight miles to be closer to it, only she couldn't do that to Lydia until she had finished school and was in a position to move anywhere.

She knew she was putting it off because she wanted her family home to be complete again, hoping that her husband would wake up to the change and fight for them, but unless he changed his ways drastically there was no hope of that at all.

The meeting was tense, for her at least, because her solicitor prided herself on being one of those bloodthirsty practitioners of law who liked to brag about winning. Winning wasn't something anyone did during a divorce as far as Abbie believed, except perhaps the solicitors who got paid extortionate amounts of money, and she tried to make that clear at every meeting.

"But if you stick to these childcare arrangements, then you'll be entitled to—"

"I'm not after his money. I earn a lot more than he does anyway, and I need him to be able to afford somewhere that Lydia can stay if she wants to."

The look she received made it obvious that the woman thought she was being a fool for missing a trick, but Abbie wasn't going to allow herself to be phased by it. She was forty-one years old, successful, and she wasn't about to be brow-beaten into kicking her husband when he was already down.

"I'm not divorcing him because he's a bad person or to get back at him, we just need to close a chapter and move on. Nothing more."

The judgemental look softened, as if to say that her solicitor still disapproved of the tactic, but client instructions were issued, and the childcare agreement was drawn up to be presented.

"When is he due to have your child next?"

"Lydia. He's due to have her on the fifteenth."

"And you have arrangements in place should she decide not to go to him? Given her age, the court is obliged to hear her thoughts on it, and I can arrange for someone to speak to her at school or—"

"No. No need for court, and yes, she is going to see her father."

"And how about things between him and yourself?" the solicitor asked pointedly. She was getting to the point as softly as she could manage, but Abbie wasn't going to be embarrassed into avoiding the response.

"You mean after the police arrived when a neighbour called them?"

"I did read something about it…"

"Well, he was drunk, he wanted to talk to me, and I said no and shut the door on him. He stayed outside, the police turned up and arrested him because he said he didn't have anywhere to go when he did."

"Soooo he didn't assault you in any way?"

Abbie bristled at her words and rolled her shoulders back, imagining for a fleeting second that the unlikeable woman was a heavy bag at the gym.

She took her in with a single glance, seeing fingers unadorned with rings and frizzy hair that wouldn't know conditioner if it pulled a knife on her. She saw an angry woman who hated men, and her way of righting the world's wrongs was to attack those men by proxy through her work.

As proud and unashamed as she was, there were things she didn't need to explain to anyone. The police had tried to elicit a complaint from her, and when she didn't give them anything, the neighbours were canvased – at one in the morning – and they obviously found someone willing to tell a long and elaborate story based on curtain-twitching of the highest order.

"Look, Abbie, with the court issuing an interim protection notice, he could be looking at long term conditions that could affect—"

"I'll deal with that as and when. Is there anything else you needed for the childcare arrangements?" Abbie asked, gathering up her bag and preparing to leave.

The afternoon went as well as the morning had, and as people started to leave the office, she was still worrying over all the things she needed to finish when her phone screen blinked to life.

It was Lydia, texting her the simple yet heart-wrenching words displayed on screen.

"Are you ever coming home?"

She dropped her phone on the desk, hitting save on her current document and locking her computer to leave. Passing someone carrying two coffee cups in the office, she tried not to roll her eyes as he spun theatrically towards her and tried to flick a wavy mess of hair out of his eyes.

"Oh, boss, I was just looking to catch up with you about that thing? You know, just touch base…" his eyebrows flickered once when he said the last words of his sentence, and that tiny motion, that arrogant assumption that she would be interested – flattered even – tipped her over the edge.

"No. I'm going home to my daughter. If you need to speak to me regarding a work matter, schedule an appointment tomorrow with Rebecca."

Ed, for all of his lack of skill in the job he barely held down, exposed himself as a pushy misogynist for bonus points.

"This isn't exactly a *work* matter, you feel me? I'm just saying, at your age you can't afford to waste time playing the field. You're not twenty-one any—"

"One more word, Ed. One more fucking word and I won't just sack you, I'll smack you so hard that ridiculous quiff won't ever stick back up again. Drop it, or I'll drop you, *you feel me?*"

She pushed past him, leaving him dumbstruck and shocked as she headed for the stairs and drove her car down the road towards home far quicker than the posted limit allowed.

She passed the gym again on the way home, no longer suffering a long line of traffic as the post-work rush had already subsided, and felt the burning desire to go inside and let out the pressure she was building up.

Getting home, she walked in to find Lydia sitting up to the breakfast bar in the kitchen finishing her homework and their dog sitting faithfully under her stool.

"Oh, hi," she muttered, trying to hide her happiness behind teenage angst. Abbie didn't allow it to affect her and gave her daughter a squeeze which she tried to resist again, only giving in far quicker than she had that morning.

They ate pizza from the freezer, and when Lydia went to bed Abbie pulled a bottle of red wine from a cupboard in the pantry and a new glass to replace the one she'd fished the broken pieces of out of the sink.

She still wasn't used to sleeping alone, not even after almost a year of him no longer living with them, and the wine helped her. The irony of the situation wasn't lost on her, but neither did she find it amusing,

After she drank half the bottle and went up to bed, she lay

there staring at the same irrelevant nothing on the screen when the display changed to show a picture of a man under the name Shaun. Her right thumb hovered over the red circle, knowing it was the right thing to do, only she changed her mind and answered the call.

"Hello?" she said when there was nothing on the other end of the line.

"Hi…"

"Shaun, it's late. What do you need?" she said after a pause to consider what she should say.

"I… I just wanted to hear a friendly voice. One that wasn't Scottish at least," he said, with a weak laugh.

She sighed, thinking he had been drinking again.

"Shaun, you know you aren't supposed to contact me—"

"I buried him today. Well, cremated him…"

"Shaun… I'm sorry, I really am. Look, it's late and Lydia's just gone to bed and—"

"I was… I was hoping I could talk to her," he said. He sounded so lost, so lonely that it almost broke her. She stayed strong, knowing that until he got his life together by himself, then no good could come from them getting back together. She had tried to help him, she'd tried for the last four years, but he had to fix this by himself, and the only thing she had left was to take herself away from him and hope that he could mend.

"Shaun, it's not a good idea… I'm sorry, you shouldn't have called. You can pick her up on the fifteenth like we'd arranged. Goodbye, Shaun."

CHAPTER THREE

Three days before the collapse

B reakfast consisted of the usual tasteless selection of cereals and budget yoghurts, pastries that looked like yesterday's leftovers, and the expected array of acidic fruit juices sitting inside their churning dispensers.

Shaun poured himself three small cups of coffee to save going back for more, threw Weetabix into a bowl and scattered a scoop of dried raisins over the top before adding milk.

As he was taking a seat and spooning the cereal into his mouth, a waiter appeared with a pad and pen.

"Full English?" he asked, ignoring the irony of asking that question in such a broad Scottish accent.

"Please. No tomato, though," Shaun answered, covering his mouth with the back of his hand in case wet Weetabix sprayed out.

"Room number?"

Shaun told him, and the waiter scribbled on the pad,

finishing with a passive aggressive swipe of the pen as he walked away to give the impression that he'd somehow provided the incorrect answer.

The wait for the hot food was filled with a small mountain of pastries and the second cup of coffee. He'd always treated hotel breakfasts that way: filled up for the day on the unlimited food he'd already paid for. It was something of a personal challenge to him, and by the time he'd made it back to the room, he felt so full he was ready to go back to bed, only duty called.

He checked his messages, emails, and calls, finding nothing that he wanted to see. That included two quotes for cleaning, one of which was astronomical and the other simply steep. Showered and changed into jeans and T-shirt, he sat on the bed to lace his boots and left the hotel room without a second glance.

The drive east looked different, as if the grey sky and storm clouds of the day before had lifted to give him a break. Finding the cottage only slightly easier than the first time, he was reminded of the dread he'd felt on first seeing it.

That drab vision was marred by the scratched and dented yellow skip large enough for him to drive the rental car straight into.

Repeating the same process of lifting the gate to walk down the slippery path, he shouldered the front door open again and braced himself to start the hard work.

He began at the front door, pulling out the furniture piece by piece and dragging it to the skip. The front room took him all morning, forcing him to break into a sweat and strip off his jacket even though it was still raining on and off.

He was forced to put some things aside, unsure if they were valuable or not. Some of the paperwork he uncovered might be important, so he set that aside into a box for reading through when he had the time.

Braving the garden shed and fighting through overgrown weeds and branches, he found a small selection of old tools and a set of thick gardening gloves gone stiff through a lack of use. He soon worked them back into shape as he used a crowbar to pry up the ancient gripper rods keeping the ruined carpet in place.

By the time the afternoon came around and he was starting to imagine the sensation of hunger creeping back in, he sat in the other armchair that he'd managed to rescue from beneath the junk piled on it and looked at the old tv set.

He imagined himself as his father, sitting alone in what was effectively the wilderness to all intents and purposes, and wondering if he'd been there because he wanted to be shut away, if he'd wanted to turn his back on the world, or if the world had turned its back on him.

Just as he had, so many years before.

"What were you doing, old man," he said to himself. "What the hell were you doing?"

———

The next day he repeated the process, and he grew more tired and felt more isolated for the simple fact that he didn't speak to anyone other than to order food when he got back to the hotel.

The end of the second day spent filling the skip and discovering unpleasant surprises in every corner. Each morning he'd stopped at a supermarket and bought budget items to replace the old, worn items he'd thrown out. Sitting in the new, but very cheap dining chair and drinking tea from the most inexpensive mug he could find, he brought up the email detailing the quotes for cleaning and picked up the old landline to place the call.

The white plastic was stained by years of dirty hands using it, and the oversized buttons reminded him that his father had been an old man the last time he'd seen him.

When Lydia was just a newborn baby.

"Hello?"

The accent was English, which threw Shaun long enough that they spoke again.

"Hellooo?"

"Sorry, it's Shaun Taylor. You emailed me a quote the other day…?"

"Yes, the house clearance job. Did you want to book it? Only I have a cancellation tomorrow if you still—"

"Yes, please! Please. That would be great, thank you," he interrupted, sounding just as eager for help as he felt. The price tag attached to the quote was intimidating but having not seen how bad it was, he feared she might have underquoted.

"Okay then! Can you give me the full address?"

"It's not that easy to find… how about I email you the directions later? I'd do it now but there's no mobile signal out here."

He took the rest of the day a little easier, concentrating more on throwing stuff out than cleaning as he went. Heading back earlier than he had the day before, he spent the night in the hotel room drinking the tea and decaff coffee sachets in the room while watching obscure eurotrash on the television.

Because he hadn't had anything to drink, he struggled to find sleep, instead rolling over his life decisions and multiple mistakes until he'd twisted the sheets up into a mess that required him to get out and fix them again.

Tractor pulling, that was the last thing he recalled watching before he passed out.

As far as he could make out, it was like drag racing, only it wasn't... Spanish commentary with English subtitles that didn't make sense influenced his dreams in odd ways.

After a few hours of twisted REM sleep, he followed his breakfast regime, feeling the same Groundhog Day disapproval for his hot food order, and drove the route on memory this time.

The sun was shining that morning, which far from making him happy made him feel suspicious, and he pulled up to see that he might have been done a favour by being conned into renting the larger skip, because the tangle of disgusting furniture and rolls of decrepit carpet was showing over the loading lip.

A small, white van sat on the gravel driveway, making Shaun check his watch as he climbed out of the little Fiesta.

"Don't worry, I'm early," a singsong voice said from the driver's window of the van. "I'm Libby. You spoke to my mum on the phone?"

"Oh, yeah. Shaun, thanks for coming out at such short notice." He smiled, offering his hand to the young woman who stepped out and stood tall. She had mocha skin and a shock of tight, light brown curls on her head. Freckles adorned her cheeks and her smile was like a hint of sunshine in an otherwise drab landscape.

Tall was the operative word. She was almost at eye level with Shaun, who was above average height, making her very tall for a woman.

She wore a company T-shirt bearing the logo of a maid dusting something. He put her at least twenty or maybe twenty-three years younger than he was, and like the woman he'd spoken to on the phone, she spoke without the local accent. When his thoughts moved to her age, he forced himself to drop the smile and be professional.

"Have you bought the place as an investment? Holiday rental?" she asked, smiling at the size of the skip.

"No, I'm selling it for my father. He... he passed away. A few weeks back."

Her face dropped, showing that same guilty, apologetic look that everyone wore when they found out why he was there. Instead of a weak apology and the ensuing awkwardness, she rolled her shoulders and sucked in a breath.

"Right, I best see what I'm in for then! Shall we?"

Striding up the path past the gate he'd left open, she opened the front door and stalled, leaning into the old wood and lifting it by the handle. He opened his mouth to tell her it needed a shove but said nothing as he witnessed brains overcoming brawn. He decided in that moment that he liked her.

Walking through the front room that had been stripped down to the floorboards, she glanced at the lonely chair and the old television set but said nothing. The kitchen, mostly empty, raised both of her eyebrows but still she said nothing. Only when she walked up the stairs did she speak.

"Sweet Jesus!"

"Yeah, I haven't even started on the bedroom yet. Sorry. I'll get it cleared out if you wanted to start downstairs?"

"Well, this is going to call for the heavy gear," she said, turning back and shooting a smile at him that said she liked a challenge, no matter how bad it smelled.

He followed her back outside, watching as she opened the back of the van and pulled out a white suit that forensic investigators used at a crime scene. She added one of those clear face shields like she was about to perform surgery and snapped on a set of thick gloves.

Shaun watched on, impressed, as she began to select her tools. She poured chemicals into buckets, and produced a cordless drill and attached a wide, circular brush to it with stiff plastic bristles.

Turning to face him she gave a smirk that he couldn't help but reflect. Zipping the drill twice she bounced her eyebrows and headed back inside, leaving Shaun powerless to do anything but smile and head back inside to start clearing the hoarded junk from the bedroom to the skip.

He worked hard, enthused by the presence of another person, and shamed into working harder because she was like a one-woman whirlwind. She almost jogged in and out of the house as she fetched new chemicals and tools to scrub the surfaces.

By lunchtime he'd carted everything down from the bedroom after resorting to opening the window and forcing the stinking mattress out to drop into the overgrown front garden.

Taking a break, Libby approached him wearing a serious business face.

"Listen, I know you only wanted a day's work, but honestly there's no way I can get the upstairs done unless I stay all night."

Shaun guessed as much, and although he hated shelling

out more money, he figured he was still saving on the quote to have a company clear the cottage out for him.

"Do you think you could come back tomorrow?"

She didn't answer right away, just dug into a pocket inside her white protective suit and pulled out her phone. With a deflated sigh she slipped it back into her pocket.

"No signal out here. No data either. Don't suppose there's Wi-Fi?" she asked. Shaun smiled and shook his head.

"I don't even think my old man knew what Wi-Fi was. He was still watching terrestrial TV!"

"Oh, is *that* what that big, old thing is?" she said with heavy sarcasm. Shaun laughed dutifully and jerked his head back towards the front door.

"Use the landline if you want."

She did, placing a call to her mother who obviously ran things from their command centre, wherever that was, and stepped back outside with a smile.

"Right, I'll finish up the downstairs and be back in the morning..." she frowned, looking as though she wanted to say something but didn't want to cause offence. "The stair carpet. You don't expect that cleaned as part of it, do you?"

"Libby, I wouldn't expect *anyone* to touch those carpets even if they were paid for it. No, I'll strip the lot of it out down to the floorboards."

They worked for the rest of the afternoon, scrubbing and discarding everything that couldn't be reasonably cleaned. Shaun was forced to break the bed frame into pieces and throw it out of the window after the mattress but the wardrobe, old enough to be classed as vintage or whatever other word people used to sell things for extortionate prices, was simply too big and heavy to move.

He left it there, along with a few other pieces in the house that he convinced himself could add to the rustic aesthetic of the property, and when Libby announced that she was done for the day he waved her off and checked downstairs to see the transformation.

Everything smelled of sweetened bleach, which he liked, and it had been power-scrubbed with her drill brush so that the original colours of the kitchen had returned. That wasn't to say it was a welcome sight, given that the kitchen was probably installed in the late seventies and had all the sickening charm of that era's colour scheme, but it was clean, and it was serviceable.

Deciding on an early finish, he locked up and set off back towards the city outskirts.

————

A much-needed shower later, Shaun tried to figure out the hotel's laundry system from the card and plastic bag left in his room. Dumping half of his clothes into it, not counting the crumpled black suit, he left it outside his door and got dressed with his mind on food once again.

Deciding on a little variety, he took a short walk away from the hotel and found a small, non-chain pizza and kebab place nearby where he could sit at a bar in the window and watch the Friday night revellers beginning their journey. The place stank of grease, but it was a comforting kind of stink.

Watching through the window, Shaun bore witness to the same story played out in every UK town and city. Small packs of young men dressed in tight jeans and white shirts roamed like pack animals, as if their own wardrobe had been deemed useless and they were forced to borrow from their younger sisters.

With their eyebrows and their chests waxed, with their bare ankles showing between their boat shoes and their pedal-pusher skinny jeans complete with tactical rips, Shaun felt very old as he saw the lines blurring more than he was comfortable with. He was all for people being who they wanted to be, live and let live being very much his mantra, but he simply couldn't understand the trend in fashion.

The women, or girls as he corrected himself, all seemed like catwalk models walking on impossibly high heels and looking as though they started getting ready maybe Wednesday afternoon to appear so perfectly sculpted on Friday night.

Wiping pizza grease from his chin, he allowed himself an internal chuckle, knowing full well that very soon a lot of those girls looking so utterly and absolutely perfect now would be carrying their shoes and walking barefoot come the early hours. They'd be smearing kebab over their mouths and screeching like banshees to get a taxi home, which made him wonder what the purpose of going out was anymore.

He saw it as a waste of time and money, getting all dressed up to go out and pay ten times the cost for cheap alcohol after waiting outside for the privilege of entry. He much preferred to have a drink at home, and that sobering thought held a mirror up to him.

He saw himself as his father had been. Alone, drinking cheap spirits in search of sleep and oblivion, yelling at the television for showing him things he didn't like and didn't understand.

A bang on the plate glass window made him jump. Cursing himself inwardly, he carried on eating as two young men squared off against one another while their support acts bounced around the edges. They were like excited primates each with little erections in anticipation of violence.

Shaun leaned back, finishing the last slice of pizza and wiping his mouth with a napkin to turn it orange as he watched the nature program unfolding outside his personal TV to the world. He smiled as Attenborough's voice began to narrate in his head.

Here… we have… two adolescent males… engaged in a display of testosterone. Watch how one of these males… emboldened by his pack… seeks to show the other male… how big his little dick is…

The window banged again, startling him.

"Eh! What are you fuckin' laughin' at, ye old bastard?" one of the backing singers yelled. Finding an escape in a common enemy, the two groups turned their combined attention on him as if diverting their rage made for a way out of the situation.

Shaun ignored them, turning away and standing to put his pizza box in the bin and slurp the last of his flat drink.

A buzzer sounded as the front door opened, and even with his back turned Shaun could tell the situation was about to escalate.

"I'm fuckin' talkin' to *you*, old man. I said, what's so funny, eh?"

The voice was young but deep. It carried with it every ounce of insecurity a young man had riding on his back, and combined with the expected low intelligence it expressed itself through aggression.

Shaun continued slurping, giving himself time to think and react to the challenge calmly. Slipping both drink and discarded pizza box into the bin, he turned and looked at the man, now supported by four of the group looking over his shoulder and doing their level best to appear intimidating.

"Me?" he asked innocently.

"Yeah, ye fat twat. *You.*"

Shaun frowned in confusion but didn't react. He may have grown comfortable and not been the lean man he was ten – okay, *fifteen* – years ago, but he could hardly be accused of obesity. Old was one thing; inaccurate personal insults were another.

"Nothing. Just finishing my pizza and leaving."

"Hey! Buy some food or get out," the man behind the counter demanded. Unlike Shaun he *was* fat, and at well over six feet tall he looked ready to throw the entire bunch of them out on the street with ease.

Mister Angry in the lead turned his attention on the proprietor, aiming a finger protruding from a clenched fist at him.

"You're fuckin' next if you don't mind yer business."

"I *am* mindin' ma business. This shop *is* ma business, and if you're no gonna buy a pizza, ye best fuck off now," the owner said, laying it down for them as plainly as he could.

Angry seemed to hesitate, looking behind him to see if he still had the full support of his backing singers.

"I'll make it easy for ye," the owner said. "Ma Mrs has just called the po-liss."

Shaun saw it then. Saw the hesitation of a boy, desperate to be an alpha, not wanting to lose face in front of the omegas who followed him. He'd successfully abandoned one confrontation by starting another, and now that one had escalated, he was forced to make another choice.

"Come on lads, let's leave these fat pricks to cuddle and wait for the po-liss," he said with a cocky sneer before turning and ushering them out of the door.

There was no sign of the other group, no doubt they'd slipped away to play peacock somewhere else, and with a parting shot of another light kick aimed at the window they were gone.

"Thanks," Shaun said to the owner, who just nodded as if such things were a regular occurrence. He doubted if the police had been called, but still he gave it a minute before leaving the shop and turning intentionally in the opposite direction to where the group had gone.

He had a feel for the part of the city outskirts he was in after a few days, and like he always did, he tried to navigate through memory and his general sense of direction that rarely let him down.

He chalked that up to knowing how to interpret a map, feeling sorry for the generation who only knew how to search their phones for what they wanted and be told what to do by their Siris and their Cortanas.

Cutting off the main drag, he walked down an unlit street between the backs of places open late into the night. Awareness wasn't something he lost once he'd gained it, so when the hushed voices and scuffs of shoes far behind him grew louder, he put his head down and sped up.

There was nothing to say he'd been followed, but an assumption of coincidence led to people being taken by surprise. The word 'suddenly' related to things like a lightning strike in his world. They didn't relate to the actions of people because 'suddenly' just meant the person wasn't aware enough to see it coming.

An empty bottle was kicked along the cobblestones and followed by an angry shushing, which told him that this wasn't a coincidence. He turned a corner, heading back towards civilisation and streetlights where there would be CCTV and occasional police vans roving the streets, but the footfalls behind him started running.

He turned, meeting the challenge head on to bring himself up to his full height.

"Think you're a fuckin' hard man, do y—"

Shaun's first strike was a solid shove of his outstretched palm into the lead man's face. He felt the nose compress beneath the hit and felt the weak impact of a shoe hitting him in the thigh as the feet came off the ground to comply with the laws of physics.

He didn't stop, didn't wait for the others to reconsider their actions, but stepped forward over the falling man who had yet to react to being taken out.

The backing singers had more confidence than he'd anticipated, but that didn't deter him. He ducked under the wild swing of the nearest one who he guessed had never connected such a haymaker before in his life. Had his fist struck Shaun's skull, he would have broken a few bones in his hand, but the young man never had the opportunity to experience the pain that would cause. He wouldn't, because Shaun's boot made contact with the back of his calf in a vicious upward swing, as a big hand slapped downwards onto his exposed neck to slam him down on his back.

The third one hesitated, but still Shaun moved forwards, advancing on him with determined strides. The young man slipped, falling to his backside in the alley and scrambling to regain his feet while moving away from the unexpected violence – unexpected on the part of their victim, at least.

He was up, regaining his feet and running along with the fourth attacker before Shaun could reach him. His personal standards forbade him from running after them, so he turned his attention back to the ringleader, who had staggered back to his feet and was dabbing a hand at his face to check for blood.

He saw Shaun approaching him and switched, running at

him and snarling angrily. Unintelligible noises came from him before a jump and an attempt at an amateur flying kick, the likes of which you saw in footage of football violence.

Shaun stood his ground, letting the man sail past him before balling his right fist and delivering a short but brutal hook shot between his legs.

Little Mister Angry hit the ground in a heap, growling a scream that sounded as if he was in labour. The one he'd laid out on his back had regained his knees but there was no fight left in either of them then.

Shaun walked away, chest heaving, hands shaking, and heart hammering, making it back to the hotel and walking straight to the bar area to order himself something stronger than a beer.

CHAPTER FOUR

Lights in the Sky

M orning came with a headache, a sour gut, and a sinking feeling of dread. The events of the previous night flooded back to him, and he pored over the memories, searching for anything he did that couldn't be justified. He checked his phone, worried that he might have called or text his wife and made the situation worse, but blessedly the only action he couldn't recall had been on his Internet browser.

Finally convincing himself during his shower that he had been in the right, Shaun went downstairs for his last breakfast in the hotel. On his way back to his room to pack up, he passed the reception desk which was occupied by the same girl he'd first met when he arrived.

She was talking to a uniformed police officer and her eyes widened when she saw him. It was too late to pretend otherwise, because the officer had seen it too, and turned around.

"Excuse me," he said cheerily. Shaun stifled the groan and made sure to keep his shoulders upright.

"Me? How can I help?" Shaun asked with a polite smile.

"Gentleman matching your description was seen returning here on CCTV last night. There was an *incident* in town, and I'd like to talk to you about it."

"Am I under arrest?" Shaun asked, seeing the officer smile and hold both hands up.

"Nooo. No, no, there's no need for all of that. Listen, an allegation has been made against you of assault, but I think I know what really happened..."

"Against *me*? Shouldn't you caution me or something?" Shaun asked, racking his brain for the subtle changes in legal procedures either side of the Scottish border.

"Not unless I need to, no. Listen, I'll level with you right now, Mister...?"

"I'm not sure we should be having this conversation in public like this," Shaun said, seeing the look on the officer's face darken. He was no fool, and they both knew that the friendly act was only serving the interests of one of them.

"Listen..." the police officer looked over both shoulders before gesturing for them to step away from the desk, even though the receptionist had respectfully made herself scarce.

"Let me tell you a story, eh? Four lads have themselves too many bevvies, pick a fight with a few groups in the town until they decide to start on a guy on his own enjoying a pizza. This guy makes his way peacefully, only these idiots decide they fancy having a crack at him when nobody's there to call us, right? Say those lads get a few bruises and run away to make up a story about how this guy attacked them with a baseball bat, only muggins here—" he pointed to himself and rolled his eyes theatrically, "—knows what *actually* happened. Long and the short of it is that I need your account on record, and to do that I just need you to come and talk to me in your own time."

Shaun smiled politely, letting out a sigh and nodding.

"That's certainly a story. Assuming it involves me, why aren't you arresting me?" Shaun asked. He saw the disappointment on the man's face. The kind of disappointment someone suffered when their attempts to cut a corner or three are thwarted.

"Because it's a local scumbag just out of clink running to the police when he picked a fight and lost. I have no doubt in my mind that you, or whoever was in that alleyway, defended themselves well within the limits of the law. I just need that on record, and I might be able to breach his release conditions."

Shaun thought about it for a few seconds before nodding.

"Listen, I don't know what you're talking about. I have a few things to sort out urgently. You see, my father passed away and I'm here to sort out his house."

"I'm very sorry for your loss. You have my condolences. I'm happy to make an appointment for you to come and see me in a couple of days' time. How's that?"

The officer handed over a business card with his contact details at a station nearby.

Shaun looked at the card before taking it. Deciding he didn't have time for this, he set out his stall.

"Look, I don't know what you're talking about, and I don't think it's legal to discuss an incident like this right here. I'm sorry, but I don't have the time to deal with this. Now, if you'll excuse me."

Having laid down the gauntlet, Shaun feared he would be arrested on the spot as soon as he walked away. Perhaps it was his tiredness, or just his general mood that made him belligerent. Perhaps it was the recent memory of the local idiots having a go at him. Either way, he had no intention of grovelling his way to a police station to justify defending himself.

With that hanging over his head, Shaun packed up his gear and left the hotel a free man.

Libby was already at the cottage when he arrived, only she wasn't waiting for him this time. Walking in through the front door which, miraculously, no longer stuck and required no brute force, he called out so he didn't startle her.

"Hello?"

"Upstairs!" she called back, before the sound of a power drill started up. He guessed she was in the bathroom, conducting a thorough decontamination, and shuddered at the thought of being in that room.

He turned his attention to the gardens, lacking the tools or the will to restore either to anything resembling attractive, and satisfied himself by finding an ancient, rusted set of heavy shears and cutting back the overgrown branches from the paths.

Looking up at the sky to see another clear day devoid of rain, he considered staying on for another week. He could call work, use up some sick leave, and still be back in time to collect Lydia for the school holiday.

His mind wandered, considering repainting the interior and adding a few pieces of furniture so he could stay there. He even imagined himself decking out the little cottage as a place to get away to and enjoy some peace and quiet. Maybe he could take Lydia there, he thought, but imagining his daughter an anxious mess at the loss of the Internet connection to her phone made him abandon the idea. As if matching his mood, the sky had turned grey, and patches of dark cloud rolled towards them from the west.

He knew that if he didn't sell this place and close the door on that chapter of his life, then he'd end up sitting alone in squalor, having developed an incurable taste for cheap alcohol and solitude. He'd repeat history in full and become the man he'd given up on.

"Shaun?"

Libby's voice cut through his daydreaming like a brick through glass. She spoke as if worried, only she remained calm at great effort.

"What's wrong?" he asked, dropping the shears and walking through the back door to see her standing stock still on the front doorstep. She was looking up, staring north, with her brush drill in one gloved hand and bucket in the other. Shaun emerged behind her, ducking under the lintel in time to look up and see the sky above the rolling grey flash white.

The light was impossibly bright. It was like looking directly at the sun when somebody flipped the switch to activate it. They both shied away and covered their eyes, Shaun hissing in pain as stars danced in his vision.

"What the hell was *that*?" she asked, her voice a mix of fear and incredulity.

Shaun looked, seeing what she was talking about, but he didn't have the first clue what it could be.

The white flash was still there, only it was fading in intensity and turning orange at the edges. Flickers of blue and green rippled through the light show above the clouds, and Libby pulled off a glove to root around in her pocket and retrieve her phone.

Grunting in exasperation, she held down the side button to try and turn it back on, but the screen remained stubbornly black.

Shaun frowned, pulling his own phone out of his pocket, and finding the same thing.

"That's bloody odd…"

He tried again, but the device flatly refused to switch on.

Libby gasped, pointing off to her left as another pinprick of bright, white light erupted and blossomed far to their south.

"What the hell…" Shaun said, his mouth hanging open as his brain tried and failed to catch up with what his eyes were feeding back. His belief in the untrustworthiness of coincidences told him that what he was seeing was wrong, coordinated somehow, as if the flashes in the sky and their phones had to be linked in a way that he didn't yet understand.

He turned on his heel, walking back inside to click on the old television set. Perhaps the news had answers. Perhaps the mobile telephone network had somehow gone down.

"Maybe there's something on the news…"

The TV didn't turn on. He checked the cable, flipping the plug switch off and on again, but the screen stubbornly refused to come to life.

"I'll try the car radio," Libby said from the doorway where she watched him slapping the side of the old box as if that had ever made anything work.

"Err, Shaun?" she called out.

He walked outside, striding to where the driver's door of her van was open, and avoiding her right foot that still rested on the gravel. He leaned in, seeing her turn the key in the ignition repeatedly as if starting from scratch each time could make it work.

"Maybe the battery's dead?" she asked, but something in her tone made that sound like a hopeful best-case scenario.

"It's not even clicking over. No way it could've fully

drained so fast," he said, rummaging in his jeans pockets and coming up with his own car keys.

Pointing them at the Fiesta he clicked the unlock button, but nothing happened. Pressing harder, repeating the action just as Libby had, as if their belief in technology was so ingrained that the thought of it ceasing to work left them confused and powerless, he gave up and flipped out the folding key to unlock the driver's door.

Just as with her van, his car was completely dead. Not even the dash lights would come on. Dread sank over him like a blanket, pinning him to the uncomfortably small car seat and threatening to keep him there if he didn't summon the courage and energy to move.

He climbed out, feeling lightheaded and unsteady on his feet, to stagger towards the cottage and burst inside. Snatching up the landline, he smelled bleach as his shaking hands held the freshly cleaned white plastic of the handset. Putting it to his ear, he held his breath, listening for the familiar reassurance of a dial tone.

Libby stood in the front doorway watching him, her gloveless hands held near her mouth as she waited.

Shaun slowly returned the phone to the cradle and closed his eyes, breathing and just thinking for a moment as he gathered his thoughts.

"So… the mobile phone grid and the power is out, so is the telephone network…" he spoke softly, as if working it out with himself. "But that doesn't explain why the cars are dead…"

He had no idea about the maintenance of hire cars but given how the one he was driving had less than ten thousand miles on the clock, he doubted it could be a mechanical fault. Not even his own twelve-year-old car would misbehave like that.

Libby's van was less than five years old judging by the number plate prefix, and it seemed well cared for.

"It could be a coincidence," Libby tried, only she didn't sound as if she believed her own words.

Shaun almost told her that he didn't believe in coincidences, and that unexpected things happened to people who weren't paying attention to the world around them. Consequences were 'suddenlys' in his opinion.

"No… No, it can't. The landline and the power? Yeah, maybe. The phone grid dropping at the same time too, but for both our phones to be dead?"

"But why won't the cars start? It's never done that to me before, and… I filled it up last night. It's got a full tank of diesel…"

She sounded younger now, as if she was frightened of what was going on. Shaun was frightened, only he didn't understand enough about what was going on yet to know just how frightened he should be.

"Probably some kind of electrical storm or something," he said, trying to sound confident and reassuring. She seemed to relax a little, as if convincing herself to accept the explanation.

"Probably, yeah. The power'll come back on soon."

Shaun was at a momentary loss for what to do. Part of him wanted to bury his head in the sand and get back to work. To whistle as if nothing was amiss and carry on in the great British manner of ignoring a problem. Part of him couldn't take one more bit of shit going wrong in his life, so it made him want to blank it.

He abandoned that weak thought as soon as he had it.

"Listen, I'm going to walk to the village, see if they're affected by it too," he said, picking up his jacket in anticipation of rain.

"I'm coming with you," she said, unzipping the white paper suit and twisting to free her shoulders from it.

Shaun almost asked if she had a coat but decided not to try and parent her. He placed each foot in turn on the front tyre of the Fiesta and retied his bootlaces, sensing her presence beside him as she waited to set off.

They walked down the rutted track towards the road in silence, turning right after checking both ways as if the single lane carriageway would suddenly have developed traffic. They walked, Shaun setting the pace and walking on the correct side of the road to face oncoming vehicles should they encounter any.

The road grew wider as they approached a junction with faded, white paint marking the give way line. Still neither of them had spoken during the few minutes they'd been walking for, and Shaun was heating up to the extent that he was forced to remove his jacket and carry it.

"That's weird," Libby said, breaking the silence.

"What is?"

"Can you hear that?"

Shaun stopped, listening to the environment intently. He heard nothing but his breathing to begin with, until a faint whistling sound began to grow in his mind. His heart thumped because it sounded like a bomb falling to the ground, and his eyes scanned the grey skies desperately as if seeing his demise would somehow save him from it.

"There!" she gasped. He turned, saw her pointing up to the sky, and followed the line of her outstretched hand as she danced on the spot and let out a whining, keening noise of terror.

Shaun's mouth fell open as the shape of a plane emerged from the dense cloud cover. It wasn't a small plane, but a large passenger liner that could hold hundreds of people.

He didn't know plane models or numbers, but he knew it was big. He couldn't see the tell-tale bulge on the forward section of the fuselage, but the sheer size of it passing through the sky told him it had to be close to the size of what he called a jumbo jet.

Size and speed are deceptive over distance, so what seemed like a huge plane so close was actually far enough away that they had no chance of being hit by it falling, and there was no doubt in his mind that it *was* falling.

At that distance they should be deafened by the scream of the four engines. They should hear the doppler effect of them humming as it passed by, only the sound was just a shrieking whistle as it cut through the air unpowered.

"Oh my god," Shaun said, unable to think of anything else to say.

They both watched as it carried on, plummeting lower to the ground as it seemed to crawl across the sky from right to left, until it went out of sight behind a patch of higher ground.

"Maybe they were gliding in to land—"

A fireball erupted in the distance, followed a second later by a rolling boom like thunder. Libby shrieked, covering her mouth with both hands and bursting into tears. Shaun turned to console her, to console himself for what they'd seen, but she flapped her hands at him and danced backwards.

"We need to help! We need to call someone!" she sobbed, pulling her phone from her pocket again and collapsing to sit on the damp road surface when her phone hadn't miraculously returned to life.

"There's nothing we *can* do," he told her. He felt emotionally numb. Cold. Like what was happening was so surreal that it hadn't truly sunk in. He knew that wasn't true. He knew it had affected him deeply.

It was as though the stress of the last ten minutes of their lives had hardened him when so many would fall apart, just as Libby was in danger of doing.

"Come on, we need to keep moving," he told her, offering a hand to help her up and wondering where the words came from. More surprisingly, they came out confident and believable, even to him, and Libby took his hand to be hauled to her unsteady feet. She cuffed at the tears on her cheeks with the heels of her hands, giving him a nod that said she was ready. That she understood.

They turned right at the junction, Shaun following her lead now as she knew the area, and within a mile they encountered another problem.

"You see that?" she said, pointing desperately again as the scene started to make sense to her. Shaun was already running, boots thumping heavily on the wet road, towards the back end of a car sticking up in the air. The nose had dropped into a short ditch and struck a stone wall, steam and smoke rising from the crushed front end.

He reached the car, looking through the window to see the driver slumped against the wheel with a line of bright blood running down the right side of his face. Yanking on the driver's door he was yelling, telling the driver that he was there to help and that it was going to be okay.

"It's locked," he said out loud, stressed and unsure what to do, but Libby was beside him with a rock the size of both fists which she hefted and banged against the rear passenger window.

The glass gave way on the second impact to shatter into a million pieces. She dropped the rock and reached inside to fumble at the locking pin before eventually freeing it for him to pull open the door.

"It's okay, you're going to be okay," Shaun said as he

leaned inside to check the driver. He put his ear close to the man's mouth and froze, holding his breath to listen.

"Is he okay?" Libby asked nervously, tears threatening to return to her.

Shaun said nothing, just slowly retracted himself from the car and placed two fingers to the side of the man's neck. At the slight pressure of his touch, the driver's head flopped away to rest at a grotesque, unnatural angle.

Libby screamed, running away a short distance, leaving Shaun looking at the scene to figure out what was wrong with it.

The car was new, less than a year old, and being a premium brand, he couldn't understand why it wouldn't have all the options to make it as safe as possible.

That said, none of the airbags had deployed, and the absence of a seatbelt explained how the driver had been killed when they hit the wall at what must have been a decent speed.

Turning off that part of his brain that responded to emotional distress, he leaned back inside and dug around to look for the driver's mobile telephone, eventually finding it in the passenger footwell.

It was a similar model to his own, so he knew where the power button was. Trying it, he found the expected results before attempting to switch on the ignition for the car and see if any dash lights showed. Nothing did; the car was completely dead. He turned to tell Libby what he'd found.

"Phone's dead. So's the car," he told her, wincing at his choice of words.

She sat on the ground again, staring off into the distance almost catatonic with shock.

"Libby, we need to—"

"I need to get home."

"How? How far away is it?"

"I need to get home now!"

"Okay, how do we—"

She scrambled to her feet and started jogging, weaving along until she picked up more speed and followed a straight line. Shaun took another look inside the car and snatched the raincoat off the back seat on impulse before grabbing his own jacket from where he'd dropped it and he followed her.

CHAPTER FIVE

Brace, Brace, Brace

"I'm telling you, Gurj, the results they showed me can't be wrong," Doctor Charles Davidson said into his phone. He'd been told twice to end his call, politely, but as almost everyone else he saw was still texting or scrolling through the endless, pointless world of social media, he thought he was okay for a little while longer.

"You sure you're not just overreacting, Charlie? Need I remind you about last time?" Gurjit Sidhu, his supervisor and Midlands regional director of Public Health England said.

"That was different. Nobody could've anticipated how a virus like that could affect a broad spectrum of—"

"Charlie, I'm just asking if you aren't looking *for something, you know?"*

"I'm not, seriously. They can't explain it either, which means it's either a new mutation or it's engineered."

"Sir, I must ask that you turn off your phone now," the air

stewardess said insistently. Davidson smiled and nodded at her, wearing a look that he hoped was sufficiently apologetic on his face. The stewardess was not convinced that he would comply, and even from underneath a heavy layer of perfectly applied makeup, her annoyance was flashing like a warning beacon.

"*Now*, please, sir."

"Gurj, I have to go. We'll be back in Manchester in a couple of hours—"

"*Manchester?*"

"It was the first flight we could get. It's quicker to get a ride from Manchester than it was to wait for a flight to Birmingham International."

"*I'll send someone for you. Text me your flight details.*"

"Will do."

"Sir! I need you to terminate your call immediately. We're about to begin our departure," the stewardess snapped. Davidson held up his hand in surrender and hit the red button to kill the call. She smiled and walked on, checking laps for seatbelts prior to the obligatory choreographic display that annoyed him.

He switched to the message function, sending the flight details from memory to Gurjit so whoever he would send could get live updates on their arrival.

They taxied out, waiting another six minutes for their slot to accelerate along the runway, which annoyed Davidson because he'd had more than enough time to finish his call in spite of the stewardess insisting he cut it off.

As the plane gathered speed he felt the rush of power, but that rush was replaced by the irrational fear of the moment when the tyres lost contact with the ground, and they took off.

That threshold, that time when the pilots could cut power and keep them on terra firma, always gave him chills because it was the point he had no control over. Davidson disliked not having control, even though he mostly believed that control was an illusion, so when he opened his eyes after they were airborne and he could relax, he felt the seat beside him shaking.

Glancing over at the other person from his office to have joined him on the trip, he raised a quizzical eyebrow.

"You know it's safer to fly than cross the road, right? I mean, cows kill more people every year than aviation related mishaps do," Roz said. Davidson tried not to sneer at her. He resisted the urge to make a derogatory comment about the awful scarves she always wore to disguise the wobbling turkey neck, to point out that not a single one she ever wore matched her outfit, but he suspected that the insult would bypass her anyway.

Someone who prided themselves on being disliked built up a kind of immunity to insults, often getting them in before their competition did. She was one of those people.

He'd flown all over the world for seminars and the sharing of results with other organisations, but the need to travel fast in response to the invitation from the World Health Organisation had resulted in his office sending the two most available people.

Davidson was available because he was single and had little to entertain him beyond his work, but Roz was available because she apparently hated her husband and children.

Davidson assumed that those feelings ran deep in both directions, because she was one of the most unlikeable people he'd ever met.

"A subject you're an expert in the field of?" he asked drily.

"Cows or aviation disasters?" she asked smarmily.

Davidson ignored her, knowing that if he likened her to

something bovine, she would only goad him to carry on, then report him to HR on return and make his life more difficult than it already was.

She seemed to have no interest in the science, more that she was only concerned with the economic side of public health. He had no time for the penny pinchers, for the people who asked how much vaccines cost and if there were alternatives, because the science was pure.

The results he'd seen in Copenhagen were pure. Purely terrifying if what he'd seen was ever allowed to spread on a continental scale.

The isolated cases presented were from Egypt, Turkey, Poland, and Norway. He was sure there would have been others, but the countries he still considered as former Soviet states were less than forthcoming with their reports, much like Russia itself. The likelihood of yet more cases in what his office unofficially called "the Stans" was high, but they could only work with what they had.

Conjecture doesn't provide lab results, he thought, but the lab results he had seen were concerning.

It was Marburg. Without a doubt. Only it *wasn't*…

That was the part of the science that he couldn't explain with clear, factual lab results. It was also what told him that this wasn't just some random mutation caused by yet another cross-species, zoonotic variation. This was different. This was much worse.

"I can't get my head around the lack of incubation period," he said softly, ignoring the fact that he strenuously disliked his colleague for the moment. Roz rolled her eyes and let out a groan worthy of someone forty years her junior.

"This again? So what? A week, a day? What's the difference?"

"About six days," Davidson answered flatly.

"You virus freaks are all the same; you want everything to be the next global threat, just like you think every plane is going to magically fall out of the sky just because *you're* on it. Get over yourself."

Davidson sucked in a loud breath through his nose and held it, save he said something that might get him invited to a lecture on dignity and respect in the workplace on their return.

He was barking up the wrong tree by talking to her, he knew that, so he would just have to wait until he got back and could discuss his findings with someone willing to comprehend his concerns.

Someone who understood the beautiful terror of viruses

He pulled the wireless earbuds from their case and carefully inserted them one at a time before swiping open his phone and selecting the audiobook he was relistening to for the tenth or eleventh time. Roz leaned over to look, seeing the well-known title by Max Brooks, and scoffed at him as if his choice in literature made her point for her. He ignored the woman, closing his eyes and wishing away the two hours it would take them to fly back to the UK.

———

It wasn't like the films. It wasn't some sudden jolt of turbulence that woke him as in every television depiction, but more the sudden *absence* of the sounds he expected to hear.

Gone was the drone of the plane's engines. Gone was the low vibration felt through his seat and gone were the calming tones of the narration cast that had lulled him into sleep.

Hushed voices rattled insistent words, and the only thing Davidson could make out was the sense of shocked panic he felt from those speaking.

He expected to hear the chime run through the cabin, to see the fasten seatbelt sign illuminate above his head, for an overhead locker to pop open with a rattle and eject a bag, but none of those things happened.

He expected the pilots to announce their descent, to thank them for choosing the airline in that bored tone of a glorified but highly qualified taxi driver, but it didn't come.

He pulled the earbuds out, glancing at his phone to see the screen had gone black. He tapped at it, annoyed that his battery had run down in such a short time, especially when he knew for a fact that it was almost full prior to boarding.

Sound came to him then, only it took a while to place because he'd never heard it on a plane of that size.

He heard the sound of rushing air.

The only thing he could liken it to from his experience was when a colleague insisted he take a ride in his new electric car. The sensation of driving without a traditional engine was alien to him, and all he could hear was the whining rumble of tyres and the rush of wind as they cut through the air of the M42.

"What's?" he started, only when he glanced at Roz to ask the obvious question, he saw that she was fumbling with her seatbelt, trying to breathe in for the clasp to fasten over her gut.

Her panic was obvious, just as was that of the other passengers who were doing the same.

"Seatbelts! Please, fasten your seatbelts!" the stewardess who had berated him for being on the phone cried out from the front of the plane. He stared at her, his gaze lingering on the place where she had been even after she ducked out of sight.

He felt the seat under his thighs fall away, signifying the terrifying fact that they were descending without power. He expected another noise; that of the dive-bombers from every Second World War film he'd ever watched, but it never came either. He expected that gathering scream of their uncontrolled return to the Earth, but all he could sense was the whoosh of the air outside as they silently glided down, caught as collateral in the crossfire of the inescapable fight between gravity and inertia.

"Oh fuck," he muttered, scrambling with the buckle to tighten it with clammy fingers. "Oh, fucking hell."

"Brace for impact!" someone yelled from towards the front of the plane, and Davidson was caught by the horrible realisation that for so many people, those words would be the last they would ever hear.

There were no blaring alarms like the films always sounded. No oxygen masks dropping from the panel above his head, but there was screaming. Lots of screaming. That was one thing the films got right, and it was the one thing he wished they hadn't.

"Brace for impact!" the voice shouted again, as if repeating the instruction could make any part of their shared situation any less terrifying.

He sat as far back in his chair as he could before bending at the waist and wrapping his hands over his head. He didn't know if he was doing the brace position right, because even though he'd flown dozens of times all over the world, and even though he'd only recently leafed through the cartoon of smiling people depicting the correct actions to take, he couldn't for the life of him remember what the proper position looked like.

He almost wished for the audible alarms, for the screaming dive-bomber sound, because the rushing wind and terrifying silence marred only by the screams of frightened passengers made for a horrifying backdrop to his last moments.

"Brace for impact!" the same woman yelled, only this time her words had morphed from the strong, commanding tone of before into a wail of desperation.

Davidson turned his head, trying to see out of the nearest window.

He wished he hadn't, because instead of seeing clear skies or the rolling, steel grey of the North Sea, he saw high-rise buildings far closer than he ever expected to see from inside an aeroplane.

"Brace for impa—"

With a boom so loud and what felt like a hundred car accidents in one, the world went black and took his consciousness with it.

CHAPTER SIX

Power Out

She was enjoying a relaxing Saturday off, meaning that her work emails were encroaching on her private life and Lydia was already nagging at her that they would be late for her training session.

Although she was a shy girl at heart, both Abbie and Shaun had agreed that martial arts would be good for her confidence throughout her entire life, so when she had shown an aptitude for Judo at age six it had been a natural progression for her to learn other disciplines alongside it.

When she had shown more aptitude by combining Judo and Ju-Jitsu, and ultimately upsetting the sensei at both clubs, she had surprised her parents by asking to abandon both disciplines and train in Brazilian Ju-Jitsu at a local gym designed specifically for training mixed martial arts fighters.

She had presented her reasoning well for a girl of nine, and four years later she still trained and competed. It had got both Shaun and Abbie into the sport, and while one showed a great aptitude for brawling, the other unleashed her disciplined side through the training. Abbie had shed a stone of weight that she didn't seem to be carrying anywhere and had toned as a result of an activity she had enjoyed.

When Shaun had begun to lose interest in everything, the first thing he had dropped was attending classes and the gym completely.

"Mum, seriously, there won't be anywhere to park if we don't go now," Lydia whined, huffing and displaying stereotypical teenage behaviour.

"Alright, I'm coming," Abbie said, slapping down the lid of her laptop and draining the last of her coffee, which had gone cold.

She lifted the dog's lead from the hook by the front door which, although it made only the slightest of sounds, sparked a desperate scrabble of claws on tiled flooring as their Labrador came charging toward the exit and freedom.

He had been a rescue puppy and came with the moniker of Chuck, but Shaun had always called him Chunk and got him to howl along by repeating, "Hey yoooou guuuuuys!" at him.

Abbie pointed out that the character who said that was Sloth, but Shaun didn't care, and Chuck became Chunk.

"Someone say food, Chonk?" Lydia added, rubbing the back of the chocolate-coloured food monster who never seemed to tire no matter how much he actively chased obesity.

"Don't call him that," Abbie chided, knowing that it was pointless to fight the girl's use of vernacular, but feeling duty-bound to defend the dog's honour.

Especially when Shaun wasn't there to do it.

· · ·

They piled into Abbie's VW Golf, with Chunk taking the back seat and switching between drivers to passenger side windows before they'd even set off to maximise his viewing pleasure.

Abbie cracked the rear windows just enough for him to poke his greedy nose out and smell the world passing by before they drove into the Saturday traffic.

The club was on her route into the city that she usually drove for work, and as she settled into the familiar route her phone buzzed and beeped in the centre console.

Lydia closed her eyes and threw her head back, shrieking, "*I've got a teeext!*".

"*Really* wish you wouldn't do that," Abbie grumbled, reaching down for the phone and holding it up to dash level so she could see it without catching the eye of any alert police officers who may be watching.

"Mum, that's illegal," Lydia moaned.

"Yeah, well, so's your face…"

She trailed off as she read the text, swerving slightly until she looked up and braked in time to stop the nose of her car wandering into the middle of the road. Stopping behind three cars at a set of lights she read the message again, leaning closer to the phone.

Lydia leaned over to read the message, but she clicked it locked and the screen went black.

"Nosey, aren't you?"

"Who's *Jez*?" her daughter asked in an accusatory voice.

"Jez is a friend of mine."

"How long have you known *Jez*?"

"Long enough."

"Long enough for *what*?"

Abbie snapped, not wanting to answer questions she didn't know the answer to herself.

"Mind your own business! I'm allowed to have friends, aren't I?"

Lydia was silent for a while, looking out of her window saying nothing. Abbie was accustomed to her style or arguing and she knew that the next one of them to speak would be the one to lose the argument.

She wouldn't back down because she believed she was completely in the right, and regardless of what happened with their family situation in the long run, she was entitled to have some privacy in her life. She deserved some attention, some fun, just some part of her life that was hers alone.

She drove in silence, intentionally putting music on that she knew Lydia would want to pass comment on, while behind her Chunk switched from side to side to check both windows for anything worthy of a bark.

Arriving at the gym she found a place to park on the road nearby and clipped the lead to Chunk's collar. As they walked towards the gym her phone beeped again, only this time Lydia offered no comedic commentary.

She slipped it from her back pocket and started to read, slowing her pace to a stop before Chunk carried on without her and jerked her arm forward. Lydia stopped and glared but still said nothing.

"What the…"

Lydia still wouldn't say a word, still sticking to her stubborn guns, but she couldn't help her inquisitive nature and she stopped to stare.

"Mum!"

"Just go ahead, I'll take Chunk around the block and catch you up," she said distractedly, not looking up from her phone. Lydia huffed again and stomped off, jogging up the steps to enter the gym leaving her mother standing there reading the text over and over as if it would change.

*I   NEED   YOUR   ADDRESS.   SERIOUS   SHIT   IS
HAPPENING AND WE MIGHT NEED TO PICK YOU UP!*

She read it, sitting below the previous message asking for
the same information only worded less desperately.

What's going on? She messaged back. It turned to 'read'
status immediately and the rolling ellipses started up straight
away.

Can't say, just need your address. Please.

Abbie's lips set in a tight line. She'd been talking to him
after meeting on an app but having only met him in person
once, she was worried about this turn of events. He was a
Royal Marine working at the training camp outside the city,
so he would likely know if something big was going to
happen, but without more information she wasn't comfortable
with it.

I'm not sure, you're being a little weird.

The ellipses started immediately.

*Devonport naval base. If it all goes to shit, go there. Give
them my name.*

A jolt of fear went through her body. She tried to think
what could be going so wrong that she would have to flee to a
military base and seek the protection of a royal marine
corporal.

She slipped her phone back in her pocket and walked fast.
Her arm jerked as Chunk decided to conduct a more thorough
investigation on the post of a street sign before lazily lifting
one back leg enough to squirt a few droplets in the vicinity.

"What were you *thinking*?" she chided herself as she
walked. Her recent foray into dating aps had resulted in a
plethora of appalling attempts to chat to her by message,
along with far too many visual examples of unimpressive
male appendages.

She had spoken with a few men, all of them who had

selected her profile were far younger than she was, but of the few who were over thirty, she did end up having meaningful conversations with a couple of them.

She had waited eight months after Shaun had moved into his own place, but still she felt that it might be too soon after fifteen years of marriage.

No, I worried that other people *would accuse me of moving on too soon,* she corrected her thoughts angrily.

She had no intentions of seeking anything substantial, nor was she interested in what the kids called *hooking up*. It was more that she wanted some conversation and a little attention to pass the little amount of free time she had. Only an attractive woman of forty was like a red rag to an army of floppy-haired twenty-something bullocks who clearly wanted to replace their own mothers with a sexual partner.

Jez Hallam had been different. He'd actually been a gentleman about making contact with her, and only when she actually agreed to meet him for a drink one night did he let on that he was a Royal Marine. She thought that if he was simply using the app as a takeaway menu of potential sexual partners that he would likely lead with that information whether it was asked for or not… like every man who did CrossFit. Or every firefighter she'd ever met. Or vegan.

Jez was based near the city as he was posted as training staff for the new recruits, and as such he didn't have a lot of evenings spare for a social life outside of the base or barracks, or whatever the marines called it.

This turn of events didn't seem right, like it was out of character. But then she remembered that she had known the man for a couple of months, meaning she didn't really know him at all. If she was to take him at his word, and nothing he had ever said or done had given her cause to doubt that, then something bad was happening.

By the time she came to that worrying realisation, she'd lapped the block and was back outside the gym. She cracked the rear windows a few inches and put Chunk in the back, where he knew the drill well enough to wait until she'd walked away before jumping over to sit behind the wheel.

Inside the gym she watched Lydia rolling over the mats, her mind distant and wandering as she intermittently checked her phone. She considered texting Jez again, but when she tried to message him, he was offline.

She scrolled through her messages, tapping on the profile picture of Shaun to bring up a text exchange that was almost six weeks old. She started to type, deleting the first word and swiping off the message, cursing herself internally for running back to him when she was scared.

She didn't even know what she was scared of, or even if there was actually anything to *be* scared of, but she hated that her first thought was to contact him as her security blanket.

She knew he'd never get a grip of his own life if she still needed him like that, and she knew she wouldn't be able to let go unless she stopped seeing him as the one to be there for her.

She watched Lydia flat on her back with another girl a little older than her pinning her down to the mat. She wasn't squeamish like other parents would be, because she trusted the trainers not to allow anything bad to develop and she trusted Lydia to know her limits.

The girl on top moved, exploding to swing her left leg around the back of Lydia's neck, but instead she fell away and rolled desperately to her side before slapping her right hand hard on the mat three times.

The session came to a close and a sweaty, red-faced Lydia bounded up to Abbie wearing a smile of satisfied pride.

"Did you see me?"

Abbie smiled warmly.

"I did, but it was a bit of a blur," she lied.

"She had me pinned, but she tried to go for the triangle too soon and she didn't have both hooks in. I blocked off the hip, grabbed the toe hold and when she tried to out, I rolled with her!"

She was excited, exhilarated by the win, but Abbie was lost.

"It was too fast for me, baby. Sorry."

"She thought she had me because she weighed me down. I could've snapped her ankle…"

The way she spoke brought a frown to Abbie's face. She hadn't heard her daughter sound so bloodthirsty before, and she hoped it was down to the adrenaline of winning.

"Hey! Nice work, kid," a proud voice said from behind them. They both turned to see the gym owner, tall and lean with a nose that probably couldn't recall how many times it had been broken, smiling at them.

"Thanks," Lydia said, adopting a more quiet and shy approach now that she was under the microscope.

"Really good reversal. Impressive!" he said, resting a hand on Lydia's shoulder in such a fatherly way that Abbie felt a pang in her heart.

"And when are you coming for another sparring session?" he asked Abbie.

"It's just crazy busy at work…"

He held up both hands to ward off any excuses she might give.

"I get it, life gets in the way sometimes. Just don't leave it too long, otherwise you'll forget how to fold clothes with people still inside them."

His rueful smirk at the joke she'd heard a hundred times before was infectious.

"Yeah, I know, I'll be back for more yoga without consent as soon as I can."

He smiled, knowing that she had been avoiding his gym because Lydia's father had been going through sporadic bouts of training every day for a week and then disappearing for a month at a time.

They left, and the time spent apart had ended their disagreement by both of them pretending it hadn't happened.

Chunk sparked to life as soon as they returned, having given up his spot behind the wheel to stretch out on the back seat.

The traffic was lighter on the way back, and Abbie's mind was in turmoil keeping her quiet. Lydia's mind was clearly on food, as she made an excited noise and pointed out of the window, hopeful for fried chicken.

Abbie checked her left mirror and signalled to move over, swerving back into the right lane with a yelp from Lydia as a trio of black Audis blasted through nose to bumper.

Small blue and red lights flashed inside their dark, tinted windows, and the warbling doppler effect of sirens all playing different sounds disappeared fast.

She checked the lane was clear again, looking back over her shoulder this time, and pulled up at the drive-through.

"You okay?" she asked Lydia after calming down herself.

"Yeah. *They* were in a hurry though, right?"

"Yeah…"

She moved along the line of cars robotically, still unable

to shake that feeling that something bad was going to happen, so when the box beside her open window crackled to life, she jumped in her seat.

"*Hi, can I take your order, please?*" Came the single word blurted out by the expectantly bored operator.

Abbie stuttered her way through an order and shuffled her Golf around to receive the food and pass it over to Lydia, who had to turn her body to stop Chunk from sniffing the bag into wetness.

"Gerroff!" she said, but fished out a coated chicken breast which the dog greedily took from her, exchanging the meat for a small deposit of drool as if some slick, practised transaction had taken place. Lydia made disgusted noises and wiped her hand on Abbie's thigh, but her mother just drove out without responding.

"Mum, what's up?"

She didn't answer, just leaned forward to check for oncoming traffic and accelerated out onto the road.

"Mum!"

"Hmm?"

"I said what's wrong?" Lydia asked, her mouth full of hot chicken.

She didn't get the chance to answer, because the car shuddered and lurched. The wheel went stiff as the power steering died, and when she tried to pump the brakes she found the pedal stiffer than expected with far less effect on stopping the car than she liked.

Panicking, shuddering to a stop, Lydia shrieked as Chunk tried to join them in the front seat through sheer inertia.

Relaxing, sucking in the first breath post near miss, they were both jerked back in their seats as a car behind clipped them, shunting them up the kerb and onto the pavement.

"Lydia! Are you okay? Are you hurt?"

"No… I don't think so…" Lydia's eyes were scrunched up, but they widened when she looked at Abbie. Spinning her head too fast and sending pain all down her body, Abbie saw the cut on her forehead, high up in her hairline, and the stream of bright red running down her face.

"It's nothing," she said, twisting painfully again because Chunk had started barking out of fear or confusion. She reassured the dog, climbing painfully out of the car to try and force open the back door and get him out. She grabbed his collar, calling for Lydia to find his lead, but the driver of the car that had clipped them was already yelling.

"What the hell did you stop for?" he roared. "Stupid bloody woman, you know how dangerous that was?"

Abbie almost apologised reflexively, almost started to explain that it wasn't her fault, and that her car just went haywire, but the scene around her overrode her decision to speak.

She rotated, seeing cars stopped or crashed everywhere, but the man who had clipped her car was blinded to it by his anger.

"Oi! I'm fucking talking to you! Are you thick?"

"Wait…" Abbie said, still looking around and trying to understand what was going on. He didn't wait. He advanced on her car and kicked the passenger door which made Lydia scream in fright and sent Chunk into an apoplectic rage.

"Hey! Back off!" Abbie yelled, rounding the front of the car to draw his attention away from her daughter. Lydia might be accomplished on the mats for such a young girl, but she wasn't deserving of aggression from a grown man.

"You wrecked my fucking car!" he yelled, advancing on her as he pointed behind at the steaming Mercedes blocking the other carriageway. Abbie put her hands up and backed up equal to each pace he took towards her. Lydia screamed louder, but when the man reached out and took hold of her by the jacket, something in her switched.

She may not have trained for a while, but the muscle memory kicked in and as soon as he grabbed her with his right hand, she threw her left up and over his arm.

Before he could react, she'd slamming her left hand – fingers splayed out for added power – up under his bicep to lock his arm out painfully.

He let out a noise somewhere between surprise and pain, but she didn't wait for him to figure out what was happening. Turning her right hip, she stepped through and kicked back to take him down.

He fell back, shoulders hitting the front of her car but not before he'd lashed out and caught her a numbing blow on her right cheek with his free hand.

She backed off, shaking hands fumbling in her pocket for the phone she had left in the centre console.

"Lydia! Call the police!" she shrieked, trying to decide whether to get back in her car for safety or get her daughter and her dog to flee. As he started to climb to his feet at the front of the car, she got back inside and tried to lock the doors, but the central locking wasn't working.

"Mum, my phone's dead! I charged it last night but it's dead!"

"Find mine!"

They both tried to look, banging their heads together as they reached under the seats to make Abbie's head ring and let more blood run into her left eye from the cut on her head.

"Got it," Abbie said, almost yelling exaltedly as the other driver got up. Lydia screamed, pointing as the man staggered around the car and slammed both hands onto the bonnet in anger.

Chunk barked loudly; fear and distress making him sound

aggressive. The noise he generated gave the man pause, but it didn't entirely deter him from getting at them.

"Bitch!" he yelled, kicking Abbie's door and adding more vulgar insults as he increased the volume and intensity of his attack. Yanking on the unlocked door she screamed and pulled it closed with both hands.

Lydia retrieved the phone and fumbled with it, desperately trying to make it work with shaking fingers and sobbing that it wouldn't work. Abbie only heard noises because her focus was entirely on keeping the door closed, but the man's size and weight won over and he tore the handle from her grip.

Lydia screamed louder as hands grabbed Abbie. The air was cut off as one wrapped around her throat and pain exploded in her scalp as the other grasped a handful of her hair to drag her from the car.

A snarl erupted directly behind her ear, and it took her a few seconds to understand that the sound came from Chunk. She had never heard anything like that come from the daft, cuddly animal before, and the yell of agony as teeth connected with a wrist shocked her further.

Her attacker fell back, yelling in pain as he tried to tug his bitten hand free from the dog but unlike the contest over the door, he was outweighed in terms of muscle this time.

When Chunk finally released his grip, the man landed hard, snarling curses at them as he backpedalled and reached for his phone from a pocket with his uninjured hand.

Abbie didn't wait. She threw herself from the car and ran around the back, pulling open the door and half dragging Lydia from the seat. Her daughter protested, but she didn't hear the words.

"Mum! Chunk!"

Abbie froze, turning back and opening the back door for

the solid dog to drop down to the road almost frantic. He whined and barked as all four feet hopped on the spot to betray his anxiety.

Ignoring his lead left behind in the car, she yelled at him to 'heel' and ran with Lydia's arm clamped in her hand.

CHAPTER SEVEN

Chaos

"Libby… wait!" Shaun gasped. He'd kept up with her for close to a mile when his lungs began burning so much that he couldn't breathe. He broke down in a coughing fit, forcing him to stop and bend over double.

"Stand up. You need to open up your diaphragm," she said, barely out of breath. He hadn't noticed her stop and come back to him. He did as he was told, putting both hands behind his head, and stretching upright with a grimace.

He instantly felt better, even if he was sucking in air like he'd been suffocating. Looking at her, he saw her shrug and stare off at nothing on the side of the road.

"My daughter has asthma," she said by way of explanation.

"Your daugh…. Where's home?"

She pointed back in the opposite direction. Shaun looked

behind him, seeing nothing but angry, grey clouds tinged with the occasional hint of blue and green, above an empty road and greenery on both sides.

"We can't walk all the way back there. We need a car," she said, continuing the theme of explaining. Shaun nodded and began walking in the direction they'd been running. She matched pace beside him, anxiously stepping fast like a sheepdog trying to keep an old ewe heading in the right direction.

She showed the same barely contained hyperactivity as before when she had been cleaning. She was like a performance motorbike forced to drive at the speed limit, like she wanted to rip off under full acceleration all the time. Shaun recognised that, now that he knew the reasons behind it, and tried to walk faster.

"The village is just up there," she said, but Shaun's exhaustion hadn't prevented him from reading a road sign at the last junction. The correlation between 'just up there' and the number four beside the village name.

A sign for a golf course gave another few miles after that, which became his fluid plan B should the village not be of any help.

He recovered sufficiently to pick up the pace after a while, and when they rounded the bend to bring the village into sight his heart sank.

Another crash blocked the road, this time a bakery truck – large and fixed-axled – had ploughed into a small Nissan and pinned it to a stone cottage at the side of the road. His heart sank further, expecting to find more death there, but as they approached it became clear that all the involved parties were walking wounded.

The lower speed limit of the built-up area, such as it was

with only a dozen buildings either side of the road, had saved their lives. Unlike the BMW driver who had probably been progressing at a comfortable sixty miles or hour or more before the ditch and the wall had ended him.

Libby put a hand out to stop him as they approached, keeping them back from getting involved. He looked at her, seeing a frown on her face, and started to question why.

"The same thing happened here. Look," she said quietly, pointing at the abandoned cars and confused people milling about in the lane, confused about what was happening.

She scanned around, tugging his sleeve towards the stretch of pavement near a tiny shop.

Shaun went with her, not realising what she was about to do until it was already happening. If he tried to stop her, he would attract the attention of the villagers, and he didn't think adding flaming torches and pitchforks to their day would help.

He looked around, checking for anyone dressed for cycling, but saw nobody. Looking back at Libby, he saw her making desperate eyes at him to help as she wrestled with two mountain bikes resting against the wall.

Shaun helped, actually tiptoeing forward like a comedy burglar, and the two of them settled uncertainly onto the unfamiliar bikes to start pedalling away with a wobble.

"Oi! That's ma bike!" came the shouted protest from far behind, but they were already accelerating away around the corner and back the way they'd come.

The return journey seemed to take only a couple of minutes, passing the car in the ditch just as they'd left it.

A column of black smoke rose in the distance where the

plane had crashed, and they both ignored it as if by unspoken agreement.

Shaun was overheating, sweating despite the light, stinging rain that had started up again. He was grateful for it, for the first time ever, and would've attempted to strike up a conversation about how he lived in one of the driest parts of the UK. Would've drawn a parallel between the Scottish weather and sunny seaside he was used to, only he needed to save his breath.

The seat was slightly too short for his height, forcing him to put undue pressure on his knees or else stand up to pedal. When he could no longer take it, he called for her to stop.

They pulled up at a sheltered bus stop made from steel and Perspex; the only feature in an otherwise abandoned part of the world. The electronic board powered by the solar panel device on the roof was blank, displaying nothing.

Stepping stiffly off the bike he bent over again, looking under the seat and finding relief that it was fitted with a quick release bolt. Unfastening it and lifting the seat higher, he bent over again to catch his breath before remembering her instructions. He stood straight, bike rested against his body as he looked at her and panted.

She seemed flushed, but otherwise unaffected by their exertions.

"I'm too old for this shit," Shaun said, hoping his attempt at humour to lighten the terror of the situation didn't upset her.

"Age is a number," she retorted robotically, like she was repeating a mantra she'd heard over and over.

"Yeah, but my number starts… with a four… and not a two," he said, still breathing heavily. She shrugged as if his answer didn't matter.

"You some kind of… fitness freak or something?"

She shrugged again, unsure if she agreed with the terminology but not denying it.

"I do triathlons."

Shaun nodded, accepting the explanation without question. In his opinion, anyone who spent a day off running, cycling, *and* getting in cold water for fun had to possess a level of dedication he had never experienced.

"You okay to carry on?" she asked, nervous tension creeping into her words. He nodded, feeling more like curling up under the bus stop shelter for a nap than continuing. He nodded, swinging his left leg stiffly over the saddle and settling on the bike with a wince.

He wasn't dressed for this kind of activity, and wet denim jeans made for uncomfortable cycling gear.

"It should take us about an hour from here," she said, speaking with the confidence of someone who rode long distances and could be trusted to make that kind of estimate. She looked at Shaun for a beat and amended her guess.

"Maybe an hour and a half."

"Sorry, you go ahead if you need to. I don't want to slow you down."

She paused with her right foot ready to start pedalling and looked at him seriously.

"You'd leave a young woman on her own when all… all *this* is going on?"

His sense of chivalry sufficiently injured, he stood a little straighter on the bike and started pedalling in the direction of the city with a renewed sense of purpose.

———

Even two miles out from the outskirts they could see, smell, and hear the carnage enveloping the built-up area.

Random fires burned, and more and more dead cars were abandoned all over the roads.

The bikes were a good idea, as they had to weave in and out of blockages that would have left any working car facing a long detour. People shouted, waving their arms in the streets, arguing, and complaining that nobody had fixed the problems yet.

There was no power, and that meant no Internet. Without Internet people couldn't work, couldn't entertain their children, couldn't watch television, or access any information.

Shaun heard snippets of conversations as he concentrated on not overheating and keeping up with Libby, who seemed not to tire at all.

He was exhausted, his mouth was dry and his throat burned so much he fought the constant tickle of a cough, he was wet through with rain and sweat, and his belly was grumbling despite the routine breakfast he'd forced down.

All he wanted to do was get a shower and go to bed. Maybe he'd wake up and everything would be okay? Maybe he'd just imagined having his hands on a dead body behind the wheel of a car he couldn't afford? Perhaps the aeroplane falling from the sky before his eyes had been a hallucination or something?

"Watch where you're going!" an angry woman screamed at him. He swerved, avoiding her walking across the road with her arms stuffed with items.

He looked back over his shoulder, seeing the mess of people all pushing to get in and out of a small Co-Op with whatever they could carry. Shaun shook his head, disappointed in his own species for their dumb, animalistic behaviour.

It was the evolution of panic buying, only without any electronic trace of stock or the ability to identify people with

CCTV, it was just panic. It was looting, pure and simple, and it wasn't as though there had even been long enough since the power went off for people to be worried in anticipation about providing.

People carried crates of canned beer and bottles of alcohol. He saw one man on his knees beside the road, attempting to stuff the thousands of pounds worth of cigarettes back into a bag that had split from being overstuffed with heavy items.

Shaun's concentration split, he failed to notice that Libby had braked hard in front of him and crashed awkwardly into the back of her. Hissing and grunting curses as the pedal spun and slammed into his shin, he half fell from the bike to regain his feet and look at what had caused the obstruction.

Two men, both young, who under any other circumstances would appear to be normal, decent members of society, stood blocking their path.

Both held knives – simple kitchen knives that seemed so innocuous when viewed in their familiar habitat – and both wore a look of desperation.

"Give us the bikes," one demanded.

"No! I need to get my daughter—"

The one who hadn't spoken yet stepped forward, knife held out in front of him like some warning talisman, and put his free hand on the handlebars.

Libby froze, backing off the bike awkwardly while keeping her eyes fixed on the shiny blade.

"You too," said the first one, jerking his weapon in Shaun's direction. Shaun said nothing, just tugged at Libby's arm and backed up to watch as the men took the bikes, warily keeping their eyes on their robbery victims, and rode away.

They stood in the roadway, shocked at how suddenly their situation had changed, until shouts and a scream announced a fight breaking out behind them.

"We need to move," Shaun said, tugging her arm again to lead her off the main road until they were relatively alone.

"How far?' he asked, but Libby seemed lost in a trance again. He shook her gently, both of his big hands on her slim upper arms. That brought her back and their eyes met. It took her all of a second to switch back on after the stress of being threatened with a knife, and she looked around to check her surroundings before pointing in a direction and setting off.

They cut through the streets, keeping away from any big areas of activity that seemed to be centred around shops ripe for looting. Shaun simply couldn't understand how society had broken down so fast, why people were acting this way only hours into a power cut, but the fact that everything electrical was irreparably down over such a widespread area worried him deeply.

He struggled to keep up with her, unsurprisingly as she was a runner, but she was careful not to leave him behind. Her comment about him suggesting they split up had already been proved a risk, even though him being with her hadn't necessarily made the situation any better.

Away from the more commercial areas, they saw people out on their front lawns or driveways discussing the novelty of the power cut with neighbours, but other things Shaun saw gave him reason to worry.

One man, desperately throwing things out of his garage to uncover their own bicycles, yelled intermittently at his family to hurry up and pack their bags.

"Don't bring anything you don't need! Water and food, come on, let's go!"

"Excuse me?" Shaun tried, but the man rounded on him and pulled a short-handled wood axe from his belt. Shaun held out his hands, palms facing the man, and tried to show he was no threat.

"Fuck off. You'll no find anything here you want, pal."

"I'm not trying anything, I promise. Do you know what's happening?"

"Fucking Russians. Or the Chinese, who knows. If you know what's good for you, you'll be away from here as fast as you can."

Shaun carried on backing up, joining Libby back on the road as they carried on in the right direction.

"What was that all about?" she asked.

"Whack job. Probably thinks the Cold War never ended," Shaun told her, trying to sound upbeat and failing. In truth, he was concerned more by what the man had said than he was letting on. He recalled reading some clickbait article in the hotel maybe yesterday or the day before about tensions between East and West like it was fifty years before. He'd been born ten years after the Cuban Missile Crisis, when it looked like the world was about to devolve into nuclear war, but he knew tensions didn't magically disappear when the Soviet Union fell.

"It's not far," Libby said, shaking that thought out of his head. He realised he hadn't even asked where they were going, but wherever it was, it was better than being on the street and far better than being stranded in a stripped-out cottage in the middle of nowhere.

A few minutes later and they turned into a cul-de-sac filled with a sweeping curve of new builds, and Libby made straight for a large, detached house with a double garage protruding from one side.

In the driveway sat another van like hers, and she ran straight up to the front door only to bounce off it when it didn't open. She hesitated, confused for a second, then started hammering on the door desperately.

"Mum! *Muuum!*" she yelled, stepping back away from the door and looking at the upstairs windows above the garage. The sound of locks unfastening and the chain being slid out of its metal housing inside the door reached them, then the door opened and a woman appeared who looked so different and yet somehow similar to Libby.

She was white, at least a foot and a half shorter than her daughter, and her build didn't imply that triathlons were a family hobby at all. On her hip, frizzy hair sticking out like she'd suffered an electric shock, was a little girl Shaun guessed was on the verge of school age.

Libby sobbed, making noises of relief and terror all at once as she took her daughter and hugged her tightly. The girl frowned and squirmed, unsure why the emotional outburst should affect her, but the older woman ushered her back inside before looking at Shaun and freezing.

"Who's this?" she demanded with a stern frown on her face.

"Shaun. The client from today," Libby said as she stepped over the threshold. Shaun smiled and took a step forward, but the mother planted herself in the doorway and pulled the door half shut so she blocked the entrance.

"Mum, it's okay, really," Libby said from inside.

"We… we spoke on the phone?" Shaun said, trying to engage the woman and offer some reassurance that he wasn't some piratical marauder looking to steal her canned goods. The woman hesitated for a few more seconds before Libby whispered something in her ear that Shaun couldn't hear.

She released the door reluctantly, looking down briefly as she stepped aside and admitted him entry.

"Thank you," Shaun said gratefully, not realising how

desperate he was to get off the streets. With a cautious glance behind him, he stepped inside and shut the door, automatically turning the key in the lock behind him. He spun around, seeing the older woman looking horrified, but he smiled to try and show he wasn't a threat to them.

"Sorry... it's not a good idea to leave it unlocked, though," he said sheepishly.

"Mum, I wouldn't have made it back here without Shaun. Shaun, this is Amanda."

Shaun smiled again like a demented idiot and bobbed his head, muttering some pointless lie about it being nice to meet her.

"It's... it's gone mad out there," Libby said sadly. She sounded younger again, as if proximity to her mother when she was a mother in her own right had somehow regressed her personality.

"It's gone mad everywhere. You know what happened?" she asked. Libby shook her head and walked through the house, which was immaculate like a show home, to the kitchen where she sat her daughter on the worktop and opened a cupboard to retrieve two pint glasses. Running the cold tap, she filled one and handed it to Shaun, who took it gratefully.

As he gulped desperately to kill the burn in his throat, Amanda filled the silence.

"I had the news on before everything went out," she said, not continuing. Shaun stopped drinking, expecting to hear something dreadful, as Libby drank and watched her mother for more.

When she said nothing, Shaun was forced to ask.

"What did it say? Was it a solar flare?"

Amanda frowned at him, her mouth hanging open slightly as if she couldn't comprehend how stupid his question was.

"Or a... a corona mass something-or-other?" he tried; unsure what terminology the newscasters would have been given. He'd been thinking about it after their bikes had been stolen – or *re*-stolen, more accurately – and landed on the only thing he could imagine having caused such widespread electrical malfunctions.

"A coronal mass ejection," Libby said, obviously on his wavelength but just as obviously repeating terminology she'd heard.

Amanda looked between them dumbstruck, seemingly unable to fathom what they were saying.

"What are you two on about? You mean you don't know about the missiles?"

Shaun choked on his drink, spraying water inside the glass and having to rest a hand on the worktop to cough and burp until he could breathe again.

"Sorry," he croaked, more annoyed at himself for interrupting the conversation than they seemed to be.

"Mum, *missiles*? What the hell are you talking about?"

"Well, I wasn't really paying attention... I was working, I only had the TV on as background noise really. I usually listen to the radio, only this little one wanted to sit with me, and I had her programmes on, then the news cut in and the power went off."

Amanda rambled, clearly flustered and frightened, so when Shaun spoke, he tried to sound calm and reassuring.

"Amanda, what did they say about the missiles?"

"Something about China mobilising troops or something, and the US launching a counterstrike. Said Russia had fired something— I don't really know, like I said, it was just background noise—"

Libby burst out in tears, putting her glass down and

hugging her daughter, who returned the squeeze but had no idea why her mother was so sad.

Shaun felt lightheaded, fearing that his knees would refuse to hold him upright any longer. He pulled a chair out from the table in the kitchen and sat down heavily. His eyes were wide in shock as he rearranged all the information he'd heard to try and make it make sense to him.

His mind pulled him back to that clickbait article he'd read. It felt like a year ago, even though it could only have been in the last two days. Something about thermonuclear detonations in the upper atmosphere. Or was it in space? Either way, the simulation video he'd watched through sheer boredom had shown what would happen to the population when something like that happened.

It was little more than guesswork based on some sketchy Internet sensationalism, but all the pieces fit.

"EMP," he said.

"What?" Amanda demanded, speaking as though the stranger in her house was insane.

"An electromagnetic pulse, mum. It fries everything electrical. Phones, computers, cars… it's all useless." She turned to Shaun, asking him as though he was an expert on the subject.

"It is permanent?"

"I… I have no idea…"

"What about radiation? Will there be, like, *fallout* or anything?"

Shaun again protested that he didn't know, wondering about that very fact himself.

Images of radioactive ash falling from the clouds filled his imagination, the unknown results of such an occurrence terrifying him. He wished he'd known more, wished he'd paid attention or even been one of the doomsday types who spent their lives waiting for some catastrophe to befall humanity so they could run to the hills and live off the land.

"Well, I'm sure the government or the army or whoever will sort it all out," Amanda said with a smile, as if a positive mental approach could solve any problem. That smile slipped, making it clear she didn't wholly believe her words.

CHAPTER EIGHT

WTF

A bbie led Lydia through the streets, heading for their home. Lydia had regained enough of her senses to untie the belt from her Gi and tie it through Chunk's collar so they didn't lose their loyal waste food recycler.

He still skipped and barked as they walked, but his distress after the crash had faded.

Abbie's distress had not. Not at all. If anything, it was worse now that she was calmer and more aware of their surroundings.

No cars moved. Nothing flew in the sky. No lights were on anywhere and every street was filled with people frowning at their phones while repeating the same actions to try and make their lifelines of connectivity work again.

She had abandoned hers, leaving it stuffed into a jacket pocket as a thousand pounds' worth of paperweight, but

Lydia still checked hers intermittently as if by some miracle it would come back to life.

A commotion behind them made Abbie turn to see two men fronting up to one another. It was all alpha male peacocking bullshit, because going nose to nose with anyone was an invitation for that nose to be broken. She ignored the intimidation tactics, unable to hear what their disagreement was over, but encouraged Lydia to pick up the pace.

"Come on, let's jog for a while," she said, forcing a smile that she didn't believe in.

Lydia saw it and returned one of her own, although with far less effort to make it seem genuine. The two of them upped the pace with Chunk cantering happily alongside. He ran with his body diagonally, looking more like a padded rocking horse than a dog, and looked up at them excitedly as if the confrontation was already forgotten and he was having the best day ever.

"Mum… they won't… they won't put Chonk down, will they?" Lydia asked.

"What? No! Why would you say that?"

"Because he bit that man. When dogs bite people, they have to be put down, don't they?"

"If a dog is bad and bites people for no reason, but Chunk was defending us, right?"

Lydia seemed to accept the answer, but Abbie knew the question came from a place that had no comprehension of what was happening. The fact that she still thought of there being anyone who would track them down and prosecute the incident showed that she didn't understand the severity of the situation.

Everywhere Abbie looked she saw more and more concerning signs of this being far bigger than anyone could imagine, and the text exchange with Jez had only made her nerves more fraught.

She cut them down an alleyway, aiming to cross a public field to get to their housing estate and cut out a couple of miles of streets filled with crashed cars and confused, angry people.

She briefly considered turning back, heading for Devonport docks like Jez had said, but the compulsion to be in her own home was too strong. She needed those four walls, needed that security blanket of familiarity, and part of her still hoped there would be a resolution to the whole mess if they could just get home and hide from it.

Lydia groaned as her white trainers splashed in the muddy edges of the footpath, but Abbie had far greater concerns on her mind. Chunk pulled hard on the makeshift lead, wanting to have fun and run across the damp grass, and Abbie looked around and seeing nobody else, she bent and untied the knot.

Chunk tore away, propelling his bulk like an overladen motorbike away from the lights, and Abbie automatically looped the belt diagonally over her torso as she did with his lead.

"Mum, what about the car?"

"I… I don't know."

"Can we go back and get it later? Or can a recovery truck collect it?"

"We'll see," Abbie said, brushing her daughter off with the non-committal answer. It seemed to work because she stayed quiet for a while.

"What's that?"

Abbie looked at her, following the outstretched hand to see her pointing out into the wide stretch of water leading to the English Channel. Abbie squinted, her eyes not as sharp as her daughter's at such distance, but she made out the shape of a large boat sitting unnaturally in the choppy waters.

It was leaning over, something her mind told her was called listing, and each consecutive wave to hit it from the direction of open water seemed to push it over more.

"It's a boat," she answered flatly, hoping Lydia wouldn't carry on asking questions and force her to admit that people were in danger and there was nothing either of them could do to help.

"But… it's sinking," Lydia said hesitantly, as if unsure that she was even seeing what was happening, like it wasn't real. Or that she *hoped* it wasn't real.

Abbie said nothing. It wasn't that she didn't care, but a sound behind them had forced her to turn around.

Four shapes, all on bikes, had entered the field through the same narrow gateway they had used, only now they fanned out to approach in a line.

She didn't know why, but Abbie had a sense that they did not want to meet these people. Not now, not here.

She kicked herself for not staying in the residential streets where loud screams could attract attention. Where a commotion would draw witnesses and bystanders who might intervene or even make a person think twice about doing something.

She knew she had a negative opinion of people in general, probably through years of partnership with her husband who saw the bad in everyone and everything, but she couldn't ignore that feeling that she had a very short space of time to avoid a terrible experience for both of them.

"Come on," she said, tugging at Lydia's sleeve and breaking into a run again while letting out a short whistle. Chunk turned direction, adding some speed as he threw up clods of loose earth behind him. She directed them off the path, heading for a patch of woodland that she knew would lead to the back of their estate.

Tall grass and brambles caught on their clothes as Abbie ignored Lydia's protests. Her daughter hadn't seen the other people yet, and she didn't want to alarm her daughter unless she had to. No more than she was already alarmed, at least.

Chunk overtook them easily and surged ahead, forcing his way through the dense undergrowth like a shark swimming just beneath the surface.

If the shark was overweight and daft.

She thought she heard a shout from far behind them, but the sound they made crashing through the dense foliage drowned it out to the point where she might have imagined it. Finally arriving under the thick, evergreen canopy of a line of massive pines, she stopped and rested her hands on her knees.

"Stand up straight," Lydia gasped. She was standing erect with her hands behind her head, sucking in air to refuel. Abbie did as her daughter instructed as a patch of nearby bushes rustled before spitting out a panting, happy, chocolate Labrador.

It took them almost twenty minutes walking under the heavy tree cover to find a break that permitted them access to the estate. Walking down a narrow footpath between two houses brought them onto a street where Abbie paused, trying to get her bearings for where they were.

She almost reached for her phone, doing it the easy way by looking at their location on the map so she knew precisely which way to head for home.

"Mum?"

She spun around, looking at Lydia in case her daughter had seen some danger that she hadn't, but she just stared back at her.

"Sorry, I'm not sure which way to—"

"It's this way," Lydia said, crossing the road holding Chunk's temporary lead. She still looked both ways before walking, as if any car still had the chance of moving.

It took them another ten minutes to reach their street, and just as Abbie remembered that her house keys were still in the ignition of her car, a shout from across the street snapped her eyes open.

"Hi!" the voice called again, and Abbie saw the man who lived opposite waving with a wide smile on his face. "Your power out too?" he asked, betraying how little he knew of what was happening.

She knew he worked from home the majority of the week, disappearing for a few days at a time in his new electric car to meetings in various parts of the world that he liked to mention whenever he found the opportunity.

"Um, yeah," she said, not sure how to explain that it was a little more serious than just a power cut.

"I hope it's back on soon, I need to fly out to Munich later this afternoon for a meeting. Don't want to have to get a cab to the airport!" he said with a chuckle, smoothing a loving hand on the roof of his newest materialistic acquisition.

Abbie smiled politely, not giving the slightest shit about his precious car, and carried on to her front door.

Looking up and down the street to see if anyone was watching, she slid the stone plant pot aside to recover the hidden spare key before screwing her face up in anger.

She had removed it, because Shaun knew that she kept a spare front door key in case of emergencies, and she didn't want him turning up drunk in the middle of the night again.

"Fuck sake," she hissed, earning a confused look from Lydia. Abbie smiled and straightened, looking up and down the street again and seeing none of the carnage they had witnessed in the city. It struck her how desperate the situation was, because those panicked people in areas where help was needed and wasn't coming would spread out into quiet places like their street before long.

As far as everyone there knew, this was just a routine power outage.

Not that such things were routine these days. Abbie had grown up knowing where the candles and matches were in her house because power cuts were common in those days, but she struggled to think of the last time the lights had been off for more than a few minutes in the last decade.

She led them down the side of the house, squeezing past the green waste bin and the half-filled recycling boxes, to reach the back gate.

"Over you go," she told Lydia, knowing that it was bolted on the inside.

"Mum, why—"

"Because I left the keys in the car, and I'd quite like to get inside," Abbie snapped, still smiling but wearing an expression that told her daughter now was not the time to be argumentative.

Lydia huffed, expressing her distaste for being used as a trained monkey, and climbed over the six-foot gate to drop down on the other side with a reverberating rattle of the lock. Sounds of scraping metal rang out as she withdrew the bolt with a wiggle, and Abbie stepping onto their patio with Chunk pushing past her legs. Untying the belt, she let the dog loose, and he immediately sought an appropriate spot in their small garden to conduct business he could easily have handled in the woods.

Abbie ignored it, looking at the small window of her utility room that was left open to vent the heat from the tumble drier.

"Lydia?"

Her daughter looked at her, then at the window, and threw a momentary strop with the accompanying noise before reaching up and jumping to grab the open edge. Abbie helped, pushing her from behind as Lydia complained and shrieked at falling into the house face first.

She slid in, landing loudly and going out of sight before popping up from behind the counter to glare at her mother, almost daring her to laugh.

Abbie pointed at the patio doors, trying to keep the frustrated anger from her body language, and waited patiently for Lydia to unlock the doors as slowly as she could without making it obvious that she was stalling and getting told off for it.

Abbie snatched open the door and stepped inside, turning back to whistle for Chunk but seeing him happily checking every corner of the garden. Leaving him outside, she went in and stripped off her jacket to pace the kitchen.

Lydia poured herself water from the tap and drank it, filling the glass with more and offering it to her mother, who waved it away distractedly. As Lydia poured it into the sink, she had a thought that running water might not be a thing for long and tried to stop her, but it was already too late.

"What?" Lydia asked, concerned that she had done something wrong.

"Nothing, it's fine. I'm going to get changed," she said, looking down at the mess she had made of their kitchen floor with her muddy boots and kicking them off before stepping out into the tiled hallway.

She ran up the stairs, nervous energy preventing her from walking, and threw off her clothes to continue pacing in the bedroom.

She stopped, hands on hips, wearing just her bra and knickers that didn't match. One was for show, the other was for comfort, and just as she became aware of the fact that her curtains were open and she was standing there in broad daylight, she looked out of the window to catch the eye of the neighbour they had just spoken to.

He looked away, pretending that he hadn't ben staring, but Abbie had already seen him and didn't fall for the innocent act.

Angrily pulling the curtains closed, she resumed pacing, trying to think of what to do. She wished she could call Shaun. All the times she had stopped herself from running to him, from asking him questions, just to prove that she could stand on her own two feet, all the texts and calls she had ignored from him in the hope that he would recover from whatever mid-life crisis he was going through and come back to them… all of that she would trade in a heartbeat to be able to speak with him in that moment.

She sucked in a steadying breath through her nose and held it, blowing it out through her pursed lips with a light whistle before throwing on a vest top and an oversized hoodie over a fresh pair of jeans.

Walking back downstairs, she went to the kitchen and opened the fridge for the wave of cool air to brush her exposed skin. She was thinking that she had just lost some ability to keep food fresh, but standing there for no real reason other than to stare at the contents, she closed the door again and forced herself to stay calm.

"Mum, what's happening?" Lydia asked. She was sitting at the breakfast bar behind her, one hand resting on Chunk's head as it rested on her thigh.

Fucked if I know, Abbie thought, but she turned and smiled reassuringly.

"And before you say it's a power cut, I know it isn't.

Power cuts don't stop cars from working, do they? Power cuts don't drain phone batteries."

"No. No they don't," Abbie admitted, deflating as she dropped the pretence of feeling confident. She moved to sit on a stool beside her daughter and rested her head on her folded arms.

"The phone batteries aren't flat. Neither are the car batteries. They stopped working all the same time and…"

"And what?" Lydia asked after her mother didn't offer the rest of the sentence.

"And I got a text from someone who might know more than regular people about stuff."

"What does that mean? Who? Was it that man you wouldn't tell me about?"

"Lydia, now's not the time—"

"Mum! What do you know? Please?"

Abbie closed her eyes again, composing herself before she answered.

"I've been talking to a man in the military. He text me earlier and asked for our address."

"You didn't give it to him, did you? Mum, he could be a psycho or something—"

"No, I didn't, but I wish now that I had. He said that if everything goes wrong, we should head to the naval base."

"Wait, he told you this was going to happen?"

"No, not specifically. Look, he just said—"

"Mum, why didn't we go there straight away?" Lydia was wide-eyed and angry at her mother. She stood, dislodging the dog who grumbled and slunk away to his bed in case he was somehow the one to have caused the anger.

"Look, we don't know what's happening. The power might come back on and things could go back to normal, then we'd look silly for traipsing through the city only to turn up at a bloody navy base and have to explain why we're there!"

"Yeah, and other people might get rescued and we could be left behind…"

Abbie watched as Lydia's expression changed from anger to fear, slowly morphing the girl into a younger version of herself. She knew what was coming because she'd already had the same thought.

"Dad. He's all the way up in Scotland…"

"I know."

"How can he get back? If cars don't work… do the planes still work? Can he fly back?"

"I don't know."

"And if we go running off to some base somewhere, then how is he going to find us?"

"Lydia—"

"What?" Her interruption was angry, born of fear and frustration, but Abbie was stressed out and close to the edge herself.

"Nothing. Forget it."

She stood and stormed out of the kitchen with no real clue where she was going. Pacing in the hallway, she stopped, hands to her face, and tried to gain some self-control.

A knock on the frosted glass in the front door made her jump, made her heart slam in her chest like a machine. Lydia appeared in the doorway, concern on her face, but Abbie waved her back before walking to the door and pressing her face to the spy hole.

Stepping back, she unlocked the door and opened it to reveal the man from across the road and his wife. Their fake smiles told Abbie they were after something – something they needed and she had – but she hardly felt in the mood to be generous.

"Hi, sorry, me again," the man said. His expression was apologetic, and Abbie didn't know if that apology was for the intrusion on her doorstep or for watching her through the upstairs window.

"We were just hoping," the woman said with a wide, awkward grin, "that we might be able to borrow your car."

Abbie was taken aback by the presumptuous request. That reaction was clearly visible in her expression because the couple recoiled and immediately started to make soothing gestures.

"I know, it's a lot to ask, only my husband has to get on a flight in a few hours, and we can't seem to get through to any cab companies because the Internet is off and both our phones have run out of battery—"

"I don't have my car. It's... it's broken down."

"It's an intrusion, we understand that, but I'd be willing to pay you double what a cab would charge," the man tried, as if money could somehow magically undo the fact that she had already told them her car wasn't working.

"I literally cannot help you, I'm sorry," she said, already moving back to close the door.

They deflated; the apologetic looks turning to annoyance that someone would deny them such a simple request. The door shut, muffling the shout as they walked away.

"Thanks for nothing!"

"Fucking pricks," Abbie groused, making sure she locked the door and added the chain for good measure.

"They don't know, do they?" Lydia asked. Her tone was quiet, and it haunted Abbie.

"No. I don't think they do."

"Why didn't you tell them?"

"Tell them what? That he isn't going to get on a plane

because nothing works? You'd think they might've figured that out by themselves."

She was stunned that her neighbours were still assuming that everything was normal, that the technology they relied on for everything would just come back to life, but the stress of deciding their next move overrode thoughts of others.

"Food. You need some lunch," Abbie said, glancing at her smartwatch for the tenth time only to find that it was still showing her a blank screen. She huffed and slipped it off, dropping it into the bowl where she usually deposited her car keys when she got in.

They made sandwiches, the makings taken from the fridge already losing the chill edge to them and ate them sitting in the kitchen in silence.

Lydia asked her what they were going to do, but when Abbie told her honestly that she didn't know yet, the conversation ended entirely.

The temperature dropped as the afternoon wore on. Abbie paced the house and Lydia sat in silence, staring at the wall to replace the phone screen that had filled her world only that morning.

Abbie was grateful for the log burner in their lounge, and Lydia pulled soft blankets from the wicker basket beside the sofa to settle down in front of the weak flames Abbie was nursing to life, with Chunk pushing in to sit and lean heavily against her as if jealous and wanting to get in on the act.

They sat in silence still, watching the fire, until Lydia's soft voice broke the spell.

"…mum…?"

Abbie turned to look at her, seeing her daughter staring

out of the window and spinning to see what had sparked the fear.

Shimmering vertical lines of green turned blue at the top, filling the darkening sky like the brightest, most vivid aurora she had ever seen a picture of.

"What is it?"

"Northern lights," Abbie said softly.

"But… we live in the south. Why is it here?"

"I… I don't know, baby. I really don't know."

CHAPTER NINE

No Plan

Shaun grew ever more aware of how he smelled. Sitting on the immaculate sofa, nestled between perfectly fluffed cushions trying not to rub his socked feet on the flawless, cream carpet, he stayed still and self-conscious.

"Shaun?" Libby said, startling him back to the moment.

"Huh?"

"Mum asked if you wanted a cup of tea," Libby said quietly. Her daughter, who he found out was called Harper despite having no official introduction, rested against her chest, half-awake as if exhausted by the stress of the adults.

"Oh, er, yes please. Only…"

"Gas is still on," Amanda explained, cutting him off. "And I'm old enough to remember how to strike a match."

Shaun got the distinct impression that the household he was a guest in neither had nor needed a male input. The three generations of family seemed wholly capable of looking after themselves from what he'd seen.

He shifted in the chair, getting an unpleasant whiff of himself as a reward for moving. He'd been drenched in sweat three times already that day, and each time it had dried to leave layers on his skin and produced an aroma that even he found unpleasant.

"Is there anywhere I can wash up?" he asked, offering an embarrassed smile by way of explanation.

"Upstairs, door in front of you," she answered softly as she stroked down the bouncy, tight curls on her daughter's head.

He stood, smiling his thanks and went upstairs with the sound of pans clanging together in the kitchen. The resilience pleased him, even if he couldn't be sure why. Like many people his age, the derision he felt for the younger generations with their smartphones and their wireless devices and their streaming on demand services was strong.

He wondered how many hipsters or Gen-Whatevers would be looking at their artisanal espresso machines waiting for the power to come back on so they could straighten their pointy beards and discuss their preferred pronouns.

He knew the situation was making him think cranky thoughts – even more cranky than usual – and he knew he was being unkind in his generalisations.

He'd been called out on a comment not long before when he muttered something about millennials and endured a loud lecture about how millennials had mortgages and preferred nights in. In his mind they were the entitled youth but factually speaking they were professionals in their late thirties.

He was still pointlessly daydreaming about the subject when it dawned on him that the hot water he was running was a finite resource. The water wasn't hot as much as warm, but he figured whatever there was left in the tank wouldn't be replaced without the power coming back on.

He killed the tap and poked around in the spotlessly clean shower for some form of soap that wasn't overly feminine. Opting for something claiming to be pH balanced, he stripped off his t-shirt and washed awkwardly over the sink.

He did the same after stripping off his jeans and underwear before rubbing himself clean with a towel large enough to be classed as bedding. When it came to getting dressed again, he had no option but to put the same damp, stiff jeans back on and return the funky smelling t-shirt over his head. As a final attempt to not repulse the others, he helped himself to some deodorant spray after weighing up the pros and cons of smelling feminine or just plain bad.

Libby's nose wrinkled when he walked back into the downstairs room, but she said nothing so as not to embarrass him. He was grateful for that, just as he was grateful for the cup of hot tea sitting waiting for him.

"Didn't know if you wanted sugar or not?" Amanda asked. She hovered in the doorway to the kitchen holding her own mug in two hands as if waiting for her brew to be appraised.

"Not for me, thanks. Can't stomach it in tea," Shaun answered, unsure why he added the irrelevant personal information. He sipped, finding that it did indeed hit precisely the correct spot, and fought the urge to let out an ungentlemanly *aaaagh*.

"Lovely. Just the thing," he said, smiling his thanks at Amanda, who nodded with a cautious grace to allow his compliment to be entered into the record.

They sat in awkward silence for a while as each of them

took sips of their tea and struggled for relevant conversation. It was Amanda, in her forthright manner that Shaun was beginning to expect, who broke the tension.

"Well, any suggestions on what to do until order gets restored?" she asked, looking out of the front window distractedly.

"We can't go back out there, mum. It's crazy. People are looting!" Libby half covered Harper's exposed ear when she spoke, as if she could shield her daughter from anything the world was throwing at her.

"I'm not sure sitting it out is an option either, not now anyway," Amanda answered ominously.

That got both Shaun and Libby's attention as she strode across the room and snatched the floor length curtains closed to peer out of the central gap. Shaun stood, not wanting to encroach, so he moved to the side and looked out.

He saw a man hurrying his family onto their bicycles, all of them weighed down with a full backpack. Shaun had imagined similar scenes playing out all over the place, as people with a plan for such events scrambled to make it to the place they deemed safe.

"That's the Corbett family out of here," Amanda said in a matter-of-fact way.

"What do they do?" Shaun asked, unsure why he wanted to know but going with a gut feeling.

"From what I remember, he does something with timber sales to the building trade. Travels a lot in that flash company car," she added with a subtle lift of her chin.

Shaun saw a nearly new Jaguar sitting uselessly on the double driveway beside a compact SUV. He followed his train of thought further.

"And what about her?"

"I *think* she does something with… oh my. She's something to do with the MOD. You don't think that means…?"

"I think that means she might know the army isn't coming to help," Libby said, picking up on her mother's earlier attestations that order would be restored along with the power.

Shaun turned back to speak to Amanda, but she was already unlocking the front door and striding across the threshold. He looked back out of the window to see her waving at the family across the street as she walked, calling out to them.

Not wanting to hear a second-hand account, he shoved his feet into his shoes and followed her.

"I'm sorry, we can't stop," the female neighbour said. Shaun picked up something in her tone, in the way she tried to sound cheery in such obvious contrast to their actions, and it worried him deeply.

"Where are you going? What do you know about all this?" Amanda demanded, not put off one bit by the breezy brush-off the woman had tried to give her.

"I'm sorry, I really can't say—"

"You bloody well can!" Amanda snapped back. "What do you know?"

The woman hesitated, hopping a couple of steps as the unfamiliar bicycle threatened to unbalance her when she stopped.

"Look…" she lowered her voice, glancing back at her two children who seemed to be enjoying the adventure. "Look, you need to get out of town. Head for somewhere smaller on the coast."

"Why?" Shaun asked, earning a flash of confusion from the woman, who didn't recognise him from the street and another of annoyance from Amanda, who didn't seem to appreciate his interruption.

"Why?" she echoed, fixing the woman with a look that said she wasn't going to relent.

"This might get worse, you understand? *Much* worse," the neighbour said in a hiss. She had dropped the pretence and looked frightened now, which made Shaun feel more worried than he liked.

"Worse how?" he asked.

"Just worse, okay? Listen, the power isn't coming back on. Most people will sit and try to wait it out, but in a couple of days the place will tear itself apart. Just… just get out of here if you can."

"Stella!" the woman's husband snapped from his place at the head of the waiting bicycle convoy.

"I'm sorry, we have to go… good luck," she said, turning and wobbling away until she picked up enough speed to settle her unfamiliar transport into a straight line.

Shaun stood in the street beside Amanda. Both were dumbstruck and confused in equal measure, and both felt a growing dread creeping over them like storm clouds rolling in.

As if expecting a peal of thunder to erupt, Shaun looked up but only saw the faint hints of green and blue above the grey clouds.

Walking back to the house, they found Libby and Harper waiting on the doorstep for them. When the conversation was relayed, Libby looked ready to burst out in tears.

"What do we do?" she asked, looking from her mother to Shaun as if either of them could magic up an answer.

To make it worse, Amanda turned to look at him and double the pressure he felt.

"I… I have no idea… maybe we should do what she suggested? Head for the coast?"

"And do what? Fish for cod and wait?" Amanda asked. Shaun closed his eyes and fought the urge to snap.

"I don't know. If we've got no power here, how long before the rest of Europe figures it out and sends help? Or America?"

"Like they've got time to waste coming here and turning our lights back on?" Amanda asked. "Missiles, Mister Taylor. *Missiles*. We're stuck in between two countries having a fight. That's what I think."

"Well, we only saw two flashes in the sky, right?" he asked, looking up to include Libby. She nodded her agreement. "So that might mean that the further south we go, the less this affects us?"

"That's your plan? Walk south and hope they've got power?" Amanda asked coldly, making him well aware that she didn't approve of his plan. He'd had enough stress and disapproval by then, and snapped.

"What do you want me to say? My family is back down south and I'm stuck up here. It's eight hours in a car, so God only knows how long it'll take without one."

He raised his voice when he spoke, throwing his arms up in the air and slapping them back down as if close to giving up.

"I'm… I'm supposed to pick up my daughter for the school holidays next Friday."

He spoke the words quietly, as if dejected and ashamed of something unspoken. His knees threatened again to give way but he stood tall, telling himself that he wouldn't give in and cry, and looking back at him were three generations of females who all seemed to convey something different in the way they looked at him.

Amanda seemed hardened to his anguish. She held the poise of a woman who had spent too many years looking after a man like he was another child, and seemed to show him no sympathy, as if incapable of it.

Shaun could see it clearly then. Could the messy divorce and the strong, single woman raising a daughter who went out and made a whole new bunch of mistakes all by herself. He made that assumption based on the absence of a man in Libby and Harper's lives, and based on his own experiences, he told himself they wouldn't be able to see anything from his perspective.

"Well then, you'd better not start on an empty stomach," Amanda said as she edged her way past her daughter and granddaughter to head for her kitchen.

Shaun was left shocked, unsure what was happening, but allowed himself to be taken inside.

"Right," Amanda said, clapping her hands together and rubbing them as if to signify that the real work was about to begin. "Libby, you fetch me everything from the fridge and freezer that wants to go off any time soon. Shaun?"

"Yes?" His eyebrows went up hopefully, grateful for any kind of direction.

"Cupboard over there. You'll find bottles and flasks. Fill them all up with water, please, and when you're done with that can you go upstairs and fill the bath and the bathroom sinks."

Shaun nodded and set to work. He knew her instructions were sensible, hacking into some deeply repressed memory of public safety videos from history. Stockpiling water was a good idea, and if the supply never went away all they had to do was pull the plug and nothing was really wasted.

He filled the bottles, trying not to get in the way of the military operation that was Amanda utilising every gas hob in rotation to cook up all the food that would spoil. He wasn't sure if it was necessary, but it felt good to be doing something to prepare for a worst-case scenario rather than sitting on a stranger's sofa wringing his hands like Mister Smithers.

He moved upstairs, seeing that the theme of the show home extended to the bedrooms, and confirmed his assumption that this family had no male influence at all.

When he'd finished running two baths and three sinks full of cold water, he returned to the kitchen where the smell of cooking meat filled his nostrils to remind his stomach that it hadn't been filled since his oversized breakfast.

The activity wasn't a priority, not that he knew what was supposed to be a priority in such a situation, but they threw themselves into it with an enthusiasm that helped mask the fear and confusion.

He joined in, still trying to be unobtrusive as he was a stranger in their private domain, and as good as the activity felt, he couldn't shake the neighbour's attestation that things were going to get worse.

Much worse.

Food was cooked and eaten. More was cooked and packed into Tupperware containers or wrapped in foil. Libby made sandwiches with Harper sitting on the worktop beside her and sealed them inside plastic sandwich bags as if they preparing for the largest packed lunch on record.

Shaun was still stressed. In fact, he felt that the stress he was bottling up was growing somehow and multiplying the longer he ignored it, but the only way he could imagine expressing it was by a screaming, terrified breakdown that threatened to explode from him at any point.

As the sky began to darken and the cooking marathon

came to an end, the sky outside through the kitchen window took on an appearance he'd never seen before.

He stared so hard that his inaction attracted the attention of the others. They joined him by the window to lean forward and look up.

"I've *never* seen the lights so bright this far south," Amanda said in hushed amazement.

Shaun's heart went cold. He'd experienced that sudden dread far too many times already that day to ignore it.

"Lights? The northern lights?" he asked, having never seen the phenomenon that was the aurora borealis before.

"That's wrong," Libby said. Her voice conveyed how Shaun felt. She stalked from the room, no longer attached to her daughter who had gone to play with her toys in the lounge. She walked to the patio doors and unlocked them, throwing them open to step outside wearing only her socks. She looked up, leaning back and staring intently at the incredible display in the darkening sky.

"Oh… oh, I see what you mean…"

Shaun turned to Amanda, concerned at her words but not understanding.

"What is it?" he asked, worried about the potential answer but unable to continue not knowing.

"It's blue," Libby said. "And the green is… *wrong*."

"Wrong how?" he asked.

"It's too green. Normally it sort of… comes *down*, you know?" Amanda said. Shaun didn't know, not at all, but he knew that the growing light show didn't look at all natural.

Blues and greens blossomed, distorted by the cloud cover to spread out the shining colours so they filled the sky more each second.

That was when he knew that article he'd seen was correct, because the testing in the sixties had made a similar kind of light show, or so he'd read. There was no doubt in his mind now. The UK had been attacked, he was sure of that, either intentionally or as collateral caught in the crossfire.

But one thing was pretty certain, and that was the fact that the lights weren't coming back on.

CHAPTER TEN

How?

Davidson blinked. His eyes stung like he had dust in them. He blinked again, intentionally scratching his eyeballs on the coarse covering as though discomfort somehow told him things were okay.

If he felt discomfort, then he wasn't dead. How wasn't he dead? He'd been in a plane crash, hadn't he? There was no way he wasn't dead. How wasn't he dead?

The discomfort in his eyes was replaced by the dizzying wave of nausea and the thumping of blood in his ears.

It took him another second to realise he was upside down, suspended from the lap belt that was so tight it was preventing his heart from pumping the blood back up to his feet.

Muttering incoherent sounds of shock and panic, Davidson fumbled for the release catch without considering the consequences of his actions. As soon as his numb fingers gained purchase on the metal catch, gravity did what it did and sent him down – or up – to slam the back of his neck and shoulders into the plastic sheeting of what had been the cabin roof.

"*Fffffffuck,*" he groaned, rolling from side to side until the pain went away. The pain in his hands and head where there was too much blood. The pain in his feet where the pins and needles stung worse than any time he'd ever experienced them before. The pain in his neck and back where he'd hit the ground – the ceiling – and the pain *everywhere.*

The only time he'd ever felt like that was when he'd been a passenger in his friend's Peugeot 206, and the idiot had tried to show off all six months of his driving experience, resulting in the car rolling into trees.

That had been over twenty years ago.

It was all too much, and he folded up in the foetal position to vomit acidic bile. It ran down his cheeks, coming out of his nose and stinging his gritty eyes even worse. He coughed, retching loudly, and making a sound that made him feel even more sick than he already did.

He didn't know if he'd passed out again, but when his senses returned to him, the former contents of his stomach were plastered in a cold goo against his face.

"Ooohh… *God…*" he groaned, trying to get back to his hands and knees. To move. To *do* something, even if he didn't have the first clue what that thing was.

He managed a form of forward momentum, crawling like Bambi on ice, when another sensation punched him in the face.

Shit. Actual human shit, and something told him it came from multiple sources. He coughed, retching again but the tank was empty, and it left him looking down at his blood-soaked hands. He stopped, checking himself over and finding nowhere on his body that it was coming from.

"Roz," he croaked, leaning back to try and lift his stiff neck up to where she had been; only he looked to his left, where she had been sitting beside him. Now that the fuselage was upside down, she was on the other side and the best he could manage was to lie down again and roll to be able to see her without hurting his neck again.

"Roz?" he asked, on his side and frowning up at the mess in the seat above him. He asked because the thing in her seat didn't look like her at all. There was a lot of blood, but he told himself that didn't always mean the worst. Small cuts could produce a lot of blood and look worse than they were.

What he couldn't comprehend was the bright white shape among the blood. It looked like the cut off end of a plastic pipe, same as the kind that the plumber who changed his boiler had used, but it looked wrong. It looked different.

And it dripped something onto the floor near his left hand, landing with a wet slap.

Davidson leaned closer to peer at the globs of... of *stuff*, recoiling when he smelled the same acidic bile that he had just expelled. Something dangled from the mess, spinning slowly around. It was angular, like a right angle but not as straight.

Looking back up again, he formed the words on his lips to ask Roz what the stuff was, but the shock faded away like clearing fog, and he saw the spinning thing was half of her lower jaw as the teeth rotated into his eye line.

Headless, still strapped into the seat, whatever had carved a straight line through the side of the plane had removed her head at mouth level and carried on going.

The top of his seat was gone; torn away to leave a tangle of moulded foam and ruined material right where his head would have been if he hadn't leaned forward with no idea if that was the right thing to do.

It had been, clearly, but he couldn't shake the feeling that what he'd already seen would be worse to have to live with than if he'd died on impact as Roz had.

As most of the passengers on the entire plane had, by the look of things.

With the sobering realisation of what he had been dangling beside, Davidson tried to move to take in the sights of other people, finding more carnage and mangled bodies in a few seconds than he could handle.

Pain momentarily forgotten, he crawled away towards daylight. He fell over strewn possessions and exploded carry-on cases littering his path, and all he could do was focus on the open end of the plane where cold air rushed in.

He made it, slick with blood and covered in so many various bodily fluids that he shuddered to think what he could have contracted during his escape.

Daylight brought with it fresh air and the refreshing blanket of light rain, for which he was grateful. He was grateful too, to escape the smells and the acrid, chemical tang in the air, and for the cleansing water falling from the sky just as he and a hundred other people had done.

With his face resting against cool, damp grass he closed his eyes and felt a sob building from somewhere down near his pelvis. It grew, getting larger as it travelled along until it forced his chest to heave and his mouth to issue a whimper.

Then it came. Long and loud and so full of relief and anguish. So laced with fear and relief. So packed with terror and elation, of guilt and giddy fortune that he ended up laughing his way through the tears that ran from him with more intensity than the rain that fell on his collapsed form.

He didn't know how long he lay there, intermittently sobbing and laughing like an escaped mental patient, but he thought it had been long enough for sirens to at least be audible in the distance as the first responders rushed to the scene.

A passenger plane coming down would be declared a major incident in any civilised country, and he had personally seen action plans for disaster events on local and national scales, so he believed that he knew more than the average person about such things.

He mentally listed off what he expected to be coming to the scene, detailing every available emergency ambulance in the area, with surrounding areas calling in every crew they had to backfill regular demand.

The multi-disciplined hazardous area response teams – the HART boys and girls – they would be forming up their specialist convoys and blasting down the motorway to get to him.

There would be pumps from every fire station in the region on their way, again with relief crews scrambling to head in and pick up the slack.

Police, local authority, military, even. All would be fulfilling their individual roles for such a disaster and yet… and yet he didn't hear a damn thing over the clicking and creaking and groaning of the shattered plane lying on a gentle slope of wet grass.

He forced himself into a more upright position as good sense dictated that he should probably put more than a handful of metres between him and the wrecked fuselage that had a more than average chance of spontaneously igniting.

Standing was possibly one of the stupidest ideas he'd ever had, proved so by the solid impact back down to the wet earth that he guessed was only a thin covering over some very rocky ground.

He tried to imagine where he could be, recalling the projected flight path west back to Manchester, but he had closed his eyes before they had even set out over the North Sea so he guessed he could be anywhere between Skegness and Stockport.

A flash of memory told him there had been building – high rise buildings – moments prior to the crash, so he could hardly be out in the sticks where he could expect the local bobby to arrive with the village GP riding shotgun and carrying his leather bag. No, he was in a built-up area, so where were all the sirens?

He clumsily put his index fingers in both ears and wiggled them vigorously, sending another wave of dizziness and nausea through his head that he had to fight against, but still he heard nothing but the sounds of so much twisted metal.

He tried to stand again, falling down before giving up and crawling on hands and knees towards… he had no idea what he was going towards, only that he was moving away from the plane and all the horrors it contained.

He rested, allowing himself a moment to lie flat on the cool ground again and let the fresh rainwater take the heat away from his face, but a new sensation sparked a fear response that he couldn't understand. He felt the ground shaking, only slightly, but it pounded in a rhythmic way that made him imagine running footsteps.

Relief hit him then, washing away the fear, as he knew that help had finally arrived.

He expected strong, reassuring hands to rest on his shoulders and tell him that he was going to be okay. He tried to remember his name so he could tell the first responders that they would be able to get a message to...

The lab results. His eyes shot wide, and he twisted like a drunk attempting to make it to the toilet bowl in time. He had to save those results. He had to show Gurjit and the others that his theory, the one he had been cooking in the back of his mind before they took off, had real merit.

It was an attack, or at least the precursor to some attack, because the results they had found and the figures he had been shown in Copenhagen didn't add up. It wasn't scientifically possible to have isolated outbreaks limited to single patients so far apart. It didn't make sense, it was scientifically impossible for such an outbreak to be natural, given the data he could extrapolate from, so the obvious conclusion was that it *wasn't* natural.

He had to get his bag. He had to retrieve his laptop, otherwise he would need the researchers at the World Health Organization to send everything they had so he could try and convince London that the threat was real.

"Mate!" a voice said. It sounded muffled, like trying to talk softly after taking headphones off blaring loud music. "Mate, are you alright? Were you on the plane?" the voice asked.

Male. Young. Evidently belonging to someone lower down the spectrum of intelligence.

"No," Davidson muttered. "I need my—"

"Fuckin' *hell!*" the voice drawled, cutting him off. He felt a wave of heat, like opening the oven but on the other side of the kitchen, then the sound he had been dreading reached him.

Whhhoomph.

Crackling filled the air as plastic, metal, and people all

burned in the discarded cooking pot that was the remains of his plane.

Panicked lowing of cattle sounded nearby, filling Davidson's head with a crystal-clear recollection of Roz extolling the dangers of annual bovine-inspired deaths compared to aviation ones.

His feet were moving, or the burning plane was reversing, because he was half sitting up and either he was heading away from the plane or it was retreating from him.

He closed his eyes, knowing that all of his notes were gone, just hoping that his brain would work when he got the chance to call Gurjit and beg for him to take his word that something big was about to happen.

His own phone was lost, having been resting on his lap before the world took a giant shit on his plans, but the person dragging him put an end to any thoughts he had of making a call.

"Tried to ring 999 but the phone's dead. Everyone's phones are dead. Happened the same time as your plane shit itself."

Davidson tried to make sense of that, but the darkness around the edge of his vision was growing thicker and harder to see through. Everything was confusing. Even the feel of the stone wall his back was now resting against was alien, as a black cow with a white face watched him with obvious concern.

"You can fuck off, too," he croaked, sounding like he'd suffered a mild stroke. "Last thing I need is a cow… killing me after… that shit…"

He slumped over, dropping onto his back because it was the only place he didn't feel like he was going to fall over, and looked up at the brightest, most beautiful aurora he had ever seen.

CHAPTER ELEVEN

Restraining Order

S haun was invited to spend the night there, being offered one of the spare rooms which was decorated more for his mother's tastes than his own.

He felt bitter, despite their hospitality. He felt bitter that his own home, hard earned and enjoying years of improvements and redecorations, was no longer *his* home. He felt bitter that every woman like Amanda insisted on keeping the massive house as a beacon of her win over the man she'd lived there with.

He knew his anger and ingratitude stemmed from stress and fear, but he couldn't escape the fact that they'd just uncovered his true feelings.

He told himself that he'd go the following day, that he'd make his excuses and leave, only he didn't have the first clue how to make it home.

Five hundred miles, that's how far it was to drive, which

was why he'd made the decision to fly and hire a car from Edinburgh airport. Even with the inflated flight and hotel prices courtesy of the match he hadn't anticipated or even been aware of, it was still less hassle than spending an entire day behind the wheel. The thought of driving back was even worse.

Now, facing far more than that distance on foot, unless he felt like walking down the motorways, he'd have given anything for an entire day behind the wheel of a working car.

The lights had been off for a day – less even – and he couldn't believe how lost he felt being disconnected from the world.

He wasn't one of those people glued to his phone for eighteen hours a day, but the simple fact that his lifeline to the world beyond his immediate surroundings had been taken away left him with a dreadful anxiety that he couldn't shift.

He didn't sleep much that night, tossing and turning until the covers annoyed him so much that he threw them off and stood to pace the room. He cupped his head with his hands on both sides before a stab of pain in his right hand made him hiss in discomfort and look at it.

In the shimmering blue-green glow coming from around the curtains he couldn't see a bruise, but he knew how hard he'd hit the drunken idiot only the night before and he knew it would hurt.

His mind raced, spinning over decisions he'd made and incidents he'd involved himself in spanning decades and jumping around without any chronological coherence.

The violent life was supposed to be behind him now, only it seemed that no matter where he went, it found him. Conflict sought him out no matter what he did, and the previous night had been the first time in a long time he had given in and accepted it.

He hadn't lost control, not like he had done when he was younger, but he hated himself for how good the memory of hitting the idiot had felt.

The bloodthirsty love of violence warmed him, but his chaotic thoughts jumped to his wife and the last conversation he'd had with her.

You shouldn't have called, she said. *You can see her on the fifteenth like we'd arranged.*

Shaun hated her for that, but not as much as he hated himself for making her say that to him. He'd pushed her away for so long that now she was out of reach.

You shouldn't have called.

He closed his eyes and pressed the heels of both hands into his forehead, feeling the pressure build and the pain blossom in his sore right hand until it took over and forced him to relax.

His breathing had gone rapid, and he couldn't calm it down. His chest heaved, making him feel flushed and light-headed. Fearing a return of the panic attacks he'd once suffered, he tried to sit on the end of the bed and concentrate on his breathing, but he couldn't even sit still.

He knew how this would end. He'd experienced it before, only usually he'd drunk himself into an angry stupor first. This time he hadn't had a drop, which made it even more frightening. The dizziness grew stronger, threatening his consciousness, until a noise outside shut everything off like a light switch had been flipped.

He stepped to the window and leaned so he could see through the gap in the curtains. Three men, clearly visible in the glowing lights shining in the sky, crept up the side of the van sitting dead on the driveway.

Their body language screamed details directly into Shaun's consciousness, creating a list of facts he knew to be true.

Males, younger than him but not kids.

Undoubtedly up to no good.

He froze, watching their body language for any indication of their intent, seeing one of them trying to open the double doors of the up-and-over garage silently. He tried for a few seconds, turning back to the others and shaking his head.

Shaun watched, still as a statue and alert like a predator as they pointed towards the side gate and disappeared.

He spun away from the window, pulling on his jeans and T-shirt but nothing else, and stepped fast for the door to the landing. He moved downstairs lightly, as if his age and bulk were no longer weighing heavy on him, and froze again in the hallway with a view through the glass of the front door and the rear windows through the kitchen and out into the back garden.

He waited to see what they would do and caught his breath in his throat when the three of them slunk past the windows. He moved fast, entering the lounge in time to see one of them leaning his weight into the sliding doors leading to the patio.

He could see them, bathed in the false northern lights as they were, but they couldn't see him until he appeared directly before the glass and startled them.

Swearing and shouting erupted as they scrambled to try and escape, but Shaun's blood was up, and he wasn't satisfied with simply scaring them off. He turned and paced for the front door, turning the keys in the lock and striding outside barefoot, cloaked in an armour of arrogant anger.

They ran past him, crossing in front of the van from his right to his left, and he only just managed to shoot out a foot in time to trip that last one to send him sprawling on the block paving with a yelp of pain and shock.

Shaun didn't let him get up. He checked his footing and threw a kick with his entire body weight behind it, connecting the bottom of his shin with the soft flesh beneath the man's bottom rib.

Even through clothing the sound of the impact echoed around the cul-de-sac along with the winded *ooof* of his victim.

The other two didn't stop, didn't turn back to help their fallen comrade, they just ran and left him to whatever fate Shaun had in store for him.

He tried to rise, but Shaun lashed out again to stamp the bare sole of his foot into the man's chest. He flew backwards, twisting as his legs were still underneath him, to gasp and make sobbing noises as he sprawled out over the neat grass of the front lawn.

He tried to get up again, his movements desperate and uncoordinated, but Shaun closed the gap and hit him across the face with an open palm hard enough to send a sharp thunderclap ringing between the houses. The man slumped into semi-consciousness as a shrill sound erupted behind him.

"What the hell's going on?" Amanda's voice shrieked.

Shaun turned to face her, intending to explain what had happened, but she checked her headlong advance and recoiled so hard she almost lost her footing. From inside the house, he heard Harper crying, which unsettled him because he'd barely heard the little girl make a sound, recognising too late that *he* had been the thing to frighten Amanda.

"I... they tried to break in. Three of them. Two ran away," he explained lamely, suddenly feeling aware of the cold

outside and the heave of his chest. With that return of awareness of his body and his surroundings came the anxiety and
the familiar aches and pains he lived with daily.

He suddenly felt his age and then some. He felt shame for
the pain he'd inflicted on another person, not because they
didn't deserve it but because he'd enjoyed it. He felt the
humiliation of a bully confronted by his victims, even though
he knew he'd held back and that the man groaning and whim-
pering on the grass at his feet had done more than enough to
deserve his treatment.

"Break in? To *my* house?" Amanda asked, her shock and
fear replaced by indignant anger. She pushed past Shaun, no
longer frightened by the man he'd morphed back into, and
demanded to know the truth from the man rolling on the
ground.

"We… only wanted… food…" he said. Shaun could tell
from his tone that he was lying. Could sense the desperation
coming off him in stinking waves as he lied and made a bid
for sympathy.

"Well, you should've gone somewhere else," she said, as
if logic could resolve the whole situation.

An awkward few seconds of silence hung in the night air
as they regarded one another in the unnatural lights in the
night sky. Shaun decided to call the man's bluff and play
along with his story.

"Why come here then?" he asked.

"Huh?" the man rolling around in pain paused to ask.

"Why *this* house? Why not that one over there, or next
door? Why not the first house in the street?"

His voice sounded different to him, as if the coldness of
his anger had hardened it somehow. His question turned
Amanda around and focused her interest on the conversation.

"I… I…" the man stammered, looking between Shaun

and Amanda as he shuffled backwards to put distance between them.

"You *what*?" Amanda demanded, but he was already turning and scrambling away. He made it ten whole yards before he managed to regain his feet properly and run upright, by which time he was too far for Shaun to catch even if he was ten years younger and wearing shoes.

"Fucking *prick!*" he yelled, wounding Shaun with the final word as he fled.

"That was Curtis," Libby said from the doorway. She sounded small and frightened again, only now there was an edge to her voice that Shaun didn't like at all. She sounded genuinely afraid of someone.

"Curtis? Anton's friend?" Amanda asked, equalling her fear. Shaun looked at them in turn, waiting for an explanation as to who Curtis and Anton were and why that was relevant.

"Inside. Now," Amanda snapped, waving her hands at her daughter and granddaughter. Shaun followed, locking the door behind him after a last glance down the street to see if the three men were gone.

Libby was sitting in the lounge holding Harper. She rocked in the chair, shushing her child who seemed to be comforting her mother more than the other way around.

"What's going on?" Shaun asked. Amanda cleared her throat for attention, and he looked at her, able to make out the barest detail of her features in the glow coming through the windows. She jerked her head towards the kitchen and walked off, leaving him to follow.

Once out of sight of Libby, he listened to the explanation.

"A year ago, Harper's... *father*... well, he got out of prison," Amanda explained. Shaun looked back into the lounge, unable to see the two of them, but doing the mental arithmetic to calculate how old Harper would've been.

"He was sentenced to twenty-nine months, only he was out after a year. There's a... an order or something. He's not allowed anywhere near Libby or Harper, or he goes back to prison again."

Shaun bit his tongue when his first thought was to laugh and say what a fat chance he had of getting arrested now. He was glad he held back, because when Libby spoke from the doorway behind them, she sounded angry and humiliated.

"It's a non-molestation order. I applied for it ex-parte when I found out he was being released early. It means he can't contact us both. At all. Did you see the other two?"

Shaun admitted that he hadn't with a sorry shake of his head. He didn't admit that he hadn't been paying attention to what they looked like but was solely focused on hurting someone.

"I bet it was him," Libby said, looking past him to her mother. He could hear the quiver in her lip when she spoke.

Shaun wanted to ask what this Anton character had done, but he was already feeling wretched enough and didn't want the conversation to become about himself.

"I'll sleep down here," he said. "You three should get back to sleep."

"Mum, what if he comes back? We can't call the police and—"

"If he comes back, I'll deal with it," Shaun said, trying to sound reassuring but coming across as menacing instead. He winced, wishing he could take back the words because the last thing this family needed was another aggressive male in their lives.

"Mum?" Libby asked, regressed once again from the confident, busy young woman he'd first read.

Amanda looked at Shaun, peering at him in the odd, low

light as if assessing whether he was good for his word and if she could trust him.

"We'll leave first thing in the morning. Head down to your uncle's house," she said.

"Where's that?" Shaun asked, looking between the two of them.

"Lake District," Libby told him. Shaun fought the urge to ask her to narrow it down. Details could wait.

"How?" Libby asked. "How are we going to get there?"

"Same way you got home today. Find a way," Amanda said, brushing off what Shaun thought was a significant problem with some more positive mental attitude.

Shaun bit his tongue yet again, and went to retrieve the rest of his clothing from the bedroom to keep watch for the remainder of the night.

CHAPTER TWELVE

Do Something

Abbie sat awake on the sofa staring at the blank, black reflective surface of the widescreen television.

She sipped at a cold coffee taken from the fridge, not enjoying the taste as much when it was just below room temperature and not chilled as it was intended to be drunk. The thought struck her that without television, what would people arrange their furniture around?

Scoffing an unamused laugh at her own thoughts, she tried to imagine a time when people sat down to talk to each other instead of bingeing on unsatisfactory box sets until it was past time to go to bed and repeat the cycle.

Lydia had slept, but before she had gone quiet Abbie had heard her sobbing quietly in the next room. She'd slept on and off herself, only without power she couldn't be sure of how long for as the only clock in the house not to require electricity was the old analogue one on the mantelpiece which had been one of the few possessions her grandmother had left her.

As a young girl she had excitedly run to it every time they visited, asking if she could wind it up. It was useless now, because she hadn't remembered the last time she had just taken a minute to wind the clock and remember people she no longer had.

Her mother and father were gone, both passing away in their early sixties within a year of one another. Shaun's father had been his only living relative, making it just the three of them.

A nudge of solid wetness at her left elbow made her feel a pang of guilt, as if the dog could somehow read her thoughts and knew he had been left out of the sum.

"Sorry, boy. You too," she said soppily, fussing the dog until he submitted to the attention and flopped onto the rug by her feet, expecting her to lean forward and continue the activity. When she didn't, he let out a grumble and followed it with a sneeze that showered wetness on her exposed feet.

"Nice," she said, but lost the train of thought as creaking floorboards above her head sounded loudly.

She found it odd, being in such a quiet world where the morning rush of traffic hadn't happened.

It was bin collection day, and she had been surprised to see that almost half of their sparsely populated street had put theirs out at the roadside as if expecting the service industry to continue under any circumstances.

Some had left on foot, deciding to walk to work in their ignorance that this was a temporary thing. Abbie laboured under no such misapprehensions, and even if she hadn't received the worrying text messages from Jez, she would know that something was very wrong.

Lydia came down the stairs, making Abbie look up to see

a mess of unruly hair sitting atop a hoodie so oversized it looked like a collapsed shelter. She recognised the top, knew why her daughter was wearing it, and said nothing.

It had been Shaun's, and Lydia wore it when she wanted to make her mother feel uncomfortable for the way things were. Abbie didn't think that was the case now; more that her daughter wore it to feel closer to her father, who was hundreds of miles away with no way of contacting them.

Lydia lifted a hand and waved weakly, flopping the hand back down to imply how exhausted she was without saying a word. She walked into the kitchen and opened the fridge, staring at the contents until something jumped out at her. She shut the door and walked over to the bread bin, as Abbie bit her tongue for watching the last of the chilled air released from the fridge for no good reason.

She took out two slices of bread and dropped them into the toaster, but before Abbie could point out the obvious, Lydia almost collapsed with a teenage groan and retrieved them.

"I can toast them on the fire if you want?"

Lydia shook her head, tumbling her messy hair over her face, and proceeded to dig out chocolate spread from a jar until she was left with roughly a fifty-fifty bread to Nutella ratio.

Chunk trotted up to greet her, dancing on the spot before sitting down and staring at her expectantly. She rewarded his efforts by tearing off the crusts from one folded sandwich and dropping it into his waiting mouth.

"Want any bread with that chocolate spread?" Abbie asked, being unnaturally upbeat and hating how it sounded coming out of her mouth.

Lydia didn't answer, just looked in her direction as if

wielding some silent magic on her mother, when someone knocked at the front door to make them both jump.

Chunk barked, more surprised by their surprise than angry that someone was at the door, and Abbie frowned before walking through the hallway to peer through the spy hole again.

"Oh, give me strength," she whispered to herself, eyes closed and head facing the tiled floor beneath her bare feet. She straightened up and opened the door, only allowing it a few inches of space before the chain caught it.

In the gap was the smiling face of the woman from across the road, clearly singing a different tune from the last time they had spoken.

"*Hiiii*, just wanted to apologise for yesterday," she said, doing a weird and awkward kind of curtsy as she said it. Abbie tried not to sneer and kept her face passive.

"Don't worry about it," she answered, not meaning a word. The neighbour let out a nervous giggle, making Abbie think there was more to the early morning visit.

"So, Jim and I were wonder*iiiing...*"

Abbie said nothing, leaving the woman to smile her way through the embarrassment.

"We noticed that you have a log fire, and we were wondering if we could, I don't know, maybe get some logs for ours?"

She stood there smiling, as if the simple act of asking would result in everything she wanted showering down on her. Abbie smiled at the thought of logs raining down on her head and the expression was misconstrued.

"Thanks, that's *sooo* kind of you. Can you bring some over and—"

"No." Abbie's face had lost the smile and the expression

that looked back at her was suddenly not as false and friendly as it had been.

"Fine, I'll send Jim over to—"

"No!"

"*Excuse* me?"

"What aren't you getting? I said no. I don't even know your name! Yesterday you two decided you could have my car. Now you want the few logs we've got for yourself, and you want *me* to deliver them?"

"Well, I—"

"No. Just… no." Abbie went to shut the door, but the woman foolishly placed her foot in the gap. Heavy door versus the light pumps she was wearing ended just as expected, and the door recoiled from the impact.

The woman shrieked, yelling all kinds of accusations as she hobbled, sobbing, back down the path to cross the road, yelling her husband's name every fake limped step of the way.

Abbie knew what would come next, so she stuffed her feet into trainers and tied her hair up with the bobble looped around her wrist.

"Mum?"

"It's fine. Go fetch me your hockey stick," Abbie answered. Lydia, to her surprise, simply disappeared to do as she was asked, retuning a few seconds later from near the back door with the stick.

"Go in the lounge and take Chunk with you—actually, leave him. Go."

"Mum, I—"

"*Go!*"

Lydia went, just as a new shape visible through the frosted glass came storming up the path to her front door.

She didn't wait for the knock, instead she threw off the

chain and yanked open the door to step out and brandish the hockey stick over her right shoulder.

Jim's face transformed from angry and indignant to shocked in a flash. Abbie could tell from that transformation, a facial representation of his balls shrivelling up inside his body, that he had been expecting to shout the odds at her and that she would have to listen.

He took a step back, still unable to find any words.

"What? What, Jim? You want all the food we have left in the house? You want to have a look through our stuff in case there's anything you want? What?"

Jim sneered, looking her up and down as if she and Shaun couldn't possibly afford to buy a house in the same street.

"Like we'd want anything of *yours*," he managed, but skipped backwards when Abbie took another step closer and hefted the stick.

"Then fuck off!" she yelled, and by raising her voice she activated Chunk into defence mode.

People think of labs as cuddly, soft dogs, when in fact Chunk was a solid ball of meat with a lot of muscle hidden beneath his bulk and a hard bite when he wanted to use it.

He bounded out beside Abbie, barking wildly at the intruder until he panicked and managed to make his feet move to propel him back across the road.

Abbie stepped back inside and slammed the door, locking it and putting the chain back on.

She had been close to making a decision even before that had happened, but the behaviour of people she didn't know acting like they could just take what she had made it easy for her.

"Go upstairs, pack some fresh clothes. Wear your walking boots," she ordered.

Lydia, a Nutella streak staining one cheek, stared at her

mother for a few seconds before jumping into action at the next command.

"Now, please!"

Abbie followed, changing her outfit and finding a bag big enough to hold a few changes of clothes and some essentials. She had finished far quicker than her daughter, and when she entered her room to see what was taking so long, she realised she had done far less than she thought to prepare her daughter for this.

"You don't need that," Abbie said, shoving her tablet aside and going through her clothing selection. Lydia sat back with a huff, muttering about doing it herself, and watched as Abbie did the entire task for her.

"Where are we going?" she asked, forcing Abbie to say it out loud.

"We're going to the dockyard," she admitted. She expected Lydia to protest, to make a snide comment about Jez, but she just nodded and looked subdued. Abbie stopped what she was doing and wrapped her arms around the girl.

"It's bad, isn't it?" she asked, sounding close to tears. Abbie couldn't lie to her, but she also couldn't say why she felt that abandoning their home was the right thing to do.

"Then what?" Lydia asked.

Abbie wished she knew, but the only thing she felt certain of was that they needed to get out of there before the meagre food supplies everyone kept in their homes ran dry, and then desperate people would be doing desperate things.

They left via the back door, climbing the fence at the end of the garden onto the thin strip of land that bordered the stream running through their estate. Chunk tried his best, but it took both of them to haul his back end over the four-foot-tall obstacle.

Abbie had no hesitation this time, having dug out the ancient A to Z of their home to give her the right bearings. The map was so old, so out of date, that it showed the sprawling estate of new builds as green fields, and she remembered these houses being erected before Lydia was born.

It did show the main routes, and just looking at it before they left had given her the right direction to head in which was enough given that the docks were hard to miss.

They retraced some of their route from the day before, crossing the same field luckily devoid of the roving gang on bikes that she was now certain she had imagined.

Not that she had imaged *them*, but that she had imagined their intentions to be bad.

They walked through the streets, crossing from residential into light commercial, and everywhere they went the atmosphere was subtly different from the day before.

There were fewer people around, and those who were in plain sight shied away from being seen by other people. That told Abbie enough about their reasons for being out and about, and she kept them away from any such contact in case someone took exception to the fact that they might witness some crime.

Some shops were shut up tight, where others had fallen foul of people's need to stockpile, and by stockpile, she meant loot.

Windows had been smashed and shop fronts had been emptied of the alluring goods on display to entice people in. They had been too enticing, clearly, because people had very much been lured in.

"Makes sense," Lydia said.

"What's that?" Abbie asked, trying to carry a hockey stick beside her body and keep Chunk from pulling ahead on his spare lead.

Lydia pointed at the electrical goods store that had clearly been ransacked. Abbie let out a laugh at the irony of the situation, but that irony was overshadowed by the fact that if people were stupid enough to loot there, what else could their stupidity make them do?

What would normally have taken thirty minutes to drive was taking far longer on foot as they threated their way through the city outskirts. More and more people were out and moving the closer they got to the centre, and while many just watched them pass by, others began to try and interact.

Abbie, being a city worker pulling long hours sometimes, had been accosted by the homeless and unfortunate more than once. She had perfected her smiling sidestep, the apologetic mutter and head shake, but it seemed that the recent changes had emboldened one particular alleyway dweller.

She watched him walking unevenly towards them on the other side of the road. He paused as if considering whether to make an approach or not, and after swinging his head in both directions as if cars were still moving, he swayed over the road towards them.

Abbie saw it, moving Lydia to her right side to protect her.

"Hey, miss. Miss! Spare change? Any spare change?" he said with a whistling lisp.

"No, sorry," Abbie said, deploying the apologetic smile and speeding them up.

It didn't work this time, and the man put on a burst of speed to stop directly in their path.

"Come on, you've got *something* for me," he said, adding an edge of nastiness to his voice as she saw his face in closer detail.

The gaunt cheeks and scabby, pale skin. The sunken, red-rimmed eyes glared maliciously at her as the cracked lips parted to reveal randomly missing teeth in between the blackened stumps of others.

Abbie had never swum in the muddy waters of the drugs world, but she knew a raging crackhead when she saw one.

Abbie wasn't in the mood to stop and discuss it, so she lifted the hockey stick in front of her to make her intentions to pass clear.

The lips cracked further apart, as if the prospect of a victim fighting back would be amusing.

Sensing the mood, Chunk started to snarl and bark, pulling on the lead as he bounced on his front feet at the man. He laughed, aiming a kick at the dog and connecting with his chest to send a hollow thud through the air.

Three things happened at once. Chunk, being of solid construction, responded to the kick by launching forwards and biting the ankle closest to him. In response to the situation escalating, Abbie swung the hockey stick upwards with perfect aim, hitting him where even the drugs in his system couldn't numb the pain.

As he yelped and groaned and leaned forward at the waist, Lydia stepped to the side of her mother and swung a roundhouse kick into the side of his head, connecting the toe of her heavy boots to the scratty beanie hat covering his skull.

Abbie didn't hang around to see what would happen next. Yanking on the lead and yelling the dog's name she pulled the three of them away, dragging their would-be assailant for a few paces before Chunk finally released his grip to leave the man wailing on the concrete.

They ran, with Chunk bounding alongside, eagerly looking up at Abbie for praise or reassurance. They didn't stop until she ran out of breath and ended up bent double before Lydia tapped at her shoulder and gestured for her to get up.

She stood tall, sucking in air and looking around to try and figure out where they were. She looked up, trying to see something higher up on the city skyline to navigate by, but the tall buildings surrounding them took away that avenue.

A noise from far behind, like a shout muted by distance and warped by echo, spurred her back into moving. She forced them along, looking up and down every street they passed, when the smell of the docks caught the breeze and turned her head to face it.

"This way," she said, going on instinct that paid off.

A small crowd of people swarmed the gates at the dockyard, and military personnel in uniform and carrying rifles stood impassively on the other side of the fence as people bayed and pleaded with them.

Abbie watched for a while, seeing where the action was happening, and resting her eyes on another gate without a crowd outside. It wasn't obvious but the small guard booth on the other side of the fence held a person sitting still.

"Come on," Abbie said, leading almost everything she cared about in the world towards it.

She was right, because when they got within thirty metres of the gate, the figure stepped out of the booth and made it obvious he was not in a generous mood by the way he held his rifle ready. It was still pointed at the ground, but the way he gripped it sent a clear signal to Abbie, and she slowed down.

Holding up her free hand still gripping Chunk's lead, she did a double take and handed off the hockey stick to Lydia who shied behind her.

"Not here, love. Sorry."

"It's okay, I'm not trying anything stupid, I just need—"

"I said not here. You want to talk to someone, go down there," he said, jerking his head in the direction of the shouting crowd, none of whom were being admitted to the base.

Abbie snapped, stepping closer to the fence and lowering her voice.

"Look, just listen to me for a second—"

"Back! Back away from the fence!" he bawled, stepping back to bring the rifle tight into his shoulder and point it at her chest.

A cold fury washed over Abbie that was oddly calming. She stood her ground, ignoring the barking dog and the frightened noises coming from Lydia behind her. She didn't know much about guns, and she'd certainly never had one pointed at her before, but she thought from the size of it, any bullet would pass through her and kill them both.

He carried on yelling, reinforcing his words with a thrust of the weapon as if she would simply go away. The commotion brought a response from behind him as two other uniformed men started running towards the gate.

Abbie saw the soldier's eyes flicker to his right in the direction of the other gate, and although Abbie dare not take her eyes off him, she guessed they were attracting attention from the crowd wanting to get in.

"Back! Get back!"

"What's going on?" the taller of the two running figures demanded confidently when he approached.

"Won't get back from the gate, Sir," the man with the aimed rifle reported.

"My name is Abbie Taylor and this is my daughter, Lydia," Abbie said, eager to make them appear as people and not faceless crowd members who could be ignored and left out in the dangerous city.

"Sorry, madam, but all public enquiries must be directed towards the—"

"Jez Hallam," she blurted out, stopping the man in his verbal tracks. Abbie seized the opportunity and continued, hoping to widen the chink in their bureaucratic armour.

"Corporal Hallam, I mean. He gave us instructions to come here."

She kept her eyes locked on the officer who shot nervous glances in the direction of the others. He seemed to tense up before a decision released that pressure and he stepped aside.

"Let them in. Quickly!"

The one aiming a rifle at her deescalated as fast as he had raised it to her, unlocking the gate to swing it wide.

"You can't bring the dog," the other one to have joined them said, but the look on Abbie's face prompted the man in charge to override him.

"It doesn't matter. Get that gate secured!"

Just before the pack of yelling, frightened people arrived dragging their suitcases and prized possessions with them, Abbie, Lydia and Chunk were hurried along the path as shouts rang out behind, ordering the people there to get back from the gate.

CHAPTER THIRTEEN

The Basics

S haun tried to remember how much water a person
needed a day. It was the kind of thing he would have just
searched on his phone had the question arisen two days prior,
but now he felt as though he was cast back to his childhood
after being given a glimpse of the future.

He thought it was around three litres for an adult. Or
maybe pints. What he did remember was that water was water
in whatever form, within reason, but still he tried to add up
how much they each needed to carry.

By the time the sun started to turn a dull grey behind the
swirling patterns of green and blue, he'd calculated what they
each needed to carry on their backs to keep the three of them
and Harper equipped for three days. He chose three days
because it sounded right.

That had them carrying ten kilos each in fluids alone, not
counting food. He knew from another recent article he'd read

that people needed between two and three thousand calories a day, but he guessed they would be doing more exercise than they were used to.

At least, that would be true for him and Amanda, because doing any kind of distance on her feet or in a saddle wouldn't cause Libby any undue suffering..

He had no idea what three thousand calories looked like in weight or volume of food, let alone what he needed to include in it to make sure they met all their nutritional needs. Sy the time the sun was about to peek over the horizon, he'd given up trying to figure it out and made the decision to haul as much as possible of the food they'd cooked.

He filled a pan with water from the sink and opened drawers in search of something to light the hob. Finding a contraption that arced a spark between two nodes, he lit the gas and cranked it up to boil enough water to make them all a cup of tea before standing at the bottom of the stairs and calling up.

"Morning…"

Libby appeared at the top of the stairs; one finger held to her lips. Shaun pulled an apologetic face and held his hands up, backing away to check on the progress of the water.

He found the gas off and the pan barely warm. He turned the dial off and on again, listening for the hiss and hearing nothing.

He tried another hob, hearing the sound he expected but it stopped before he could apply the spark to it. Trying the last two hobs, he succeeded only in making the flame last for a second before it faded out to nothing.

"Shit," he said dejectedly.

"What?" Libby asked, worry in her voice.

"The gas… it's gone off."

"Shit," she said after a pause to stare at the hob.

"Have you got any camping stuff? A bottle of Calor gas or something?" he asked, but she was already shaking her head. Amanda joined them and the information was repeated for her. Her positive outlook was missing now, and she seemed lost for anything to say. Shaun took the opportunity to suggest what he'd come up with after spending the last four and a half hours awake.

"Look, ladies, how about I go out and see if I can find us some transport?"

"Transport? How?"

Shaun explained how he knew of a cycle shop he'd seen closer to the city, but Amanda cut him off with logic and fired questions at him.

"How are you going to get three bikes back here on your own? What about Harper?"

Shaun started to explain that he'd thought about that, and that he'd just manage somehow, when Libby spoke up.

"I have two bikes in the garage. Two of us can go and bring back another one?"

"Or we can check other houses around here. Maybe someone has one they can spare?" Amanda suggested, but Shaun didn't like the idea of knocking on a person's house and asking for their possessions in the current climate. It felt piratical.

"No, borrowing from a shop is better. Maybe they're even still open? Do you have any cash in case they are?"

Amanda responded by walking out of the room and returning a minute later with a petty cash tin. She opened it to show a few hundred pounds in assorted notes inside. Shaun pulled out his own wallet and thumbed through the couple of hundred he carried.

"That should be enough, right?" he asked, looking at Libby as the resident expert in bicycles. She nodded warily.

. . .

Abandoning the prospect of a hot drink, he spoke to Amanda after Libby had gone back upstairs to change.

"Are you sure you're okay here with the little one?"

She nodded firmly, but he could see in her eyes that she was worried about Libby's ex coming back with his friends. Shaun asked a question he didn't think he would ever have had to pose to another person.

"Amanda, do you... do you have any weapons in the house?"

"My husband had a shotgun years ago, but no. I don't even think any of the neighbours here do."

Shaun nodded thoughtfully, wishing he'd joined the military when he was younger or had somehow learned how to defend himself with anything other than his fists and his feet along the way.

He tried to explain his thought process, stumbling as he said it out loud, but eventually managed to get his point across.

"It's what the woman over the street said more than anything. She obviously knows something, so the fact that they left yesterday tells me a lot. You need to get out of town and I need to get home. The way I see it, we're both heading the same direction so we might as well stick together for now."

———

Shaun rode the obviously expensive bike down the road slowly, twisting his head left and right in search of dangers. Each time he turned, the small pack on his back shifted position and adjusted the weight distribution. He carried only bottles of water and some food, along with his jacket that he had balled up tightly to force it inside the small bag.

Libby rode ahead, checking behind her constantly to show how aware she was of leaving him behind.

On both sides of the streets they rode down, they saw the evidence of a night without power and law. One house had even suffered a fire, and Shaun's mind raced with the possibilities of how it had started.

Had it been someone trying to heat water? To cook food? Had it been deliberately set?

People twitched their curtains as they passed, whereas others stepped outside their homes holding kitchen knives or other makeshift weapons to demonstrate that their house wasn't a place anyone wanted to pay particular attention to.

With each of them, Shaun felt as though these people were naïve in staying at home, just waiting for the world around them to go back to normal.

His hours spent awake on guard duty had solidified the thoughts in his head, telling him over and over that the power wasn't coming back on. If they were caught in the crossfire between two massive nations with armed forces tallying in the hundreds of thousands, then the blasts high over their little islands were strategic.

They had been blinded. They had been rendered spectators to world events without a clue what was happening, and they had been abandoned to their fate.

He believed that nobody would help them but themselves, and even though that felt as pessimistic as those patiently waiting at home had been optimistic, he had to believe it was true. He had to believe it in order to take action, to do what he thought was best, and if it all turned out okay in the near future, then he had no regrets.

None yet, anyway.

The closer they got to the city the more chaotic things became. Small convenience stores were ransacked, with plate glass windows shattered into the street. Shaun looked inside one as they passed, seeing the cigarette shelves behind the tills cleared out to leave nothing behind.

He scoffed at that, having never been a smoker, thinking how a person's priorities always leaned towards their addictions over their needs. Drug addicts would go in search of drugs, in whatever form they took, and they would ignore more pressing needs to feed their addiction.

He imagined the alcohol aisle inside to look very similar, leaving perhaps a couple of bottles of cheap spirits discarded at the back of a shelf somewhere. The alcohol-free wine would still be there, he guessed, because he saw no point in anyone looting that.

His thoughts of alcohol made him thirsty despite the early hour, and he felt a deep loathing for himself. The visions of how his father had lived and died came back to him, reminding him of the fate life had in store for him if he carried on the way he was going.

But that was before. Now he had priorities. He had a mission, a purpose, and he couldn't sit alone each night with a crate or a bottle of something and read inane articles on his phone out of sheer boredom. He couldn't avoid sleep because of the chances of unpleasant dreams.

"This way," Libby said to him, snapping him out of the daydream. She leaned to her right, going across a junction without giving way. She still looked both ways out of habit, just as Shaun did to comply with the muscle memory of an act drummed into him over four decades ago.

It was no surprise that there weren't any vehicles travelling along the road, but complacency wasn't something he thought they could afford right then.

He soon realised they were heading away from the city, and putting on a burst of speed with considerable effort, he caught up beside her and asked where they were going.

"That shop you were talking about is too far away. There's a place I use to service my bikes down here. They've got a little shop in the front but it's tucked away so hopefully nobody would've found it."

Shaun liked her thinking, and fell back to follow her as she took the twisting turns down ever shrinking streets until she slowed in a narrow access road behind a row of old terraced houses.

"The workshop is in the back. Let me go first," she said. Shaun agreed that trespassing under their current circumstances might earn a bad reaction from the owner, but a friendly face made all the difference.

They dismounted and she opened the wooden gate. On it was a crude sign advertising the business – Evans' cycles – that Shaun guessed was more of a paid hobby than a real money maker.

Libby crept ahead of him after resting her bike up against a wall and called out quietly.

"Hello? Evan?"

Shaun frowned, recalling the placement of the apostrophe in the business name and wondering if it was an error or if the owner was called Evan Evans.

She tested the door to the workshop and found it unlocked, but with nobody inside. She went down a few steps and into a tiny patch of overgrown garden to knock on the back door but that was similarly unlocked.

With a cautious glance at Shaun, she pushed the door

open and set foot inside, calling out for the owner by name again.

"He must be gone," she said by the time she'd looked through the small selection of downstairs rooms. Pushing open another door, she entered the shop front, Shaun following and finding it just as miniscule as she had described it to him.

Bikes hung tightly packed along the walls with a display line of six more sitting at diagonal angles along one wall. Libby wasted no time in selecting three sturdy mountain bikes, each with chunky front suspension forks, and began lining them up by the door back into the house.

"Can you get that?" she asked, catching his eye and looking up at something hanging from the ceiling.

Shaun followed her gaze and took in the bright fabric of a little cycle trailer. It was the kind that people used to transport young children or dogs who couldn't keep up, and he had to admit to himself the genius of it.

He got it down without much difficulty and helped her take the three bikes and trailer to the workshop where Libby brought her own bikes inside. Searching inside, she eventually located a discarded envelope and a pen to scribble an explanatory note to Evan which she left on the saddle of her own bike.

Shaun could imagine what it said, offering her apologies for helping herself but leaving him items of obvious significant value by way of collateral for the safe return of the things they needed.

There was another trailer in the workshop, but it was half built with only one tyre attached. Shaun set to work affixing the last one and checking the components for tightness of fit before figuring out how it attached to the mountain bikes.

Libby was checking those new bikes over, performing brake tests and adjusting them with practised ease.

"You might want to check the shop for some clothes," Libby said. Her eyes were down, deliberately not making contact with his, because she was embarrassed to raise the subject. Shaun knew he still smelled – at least his clothes did – and he accepted the hint with as much grace as she'd shown giving it.

Back inside, Shaun was torn between dark Lycra and the gaudy, bright colours of cycling jerseys that would make him look like a loaf of rising bread dough if he tried to squeeze into one.

Settling on the largest t-shirts he could find advertising some brand he hadn't heard of, he took a dark rain jacket with a wide reflective strip running all the way up both sleeves, and fought his way into a pair of men's leggings which were in a packet marked as extra-large.

He suspected that the packaging was either wrong, or else the cycling world had a very different idea about what constituted an extra-large person, but the end result was an uncomfortable feeling of self-consciousness coupled with the best groin support he'd ever experienced.

With a few spares under his arm, he made for the door back into the house and froze as noises sounded on the street.

He was grateful for having decided to change into his new gear on the spot, because two men appeared at the glass frontage and pressed their faces to shield the sunlight and see inside.

He froze, adopting an unnaturally stiff pose looking away from the front in the hope that his sudden inspiration to act like a mannequin was successful.

He heard them talking but couldn't make out the words. From the muffled cadence of their speech patterns, Shaun suspected he wasn't hearing them speak English to one another.

The door handle was tried, rattling the metal in the wood before a thumping sound told him they were trying to force it. Standing as still as possible, he tried to turn his eyes to see what they were doing but the sound stopped and the two had disappeared.

He ran, scrambling out of the house and into the workshop to startle Libby.

"We need to go. People are trying to break into the shop," he told her. To her credit she didn't panic. She pushed the bikes towards him one at a time, starting with the unburdened one and following with the two encumbered by their trailers. On impulse, Shaun saw a length of fresh bicycle chain and snatched it up to stuff it into the pocket of his new jacket.

Fighting the three bikes out into the narrow alley behind the houses, they set off with Libby awkwardly steering the third bike with her free hand as sounds behind them made it clear the men had got inside.

They went fast, as fast as they could so weighed down, and when the road became uninhabited for a short stretch, Libby called a halt so she could try and fix the spare bike onto the trailer somehow

Eventually balancing it correctly, they resumed their progress only to make it back and find that the brief time they had been gone had not been uneventful for Amanda.

———

Libby's gasp when they rounded the bend and came in sight of the house cut through Shaun like a knife. She skidded to a stop and dropped the bike to the roadway, running ahead to where three people stood arrayed on the driveway. Their look was hostile, like circling predators around a wounded animal that could still hurt them, and the one closest to the house yelled something before aiming an ineffectual kick at the locked front door.

Libby was shouting as she ran, cursing the man whose identity Shaun was in no doubt of, and he dumped his own bike to follow her.

The two supporting acts turned at her approach before their leader, Anton, slowly spun to deliver a look so filled with malice that Shaun felt the familiar warmth rise in his body.

He felt the calmness descend over him, and he slipped his hands into his jacket pockets as he walked towards them, only that calmness took a shot to the gut when the faces became visible to him.

"You've got to be fucking joking, pal," Anton sad nastily, looking past Libby at him.

Shaun almost laughed at how ludicrous the situation was. Anton's nose was still red and swollen, and the hurt looks from the other two gave him no clue as to which one he'd beaten up last night and which one the night before.

He felt no regrets at all for laying hands on them, but the thought that he might have made the situation worse for the family who had taken him in turned his blood cold.

Anton sauntered forwards, shoulders swinging before his arms as if he was a primate displaying his superiority. Shaun wasn't the slightest bit impressed or intimidated, and his bored tone matched that approach.

"You three need to leave," he said, as though casually reminding them that they were late for something.

"Oh? Is that so, ye fat bastard?" Anton mocked, leaning

back as he spoke as if the joke was the best he'd heard in years. He glanced at the other two, and both replaced their wary looks with ones of loyal amusement.

Anton kept sauntering his way, and from the twitchy bounce in his step Shaun was pretty sure he knew why the man was so angry and out of control. He half expected to see powder residue under the man's nose, but he doubted he could afford to waste any.

"That's right."

"I'm no goin' anywhere until I've got ma daughter, ye hear me, y'old bastard?"

"That's not going to happen," Shaun said calmly, waiting for Anton to step closer and deliver more threats.

"Oh, aye, it is. And when I've got her, you and me are gonna have a wee *chat*."

"We can do that if you like, but you are going to go," Shaun said, still speaking as a disinterested narrator to their scene.

"Or *what*, eh? You gonna try and sucker punch me agai—"

Shaun whipped his right hand from his pocket where he'd wrapped it around the end of the chain. The sickening *thwack* of the metal lashing over Anton's skull startled all of them, Shaun included, but as the blood began to flow freely from his lacerated scalp, Anton took the full force of Shaun's right boot between the legs and dropped to faceplant the driveway with a slap.

He didn't wait for what had happened to sink in for the other two. He advanced on them, chain cocked back in his right hand looking ready to decapitate the nearest one, who fled without a second glance. The last one, looking around him as if trying to decide on the best way to escape, contorted his face at his preferred option as he made the decision to attack instead.

He was fast, and Shaun let him come before swinging the chain but he was already flying through the air to hit him with a slide tackle around his chest.

Shaun was driven backwards, feeling the air knocked from his lungs as they both hit the ground only a few feet away from the bleeding, writhing Anton.

"Tommy! No!" Libby screamed, but if he heard the words he paid them no mind. He rose up, intending to pummel Shaun into the ground, but Shaun's brain worked faster than his body.

The man was younger and fitter than he was, but technique and a lifetime of dirty fighting had taught Shaun more than this boy could ever know.

He was recreating what he'd seen on television, convincing himself that he could hold his own in a mixed martial arts fight, but he had failed to secure Shaun's body on the ground in any way before he went for the haymaker elbow strikes designed to split the older man's head open.

Shaun let the first one come, blocking it with both of his forearms. Tommy rose higher, planning on putting even more power behind his next shot in the naïve belief that he had the man pinned.

Shaun let it come, rolling his head to the left and bucking his hips up off the ground to tip his attacker's momentum forward. He flinched, just catching the very edge of the man's elbow against his cheek before the full force of it struck the block paving with a sharp, splintering crack followed by a shriek and howl of agony.

Shaun tipped him off, watching as his body was held rigid in pain and the left hand clutched tightly around the right forearm. The arm wasn't disfigured, not yet anyway, and there was no bone protruding through the skin and muscle but Shaun knew what a broken arm sounded like.

Back on his feet, Shaun walked to retrieve the bikes and manhandled the three of them with their two trailers back to the house.

"We should go," he said, ignoring the pained noises from behind him.

CHAPTER FOURTEEN

Much worse

Shaun rode the bike carrying most of their supplies in the attached trailer. Of all of them, the one best suited to that task was Libby, but being trusted with their food and water was very different from being trusted with a child.

He knew they had been shocked by what he had done. He could sense it in everything, from how they spoke to how they looked at him. Far from being seen as their rescuing hero, both Amanda and Libby treated him with a wary fear.

He knew that people could be capable of great violence and still be fundamentally good, but for people who hadn't been exposed to any level of brutality, the correlation between violence and bad was oversimplified.

"What's the plan?" he asked, easing off on the pedals so that he dropped back level with them. He knew they had no chance at all of making it to the Lake District in a day, and he was kicking himself for not having a plan when they left.

In truth, he'd been so wired on fear and adrenaline, so overcome by the endorphins of besting the vile scum who appeared to prey on others as soon as the rules went out of the window, that he wasn't thinking straight.

He expected Libby to answer, expected her to be the one working out speed and distance, but Amanda surprised him by being the one to speak. She was out of breath from the exercise, but her head was undeniably screwed on.

"Peebles."

"Excuse me?" Shaun said.

"Peebles. There's a… camping shop there and… a cycling thingy," Amanda explained.

Shaun said nothing, having already been to one cycling thingy that day, but he couldn't argue with the logic of getting some camping gear.

The streets had been oddly quiet when they had cycled away from the outskirts of the city. Everywhere he looked he saw people tucked up inside their houses, nervously peering out as if expecting to see the military roll up in their street to restore order along with the power.

Shaun wasn't so naïve as that, and he couldn't even begin to put a label on the kind of stress he was experiencing. He couldn't shake off the words of Amanda's neighbour, warning them that things would only get worse.

They were the sheep, all those people staying at home and blindly trusting that life would go back to normal. They were the followers, the ones who didn't look beyond their own fence, and they suddenly offended him. He found that weird because he *was* one of them.

He went with the flow, accepted the norm, complied with the status quo in everything his life had served up.

He waited to be told what to do, because life had kicked him back down so many times that he no longer even felt the impulsive urge to offer up a new idea when so many of them had been shot down in flames.

He'd been beaten down by life, and life had eventually won. So why was he fighting against the flow now? Why was he riding a damn bicycle down a Scottish A-road with three strangers when he wasn't sure if they had kidnapped him or the other way around.

The roads were entirely abandoned, he admitted to himself. Cars were abandoned or crashed everywhere, so much so that their progress felt more like a lazy slalom race than a straight road.

They passed some people, more groups and families than individuals, and one man even stopped to put his family behind a dead car while he stood and watched them ride past. The over and under shotgun he carried, resting on his hip to point at the sky, made his stance clear.

Shaun caught his eye and gave a respectful nod before looking back to his front. He tried to convey something man-to-man, like rival animals inhabiting the same space and agreeing to avoid each other. He didn't know if he'd succeeded or not, but the man stood his ground and watched them ride past.

Shaun was infested by uncomfortable thoughts then. The man had been armed. Literally walking the streets with a shotgun that he seemed more than prepared to use on other people. Shaun was fine with him protecting his family, but where was the line? What was to stop him deciding that he didn't want to walk any further? What stopped him using that advantage to take what someone else had?

Shaun's already low opinion of humanity darkened his thoughts even further, and that building stress found its way to his feet and the pedals.

"We need to pick up the pace," he said. He hoped they could make the distance to the small town before the light started to fail. He hoped they wouldn't find the place ransacked. He hoped a lot of things, and those hopes conspired with his fears so much it threatened to overwhelm him.

"Shaun. Shaun! Slow down," Libby said. She didn't sound at all out of breath, so Shaun guessed her protests were on behalf of her mother. He slowed, twisting to look behind with a wobble as the trailer fought against the movement, and saw that the distress actually belonged to the smallest member.

Harper was so quiet, so well behaved, that he forgot she was there half the time. His own daughter had been a tornado from the first minute she could crawl, and by the time she was running and climbing, there wasn't anything nice left in their house that she could feasibly reach. Lydia had either broken it, or it had been removed to keep it safe from her.

Shaun was hit by a flash of memory when she had managed to reach the wedding picture of him and her mother, and when that frame had broken against the stones of the fireplace it had never gone back up.

Harper was crying, which threw him. He hadn't heard her cry before even when her mother had been upset, and the sound of it now broke his heart.

He pulled up, climbing stiffly off the saddle after doing more cycling in one day than he'd done in the last fifteen years, and rested the bike against the central barrier.

Libby pulled up behind him and did the same, going to

her child and saying reassuring things to her as she pulled her out of the trailer and hugged her close.

"Oh, that's why you're upset!" she said pulling her hand away from the back of her daughter and checking it. Shaun didn't need to have young children anymore to know what she was checking.

Libby used the bonnet of an abandoned car to lay Harper out and change her. She used wipes to clean her up before pulling fresh bottoms from the bag for her. She hesitated, holding the soiled pair between finger and thumb, before seeming to conclude something in her own head and dropping them at the roadside.

"It's okay, baby. It's okay," she crooned softly to the girl. She offered her snacks, restoring her to the trailer and strapping her in.

"I need a minute," Amanda said, shooting a look at Libby. They both turned to look at Shaun who took a few seconds to understand.

"Oh, yeah, want me to watch Harper while you go…"

He saw it then; the flash of fear in their eyes at leaving a child with someone they didn't know. He didn't blame them because they didn't know him. They had seen that he was a good person, at least he hoped that, but they had also seen that he was a man capable of intense violence. Worse still, he didn't seem to be adversely affected by what he had done.

"It's okay, mum. You go first," Libby said, flashing an awkward smile at Shaun as if to say that she meant no offence. He genuinely took none and smiled back to show that, but she had already looked away.

He drank water and ate two breaded turkey breasts from the previous day's cookout, wondering why he didn't need to relieve his own bladder yet. Amanda came back and swapped with Libby for her to disappear down the slight slope of the roadside embankment for the privacy offered by a large hedgerow.

When they were reunited again, Shaun swung a stiff leg over his saddle and set off to follow the road south, but before he could push off a shout from far behind them stopped him.

He turned, along with Amanda and Libby who had heard the same desperate sound yelled from back up the road.

"Please!" came another shout. Shaun peered into the distance and cursed his age for taking away the extremities of his sight.

"Come on," Amanda said, settling herself in to start pedalling.

"Mum, what if they need help? We can't just leave—"

"And what if they want our water, hmm? What if they want our food or our bikes? What then?" Amanda demanded. Libby's face slowly dropped as if she was only just accepting the fact that even good people might do bad things out of desperation. She looked at Shaun, maybe for support or maybe for confirmation that her mother was right, but what she got was the truth.

The stark, stone cold, harsh, honest truth.

"We can't take that chance," he told her, shaking himself by saying the word 'we' and meaning it.

With a resigned sadness, they set off south trying to ignore the yells coming from behind as they turned from desperate and pleading, to angry and abusive.

They passed through a village, more of a collection of houses just off the road similar to the one where they had stolen their first bikes. Cars weren't just abandoned here; they had been intentionally damaged and one had even been partially burned out. A couple of houses sat with their front doors wide open, and one had obviously been shattered open by force. They didn't stop, and when they passed through heading south, Amanda spoke.

"All this in one day?" she asked. Her tone suggested she had been expecting to see similar scenes, only not just yet.

"You're judging other people by your own standards," Shaun said. He didn't know where it was coming from, but it sounded right.

"Meaning?" Libby asked.

"Meaning after one night of no power, it wouldn't occur to you to go out and act like it's the fucking purge. Don't expect everyone else to be so decent," he said, earning a pointed throat-clearing noise from Amanda for his choice of words.

"He's right," Libby added sadly. "Anton's been out of prison for how long? He didn't dare try anything himself at first, but the second he realised the police wouldn't come, he was all brave again."

Shaun felt embarrassed by her words, as if he was being shown the unpleasant secrets behind the façade of family.

"Speaking of which, how did he know you?" Amanda asked, as if the need to flee their home had overridden the need to discuss what had happened.

"I went out for a pizza two nights ago," he explained, frowning in thought as he tried to fathom how much had happened since that incident because it already felt like it had happened a year ago.

"And?" Libby asked.

"And there were two groups of lads who looked like they were going to take a pop at each other. One of them saw me watching through the shop window and came in to start on me."

"And?" Amanda asked, sounding annoyed that he wasn't being forthcoming with the whole story.

"And the owner said he'd called the police, so they left… then I left, and when I was walking back to the hotel, they caught up with me."

"And judging by how they were beaten up and you weren't…" Libby said, trailing off as if hoping for an explanation that justified his actions.

Shaun twisted to look at her, delivering a quizzical frown in case she was criticising him for putting a violent bully in his place twice. He was no fool. He knew that people living with domestic violence – which he heavily suspected was the case with Harper's father – learned how to adapt and survive, and part of that survival was protecting their abuser. He didn't know if she was going to justify Anton's actions or condemn Shaun for his own.

"Three of them attacked me in an alleyway. I hit the first one in the face and kicked another one in the leg, then the third one ran away. If it makes you feel better, they went to the police and said *they* were the victims."

"I'd feel better if he'd still been in prison and rotted there," Amanda snarled, earning an angry tut from her daughter.

"Well it's true! What that boy put you through is unforgivable, and what he tried to do this morning…"

"It's not that," Libby interrupted. "Regardless of what he's done, he's still Harper's father. I… I still thought he might grow up one day and be able to be there for her."

Shaun's heart cracked, sending a jolt of cold through his chest. His own feeling of abandonment, of guilt for all the things he'd done wrong, his sympathy for Libby and Harper and his hatred for the man who had tortured her, all of it rushed through him like a poison.

Pushing aside the feelings of how he'd messed up his own life so badly, he pushed on to the next town.

————

Peebles was a larger place than Shaun had imagined. He didn't know why he imagined it that way at all, but without his phone or even an old paper map for reference, he was lost when it came to such things.

The first thing to catch their attention on the outskirts was smashed glass sitting on the pavement in front of closed roller shutters. The non-chain convenience store that also sold fuel had been buttoned down tightly, but evidently not before some locals had decided to help themselves.

They rode on, ignoring the protected domain of another person for fear of attracting the wrong kind of attention, and cycled on into the heart of the small town.

They passed through an estate of newer houses as they went further, and just before he saw it, Shaun smelled smoke in the air. He mentioned it, looking around as he sniffed as if able to tell which direction it came from, but the absence of an obvious pillar of smoke ended the conversation.

"Where do we go?" Shaun asked, twisting to try and see Amanda so she knew the question was directed at her.

"Follow the road into town, then turn right as if you're doubling back on yourself. It's up by the big Tesco."

Shaun was just as interested in the big Tesco as he was in the camping store, but he said nothing about it because the signs of carnage were growing the closer they got to the centre.

When they made the sharp right turn, the stink of smoke was more obvious. Another few hundred tentative yards later and the source of the fire was obvious.

A car sat in the glass entrance of the supermarket, only the glass was gone, and the white exterior was scorched from the flames that were all but burned out. Shaun's mind jumped to the conclusion of a ramraid gone wrong, and the damage to the vehicle had been too much. It had caught fire, and that entrance was a wreck.

They rode past, not bothering to even consider the supermarket as a viable source to find things they needed.

A few more minutes, now with Amanda in the lead, took them down a side street where a double-fronted shop was set up like a car boot sale. A trestle table blocked the entrance, and two tall men holding weapons flanked a woman holding court behind the table.

"Wait here," Shaun said, pulling to the side of the road opposite to rest his bike against the wall. He didn't wait for an answer and heard no protests as he jogged across the road to hear the exchange between retailers and potential customers.

"Cash only, people," the woman said gleefully. She was wearing a polo shirt with the logo of the camping store on the left side of her chest, but the two large men appeared to have been recruited for their size rather than their knowledge of the camping equipment retail industry.

"We need a camping stove, please," one woman said. The retailer patted a small gas tank with a silver contraption attached to the top and declared her price greedily.

"A hundred. Another fifty each for the gas tanks."

The small crowd erupted in angry shouts, ranging from accusations of profiteering to threats. She didn't seem to care at all.

"It is what it is, people. Take it or leave it," she said, raising her voice over their noise.

"We'll just take it then," one man answered

The woman smiled, totally unconcerned by the threat, gesturing to her two hulking bodyguards who stepped forward to showcase how bad an idea it would be to try and loot her shop.

One of them held an axe, the style used by serious rock climbers on ice-covered peaks, while the other hefted a baseball bat.

Shaun scoffed at that. He'd never seen a baseball match, in fact, he'd never even heard of a baseball match being played in England, so quite why such an item was handy now was beyond him.

The nose he made attracted the attention of baseball bat man, and his head rotated to lock onto Shaun's with a sneer that spoke like the man's job interview. He was a thug, pure and simple, and his only job was to look intimidating. Shaun saw it, not that he could explain how or why, but he knew in that moment that the man was all show and no go; he wouldn't use that bat on anyone unless he had no choice.

Then again, desperate people did desperate things, so Shaun put his eyes down and shifted out of the man's line of sight to avoid the need for any testosterone-fuelled confrontation.

"Come on," Libby said, tugging on his gaudy sleeve to pull him back away from the small crowd eagerly giving away whatever they had for just one hot meal.

He went back, swinging a stiff leg over an uncomfortable saddle to pedal away through the streets and find something else to aim for.

CHAPTER FIFTEEN

Hope
The day of the fall

"Davidson, Charles Raymond, born fourteenth of December 1979, according to his driving licence. Home address down near Birmingham."

Davidson's consciousness returned just enough to recognise the information being given like a formal handover. He recognised it but was unable to cognitively process the sounds those familiar words made to make sense of anything. It was more the *feeling* that he should know what was happening.

"Minor trauma evident and loss of consciousness post-crash, from what we were told. BP was low when we last checked."

"SATS?"

"Your guess is as good as mine."

The shadow that the words were coming from moved

away, revealing a bright but overcast sky behind them. Davidson didn't yet know words like 'overcast' but he understood the concept of 'bright' because it hurt his eyes.

He tried to speak. Tried to utter the immortal words of 'where am I?', only nothing came out.

He breathed, diving deep into the sensation as if experiencing it for the first time. Was he dead? No, impossible, why would a paramedic be giving a verbal handover if he was dead?

Paramedic.

The word confused him, as much as if he'd just started speaking fluent Latin.

Latin?

How did he even know what Latin was? What *was* Latin for that matter? Nothing made sense to him, everything was numb and confusing, right up until the moment the pain returned and focused his entire existence.

"*Mmmmmurgh,*" he groaned, contracting sore stomach muscles, and trying to sit up but failing miserably.

"Sh-sh-shh, it's okay, you're okay, just lie down for me," said a sweet, female voice that made him almost believe that everything was, in fact, going to be okay.

"Can you tell me where you have pain? Can you point to where it's worst?" the voice asked. Davison fluttered the fingers of his right hand, automatically complying with the instruction from someone obviously in a position of trust before he even comprehended the request.

On the third attempt he managed to lift his right hand, waving it groggily over his torso like a drunk indicating which vague direction he lived in.

"Okay, you just lie still, I'm going to take a look."

In the absence of any more pressing engagements, Davidson stayed exactly where he was as heavy medical shears began chomping through his clothing from waist to neck.

He was sad at that. He liked the jumper he was wearing, although it was getting a little old, and no matter how hard he looked he had never been able to find a replacement that felt the same. The wool blend was either too scratchy or too loose. The neckline was too tight or else too baggy. Nothing he'd tried on ever gave him that same sense that it fit like it was supposed to.

"Ooooh-kay," said the voice, sounding like a hint of fear had crept in via an unlocked door. The confident tones of a medical professional under pressure were wavering, only Davidson was too preoccupied to notice and worry what that might mean for him.

What he did notice was his back. Specifically, that it was cold. Not cold from the sense of he was going into shock or anything drastic, but more like he was lying on something cold.

The fingers of his right hand, apparently the only part of him willing to move yet, twitched in search of more information to send back up to his brain so he could fathom the odd sensation.

Ignoring cold hands pressing into his midriff, he found damp grass beyond a plastic sheet, and reassured himself that he was still outside. That figured, along with the cloudy sky hiding the brightness of the sun behind it, but what didn't compute was what else he saw in the sky.

He blinked, trying to make the swirling lights go away like spots in his vision after too long spent staring at a screen. He blinked again when they didn't fade, worrying that he had suffered some major head trauma. He thought it might be a good idea to let the person checking him over know.

"Mmmuh," he said, slowly smacking his lips and trying again. "Mmmmy eyes... lights..."

"You've got lights in your eyes? Did you hit your head, Charles?"

"D-don't... don't know..."

"Are they spots moving around?"

Davidson tried to shake his head, only managing to produce a tiny motion and a squeak of wet hair on plastic.

"Flashing... streaks... blue and... green?"

The shape leaning over him stopped, peering back over her shoulder at the sky above them.

"No, they're real," she said. "Started just after the light-ning flashes."

Davidson might have been half insensible. He might have been fully in shock at what had happened, and possibly even close to medical shock as a result of the plane crash, but the part of his brain that was locked away behind the pain and confusion was hammering on the walls trying to get out.

He might have been a virologist with post-graduate quali-fications in immunology and economics, but he knew an aurora when he saw one.

"Northern... northern lights?" he grunted, trying to convey more than just the words he was able to get out.

"Never seen Northern Lights in Doncaster before," she muttered darkly, as though she was aware that the phenomenon in the sky was worryingly abnormal, but that she had more pressing matters on her hands right then.

Davidson looked at the impossibly tall streaks of green tinged with purple and pink at the edges. He knew what they were, breaking down the sight into the burning of oxygen and nitrogen in the Earth's atmosphere, but understanding the science and seeing such a thing were so far apart, so discon-nected, that he couldn't wrap his mind around it.

"Charles, I'm going to tap on your tummy, and you need to tell me if it hurts, okay?"

She began rapping him in different places before he could work up a verbal response. He was sore everywhere, and he meant literally *everywhere*, but nothing she did sent any of the expected lances of white-hot agony through him.

"Charlie," he managed to say quietly. "Or... or Davidson. Nobody calls... me Charles."

She smiled at the correction and continued to check him over, running the shears up his right sleeve to expose his upper arm to wrap an inflatable cuff around it. He stayed still, which wasn't hard as he felt as though he could barely move, and waited as she used a stethoscope to manually check his blood pressure.

He found that odd, why someone would use such an outdated method when compact machines could give an accurate reading faster.

When finished, she let out a noise that didn't fill him with confidence, but before he could ask, another shadow loomed over him and abruptly asked for a report.

"Male, early forties, apparently climbed free of the wreckage and lost consciousness afterwards. BP was eighty over fifty-five—"

"Any obvious trauma?" the shadow interrupted.

"Minor head wound, capillary bleeding only by the look of it."

"Check the BP again." She did, reapplying the cuff to his arms and inflating it until he felt the heat and tightness cut off the flow. It released slowly as the cold metal disc pressed into the crook of his elbow. Silence hung over all three of them, and Davidson kept as still as possible so as not to interrupt the important people doing important things.

"Ninety over sixty," she finally said, removing the cuff and looping the stethoscope around her neck.

"Keep an eye on that. Check for any signs of internal bleeding, especially in the abdomen. Any loss of motor function or one-side weakness and you send someone for me immediately."

The shadow moved away, probably going to oversee the next injured person, as if there would be many after...

Images of a decapitated Roz flooded his mind and started a rumbling in his stomach that threatened an eruption.

"*Goingtobesick—*"

She leaned back expertly, and Davidson convulsed and managed to throw himself on his left side to eject more bile. She held him there, rubbing his back soothingly and encouraging him to get it all up.

He lay back, not caring that the acidic contents of his stomach stuck to his cheek to form another layer over the last time.

She soothed him again, saying the immortal words, "Sharp scratch," before something cold washed up his right arm. It went from cold to warm, then to tingly and fuzzy as the pain ebbed away with each laboured breath, and the shimmering lights in the sky dimmed until his eyes closed and stayed that way.

———

Davidson woke and like the last time, he felt he was peeking through a gap in a door at the world his body inhabited. He listened intently to the voices as if eavesdropping.

"Broken ribs, two of them obvious from the crepitus, and probably three or four more with minor fractures. Some severe abdominal bruising but still no sign of internal haemorrhage."

"Lung function?" another voice asked. It was older, deeper, and carried an authority that made the speaker sound almost annoyed.

"No signs of diminished capacity. I believe it's unlikely that there's any major organ damage. Pallor receding and colour returning. Seems as though this man escaped with only minor injuries."

"But not yet returned to full consciousness? Are we ruling out severe head trauma?" the deeper voice asked, making it sound a little condescending as though the woman giving the report had missed something obvious.

"No sign of severe head trauma. Minor abrasion to the scalp stopped bleeding without intervention."

"BP normal?"

"Still a little on the low side—"

Davidson lifted a hand, trying to interject politely but only succeeding in causing a minor panic as the people standing over him stepped closer as if fearing the worst.

"Mmm... my blood pressure..." he said, only his lips didn't want to work. He feared he'd suffered a stroke or similar, before a level of clarity returned to him that was a pleasant surprise. "My blood pressure... is usually... low..."

"There you go then," deeper voice said. "Mister Davidson, my name is Suren Kanna, and I'm an orthopaedic consultant. Can you tell me what happened?"

Davidson frowned, recalling recent events, and wondering why anyone would ask. Of course he knew he'd been in an aviation disaster, but the thought that he might be able to shed any light as to the causes of the crash was ridiculous to him.

"I was on... on a plane. From Co... Copen...hagen."

"And can you tell me what happened before the plane crashed?" the man evidently too senior a doctor to be called doctor asked.

Davidson thought about it for a few seconds, trying to recall any fact from those terrifying seconds before physics did its thing.

"We... we were... *gliding*. No power. No... no engines..."

Faces glanced at one another, annoying Davidson that there was something he wasn't being told. He tried to sit up, but before anyone could try to stop him, he flopped back down and panted a few breaths. His entire body was stiff and ached like he was a hundred years old.

He noticed no beeping machines, heard no hissing of respirators as he would expect in such an environment. There were no radios chirping static and unintelligible words as any major incident would dictate. No phones rang. The absence of expected noises disturbed him, and that imprisoned version of himself trapped deep inside his mind yelled warnings at him.

A power outage like that, coinciding with a plane going down, meant something widespread and severe. Like a solar flare or similar. Or like an attack. An attack that acted as a precursor to releasing a biological agent.

"I need... to get to... Birmingham..."

"I'm afraid we all have places we wanted to be, Mister Davison. Unfortunately, events are rather—"

"Public Health... England. And it's... Doctor. I work... for Public Health England. I need to get... back to the..."

His consciousness was fading again, though not induced by anything transmitted through the medium of a sharp scratch this time. The cold numbness came via his left arm, and he squinted in that direction to see clear tubes dangling from a makeshift hanging rail above the hard bench he occupied.

"You just rest now," the female voice said. "Let us take care of you for now."

He tried to speak again, tried to tell them that there was more to it, that the power outages couldn't be accidental. That what he'd seen in Copenhagen told him that something much, much worse was coming than just a plane crash.

"Please," he said weakly. "Please…"

CHAPTER SIXTEEN

Good With the Bad

They cycled slowly, their attitudes subdued after seeing signs of humanity biting chunks out of itself.

Shaun grew concerned when Scotland did what it did best and started to rain on them, reducing the low mood to abject misery. Libby seemed content – at least she seemed unconcerned with getting wet – but that was offset by the fact that Harper began to whine in the trailer as if threatening to cry soon.

"I know, baby, we'll get you out soon," she promised, twisting in her saddle to look at Shaun and her mother. He took that as his cue to make a decision about where to spend the night, but Amanda's matriarchal spirit beat his reluctant leadership to it.

"There," she said, lifting her head as if gesturing to the general world in front of them. Shaun looked, seeing road signs but nothing obvious. Turning back to look at Amanda quizzically he wobbled without his eyes on the road ahead and that prompted a laugh from the woman.

"Eyes on the road," Amanda chuckled. "The brown sign. Golf club three miles ahead."

"Since when did you like golf?" Libby asked, only her delivery of the joke was so convincing that Amanda took it seriously.

"I don't. Never have. But I know your father didn't spend seven hours at a time walking around and hitting silly little balls with his silly little clubs. They'll have a clubhouse with at least one bar and a restaurant, trust me."

Shaun, who shared Amanda's sentiments on the sport – and he used that term very loosely – smiled, unable to fault her logic. He'd never played a single round in his life, had never even had a lesson, so now that he was forced to analyse his opinions, he realised he had very little to dislike golf for.

With an open mind, he cycled onwards, eventually leading the way off the road and down a neatly trimmed, two-lane driveway with manicured grass on either side of the orderly fences.

Halfway down the drive an obnoxiously large vehicle blocked the road. The nose faced in their direction, so no doubt the driver had decided to head back to the clubhouse. Likely with very little anguish over the decision.

They filed past the Bentley, Shaun catching the bright yellow of his reflection in the waxed, pearlescent paint and feeling none of the jealousy he'd have experienced only a few days ago when he saw people demonstrating how much disposable income they had.

He wondered what the guy did. Lawyer? Footballer? Some self-made millionaire property tycoon? He satisfied himself that the guy was probably a dentist and had the car on a lease, giving in to the residual jealousy that had begun to creep back in, reminding him that he hadn't completely changed.

By now Harper was crying properly, only to Shaun it didn't sound right. He only had his own daughter to hold a comparison to, and she'd passed through that stage a decade ago, but he knew the difference between unwell and unhappy.

Libby still made soothing noises and spoke to her as she rode the bike down the sweeping stretch of tarmac towards the long, low building ahead.

A car park filled with all the expected sights greeted them. A handful of BMWs, all five and seven series with the exception of a large SUV, sat among the Jaguars and Audis, but the majority winner seemed to be club Mercedes. Shaun hadn't seen that many E class cars in one place since the last time he passed a dealership.

They stopped, hesitating as there seemed to be nobody around. Libby fussed at Harper with Amanda shushing over her shoulder, leaving it down to Shaun to address their reason for being there.

He walked to the front doors, but something in him made him hold back. The fact that he wasn't a member was a weird thing to consider given the gravity of the situation they faced, but he still held back for precisely that reason.

Unless invited, he was trespassing. Not that he considered trespassing a serious issue, especially given the obvious explanation that was only underlined by the crying child, but he wasn't sure how people would react to uninvited guests, given the recent changes in the world.

The saying went that an Englishman's home was his castle, but they weren't yet in England, and the vast majorities of castles in the UK were in Scotland which, historically speaking, was *because* of the English occupation. At least that was what he thought.

Those thoughts still occupied his mind when a kindly, crackly voice offered a greeting.

"Hellooo?"

Shaun jumped out of his skin, returning to the Earth doing some snippet of a Michael Jackson impression that he was certain had made him look like a grade A twat.

He spun away from the front doors to round on the source of the voice, laying eyes on a wizened, thin man with a slightly bent back and wide smile of genuine warmth. Shaun felt instantly angry with himself for being startled and tried to return the smile.

"Hi, sorry, hope you don't mind us barging in, only my—"

"Don't think I know you. Are you a member here?"

"I'm not, no. Sorry, I hope you don't mind..." Shaun bumbled his way through the botched greeting, stammering out random apologies until the old man calmed him with a gesture from both hands.

"Let's everybody take a breath, shall we? Now, is that a wee bairn my ears hear? Is she not well?"

He walked past Shaun; one leg slightly bowed to give him a walk that seemed more at home on the deck of a windswept fishing vessel than on the soft, green land of a golf course.

"Oh, deary me, whatever's the matter, little one?" he said, softly crooning at Harper who sobbed through a face full of running snot over Libby's shoulder.

The way he was with her, the way he spoke and acted with such effortless sympathy and kindness, took every bit of possible sting out of his next actions so that nobody, no matter how protective they were, could be justified in recoiling or challenging him.

"Oh, ye poor wee thing, you're burnin' up a treat. Come

on, lassies, let's get you all inside, shall we? Get the poor wee mite a drink, eh?"

He led the way, his swaying gait as hypnotising as the hips of a full-figured woman only in a very, *very* different way. Shaun followed, unsure what to do about their bikes and supplies. He made the quick decision to pull his bike and trailer inside the doors that the others were walking through to keep the food protected from the elements at least.

He had to jog to catch up, reminding him that he was the wrong side of forty to be doing so much exercise in one day without building up to it, not joining them until he pushed through a set of wooden double doors to a sea of plush chairs and dark wood that formed the bar of the clubhouse.

"Pop the little lady down here and let's see what we've got for her," he said, waddling away behind the bar to talk to himself as he bent under the counter. Coming back up with a selection of small, glass bottles he returned to them, offering Harper a choice of expensive fruit juices and sparkling drinks. Harper just turned her face into Libby and cried harder, making the kind, old man pull back with evident sadness all over his face.

"She's not right, mum, feel her," Libby said. Her voice had lost that confident edge like the first time he'd heard her frightened in front of her mother. Even though she held her own child, Libby regressed again in the presence of someone she had total confidence in.

Amanda leaned over, pressing a flat hand over Harper's forehead and pausing to frown at the sensation.

"Strip her off a bit, let her cool down," Amanda said, but the young girl was so clingy that trying to pry her away from her mother to bring her temperature down was just distressing her more.

Feeling awkward and useless, Shaun backed off to give

the family space. The old man did the same, and the two of them retreated half a dozen steps. Shaun leaned over, extending his right hand open to shake.

"Shaun Taylor," he said quietly.

"Angus McBride," came the equally quiet response as the hand was gripped tighter than the frail, old frame might have suggested.

"Good to meet you," Shaun said, but the old man didn't let go of his hand. He turned to see a questioning look hiding behind a weak smile, and Shaun was left with the impression that he'd missed something.

"Um…"

"Not a golfer, I take it?" Angus asked, still smiling. Shaun felt embarrassed to have turned up there without knowing anything of the… sport… and gave an apologetic shrug.

"Ach, its fine. Most folks aren't old enough to remember me anyway," Angus said, letting his smile fade a little as his eyes glazed over in some flash of nostalgia. "I played a bit in the eighties. Taught all over for years after and ended up back here looking after the place."

Shaun didn't know what to say. He'd never met a minor sports celebrity before, let alone one he couldn't have recognised if his life depended on it.

Harper was eventually wrestled out of her layers and calmed down enough to have a drink, but it was clear to Shaun that the girl wasn't well. Coming down with a fever at such a young age was bad, he knew that, but without any way to call for help if her condition – God forbid – worsened.

"What do you know, Angus?" Shaun asked. As though the subject was a difficult one to answer, Angus limped his way around the end of the bar and stood locked in thought before selecting one of the finer bottles sitting behind the bar. It wasn't the regular stuff in the big bottles locked into the rack of optics, but the sound of the cork squeaking wetly from the neck made Shaun's mouth water.

"None for me, thanks," he said hurriedly, before the man cold pour two glasses and he wouldn't be able to say no.

It was strange, he realised in that moment, that he hadn't even thought about taking a drop since everything started to go wrong. It was all he could do most days to keep it limited to one or two beers, let alone uncorking a bottle and knowing he wouldn't stop until his consciousness fled, or the bottle ran dry.

"Suit yourself," Angus said happily. He poured himself a modestly small amount and carefully restored the bottle, reaching under the counter again to pull out two small bottles of mixers. Shaun indicated the orange juice with a grateful point and nodded his thanks as the lid was popped off and the bottle handed to him.

Angus lifted the glass slightly, as if contemplating a toast, but simply nodded and took a sip. Shaun drank too, not enjoying the warm juice but feeling as though he needed the sugars and the hydration.

"Let's see… yesterday, late morning I believe, there was a big flash in the sky and almost everything electrical died a death. That's about it. People realised their cars were no good, so some folks here waited it out for a few hours before they gave up and started walking home. Not had anyone come back since, so it's just me here."

He finished with a shrug as if the simple facts as stated weren't up to much.

"And before? Did you see any news broadcasts or anything?"

"Sorry, friend, I was ridin' a lawnmower at the time.

Damn thing crapped out on me and left me with a mile and a half of rough to traverse to get back here."

"Dammit," Shaun said, eyes cast down into his Britvic orange as he tried to think.

"What about you? I can tell from the lost look you're no local…"

"Yeah, I… I flew up a few days ago."

"For the rugby?" Angus asked, smiling. Shaun vaguely recalled a narrow win in favour of the hosts, so no doubt was about to receive some lighthearted teasing as if he cared about such things.

"No, I came to bury my father and deal with his estate."

Angus' face dropped like he'd had a sudden stroke and Shaun suspected he might start babbling an apology. Instead, he raised the glass again and intoned solemn words.

"To your father, God keep him well."

Shaun doubted that his father had ridden the escalator up and not down when he passed, but returned the gesture and drank tepid, bitter orange juice again.

"And now you need to get back home," Angus said, stating obvious facts.

"I do. I… I have a wife and daughter I need… they need…"

"I understand, friend. I understand."

Shaun knew for a fact he didn't understand. If any of them knew the truth behind his desperate need to reunite with his family, they might not look at him in the same way. He drank again to cover time and create a natural silence before the words Angus had used earlier came back to him.

"Wait, what do you mean *almost* everything?"

·   ·   ·

The door of the old, refrigerated trailer unit protested as the two men hauled it open. It had been an articulated trailer when it was still in service, and now it sat on a low foundation of stacked bricks to keep the fibreglass off the ground.

"We keep the spare batteries in here. Don't ask me why, this thing was here before my time and it'll likely be here much longer after me too, but it keeps the batteries dry and safe."

Shaun climbed up and looked around, seeing stacks of what looked like car batteries but clearly weren't. Looking at the ceiling of the trailer, he guessed the thing was lined with metal to keep the cold in, given how old it was.

"Lead?" he asked Angus.

"Aye, probably. Likely a load of asbestos too, so don't be pokin' yer finger in any holes now!"

Shaun thought. Asbestos was the absolute least of his worries at that point.

"And they still work?"

"Well, after I walked myself back here, I thought I'd take a run around the course to make sure none of the players got themselves into any bother when the flash came. You know, rolled off into the bunkers and got themselves trapped under the buggy or something like that," he said, seemingly unable to provide any answer limited to the words yes or no.

"Anyway, I grabbed the buggy I use but the thing was dead as a doornail, so I took the battery out to charge it, intending to swap it out for a new one, only the old battery wouldn't hold a charge and the charging station was also like said doornail."

Shaun got the point. These batteries were protected from the EMP by effectively being sealed in a freezer.

"Angus, how far can I get on a single battery?"

"Depends… just you on your own as you are? Maybe

forty miles? Two of you with all your gear would make that thirty if you're lucky."

"And how fast do they go?"

"Again, that's relative. Just you, maybe fifteen? Weigh it down and you'll crawl along at eight."

"Average walking speed is three, at least I think I read that somewhere... eight and not burning calories sounds like a dream to me."

As if talking about the exercise of riding a bike, Shaun's body ached all over now that he'd mentally opened the door to it. The second wave of that attack his own body made on him was to send a rumble of thunder through his stomach loud enough to interrupt their conversation.

"That settles it, you need a bacon sandwich, young man," Angus said as he prepared to seal up the old freezer trailer again. Shaun didn't argue, mainly because he did indeed need a bacon sandwich. Maybe even two.

"How can we cook bacon?" Shaun asked after a few moments of walking in silence, but Angus chuckled before he spoke.

"Ah, you young folk. Watch and learn."

A cast iron skillet sat atop the wide log burner in what Angus called 'the study' but was in fact about twice the size of Shaun's entire two-bedroomed apartment back home.

He assumed it was where the VIP members were permitted to smoke cigars inside or something, where they were served fifty pounds' worth of single malt or brandy without having to leave the wing-backed Chesterfield after a round of business talk.

Savage jealousy set aside, Shaun's mind returned to the moment as the fat slabs of cured pig began to sizzle in the fat.

As that sizzling rose to a crackle, Angus let out a satisfied noise.

"Aaah, sing for me, you little beauties!"

Shaun wasn't sitting idly as a useless guest. As Angus monitored the ritual burning of meat, Shaun was buttering fat slices of rough-hewn bread retrieved from the kitchens along with the bacon and sauce.

When a plate of sandwiches had been made, he carried them ahead of Angus back into the clubhouse, only for Amanda to stop him from advertising their achievement with a finger pressed vertically against her lips.

Shaun paused, seeing Harper asleep on the seat beside Libby. Her chest rose and fell rapidly which alarmed him for a second before he recalled how small she was, but it was clear from a distance that the young girl wasn't right.

Shaun retreated with Angus again to a respectful distance where he put the plan he'd been thinking up into words.

"Where's the nearest town?"

Angus leaned back and chewed pensively, still unable to offer an immediate answer to any question. He listed off three places, verbally examining the pros and cons of each given their current situation.

"How about a pharmacy? Or any shops that would have that kind of stuff?"

"Aye, that'll be about four miles away. But you'll be wanting to rest for the night first, no doubt," he finished.

Shaun was exhausted, physically and mentally, and a night's rest would be appreciated. He put that aside because Harper needed medication and there was nobody else he could expect to go.

Shaun leaned to look at the sky outside the large windows, seeing that the sun was already beginning its journey down, and knew he couldn't delay.

"No, I think I need to get going now."

He told Amanda and Libby where he was going, ignoring their protests that he didn't have to. He did, for many reasons, but the primary one was that he was of no use to anyone there. He could do something to help by going out and getting what they needed.

Amanda gave him a list which he repeated to himself over and over until the sequence was set in his memory.

Emptying out the wrapped and boxed food supplies from the trailer, he awkwardly turned his bike around and headed back up the long driveway.

CHAPTER SEVENTEEN

Still Good People

S haun cycled down the road, following the directions he had committed to memory along with the shopping list.

Being alone made him more nervous than he'd expected, as if the world would suddenly sprout roving gangs of cannibals after a couple of days without power.

He shuddered to think what crimes were being perpetrated back in the larger towns and cities. He imagined Anton and his cronies swaggering around, intimidating people with the threat of violence like the weak, little pack hunters they were.

Then he imagined that they probably weren't doing much. One had a broken arm and he'd be surprised if Anton was even back on his feet after the bike chain had turned his world the wrong way up. He allowed himself a small smile at that, quickly wiping it away because it showed a side of him that was a little frightening.

He'd taken the bike for the added speed, thinking that he could get in and get out, and then considered that his top speed was variable depending on how much effort he put in.

His legs burned; calves and thighs protesting with every extension to turn the pedals. He forced his mind out of his muscles and back into his surroundings, feeling the eerie silence of a world without power and appreciating that it was far more threatening than he'd imagined.

If pressed a week ago, he'd likely have said that a national power cut would bring some peace and quiet, but instead of that back-to-nature kind of feeling, he was left with a brooding sense of threat everywhere.

Every hedgerow was a hiding place. Every blind bend could conceal a roadblock.

With every obstacle like that he passed, his mood grew even more tense, when the fact that nothing bad had actually happened yet might have relaxed him instead. He knew his view of the world was a negative one, that he saw no good in people in general and that society was a stinking shitpit of selfishness and cruelty, but he had to admit that he hadn't seen the devolution he might have expected.

Only the knifepoint robbery, looting, attempted kidnapping of a child and shameless profiteering marred the last few days, and while that would be more than enough to scar a person for life under normal circumstances, he still expected much worse.

That had been the result of the behaviour of only a few people, and when he tried to calculate the hundreds of thousands of people still sheltering in their homes waiting in hope for salvation, he was forced to admit that the vast majority of human beings weren't the piratical scum he thought they were.

Those idle thoughts diminished the sting of the fear

caused by bends and hedges, and progressed him closer to the small town. He slowed when he found evidence of the outskirts; a change in speed limit from fifty to thirty, marked by the gateway effect of twin signs and a lot of red and white paint on the road.

He rolled slowly, shooting nervous glances to either side, seeing the familiar evidence of a world suddenly without electricity.

Cars were abandoned. Curtains twitched as he passed, betraying the existence of lurking people hiding and waiting.

He found the place Angus had described and checked all around him before pulling up outside. Cursing his stupidity for not having a lock to secure the bike with was short-lived when he recalled the circumstances of acquiring the bikes in the first place. He felt even more stupid when he tried to imagine himself making a rapid getaway after unlocking it.

As expected, the front door was locked. Undeterred, Shaun walked around the side of the line of terraced shop fronts and made two right turns before counting the buildings down and finding the back of the one he wanted.

Opening the back gate tentatively, he peered inside to find large commercial bins and a sharps repository. The smell of waste screwed up his nose with the sickly, sweet tang and he leaned away from the bins as if he could catch hepatitis through sheer proximity.

The back door was also locked, and he hung his head at yet another schoolboy error because he hadn't even thought to bring tools that could open doors.

As he stood there cursing his bad luck, he felt stupid twice over because he had forgotten the one thing that he really knew. The majority of his working life was spent behind a desk managing people who wanted their decisions ratified – something else his wife had always complained about – but he had come up through analysing structures for safety and security requirements.

It had been a very long time since he'd conducted a site visit and prepared a quote, but his mind automatically began running through the process before he had even made a conscious decision.

CCTV cameras; one on the back door and.... *There it was*. One facing the back gate, both screwed, obviously.

He checked the solidity of the locks, just as he would when recommending an upgrade that his company could supply and fit, before turning his attention to the accessible windows. The two on the ground floor were barred; covered with a solid grate and fixings that had been welded tight, so even with tools he wouldn't be able to budge them. What he needed, he thought, was an acetylene torch but the chances of finding one were slim.

He began running through the buildings he had seen already, scouring his sh0rt-term memory for a garage where such an item could be found, when he stopped himself, wondering why he had become so fixated on *this* place when there were others that could offer no resistance.

He still held out hope that he could purchase what he needed, although he was already starting to see that cash was a defunct item in a society that had become largely contactless.

Returning to the front of the shops, he stood still, staring at the spot where he had left the bike and trailer only to see nothing but empty pavement.

"Well… fuck me," he said sadly, having lost what little faith he had recovered from meeting Angus and being shown kindness.

"Fucking hell," he exploded, kicking the nearest object which happened to be a bin that was far more solid than he expected it to be. Hopping from the pain lancing up his foot, he spun around a few times on the spot, only on one of the rotations he saw a face in the window of the very shop he'd been trying to get into.

He stopped, taking two steps up to the glass and knocking on it gently but insistently.

"Please! I need medication! It's for a little girl."

He waited, hoping, and the face reappeared from behind the counter.

"Are you alone?" came the muffled question.

"Yeah. I had a bike with me but that's grown wings and fucked off all by itself," he groused, saying the second part too quietly for his words to carry inside.

"What medication is she on?" the man asked. He was slim, with dark brown skin and a neatly trimmed goatee below thick, rimless glasses. The accent was local, which always threw Shaun no matter how cultured he thought he was becoming. He expected the stereotypical Indian shop-keeper, not the soft, melodic drawl of southern Scotland.

"She's not... she's got a fever."

The man came up to the glass, concern riding the wave of concentration on his face.

"Did the fever come on after exercise or exertion, and is she out of breath?"

"No... no exercise, but she has had a couple of frights with all this going on," Shaun answered, trying to keep his voice down as if anyone left outside would be more interested in someone's personal business than what was happening in the world.

"And is she breathless?"

"No, I mean, she's breathing fast but she isn't struggling or anything."

"And is she still eating and drinking? Playing as normal?"

"She's had drinks… I'm not sure if she's had anything to eat. She's not herself at all."

"Any choking or smoke inhalation in the last twenty-four hours? Any cough?"

"No and no," Shaun said, starting to feel annoyed at twenty questions through the glass.

The man's eyes flickered to something behind Shaun, making him spin around, fearful of someone coming up behind him as if he was worth robbing. He saw nobody, but the click of locks from in front made him turn back. The man hesitated on the final one, looking directly at him.

"I have your word that you're not here to rob me?"

"What? Yes, of course!"

The final lock clicked, and Shaun stepped inside only for the door to be barred again in case anyone else tried to gain entry. The shopkeeper paused a while longer, staring out into the street before spinning on Shaun and resuming the questions.

"Does she seem confused at all?"

"Not that I can tell… she's very sleepy, I know that much."

"And has her breathing been this bad before?"

Shaun didn't know the answer, but something Libby had said what felt like a month ago came back to him.

"Asthma! She's asthmatic."

The man nodded thoughtfully, walking past Shaun as he stepped behind the counter again.

"I'll give you some spares for her inhaler. I presume she uses a spacer?"

Shaun nodded, not sure what a spacer was but thinking it wouldn't hurt.

"And what about the fever?"

"Give her five mils of this, four hours apart. Don't give

her any ibuprofen as it might make her breathing worsen," he said, holding up a large, glass bottle. Shaun recognised generic infant paracetamol when he saw it, and nodded his understanding and gratitude

The man added a second bottle after some hesitation, then carried on with his advice.

"Keep her hydrated and cool, but don't try anything drastic like an ice bath or stripping her off in front of a fan or anything like that."

Shaun bit down on the urge to ask where he would find a working fan because the man was helping him, and clearly at some risk to himself. That got Shaun thinking.

"Have you had trouble?"

"Some. Not much."

Shaun considered how fast his bike and trailer had been stolen in a seemingly empty town and couldn't shake the feeling that they were being watched. He glanced out of the windows, expecting the see half the supporting cast from Mad Max strolling down the road, but it remained ominously vacant.

"I've put some electrolyte sachets in as well – that's not for the bairn but the adults, in case you catch the same fever, okay? Just keep her hydrated and don't give her anything you'd normally give an adult."

"Understood," Shaun said as he accepted the offered carrier bag. "And thanks, I really appreciate you helping."

"Don't worry about thanking me, you just look after your daughter," he said.

Shaun's face dropped, but the man had already turned away and hadn't seen it. He walked to the front door, pressing his face up to the glass to see down the road in both directions before turning two locks and nodding at Shaun.

"Thanks again," he said as he slipped out of the open door. "And take care of yourself."

The man in the pharmacy promised he would, then locked the doors behind Shaun and disappeared from sight as though he'd never even been there.

Shaun hesitated on the pavement for a moment before setting off north on foot.

Darkness began to descend before he guessed he'd even made it halfway back to the golf club, and he worried that he wouldn't be able to find it. He need not have been so concerned, because the entrance to the driveway was framed by a pair of solar lamps.

Shaun, exhausted and parched, spent the first half of the driveway staggering along trying to comprehend how they were still working. They shone weakly, not as bright as he expected them to, but his tired thought process ran around in confused loops.

When he scuffed his feet up to the front doors the sky was fully dark, and he was so tired that his peripheral vision had all but disappeared.

Angus must have been watching, because he waddled fast up to him holding a small torch in his hand, the beam bouncing along the floor and walls as his unnatural gait propelled him towards Shaun.

He unlocked the doors, speaking in a concerned voice but Shaun didn't catch the words. He pushed past, muttering what he hoped came out as an apology.

He bounced down the corridor, knocking off at least one framed picture of men wearing ridiculous trousers and only one glove as he went.

Crashing into the club room, he was met by Amanda, who

demanded to know what had happened. In answer he held up the bag.

"Five mil of this every four hours," he said, gasping for breath through an exhaustion worse than anything he had experienced in as long as he could recall. "Keep her... hydrated, and don't try to make her cold."

He collapsed on the nearest couch, eyes closing through utter exhaustion, and passed out immediately.

———

Morning brought with it a crippling ache that started in his lower back, travelling down to the arches of his feet where they burned like electricity. The pain shot the other way too, finding the gaps between every one of his ribs.

In the films, this would be the part where he gasped and sat up theatrically to find concerned faces watching over him. In reality, the world moved differently.

"Urrrgh! Fucking... hell..." he groaned, rolling off the couch and kneeling on the ground.

Angus appeared beside him, the old cowboy gait announcing his identity. Shaun opened one eye, turning his head on a stiff neck to blink and focus on a cup of coffee.

He managed to fight his way back onto the couch and tried to stretch, but a loud pop from somewhere near his left hip threatened to send him back to the carpet.

"Shit," he gasped, taking a few steadying breaths before reaching for the coffee. Angus' other hand opened up, showing him four white pills which he took and threw into his mouth without even asking what they were.

"Steady now, they're the strong ones," Angus warned lightly. Shaun didn't care if it was heroin at that point, and just wanted anything to numb the pain.

With a groan worthy of how Shaun felt, Angus settled himself onto the seat beside him and leaned back.

"So, how did you leave on a bike and come back on Shanks' pony?" he asked. Shaun couldn't help but smile at the terminology he hadn't heard for years. Not since his father had been more present in his life. More present in general life, in fact.

"Bike got nicked," Shaun said, sipping the coffee and letting the caffeine infuse.

"Ah, bad luck."

"But I found the pharmacy, and the guy gave me… Shit, Harper, how is she?" he said, sitting up tall and looking around.

"They're in the study. The wee bairn's sleeping."

"Has she had the medicine?"

"She has. Amanda reckons on her fever coming down, but she won't be going anywhere for a day or two, that's for sure," Angus said.

Shaun relaxed, knowing that he had achieved something even though he had been caught out so badly by the world they currently inhabited. He tried to understand how he had been in such a state, how he had been barely able to remain conscious long enough to retrieve the medicine Harper needed.

He thought back over the last few days, about how he had barely had any sleep and had done more exercise in two days than he had done in the last two months. The stress couldn't have helped, he knew that, but still the near collapse had shocked him.

Angus seemed to sense that, and rested a reassuring, fatherly hand on his shoulder.

"You did good, laddie. You did good. Just you sit yourself

there and let the good stuff start working. I'll put the bacon on, eh?"

"Thanks, Angus. Really, thank you. I... I don't..."

"Don't what? Don't tell me you don't like bacon after all?" He put a hand to his chest in mock horror. "You're no *vegetarian*, are you?"

"God, no," Shaun chuckled, unable to resist the old man's charming humour.

"Good. Rest up, and when you're feeling yourself again you can help me with a wee project I have my eye on for you."

CHAPTER EIGHTEEN

Safely Behind the Wire

Twice more they were told that Chunk couldn't come with them, and both occasions ended up with the people dressed as soldiers capitulating when Abbie's argumentative side put her firmly in the 'too difficult' box.

They were ushered along, the solders eager for them to become someone else's problem, until eventually they joined the back of a line of people waiting for something.

Lydia asked what was happening, but after Abbie's third response that she had no idea her daughter gave up and waited in nervous silence. That silence was punctuated every few minutes by the shout of, "next!"

Armed men and women in uniform watched the line from a distance, all of them standing back against the walls in the large building as if trying to blend in, but the bulk of their rifles and magazines was all too obvious.

Some time later – neither knew how long because neither

had the means to tell the time – they neared the front of the queue and saw a long table behind which sat two people, one male and one female, in uniform. She didn't know insignia, but she guessed from their demeanour that they were officers.

They weren't wearing the camouflage get-up she expected, and her muddled, overloaded brain finally had enough clarity to remind her she was inside a naval base, so the dark blue shirts made more sense.

"Next," announced the same voice, as if it was a pre-recorded sound bite being replayed.

Abbie put her free hand behind Lydia's back and stepped forwards.

"One at a time, please," said the woman sitting behind the desk.

"She's my daughter," Abbie said, offering no further justification for ignoring the order.

"She can answer her own questions after you—"

"She's thirteen, so no, she can't."

The uniformed woman looked Abbie up and down, resting her gaze on the daft chocolate Labrador panting away happily beside her legs. With a small shake of her head, she too put Abbie in the too difficult box and leaned back in her chair as if letting it go.

The female officer pointed at Chunk.

"First off, that dog can't—"

"He's my support dog. You can ask my GP," Abbie said, bullshitting like a professional, knowing full well that there was no way anyone could check anything. The woman watched her for a few seconds, waiting for the lie to expose itself. When it didn't, she shook her head and muttered something unintelligible.

"Name?" asked the man, his eyes down to a pad of paper as if fully focused on the task and not the people.

"Abbie and Lydia Taylor."

"And Chunk," Lydia whispered loud enough only for her mother to hear. For some reason Abbie found that hilarious, laughing quickly before she composed herself to receive an annoyed look from the man, who deigned to look up briefly.

She didn't know where the outburst had come from, suspecting that the stress of recent events had pushed her slightly out of kilter with reality.

She gave their dates of birth, their address, occupation, until the question was asked that threw Abbie.

"Name of your sponsor."

Abbie hadn't heard the terminology used but took a gamble on the only link she had to the base.

"Corporal Jez Hallam."

The two officers exchanged a look which made her question a lot of things, but the conversation moved on quickly.

"Go that way," the woman said as she handed over two identification tags on plain, red lanyards. "Wear these at all times when on base."

"What's through there?" Abbie asked, not budging from her spot in front of the table as she looked in the direction the woman had pointed.

"You'll be searched," she answered, glancing at the hockey stick Abbie had tried to disguise as a walking aid, "and you'll be placed in temporary accommodation."

"Temporary until when?" Abbie asked, earning an annoyed response from the man.

"Until decisions are made as to where to house refugees. Now, move along, please. Next!"

Lydia tugged her mother's sleeve to move them away from the table, heading through a set of double doors where they waited in line again to be searched and have their bags rifled through.

A large, plastic bin sat behind the searching station, filled with kitchen knives and other makeshift weapons that people had evidently armed themselves with just in case. Abbie led with the hockey stick, handing it over with an embarrassed smile.

"Didn't have to use it, then?" anther blue uniformed man asked. Abbie smiled her response, not wanting to explain that she had used it to cripple a crackhead and make good their escape.

They were searched, Chunk pacing on the spot nervously when they went out of sight behind the curtain to remove part of their clothing, before they moved along the line in the meat factory to complete a medical questionnaire about current prescriptions and conditions. They seemed to pass that with flying colours, pleasing the medical service-woman, before they were escorted by a frantic young man clutching a clipboard as though it would protect him from anything.

"I've allocated yous... err... B-twelve and B-thirteen," he said in a Newcastle accent that would have seemed out of place had it been a normal day, speeding up his walk to a pace they couldn't hope to match. He stopped before they could catch up, indicating two camping cots placed about three feet apart under hastily written signs indicating the allocation.

He smiled, looking up from the clipboard for a second before starting off back the way he had come.

"Excuse me, sorry, what do we do now?" Abbie asked, confused by the whole situation.

"Wait," he said with a shrug.

"But wait for what?" Abbie asked, undeterred by a non-committal answer.

"Well, scran for starters, after that..." he gave another

shrug before walking away, leaving both of them more confused than before he had explained.

"Mum?" Lydia said questioningly. Abbie turned to see her sitting on the camp cot fussing at Chunk, who submitted to it without resistance and flopped onto his side to receive the scratches.

"Hmm?"

"What's scran?"

"Not a fucking clue," Abbie said, resting her backside on the empty cot and testing it for strength before lying down and letting out an exhausted sigh.

Scran turned out to be food, and the food turned out to be basic rations heated up over large metal vats sitting atop little gas burners. It reminded Abbie of all-inclusive holidays, where the food serving sessions went on for so long that it actually cooked more throughout. Arriving late for breakfast ensured the bacon was crispy, but in this case it ensured that the gelatinous gloop being mis-sold as macaroni came in bricks instead of scoops.

Abbie tried to ask a few people what was going on, but after none of them had anything other than fearful or excited conjecture to spread, she gave up asking and started listening.

"Yep, definitely the Chinese," someone opined, failing to elaborate on what the Chinese had definitely done. For all Abbie knew he was deciding on the source of his upset stomach.

"Fuck off, it was Russia. Cold War never ended, mate, believe me," came the response.

Abbie tried not to look behind her at the two men discussing nothing but their personal prejudices by the way the talked, but the next comment prompted a glare that silenced both of them.

"Either way, these cunts have done us right over—"

The way her head spun to lock on to the speaker made his mouth shut with an audible clap. He glanced slightly down at Lydia, mouthing "sorry" at Abbie in the hope that she would leave him alone.

She tried to ignore their conversation and focus on others as they shuffled along, awkwardly holding on to Chunk's lead as she tried to manoeuvre the plastic tray along.

The slab of solid set macaroni was accompanied by a sealed bottle of water and a cereal bar, both off-brand and possessing the look of items that had been stored for a long time.

"They can't keep us here," a man slightly ahead of her complained, before a younger woman hushed him and glanced around in case anyone had overhead.

"They *can't*, it isn't safe," he hissed in a lower voice, but still loud enough to carry to Abbie's ears. She tried to listen, tried to watch without looking, but her eyes went wide when she recognised the speaker.

She didn't follow politics. She couldn't care less about the corrupt bastards in parliament making dodgy deals with public money to line the pockets of their friends. What she *did* know was he had been at the centre of a local scandal about a year before.

It revolved around two escorts at a private party, that much she could remember, but seeing his face plastered on the local newspaper's front page had stuck with her. She'd taken one look at him and decided that, whatever the allegation was, he had definitely done it.

He was that person people think of when they ask, "You know when you just look at someone and think, 'prick'?"

He caught her eye, saw him looking at her, and totally misread the situation. He smiled at her, trying to ooze reassurance, but only managed to appear falser than she already assumed he was.

Still wearing the smile, he turned slightly away and kept the rictus grin on his face as he muttered angrily at the younger woman. Abbie didn't hear what he said this time, but he'd already said enough.

They took their food away to sit on the end of a folding table where she stabbed a plastic fork at the bouncy lump that promised to taste just as awful as it looked. If not worse.

"Mum, what's wrong?" Lydia asked.

Abbie didn't know where to start. She didn't want to unburden herself to her daughter and force the weight of adulthood on her before her time, but there was nobody else she *could* talk to.

"I don't think we should stay here," she said softly. She stabbed the fork down to fill the stunned silence, prising off a lump and sending it off the end of the tray for Chunk to catch before it could hit the floor.

"You're kidding, right?" Lydia asked angrily. "I said we should stay at home and wait, but *you* said we had to come here because *Jez* told you to."

"That's not fair. Staying at home wasn't an option, not with people about to start acting stupid, but—"

"And where is he anyway?"

"That's not the point, we couldn't—"

"You get one text, and we run off here. How is dad going to find us when he gets back? Did you even leave him a note?"

Abbie stopped. In all the excitement and fear of fleeing their house she hadn't paused at all to think of what Shaun would do.

There was no way he wouldn't be trying to get back to them. The first and only place he would think to look was their home; the place where all of their shared memories as a family were rooted.

Lydia went on angrily, but Abbie no longer heard the words. How could she be so thoughtless? Had she truly fallen so far out of love with him that he hadn't even entered her thoughts? Had she been too quick to run off for another man to protect her?

The last thought hurt her the most, because she was and had always been a strong woman in her own right. She told herself that she had come here for the protection of the military, to get answers, but all she had done was condemn them to become part of the machine that ground out pieces of shit like the member of parliament she had seen in the queue.

"Well, did you?" Lydia demanded, banging her hand on the table and raising her voice. Abbie jumped, startled out of her introspection by the action, and her expression darkened.

Lydia realised her mistake, her own features melting from angry to fearful at the anger she had sparked in her mother. Abbie didn't raise her voice; she just leaned across the table and spoke in a low tone that promised consequences.

"No, I didn't, because I was more interested in getting you out of there and somewhere safe before more people came knocking to ask for our things. I wouldn't be surprised if our house was already broken into, and I didn't want either of us there when that happened."

Lydia's eyes narrowed in challenge, but her words came more softly this time.

"I did."

Abbie was torn between relief and the anger she still felt at being spoken to the way she had. She became aware that their interaction had attracted attention, and as she sat up to look at the other nearby diners, all but a few of them looked away.

One could only be described as a weirdo, but the other to meet her gaze was the politician. Details of the alleged scandal came back to her now that she wasn't trying to actively recall them, and she also remembered how it had all gone away and stopped being news as if the media and the government all worked from the same office.

He smiled, trying to appear fatherly and sympathetic, but Abbie wasn't in the mood.

"Why isn't it safe here?" she asked, loudly enough to gather more attention than her argument had. People looked, twisting in their chairs without a care for who saw them as they tried to locate the person she had challenged.

"Safe? It's perfectly safe here—"

"You just said it wasn't. I heard you. Where do you think we should go?" she demanded. His face dropped. Gone was the politician's smile, and in its place was the angry visage of a man being publicly shamed.

"I was merely having a *private* conversation with my assistant regarding certain contingencies for members of the government. If you must know, I should be in London where the cabinet is protected—"

"Oh, so you're important enough to be somewhere safe and we aren't, that it?" she said, nailing him to his chair with the reasonable accusation based on his choice of words.

"Madam, that's not what I said, I *meant* that—"

"Or is it just that the escorts here aren't underaged enough for you?" she asked, fixing his eyes with her stare, earning hisses of shock and laughs from others who must have recognised him.

He glared at her, so obviously wanting to say something vile as a comeback, but still he forced on the mask of public persona. She could see a vein bulge in his neck as his eyes narrowed above flaring nostrils.

Instead of saying anything, he simply stood and walked away, abandoning his tray of food where it sat.

His associate followed, keeping her eyes down to avoid the accusatory glares from anyone she might encounter. Abbie guessed from her age and the way she looked that there might have been other candidates better for the job she had landed, and she chose to apportion the shame to that fact among others.

"Feel better now?" Lydia asked sarcastically.

"Actually, I do," she answered, but before Lydia could resume their argument the doors to the large room opened again and a dozen or more people in green camouflage walked in.

They were dressed for battle, with weapons and helmets, but their intention was clearly more culinary than military. They lined up, one person handing back a stack of trays for the first half of the group to hold one each, and Abbie stared at the man second in line.

She couldn't be certain, especially not at that distance, but she recognised the frame and shape of him. Telling herself that she wouldn't be able to do that with someone she didn't know, she stood to get a better look.

He saw her, putting the tray down and muttering an explanation to the man beside him before walking across the hall in her direction.

He didn't carry the same rifle as she had seen in the hands of those guarding their entry or carried by those on the gates to the base. His looked more like what she imagined the American forces to use, like the iconic M16 only shorter, more modern, and sprouting a short telescopic site along with a few other gadgets bolted to it.

"Abbie, you made it," Jez Hallam said. He slowed as he approached, seeming to settle himself before Lydia turned to appraise him. When she had met him before he had seemed big, like the musculature frame had taken years to earn and little to maintain. In full action man get-up, he looked huge.

"And you must be Lydia. I've heard a lot about you," he added kindly.

"Funny, I haven't heard anything about *you*," she muttered, turning her back and demonstrating an ability for acidic disdain that she could have learnt from either parent. Abbie rolled her eyes, but Jez waved it away.

"I'm glad you got here okay anyway. When did you arrive?"

"I want to say a few hours ago, only…" She looked at her bare wrist and shrugged. Jez fumbled around in the many pouches he was adorned with, coming up with something on the second one which he handed to her.

"I've got it aaaaaas thirteen-eighteen," he said, looking up as she checked the watch face on the analogue timepiece. She gave it a few turns to wind it and told him the time like a normal person.

"Twenty past one."

Jez nodded, happy at the translation between military and civilian.

"Just missed us then. We've been out rounding up people on the list."

"What list?" Abbie asked. Jez glanced around, seeing lots of people suddenly not interested in their conversation. Stepping closer he lowered his voice.

"A list of all the key people we need to evacuate from the area. We can't stay here for long."

"What? Why? Where is there to go?" Abbie asked, keeping her own voice too low to carry far. She envisaged setting sail, heading out to sea on a warship, but Jez's next words put that idea firmly in the ground and left it there.

"Inland. There's certain sites that are kept for... for in case stuff happens."

"No ships then?" she asked. He shook his head sombrely.

"Nothing works. They'll all sink soon without power to the pumps."

"What? How? How can navy ships sink?" she asked, realising after she'd spoken how stupid those words sounded coming out of her mouth.

"The EMP. It knocked out *everything*. Even some stuff that was supposed to be protected."

"EMP? So it *was* an EMP. Does that mean it was an attack?"

Jez looked over both shoulders again and took another step closer so that the rifle hanging down his chest rested close to Lydia. Even though it had the... she wanted to say *magazine*? Clip, maybe? Even though that was missing, it was still far too close to her daughter for comfort.

"Yes, only the bosses don't think we're the target. They've hit us so we aren't a viable go-between."

"What the hell does *that* mean?" Abbie blurted out, forcing her voice back down to an insistent whisper. "What do you mean?"

"The Yanks are going at it on their west coast. Western Europe's been bloody fried to keep a buffer or something, I don't know exactly."

"Who does? Who can I talk to—"

"This isn't a restaurant, Abbie. You can't just ask to speak to the manager!"

"Well... we'll go home then. We'll leave if nobody is going to tell us what's going on."

"I don't know if they'll let you. Look, going home isn't an option, we—"

"Why not?"

"The protocol for this is to abandon the key military facilities and major metropolitan areas—"

"We're leaving."

"Abbie, you can't, it's getting crazy out there. You can't leave."

"*Why?*"

"*Because they'll hit us again!*" he hissed, retreating slightly and glancing around again in case anyone had heard him. He was certain they had, but nobody looked at him.

A whistle sounded from the other side of the room making both of them look. Abbie saw the other marines putting their trays down and scrambling to put their helmets back on. Jez didn't look back, just ran from the hall leaving her with more questions than before he'd entered.

CHAPTER NINETEEN

Killing Time

S haun had fallen back asleep in spite of the coffee being strong enough to make his blood itch. He woke again around midday, as dictated by Angus cooking yet more slabs of bacon on his skillet, only this time the bread was very distinctly starting to taste and feel a little stale.

Harper was better, in that she was sleeping peacefully beside Libby, who looked as though she hadn't slept at all, and Shaun felt a stab of pride that he had been in some way responsible for the girl being in less pain and distress.

Amanda returned to the lounge towelling her hair dry. Shaun wasn't sure how she'd washed her hair, but the sight of her looking fresh and clean made him feel pretty bad about how he felt and smelled.

Asking Angus where he could wash up, the old man wordlessly beckoned him to follow and limped away through the back of the clubhouse to the changing rooms.

Shaun had seen rooms decorated like that before, only they had been in hotels and not changing rooms. Hard wood lined the walls as each locker was comprised of solid mahogany and not veneered chipboard or plastic like the places he had been able to afford to visit.

"Water's cold, but a big lad like you won't feel it, I'm sure," Angus said with a smile.

Shaun wasn't so sure, but he returned the smile and prepared himself for a quick wash before hypothermia set in.

Stripping off outside a cubicle, he leaned in and spun the dial, hearing a laboured bubbling noise as the water forced its way through.

"It'll take a wee while, the fancy pumps aren't working," Angus called out from somewhere in the changing room. Shaun bit down on the urge to make a noise at how obvious his observation was, stepping under the water and letting out a very unmanly yelp as he shuddered and forced himself to stay under the weak stream.

Quickly pumping a handful of soap suds from the dispenser attached to the tiles in front of him, he scrubbed the soap into his hair and moved down to his armpits, feeling the cloying sting of dried sweat on dried sweat being washed away to leave the clean skin beneath raw and tingling.

He took long, slow, steadying breaths against the cold and pumped more soap out, scrubbing himself rigorously as if movement could stave off the threat of exposure, and he was shocked to find that, after about half a minute, it actually did.

He was either growing accustomed to the flow of cold water or else he had died without noticing, because he no longer even felt the sting of the icy fluid washing down his body.

He smelled coconut, bitterly thinking that the stuff the club gave away to its members by the pint was of better quality than he could afford. That wasn't true; he could afford better, he was just too cheap to buy it, and without Abbie telling him what he needed, he didn't have the first clue.

That thought sobered him. He usually grew angry when his mind wandered back to her; anger at himself for being a miserable piece of shit that she couldn't stand to be around any longer and anger at her for hating him.

He didn't know when he'd changed. He wasn't even aware that he had changed, not even when it was pointed out to him with the ultimatum that he needed to address it, get help, or else he would be gone.

He either hadn't taken her seriously or else his head had been too far up his own arse for the words to get through, because she'd stayed true to her word.

The drinking didn't help, but it wasn't the cause of the problem. Most men hit their early forties and bought an old Mazda MX5 or else they burned what little savings they had on a motorbike, like they could relive their glory days of the early nineties all over again.

Most men didn't fall into a hateful pit of misery and take it out on everyone else around them until the drink was the only friend they had left.

He wasn't an alcoholic. He didn't even have a problem with drink, because he was always in total control of when he would let a drop touch his lips. What he did have was a problem with himself, and sometimes he used drink to drown out the sound of his own damn hateful thoughts.

He shut off the water, shivering from head to toe. Stepping out of the cubicle he rubbed at his body with the towel so hard he made his skin turn red. He kept scrubbing, muttering angrily at himself as he did.

"Stupid, stupid, *stupid…*"

"What's that?" Angus called out from around the corner.

"Nothing, just… bloody cold," Shaun answered, forcing some false laughter into his words. Angus either knew it was faked or he didn't. If he knew, then Shaun liked the smiling old man even more for letting him pretend.

He dressed, having chosen the least offensive clothes he could find in the club shop, only to end up wearing grey trousers with a wide, checked pattern and a pale blue shirt. Over that he wore a navy jumper with no sleeves, and a light rain jacket to complete the look. Angus had offered him a flat cap, smiling as he obviously knew what the response was going to be, but Shaun elected a black baseball cap to complete the outfit.

"Well?" Shaun asked, taking a comedic spin to show off his new gear.

"Less Tiger Woods and more Stray Cat Woods, but you'll pass muster," Angus laughed back at him. Had Shaun known the man better, he would have invited him to fuck off at that point, but he wasn't so sure the old man would take it how it was intended.

"And by stray, I mean one of those mangy, flea-bitten bastards with one eye who looks like they've done hard time, you know?"

"I get it, thanks—"

"Probably had a few nasty STDs in its life too, no doubt."

"Alright, calm d—"

"The kind of cat that makes responsible owners take one look at it and get their own spayed, if you catch my drift?"

"Fuck off!" Shaun blurted out, unable to stop himself laughing.

"And the man's back," Angus said happily, slapping both hands on his thighs and standing with a groan that lasted until he was upright.

"Now that you're properly attired, you can help me with

that thing I mentioned," he said, leading the way out of the changing rooms and through a door marked 'staff only' which led through the back of the shop until they stepped outside via a storeroom.

"Now, I managed a few while you were getting your beauty sleep, but ma back's not what it was," Angus said as he stopped and gestured at his creation.

Shaun laid eyes on a golf buggy, but the extra batteries strapped down on the back shelf where the clubs would go snaked wires under the seat.

"I see you went for the extended range model," Shaun said approvingly.

"No, this is the performance-plus deluxe super, laddie," he answered with a smirk that was almost unruly.

"What did you do? Slap on a supercharger? You go full Paul Walker on me?"

"Not quite. I might've messed with the speed governor a smidge…"

"So, what am I looking at here? 0-60 in sub five?"

"Under five minutes, aye. And maybe not sixty…"

"How long do you reckon it'll go?" Shaun asked, still smiling but dropping the comedy act.

"Somewhere between seventy and a hundred miles, depending on how hard you go at it and how much you carry. It's not as fast as your bike… *was*… but it beats doing it yourself."

Shaun was fully supportive of that mentality, especially as the tablets were beginning to wear off a good couple of hours before it was safe to take more.

"Now, if you're all done gawkin' at ma handywork, I need four more of those working batteries from the lockup.

. . .

Shaun suggested driving the cart to retrieve them, but Angus pointed out every minute spent joyriding around the club was another minute he wouldn't be heading south without walking, so Shaun began carrying them one at a time back to the workshop where Angus was hard at work modifying three rides for them.

When he walked back with the fourth and final one, already breaking out in a sweat to ruin the feel of clean skin under clean clothes, Angus called a halt to work.

"I need to stretch ma back," he said, leading the way around the back of the workshop to where the staff-only area met the driving range.

Shaun stopped, looking down the long, flat lawn that he knew had another word but couldn't for the life of him recall what it was.

"You've never done it?" Angus asked.

"Never. Didn't see the point if I'm honest… no offence or anything, but I'd rather have the—"

"You'd rather have the walk without the expense, yeah, I've heard it all before. Go on, take a swing."

Shaun looked around, seeing a club with a fat, misshapen head and deciding that was what he needed. He found a bucket of balls of varying colours but predominantly white, and dropped one onto the worn AstroTurf mat.

"You'll want a tee," Angus said.

"Lovely, thanks. No sugar and just a little milk," Shaun quipped back, looking around until he found the little plastic spike and sinking it into the ground.

Shaun settled himself into what he thought was a good pose from what he'd seen on television. He shuffled his feet in search of the perfect position before taking a huge back-swing and holding it, then swinging the club as hard as he could.

He heard the sharp *click* of metal striking ball. He looked up, expecting to see it sailing dead ahead, but movement off to his left showed the pathetic progress of the ball skittering along the grass, heading for his ten o'clock.

Angus, bless him, didn't laugh.

"Go for another one," he said impassively, offering no judgement on his lack of ability.

Shaun lined up another, did the same shuffle, only this time the ball hooked even harder to the left and moved about thirty feet.

"Try setting the next one a little higher from the ground," Angus suggested mildly. The way he spoke made him sound like he was Shaun's conscience instead of a shrivelled, old Scotsman standing still as a statue in his blind spot. He didn't acknowledge him for fear of breaking the spell, but he did set the tee a little higher than before.

"Now, try to keep the ball inside your left foot and open up the face of the club slightly…"

Shaun didn't understand the words or how to compute them, but he got the sense that he *felt* what Angus was trying to tell him.

"That's better… shoulders back a little… little more… now, keep that front foot planted, and away you go."

Shaun took another swing, shocking himself that the ball flew through the air and not along the ground. It still hooked left and went nowhere near as far as he felt the power of the swing should have sent it.

"Try again, but this time don't hold it like a baseball bat. Overlap your hands."

Shaun broke the spell then, turning to give Angus his best 'what the fuck are you on about?' look.

"Trust me, interlock your hands to stabilise your swing,"

he said, twirling his finger to tell Shaun to get his mind back on the task.

Shaun set another ball on the tee, trying to recall everything he'd been told in sequence until he couldn't keep the information straight in his head. He had to feel it, had to put into practice everything Angus had muttered to him to correct his form, and swung.

The ball made a solid sound against the club and sailed away, rocketing up through the air and only hooking left slightly.

Shaun turned, elated at his prowess, only to see Angus smiling at him the way a parent laughs at someone unable to get back to their feet drunk. Shaun's smile dropped away.

"Shaun, you drive like my mother, and she's been dead since 1980."

"Bit harsh," Shaun grunted.

"No, I'll give you that. Third ball you hit, and it wasn't a total failure. I reckon inside of a month with regular lessons, and I'll have you hitting eight out of ten in the right direction. And that's before we even talk about progressing you onto wedges and irons."

"Alright, enough about wedgies and ironing, you old bugger," Shaun grumbled.

———

Work resumed on the carts, and after that it was time to address their gear transportation. The addition of netting and hooks to hang bags resolved it, but there was little to do other than that.

They were ready to go, but Harper's condition hadn't improved at all. She hadn't eaten in over a day, and all she wanted to do was sleep and burn up. She hadn't done anything in her nappies, which concerned Libby and Amanda. Keeping her hydrated was hard because she cried and pushed all offered drinks away.

"I just wish she could tell me what she was feeling," Libby said. She sounded beaten and exhausted, and Shaun felt the sting of helplessness both for her and for himself.

All he could do was wait, but all he wanted to do was get back on the road and head south as far and as fast as possible.

———

"What about antibiotics?" Shaun suggested.

"Pointless if it's viral," Amanda said.

"But would it do any harm?" he asked.

They shrugged, exchanging looks as if one of them would have the knowledge available to answer the question. Angus broke the tense silence in the end with his characteristic double thigh slap.

"Well, I have good news and I have some not so good news," he announced seriously.

"Bad news," Shaun said, betraying more about his personality than he realised.

"There's not much bacon left and we're down to the last of the bread."

"What's the good news?" Libby asked, making Angus smile widely before he answered.

"We've just enough bacon and bread for more bacon butties!"

He stood, slowly, creaking and groaning until he reached a vertical state and set off in the direction of the kitchens.

"I'll help," Shaun announced, getting up to follow him only a little faster and with just as much groaning.

"Is a bacon butty the only thing you know how to cook?"

Shaun asked, hoping to lighten the mood but Angus was uncharacteristically subdued now that they were away from the others.

"No, but it's the best I can do with what we have."

"Angus, you're going to come with us, right? You can't stay here on your own."

"Shaun, laddie, what's out there for me, eh? Tell me that. No, I'm an old man, I've had ma time and I've enjoyed most of it. Either the world will start turning again or it won't, but either way ma part's almost done."

The way he spoke was final, a decision already made and beyond the ability of both of them to affect the outcome.

"What are you going to do when your food runs out?"

"I'll manage. Don't need much to keep this old goat bleating."

"Angus, mate... this is going to get much worse. I don't know how, but I know it isn't just going to get better by magic. Come with us, please."

Angus smiled, resting a hand on Shaun's shoulder with difficulty because the old man was bent over.

"You'll get home to your family, I can feel it in ma bones."

"That's just the arthritis," Shaun joked quietly.

"This ain't got nothin' to do with that Arthur fella, whoever he may be. It's down to you, y'hear me? *You*. And nobody else can stop you unless they kill you... the world's gone to hell in a Glasgow prozzie's handbag, but you do whatever you have to. Promise me that."

CHAPTER TWENTY

The Value of Life

Shaun felt an odd sense of loss as he drove slowly away from the golf club. He had known Angus for two days and change, but in that time he had felt a bond with the old man that dressed itself as everything that had been missing from the relationship with his own father.

Maybe it was the recent loss, or more likely it was recent events, but he didn't want to leave him behind on his own.

He had assured them he would manage just fine, that he'd suffered worse hardships in his life and that he was already an old man with far more time behind him than ahead.

Amanda and Libby tried to convince him to come along too, but he had smiled kindly and deflected all of their efforts without getting cross at their persistence.

So it was that the three and a half of them said their farewells and rolled out behind the wheels of the oddest convoy Shaun had ever laid eyes on.

.   .   .

As their laden golf carts hummed down the smooth tarmac, promising a hundred miles of jogging pace without the need to use their own two feet, Shaun tried to shake that sense of loss and focus on the old man's words of wisdom.

Libby, Harper and Amanda weren't his family, but they had shown him trust and kindness when they didn't need to. True, he had returned that trust with actions that had protected them more than once, but he wondered when and where their bond would end.

Harper was still subdued, but her fever had broken, and she looked a normal colour. Libby thanked Shaun every time they spoke, but he considered riding into town for some medicine to be nothing, in spite of how terrifying such a minor task had been.

He led the way, aiming them further east before turning south to pick up the main road and avoid interaction with people in towns and villages along the way.

Angus' directions had been flawless, bearing all the accuracy of an old man who had driven the same roads for decades. Most people gave directions through road names and numbers. Women – at least in Shaun's experience – navigated by directions to known places and used landmarks. Men did that too, only they used pubs as the landmarks and were more likely to refer to the roads by their numerical designation.

Angus had told him to head straight for the rising sun, which he took as east, easy given that they were leaving first thing in the morning, and when they passed the second cross-roads they were to take the next right and head past the Old Lion.

The Old Lion, it turned out, was a derelict country pub which had no doubt suffered a slow death after the country's attitude went from accepting drink driving as being just one of those things, to society knowing without a doubt that drink drivers were worse scum than crack addicts stealing babies.

Shaun had many a fond memory of such places, even after they had been forced to become food pubs as a way to make up the cash lost by the hardened drinkers making home their local. Some had succeeded where many had failed. Some had sold out to become restaurants, prompting a strange spike in Indian and Chinese cuisine reaching the countryside, but many of them had died away too.

The old Lion, though, had never sold out by the look of it. It had died hard. It had died alone, and its remains sat there glowering at anyone wanting to pass judgement.

Much like his father had.

When the bones of the Old Lion were behind them, Shaun returned his attention to the next phase of Angus' directions, sending them down a dead straight, single-track road that eventually met up with a modern dual carriageway.

Shaun made a point of leaning out to see if anything was coming, following it up with an exaggerated gesture of indicating his intention to merge with traffic by holding out a hand like a cyclist.

He thought he heard Libby laughing in the buggy behind him, Harper sitting in her makeshift restraint beside her.

The road was empty. It was like one of those television programs where the film crew closed a road at four in the morning at the height of summer, then added a filter to make out like it was an empty world instead of a world that had only just started to wake up.

He cruised along, happy with his fifteen miles per hour, and smiled when Libby pulled her cart up alongside his. He thought she might have caught up to say something, but the smile on her face made it clear that she was enjoying being moving just as much as he was.

Amanda, taking the lead from her daughter, pulled up on his left so that the three of them buzzed their bumpy way down the major trunk road in some bizarre mockery of the iconic Ford triple at Le Mans.

He was hardly dressed as a racing driver, with his chequered-pattern golf trousers and his muted pastel colours, but he did feel a sense of thrill in that moment.

His plan only extended as far as the next hundred or so miles heading south, but that was a hundred or so miles closer to Abbie and Lydia.

His mind turned to them, darkening his mood and killing his momentary happiness so obviously that the other two carts fell back into line, as if his mood darkening signified the end of their fun.

He imagined them sitting at home, waiting for help to come in the form of the police or military going door to door and telling them only to bring what they could carry on their backs. He hoped they would let Chunk go with them, because the daft, old waste recycler was the most loyal boy he'd ever known. It hurt him to be away from the dog as much as it did his wife and daughter, but he'd lost that privilege when he was unable to change back into the person that deserved to be in their lives.

That sullen mood, that self-directed anger, took them past a dozen turn offs. Amanda called a halt, citing the need to find a bush, and Shaun was happy to take a break and made sure everyone ate and drank.

They could clearly sense he was unhappy, and he felt

guilty because either they had no idea what to do or say, or else they feared they were the cause of it. Amanda put that into words before they set off again.

"You can go on ahead when we find the next place," she told him. "I can see you want to get home and not be carting us around with you."

Shaun was mortified, stuttering an apology and telling them he wasn't looking to dump them off.

"It's me, really. I… I don't feel like I deserve to be around people much."

"Why would you say that?" Libby asked, looking like she wanted to hug him. His heart broke even more then, because these people, these good, decent people only knew the smallest amount about him. He didn't know why, but the outpouring of self-loathing came in a torrent as if admitting that he was a fraud and had been all along.

"My wife kicked me out months ago. I was angry all the time, nothing was going the way it should, and… look, there were people my age driving Range Rovers and living in million-pound houses in the country. They had second homes they flew to in the school holidays. I spent my life making ends just about meet, working myself to the bone, and for what? So I could buy a five-year-old car on finance? So I could afford to take my family away every two years to *Costa Del Best I Could Do?*"

"Life isn't perfect, Shaun," Amanda said. "The only thing that's good is how you take it."

Shaun bit back the urge to ask if she'd read that on the packaging of a bath bomb or if it had come from a fortune cookie. He didn't hear the words she said, let alone understand their meaning, because he was diving down the spiral of depression all over again.

"So what if you don't have the expensive things they do?"

Libby said. "So what if you can't afford to do two weeks all-inclusive in Florida. That's not what matters. What matters is what you do with the time you've got."

"So you're saying your husband wasn't a loser like me? You didn't kick him out because you were successful all on your own? Like you didn't need him?" Shaun asked, directing some of that anger at Amanda.

"My husband," she said carefully, speaking in a controlled way that Shaun should have taken as a warning, "was a good man who tried his best. He didn't always succeed, but he never took that out on us."

"But you still left him, right?" Shaun snapped petulantly.

"Shaun, my husband, Libby's father, died. He died when she was thirteen, and the success you apparently saw was how I spent the money from his life insurance policy."

Shaun wanted the ground to open up and swallow him whole. He almost wished for another plane to come down, to plummet from the sky and flatten him against the road like he deserved.

"I…" his mouth opened and closed but nothing he could think of to say made up for the words he had already spoken.

"You weren't to know, so don't worry about it," Amanda said, only her expression told him he had crossed a line that would need a lot of work to get back over. He glanced at Libby, but she had already turned away to strap Harper into the seat of her buggy.

He died when she was thirteen.

The same age as Lydia was now, only Lydia had anything but good memories of *him* to look back on, unlike Libby with her father.

All Lydia knew was the pathetic, angry man who shouted at her mother and drank too much. She had seen him paralytic, had heard him say horrible things, and all because he couldn't keep up with the expectations of society for him to be investing windfalls in stocks, buying crypto, or purchasing properties to flip.

The same society that told teenage girls they should always be flawlessly dressed with a full face of makeup, that they should have a certain sized chest and a narrow waist, or else men wouldn't find them attractive.

The same concept that drove adolescents to suicide because they didn't conform to the false expectations of an online society, that was what made him fall into depression.

Depression that he was a failure, that he didn't have a fashionable beard, that he didn't drink craft ales and still have a good body after turning forty. That he wasn't *successful.*

That depression found an outlet through alcohol, and all that did was depress him more and deepen the cycle of petty self-loathing.

He didn't deserve to be around people, he truly believed that, but if he could just prove to Abbie that he was worthy… if he could make it back there, prove to them that he would cross hell and high water for them, then they might *see* him as worthy, and that might make him be better.

That way, he might see *himself* as worthy.

The thought made him want to head south at full speed immediately, but the three people he was travelling with weren't his burden; they were his responsibility.

As if reading his thoughts, Amanda added one last comment that made his decision to break away even easier.

"We aren't your burden, Shaun. We can look after ourselves."

"I know you can," he said, setting off slowly and adding quieter words just for his own ears. "But I can look after people too."

· · ·

The rain came in the afternoon as if sensing that the mood of their group had dropped. Their progress was faster than walking and more comfortable than cycling, but golf buggies weren't designed to keep the rain out.

As the afternoon wore on into an early, gloomy evening, that got Shaun thinking about where to spend the night. Amanda had evidently thought of that first, because she whizzed her cart up level with his and pointed ahead.

Shaun saw nothing but trees and the barrier beside the road, turning to give her a questioning look and receiving a sigh of disappointment. Her finger rotated to point upward, and Shaun looked back to see an advertising balloon high up in the sky.

The word blimp sprang immediately to mind, only he thought that blurting the word out might be misconstrued if it was just one of those words he used when others didn't.

"The balloon?"

"Yes. Can you read it from here?"

Shaun squinted, but other than the white body with the blue fins, he couldn't make out the single word printed on the side.

"There's a big bed place off the next exit," Amanda told him, and Shaun couldn't come up with a single argument against the idea. He knew his sore back and stiff legs were making decisions for him, but still, he couldn't argue.

"Well, sounds good to me!"

The car park served eight superstores, although only six were still operating. At least, they had been a few days ago when the power was still on.

One was a computer store, for all the good that was now. One sold household items, and that was similarly useless to them, unless anyone wanted to add a cushion to their temporary rides. Another was a DIY superstore, and Shaun already had a mind to take full advantage of the lack of CCTV, which sat beside a furniture shop and a mattress hyperstore.

Shaun had never imagined what delights would be found inside a mattress hyperstore, whatever one of those was, but he was absolutely certain that he would find an exorbitant expanse of memory foam to imitate a starfish on.

"We should go around the back," Shaun said, leading the way to the loading area so as not to advertise their presence to anyone wanting a new set of wheels. Parking the three buggies facing outwards between two shipping containers, Shaun set about disabling the buggies with what Angus had called the manual immobiliser.

Showing the others what to do because there was no sense in being the only one with the information, Shaun lifted the panel behind the seats and told them what wire to disconnect.

"Won't work at all without that. Anyone trying to pinch them will just think they're dead like everything else electrical," he explained.

"Won't they steal the batteries?" Libby asked. Shaun felt bad for her, but luckily Amanda spoke first.

"As what? Door stops?"

"Oh yeah, good point," Libby said, embarrassed by speaking without thinking first.

"Okay," Shaun said. "You three wait here. I need to go to—"

"No, we'll come with you," Amanda said flatly. She stared at him, almost daring him to say he had to go on his own because it wasn't safe for them. It was safer for them all to stay together than for any of them to split up, especially when they didn't have the means to contact one another without yelling if they were separated.

"Okay… but if anything happens, if we have to run or anything like that, then we meet back here. Got it?"

The two women nodded, making Shaun dig around in his mind for where that came from. Something from a military fitness reality show came to mind, about emergency RV points or some such nonsense, but now that he considered the real-world applications, it didn't seem so daft at all.

"What about the supplies?" Amanda asked, pointing to the three bags and three crates of plastic-wrapped bottled water.

"We'll move them inside with us after," Shaun said, hoping it was the right thing to say.

The rear shutter doors to the DIY store stood open, tall enough for an articulated trailer to back into. He guessed they were open when the power was killed, and that they had no manual way of being closed.

Leading them inside and feeling like a criminal, he caught a reflection of himself in a shiny, metal tube and saw how he was hunched over, as if he was creeping around.

Guilty body language. That was what he was displaying, and he immediately stood tall and walked in like he owned the joint.

With the faked confidence came an actual belief that he had a right to do what he was doing, and what he was doing was effectively a burglary to steal tools and items that he intended to use as weapons.

Entering the shop floor from the staff entrance, Shaun stopped and listened for a long time to check if they were alone. Harper, as always and quite unnervingly, didn't utter a sound. Libby saw an abandoned trolley, and handed Harper to Amanda while she removed the three packs of laminate flooring that had apparently been someone's project until the world decided to stop turning.

She took her daughter back and sat her in the seat, earning a happy smile and a clap of the little girl's hands. Shaun smiled at that, happy that someone was happy and jealous of the girl's ignorance of what was going on in the world. Still wearing that smile, he went to work.

He took crowbars of varying sizes, each multi-purpose, and added a decent selection of good hand tools along with boxes of large, long wood screws. When Amanda raised a quizzical eye, he smiled and whispered his answer.

"Universal door locks."

She nodded thoughtfully, and he continued on. He added two pick axe handles with an obvious application, and by the time they had worked their way back to the rear of the store after emptying the one fridge of chocolate and bottled drinks from near the checkout, the trolley was full.

"And how are we going to carry all of this?" Amanda asked, pointing out that what they had was either strapped precariously on the back of a golf cart or else in bags on their backs. Shaun thought about it, running back down the aisles at a loping jog before coming back with a couple of decent tool bags.

Not hanging around, they returned to the rear loading area to find that nobody had pilfered their stashed supplies, and piled them on top of the tools before approaching the back of the mattress hyperstore.

"Great. Locked," Amanda said, stepping back from the door and giving Shaun a defeated look.

He walked right on past her, smiling in anticipation as he selected the largest crowbar, just as Angus would have picked his favourite iron for a shot from the rough or whatever it was called. He slid the bladed end underneath the roller shutter, a much smaller version than the open one they had just walked through, and stood on the upturned tool to lever the whole door upwards with a shuddering creak of metal.

"Reckon you can get in there, Libby?"

She assessed the gap and nodded, dropping to the ground ready to shuffle in feet first.

"Wait, how will I open the door from the inside?" she asked, clearly ahead of Shaun's explanation for their plan to get in.

"Regulations. It has to be a push bar opening on a commercial building this size. You can ignore the signs warning you that it's alarmed, though."

Libby took his word for it, sliding in up to her waist and lying down to shuffle through the gap barely high enough for her face to get through. She turned to the side, muttering something about not letting it go.

Shaun waited for her verbal okay before releasing the pressure of his body weight on the crowbar, scraping the blade out in time for the door behind them to open with a heavy clunk.

Amanda said nothing about it, neither did Libby, and Shaun was happy that they neither protested the young woman going in by herself, nor did they expect him to do everything for them.

The actual need to do something, other than sit still at fifteen miles an hour and watch the horizon get closer in a measurement of days rather than hours, had lightened his mood. It distracted him from the dark thoughts that sniped accusations at him from the recesses of his mind. It added some positivity. Some cause and effect. Something that could be achieved in the here and now, and every one of those tasks was a win.

. . .

Inside the mattress hyperstore was everything it promised to be, and although Shaun said they should keep to the back of the store so as not to attract any attention through the glass windows, the mood was significantly lighter than he'd hoped for.

The toilets didn't flush, but they were still usable and there were enough of them for everyone to have some privacy. Libby even found a box of chocolates in the abandoned staff room, and the four of them shared them as the light began to fade outside.

Shaun felt like a king, sitting on a mattress costing a month's take-home and propped up on a bed of pillows so expensive he would never even entertain buying one, let alone eight.

Surrounded by the trappings of all the things society told him he should be able to afford, he finally saw them as nothing but baubles to show other people what he wanted them to think of him.

Depressed even further by the realisation that he was the richest man he knew if the things that mattered most had a financial value, he slept like a log.

CHAPTER TWENTY-ONE

Shipped Out

"You again?" said the naval rating guarding the door leading out to the fenced, concrete yard. He wore a smile on his face, but Abbie was far from in the mood to joke.

Ordinarily she would have made a joke or provided some witty comeback, blaming Chunk, who would hang his tongue out of his mouth and be happy that he was the subject of conversation.

Ordinarily, however, she wouldn't require an armed escort to take her dog outside to do his business.

The rating got the message and opened the door using a set of keys hanging from his belt, checking outside before gesturing for them to go on.

Abbie released Chunk from the lead, seeing him accelerate away in a way she could only describe as 'lolloping'. Lydia followed, her body language exuding boredom and annoyance in equal measures. Abbie didn't blame her. They'd been there for four days with nothing to disturb the monotony of hurrying up and waiting except the mealtimes.

And mealtimes were a loose description of them waiting in line to be issued with food that grew less and less appealing as the fresh produce was replaced with tinned and freeze-dried goods.

Chunk bounced along, glad of the temporary freedom, and proceeded to run a counter clockwise lap of the fenced square only to grow increasingly desperate to release a payload, because he evidently couldn't decide on the most appropriate location for it.

The uniformed man took full advantage of the opportunity and stepped outside with them, hurriedly rolling a cigarette and relishing it in a way that betrayed how many 'sneaky' smokes he'd enjoyed in his military career.

Nobody else was out there, and it had taken her a lot of arguing on the first day of what felt like internment to be permitted to take Chunk outside. It had cost her the loss of some self-respect in allowing her dog to perform the shaky squat and make a deposit near to the table where the officers running the establishment sat. After that a guard had been placed on the rear door leading to the enclosed yard, and others had grabbed the opportunity to take some fresh air and smoke what cigarettes they had with them.

Jez had returned later that first day, bearing a large sack of dried dog food. Abbie was grateful of that, not only for the evidence that he was thinking of her, but also because the scraps of stodgy human food would do terrible things to Chunk's guts, and he had no shame in releasing those gases for all to enjoy.

Lydia was quiet. She knew better than to argue that her nap had been disturbed, because Abbie had made it abundantly clear that the girl was not to leave her side under any circumstances.

She stood, thinking, worrying, absentmindedly staring at the lapping, grey water beyond the fence. She had stared in wonder the first time she had been out there, seeing a line of six submarines stacked in the harbour-equivalent of a tight car park, while to her right sat a massive warship sprouting guns and all manner of gadgetry that she had been assured was now utterly useless.

As she stared, something made her frown. Something didn't seem right, only in her semi catatonic state of stress and inactivity, she couldn't quite figure it out.

"Oh, *bleedin' fackin' Christ*," blurted out the guard behind her. She heard him say unlock the door and yell something inside, but she couldn't make out all the words. She knew what they meant individually, only in the sequence he used them it took her seconds to comprehend their meaning.

"Miss, get your arses back inside now," he said as he strode past her and pulled on something to make the rifle in his hands issue a sharp, metallic *shclack* sound.

"Lydia!" she snapped, already running for Chunk and slapping her thighs with both hands to bring him bounding happily towards her, totally unaware of the unfolding situation.

"Mum? Mum, what's happening?" Lydia said. Her voice was filled with fear and confusion, but Abbie couldn't manage an answer as well as securing the dog's lead to his collar.

The door burst open, disgorging marines with their fancy guns into the fenced area. They raised their weapons as they came out, and all of them lowered them when the barrels pointed in the direction of Abbie and her family, just as if they were playing a video game that wouldn't let them target an innocent character.

Jez was the second to last man out, his eyes going wide when he saw them, and he stepped aside to usher them through the door as it was closing.

"What are you doing here? Get inside!"

The way he spoke to her, the way he barked the orders in a voice edged with hardened steel, shocked her into instant compliance. She dragged dog and child with her, rushing to escape the situation as shouts rang out behind her.

"Stop!"

"Turn around!"

"Go back or we will open fire!"

Abbie rushed Lydia away from the anticipated gunfire that she felt certain was about to erupt, as the images she had seen managed to arrange themselves into something she could understand.

A rowboat reminiscent of the small, wooden craft that would normally be seen floating down a river on a pleasant, sunny day was overloaded with people and bags as it headed right for them.

Occupants waved their arms, shouting pleas for the marines not to shoot, but Abbie knew well enough by now that their club was invitation only.

"Mum?"

"it's alright, baby. It's oka—"

Single gunshots sounded through the closed door, cracking sharply outside to make Abbie's imagination do backflips.

Would they actually shoot civilians trying to get to safety? Would Jez do that to someone?

She hated the consequences of the last thought, imagining

that they were there on the invitation of someone who could do something like that.

They were forced into a doorway to avoid another squad of armed men and women rushing past to reinforce the potential breach in their perimeter, after which the three of them made a beeline for their cots.

Only Chunk seemed oblivious to the fear and stress, thinking that the panic was an exciting game to get back to their spot first.

Abbie lay back on her cot listening to Lydia sob quietly beside her, and for the first time in her life she didn't have the words to comfort her.

It took over half an hour, according to her new watch that she wound up obsessively, for them to filter back inside. A lot more armed personnel had gone out than had come back in, but she recognised some of the faces of the marines Jez was with.

He drew attention to himself as he stopped, scanning the large room which had filled substantially over the last forty-eight hours as he and other teams had gone out to come back with more bedraggled, frightened people and their meagre belongings.

She held up her hand for his attention, not that she wanted to speak to him for reassurance, but more that she wanted to challenge what had happened outside.

She stood, handing Chunk's lead to Lydia with a firm warning not to move, and walked to meet Jez halfway.

He smiled as he neared her, but that smile dropped when he saw the thunder on her face.

"What the fuck was that? Shooting at innocent people?"

He held up both hands and kept a larger than usual

distance from her, answering in a soft voice after checking over both shoulders for eavesdroppers.

"Calm down, it's not like—"

"Calm down?" she scoffed loudly, as if she couldn't quite believe he'd been that stupid. "Fucking *calm down*? You just shot people trying to get—"

"We didn't zap anyone!" he snarled, speaking savagely to shut her up before she ramped up and boiled over for everyone to hear. He went on in his customary quiet voice.

"Listen, I'm sorry, but you need to get a grip of shit right now, okay? This situation is worse than anything you can possibly imagine it to be."

That shut her up, reminding her that the situation was bigger than the four stifling walls she inhabited. He went on before she could arrange another question in her head.

"Look, we've almost finished getting the list of people here, and the bosses are wanting to get moving soon. It isn't going to be pretty; I can tell you that much—"

"How? How are we going to walk out of here if there's a crowd of people outside and others so desperate that they're trying to bloody *swim* in here?"

"Easy. Open the other gate and leave via the side. They'll be so distracted with the supplies left behind that they won't even notice," he said with a shrug.

"When?" Abbie asked simply.

"Today. Not sure when, but we don't have enough personnel here to keep everyone out if they start getting inventive."

"And you're leaving supplies behind? Won't we need them?"

Jez smiled, even laughed a little, which her face told him was the wrong response. He got serious and explained quickly.

"Trust me, what there is here is nothing compared to what's stored underground."

"I take it you aren't leaving any of *those* lying around?" she asked, waving a fearful hand at the rifle he held loosely with his right hand, index finger extended along the side as straight as an arrow.

"No, we're taking all the good stuff. There isn't much here, truth be told. It's mostly shipping the armoury contents off the docked ships that's taking the time."

Abbie hadn't noticed any such activity during her frequent trips outside, but then again there were a lot of things happening that she knew nothing about.

That, she realised, was the problem. She was so used to being in charge, to being in control and having all the information she wanted and needed, that being kept in the dark like one of the masses was getting to her. It was making her act even more irrationally than the situation dictated, because she needed to cling onto control of something.

"Abbie?"

She looked up, having missed what Jez had said.

"Sorry?"

"I said I need you three ready to move. It'll be soon."

"Okay… are we walking? How are we getting there?"

Jez smiled knowingly, giving her a flash of that cheeky confidence that had made her pick his dating profile weeks ago in the first place. He said nothing, just gave her a wink and turned to jog after his fellow marines.

———

The call to vacate the premises came sooner than she expected. Hefting their new, camouflaged rucksacks that were the same size as an average adult and were apparently called 'bergens', they explored all the different compartments to them.

Into those bags they packed their personal effects, along with a set number of water bottles and other rations which appeared to be the cause for a lot of distracting excitement for those not accustomed to them.

They packed their sleeping bags, apparently called 'grot bags' for some reason unfathomable to people who spoke English and not the odd, naval slang language that all the uniformed personnel seemed to converse in.

Abbie couldn't carry the full sack of dried dog food, so she managed to source two carrier bags that held enough to keep Chunk going for four or five days and had to abandon the rest where it sat.

Hoping it wasn't a mistake, she hefted the heavy pack onto her shoulder, folded the leather of Chunk's lead around her hand to shorten his reach, and took Lydia firmly by the hand to join the line of people filing out of the large room to head God only knew where.

The first thing Abbie was assaulted by was the stink of rough diesel fumes. The second thing was the tang of damp canvas, as though she'd been transported back thirty years to her Brownie annual camp where she was forced to sleep in something that was probably leftover surplus from World War 2.

She gripped Lydia tightly, feeling their combined sweat loosen their grasp for a moment before she squeezed so as not to lose the two things she desperately needed to keep.

Armed personnel stood either side of the line of civilians, hurrying them along to climb up into the backs of old, green trucks that were the vehicular equivalent of a box of old clothes in the garage. It was difficult to climb up, and the jump was far beyond Chunk's ability, so he had to be hauled up too.

The trucks stank of cold and a lack of use. The wooden bench seats they were crammed into were hard and damp. Someone wearing camouflage uniform stood at the back, speaking loudly and telling people to squeeze in and put their bergens on the floor in front of them but not to let them go.

Chunk whined, letting out a single bark that conveyed his fear at the mass movement. Abbie shushed him, squidging the dense flab on the back of his head just how he liked to be fussed, and in response he tried to climb on top of her, only managing to half mount her massive rucksack and stretch his neck out to drop his wet chin on her hands.

Lydia clung to her, silent and clearly nervous, but they were caught up in the momentum of so many people swept along with the mighty military machine moving.

"It's alright," Abbie said to Lydia and Chunk, taking some confidence from the assertion herself as if saying it could make it true.

The noise of so many big diesel trucks running in a confined area made her ears hurt, and she just sat there, hugging her daughter and her dog, wishing she had more control over the situation.

The person organising them to sit down climbed off the back of the truck and slammed the tailgate up, banging on it twice, probably to let the driver know they were loaded. The truck backed up with a shudder as the driver slipped the clutch, and Abbie leaned around Chunk's head to see someone waving them back towards a trailer that looked just like the truck, only without the boxy cab on the front. When that was connected, they waited – always waiting when the military were involved, she thought – and at some unheard signal they rolled out.

Leaving the massive hangar and going outside was a shock to her system. The wind blew violently, thumping the canvas into the back of her head and startling a yelp from her lips.

Revs built, disappeared for the clunk of a gear change, then built again with a lower note to signify their escape from a city that was on the verge of tearing itself apart, if Jez was to be believed.

She had no reason to disbelieve him, and those few people trickling in over the days they had been there had displayed more and more haunted looks as if they couldn't believe what was happening.

She had kept herself to herself, isolating her and Lydia away from people for reasons she didn't yet understand, and all the while she felt her control of the situation slipping away.

She didn't want to be reliant on a man she barely knew for their protection, she wanted to be reliant on herself, and to that end she set her mind towards the next phase of their lives.

Whatever the hell that would look like.

CHAPTER TWENTY-TWO

Good People

"I reckon today's the day," Shaun said. Amanda stared suspiciously at her buggy, having already voiced the opinion that it was starting to feel sluggish compared to when they first set off.

They had spent three nights on the road, each time finding somewhere safe and sheltered to camp and obtaining supplies on the way.

Whole towns seemed abandoned in places, where in others the hostile stares of locals kept them moving along.

"We should've stuck with bikes," Libby said, being the only one of them to be comfortable in a saddle for hours on end.

"Says the triathlete," Shaun murmured.

"True, but I'll be the one laughing if we have to run and swim…"

"Did you know that a saltwater crocodile is faster in the

water than a human, but a human can outrun one on dry land?" he asked, earning a terribly confused look from Libby. Amanda was already groaning and rubbing her forehead, but Libby hadn't figured it out yet.

"Sooo…" she asked, wondering where he was going with it.

"So in a triathlon, it's down to which one of you is the stronger cyclist," he said, keeping his face deadly serious and fighting the urge to collapse with laughter at how successful his build-up had been.

Libby's face set into a look that made it clear to him he wasn't funny, even though it was funny. Ut was too much for Shaun, who burst out laughing at his own joke.

"Anyway," Libby said, unwrapping a chocolate bar and handing it to an excited Harper. She spread the ordnance survey map out on the front of her cart.

"Reckon we could make it there by tonight?" she asked. Shaun peered over her shoulder, leaning close and not feeling any awkwardness after the time they had spent in close proximity to one another.

He peered at the point she marked with a dirty fingernail, running his own finger down the main trunk roads to get to it.

"Ambitious," he said. "Especially given how we might be running out of juice soon."

The three of them stood in silence, all leaning over the map and considering an alternative. This was the point Shaun had been worried about – the threshold between having transport and having to source an alternative.

He didn't want to be walking. He didn't want to be cycling again either, but between the two he'd reluctantly choose that over walking.

He lost concentration, feeling grateful instead that he had company on his journey south with people who had no real agenda other than finding a safe place for Harper. They had accepted early on that sitting it out wasn't an option, because already many towns were beginning to show signs of lawlessness. People had looted as much as they could, and signs of the unsuccessful were starting to become evident.

The best course of action, Shaun felt, was action. Keep moving, never get bogged down, stay fluid and roll fast.

He laughed at himself for the thought, unable to correlate the person he thought he was with this new, improved version with drive and determination.

"What's so funny? Thought of another dad joke?" Libby asked.

"No, I… was actually just thinking… never mind. It's daft."

"No, go on," Amanda said, smiling at him.

"I'm just feeling a little, I don't know, blessed? Happy that I'm not on my own, anyway."

He looked down, embarrassed at his show of vulnerability.

"Well, we haven't got much else to do, have we?" Amanda said, patting him lightly on the shoulder. The moment passed and he shook himself out of it, returning his full attention to the map.

"Well, south is good," he said, covering the silence with an obvious comment. In the absence of any other idea, they packed up their few belongings from the small campsite they had made and continued their way south.

"Just keep your eyes peeled," Shaun warned.

"For what? Roving gangs of cannibals? Road warriors wearing gimp masks?" Amanda asked ruefully. Shaun smiled at her Mad Max knowledge, but his smile faded when he recalled that storyline was supposed to happen about the time they were living in right now.

"Not everyone is looking to hurt you or steal your stuff, Shaun. There are good people out there, you know?"

Shaun grunted, unwilling to accept that viewpoint even a month ago, but he let it go and concentrated on the road ahead.

The days since the night spent sleeping on memory foam had seen them acquire a meagre amount of camping equipment from a small store off the beaten path. They now possessed a small tent each, along with inflatable camping rolls and sleeping bags.

The good stuff, the little gas cookers mainly, had already been pilfered but there was so much good stuff left behind that they no longer needed to worry about breaking into places to find shelter at night.

They were limited to abandoned commercial properties as it was, and Shaun was beginning to worry that their luck would run out if they continued that way.

The rain stayed away all morning, their journey down deserted roads marked by the masses of abandoned cars that forced them to slow their progress in places. They didn't look inside those that had crashed, not wanting to repeat the scenes they had found after the initial flashes of light in the sky.

Just when they were forced to proceed at a crawl to navigate between cars that had caused a snaggle of obstacles in the road, the expected happened.

"Well… shit," Amanda declared.

Shaun stopped, turning in his seat to see her getting out of her buggy and staring at it, hands on her hips.

"Hey Sanka, ya dead?" Shaun asked, forgetting that he

didn't know his travelling companions as well as he might. The reference was ignored, which was fine by him.

Amanda was already removing the two backpacks and the last of the bottled water from her passenger seat, and Shaun parked his own buggy to help. Putting the bags in Libby's cart, Shaun made room for a passenger and they set off again, making only another two or three hundred yards of progress before his own cart wound down to a halt.

"Well… shit," he said.

Libby rolled by, throwing up a peace sign and crowing, "So long, suckerrrrs!"

Her bragging lasted another thirty feet before her own buggy shuddered to a stop.

"Well…" Shaun said, looking at Amanda for her to finish their newly adopted catchphrase.

"Shit."

They repacked their bags, drinking a bottle of water each to lighten the load they had to carry on their backs, and started walking without a backward glance at the rides that had carried them for four days.

"Oi, sir!" Shaun said in a tone that made it obvious he was making one of his jokes. "What you doing?"

He turned as he walked, making out as though he was answering himself.

"Trudging."

"What's that from? It's…" Amanda clicked her fingers as if trying to recall the words from deep within her memory.

"A Knight's—"

"Hello?"

The interrupting voice made all of them jump, and at their startled response, Harper whined as a prerequisite of crying.

Shaun's head spun, desperately searching for the source of the voice. His left hand kept hold of the tool bag while his right hefted the pick axe handle in readiness to use it.

He didn't know why the sudden arrival of another person made him feel so frightened and defensive, but after days spent avoiding others it was an unsettling experience to be challenged without warning.

"Who's there?" he growled, sounding so forceful that he barely recognised his own voice.

"Just me, over here," a man's voice said. He turned, wooden club raised, to see a man emerging from behind a car with empty hands held out. His body language screamed non-aggression, as did his smile, but Shaun was so edgy that he took a step towards the man and lifted the wooden weapon a little higher.

"Who are you? What do you want?" he demanded.

"Roger. And I don't want anything!" the man said, still smiling but backing up a few paces. He gave off the impression that he wasn't frightened, but that he didn't want to frighten anyone else.

Shaun looked him up and down, seeing a man closer to sixty than forty. He was trim, not big built at all, and behind him was a stack of green, metal jerrycans and a funnel.

"Didn't mean to jump out on you," Roger said. "I was just siphoning some fuel and didn't know anyone was around. You scared *me* if I'm honest…"

"*We* scared *you*?" Amanda said with a hand pressed flat to the top of her chest. "Ha! I nearly wet myself!"

"Sorry about that," Roger chuckled. An awkward silence followed, during which none of them knew what to say to break the deadlock. It seemed impolite to ask what he was doing, even if he had given the explanation and the tools made it obvious, but the question still burned on Shaun's lips.

"What do you need fuel for?"

"For the old truck," Roger answered. "Well, *trucks*, technically…"

"Wait, you still have working cars? How?" Amanda asked, taking an unafraid step forward.

"Because they're old. None of the fancy electrical gizmos you get in your modern rubbish."

Shaun wanted to ask so many questions, but he feared a trap. He couldn't say why, couldn't articulate his worries, but he put a hand out to stop Amanda from moving any further away.

"Why didn't you drive here then?" he asked, looking around for an old vehicle and seeing none in their vicinity.

"No sense in wasting it, is there?" Roger answered happily. "Plus, petrol's hard enough to come by at the moment. Not like the old days when you could just siphon it out; these new cars have all that—" he waved his hands "—stuff so you have to tap into the tank directly."

Shaun leaned to look past him, seeing a Ford jacked up slightly from the road with a black, plastic tray underneath catching the trickle of liquid running out.

The awkwardness continued. Shaun wanted to ask for help, to ask for one of the two working vehicles they apparently had, but he still couldn't shake the feeling that they were being set up to be robbed.

He looked around, inspecting the hedgerows and parked cars for any sign of movement. Roger must have realised that and tried to calm him.

"It's just me out here, you have my word," he said seriously.

"Yeah? No offence, *Roger*, but I don't know you well enough to take you at your word," Shaun said, earning a sharp look from Amanda.

"And I recall we didn't know you well enough less than a week ago, but we still trusted you at your word," she said testily, making Shaun feel a little humiliated at how he was coming across.

Tentatively, almost reluctantly, he lowered the pickaxe handle.

"Sorry, Roger. I…"

"It's no bother," the man interrupted, smiling again.

His eagerness set alarm bells ringing in Shaun's mind again, but Amanda's words from that morning came back to remind him that he was a miserable, suspicious bastard at heart.

"Who else is out here with you?" Libby asked. She seemed cautious but willing to believe the man was genuine.

"Just me. Our place is just back down the way," Roger said with a nod back up the road where a small junction was almost hidden among the hedges. "Come and see." Shaun turned, looking at the others and finding himself outnumbered two to one.

"Okay, if you're sure it's not a problem," he said, eyeing Roger up.

Roger smiled. It was warm and genuine, and no matter how hard Shaun looked, he couldn't see any guile there.

Roger gathered his gear, pouring the reclaimed petrol carefully from the tray through the funnel and into his metal can. He refused the offer of help with a smile, groaning as he tucked the tray under his arm and carried a can in each hand.

The walk down the single track took them all of five minutes, and when the house came into view a woman walked out of the ornate front door casually holding a shotgun diagonally across her body.

"No, no, it's fine!" Roger said loudly. Shaun saw the woman, his wife he assumed, relax visibly and slacken her grip on the weapon, which she broke by flicking the lever over to open the breech.

"What are you doing, Roger, inviting every man, woman, and child back here?" she said, storming forward to frown at him. Roger put down his dual burdens and released the tray to drop beside them, then spread his arms wide in apology.

"I'm sorry, dear. I was collecting fuel and they broke down. And they've got a wee one with—"

He never got to finish his sentence, because the woman saw Harper peering out from behind Libby's legs.

"Aww! Hello, little lady, and what's your name?"

Harper looked up at Libby, obvious trepidation on her little features.

"She doesn't really speak yet," Libby said apologetically. "She's Harper. I'm Libby, and this is my mum, Amanda."

"Pleased to meet you," the woman said. She turned her raised eyebrows on Shaun, who flustered and managed to stumble out his own name.

"Oh, where are my manners?" Roger said. "This is Edith, my lovely wife."

Edith smiled, genuinely pleased at the way he spoke about her. Shaun guessed they had to have been together for thirty years or more, and that pang of evident love and affection stabbed at him deep inside his chest.

"You'll want to sit down, I'm guessing. Tea?" Edith said, lighting up eyes at the thought of a hot drink.

"How...?" Shaun asked, looking between Roger and Edith.

"Wood stove, and we've still plenty of heating oil left after a mild winter," Roger said. "Come on, let the ladies get a drink brewing and I'll show you around, eh? You'll not need your hittin' stick, but you're welcome to bring it along if it makes you feel better."

Shaun felt instantly foolish still holding the pickaxe handle, and he slipped off his rucksack straps to rest all of his burdens on the ground.

Roger led the way, taking great delight in showing off his chickens with a single duck among them.

"That's Edna. She's unaware that she's not a chicken, and I'll thank you not to tell her."

Shaun couldn't help but laugh. He felt his stress ebbing away with each step he took around the old man's tiny slice of the world where nothing bad happened.

After the chickens came the resident goat. It stared at Shaun sullenly, and Roger's words of caution sparked yet more laughter from him.

"That's Daisy," he said quietly. "Don't make eye contact… *she can smell fear*."

Leaving the demonic goat behind, Roger led him to an old brick barn with a sagging, tiled roof where Shaun saw the front of two vehicles that would be recognised the world over.

"Series Two?" he asked, earning a cluck of Roger's tongue.

"Series Three, and the one on the left is my son's Wolf."

Shaun walked closer, seeing the drab green of the military version of the iconic Defender. He hesitated, turning back to Roger as if asking permission, and received a smile and a nod of permission.

He took in the spare wheel on the driver's side, the conical shape of the raised air intake, and found himself wondering if there really was any other vehicle for when the shit hit the fan.

"They work?" he asked.

"Of course they do! No sense in gathering fuel for cars that don't work…"

"True," Shaun admitted. "But, what about the electrics? Aren't they fried? The car I had was dead as a doornail."

"None of your fancy ECUs and EFIs here."

"But the fuel injection and… and timing and stuff…"

"They use a pump driven from the crankshaft and all the timing gear is linked to that. Just needed jump starting and they work just fine."

Shaun wondered how many other trappings of their old lives could be revived like that, wondered how much they had all given up because they lacked the knowledge and ingenuity to make it happen.

Roger's words came back to him, and he felt as though he was stepping on toes.

"It's your son's?"

"Aye, it was…"

Something in Roger's tone, something in the distant look in his eyes warned Shaun off from pushing the subject any further.

"You're not getting some kind of sponsorship deal, are you? If this was the BBC you'd be obliged to point out that other makes are available," Shaun said, awkwardly trying to move the conversation on.

Roger smiled, accepting the weak joke for the way it was intended and letting the moment move on.

"Come on. Ladies'll have that kettle hot by now, I don't doubt."

. . .

Shaun sat quietly in the corner of the kitchen on a pine chair likely as old as he was. The uneven quarry tiles of the floor made it rock slightly, and he tensed his body to make it knock gently back and forth under the gaze of a long-haired collie dog that watched him intently. Not him, specifically, it was the fresh baked scone in his hand that was the main focus.

He tested his theory, slowly moving the scone from side to side, and smiling as the dog locked on like an automated weapons system.

The conversation in the room moved easily, with the others asking questions and exchanging information about themselves like normal, civilised people. The connection between the women was warm and effortless, and Shaun felt guilty that he was somehow denying them that connection by being the harbinger of doom and gloom.

In the world Shaun had rapidly hardened himself to, their connection seemed surreal.

"So, you need to get back down south?" Roger said, snapping him out of his trance with the dog.

"Huh?"

"Amanda was just saying how you had to get back to your wife and daughter," Roger said. "And my condolences about your father," he added.

Shaun pursed his lips and nodded, pulling that face people make when they want to say thank you, but the emotions are running too high to trust their words to come out right.

It wasn't the emotions over his father, it was rather the reminder of needing to get home to find Abbie and Lydia that threatened to force tears of frustrated fear from his eyes.

"Well, it's a little late to be on your way just now. Why don't you stay for the night, eh?"

Shaun was taken aback by the offer. Everywhere they had been, bar the pharmacist who was duty bound to help sick people, he had seen nothing but wary hostility at best from everyone they had encountered so far.

"If it's no trouble," Amanda said. "We've got our tents. If you don't mind us setting up on your front garden we can—"

"Nonsense!" Edith interrupted. "We've got bedrooms to spare and I've a loaf of bread that'll go to the chickens if we don't use it up in the morning. I've even got a travel cot for the little lady."

Shaun looked at Harper, sound asleep on Libby's lap, and felt that this kind, old couple needed them in their lives as much as they needed the offer of such kindness. He felt sad, though. Sad because he didn't feel as though he deserved to fit in with them there.

That sadness didn't linger. Because the happiness he felt at being wrong about people made it all worthwhile.

The ladies went upstairs to settle Harper and make up the beds, leaving Shaun alone with Roger, who stood and groaned as he reached up for the bottle sitting on the top shelf of the dresser beside the range cooker.

He retrieved two glasses, holding them up to Shaun with raised eyebrows.

Shaun nodded, happy to take a drink with another person to enhance the temporary happiness. It was such a marked contrast to how he had usually drunk scotch; alone and angry at himself and everything else in the world.

"Do you smoke?" Roger asked, leaning to one side and retrieving a pouch from one pocket and a pipe from another. Shaun shook his head and Roger hesitated, leaning again to put the pouch away again.

"But I don't mind if you do. It's your house."

"Aye, but Edith says it smells like a dog's arse. Shall we take it outside, perhaps?"

They strolled, with Shaun taking his time and swirling the

small measure in his glass as he stared at a sky filled with millions of bright stars and not a single manmade intrusion anywhere.

"It's beautiful out here," Roger said.

"Have you been here long?"

"Thirty-seven years this October. Moved here as soon as we got back from our honeymoon in Skegness."

"Wow," Shaun said, genuinely finding it impressive and for once being happy for another person instead of feeling jealousy. Roger sighed, puffed on his pipe and joined Shaun looking up at the night sky.

"I want you to have the spare truck," he said eventually, making Shaun splutter and cough at the offer.

"I can't, it's too much, what if you need it?"

"We won't. We've got just about everything we could need here, and what we don't have we likely won't miss. We can hold out for a long time until things set themselves right again."

"But..."

"But what if it doesn't? Then we have just about everything we need here."

Shaun started to protest, but Roger shut him down by proving that he'd considered everything already.

"There's a timber yard five miles that way," he said, pointing off into the dark. "And beyond that is where we can get more heating oil and gas burners a-plenty. We've got supplies enough, and I dare say we can hold out comfortably enough until the new year without much bother."

"I... I don't know what to say..."

"Thanks would be customary, but I know you're grateful already so don't worry about it. Now, I imagine you'll be wanting a good night's rest and a warm bath in the morning, eh?"

.   .   .

Shaun, although too large for the single bed in the spare room, slept like he'd run a marathon. Even though he'd slept enough on their journey, the fact that he felt safe and protected there made his slumber so much deeper and more relaxing that he couldn't recall a better night's sleep.

Waking fresh, blinking away the confusion of their situation and good fortune, he had a hot bath and enjoyed fresh eggs on homemade bread toast among people he hadn't known long but now considered friends.

Amanda took him aside as Libby insisted she washed up, leaving Edith playing with Harper and Roger tending to the previous night's ash from the fire. They walked outside and before she even said a word, he knew what was coming.

"You're staying here, aren't you?" He spoke as though stating a fact for confirmation and not questioning her.

"We are."

"I'm glad," he said, following up quickly lest she take the wrong impression from his words. "Not that I don't want you with me, just that you all deserve to be somewhere safe and not traipsing the length of the country with me."

"And we will be safe here. Safe enough for a long time if needs be. You'll get home and find your ladies, and we'll be just right here until this whole mess sorts itself out."

Shaun wasn't so convinced about the last part, but he accepted her belief in it.

Roger helped him load the vehicle, showing him the intricacies of how it worked and what he needed to do to keep it running. He added the necessary tools to lift cars and drain their fuel, and Edith insisted on making him up as much food as she could spare.

"You'll need to keep your strength up if you're to get back to those women of yours," she said, smiling and kissing him on his bearded cheek before Roger stepped out of the house bearing a shotgun and a small bag.

"You know how to use one of these?" he asked seriously, not handing over the weapon until he was assured that Shaun wasn't in need of a beginner's lesson.

"I've done some clay days," he replied, evidently satisfying the man enough to be gifted the precious item.

"You're sure? You won't need it for yourself?"

Roger smiled ruefully.

"Shaun, I have four more and ten times the ammunition tucked away. I'll keep them fed; don't you worry."

Starting up the old military land rover and feeling the rhythmic rumble of the solid diesel engine, Shaun waved them goodbye and headed back to the road on his own, turning left to head south with renewed energy and more than a little regret.

Just like that, he was alone. He always knew there would come a time when this would be the case, but he always thought it would be another day, and not that day.

CHAPTER TWENTY-THREE

Definitely Not Salvation

I f the harsh bureaucracy of the naval dockyards was stifling, what they encountered at the tent city was nothing short of totalitarian rule.

Men and women wearing yellow and orange high visibility vests strutted along the lines of people like overseers, bearing clipboards and pens as the weapons of their control.

These civilian leaders, the marshals as they were referred to, laid out the facts of their new life abruptly and with all the boredom of people repeating the same mundane tasks.

The place had some official designation, but to Abbie it was just a refugee camp. To make matters worse, she hadn't seen much in the way of justification for them being there.

"Name?"

Abbie jumped and turned to see a woman with greasy hair and glasses, those looking obviously like the stand-by pair of a regular contact lens user.

"Um, Abbie Taylo—"

"Speak up! Lots of people here and I'm not a mind reader!"

Abbie took a calming breath, not quite at the stage where she was going to flip the lever and press her thumb on the big, red button. Almost, but not quite.

She pulled the ID card from the lanyard on her neck, utilising the anti-strangle feature, and thrust it in the woman's face, forcing her to lean back so she could focus on the handwritten details.

Instead of asking, the woman turned an annoyed look on Lydia as if she was expected to read minds also.

Lydia, picking up on her mother's attitude instantly, shoved her own ID at the woman and set her best resting bitch face.

Copying down the information as slowly as she could to demonstrate the power of her clipboard and high vis, she finally looked down at Chunk.

"Animal passport?"

"What?" Abbie asked.

"All animals require a passport."

"Okay, where do I get one of those?"

"You should already have one from your previous site," she said, looking up from the clipboard to wield her dominance like a stick.

"Well, they didn't say that there," Abbie argued, not showing any sign of weakness in case the power-hungry woman sensed it.

"I'm saying it here. No animal passport, no entry. Sorry!" The smile she gave made it obvious to Abbie that she wasn't in the slightest bit sorry. In fact, the smile made the smug bitch look like the most punchable thing she'd ever seen.

Abbie took a very deliberate step closer, forcing the clipboard aside with her body, and lowered her voice.

"Now listen to me, you f—"

"Can I help anyone?"

Abbie snapped her head around at the interruption, eyes still boiling a thunderstorm, and was disarmed by the face of a young man that was so genuine, so... so *beautiful* that all her anger fled in embarrassment.

"I... we..."

"They haven't got an animal passport," snapped clipboard and glasses.

The man, tall and built like an athlete, bent to fuss Chunk under the chin and mutter questions to him as if talking to a small child.

"He's my support dog," Lydia said, delivering the lie with more confidence this time.

"They didn't give you a passport? Who wouldn't give a good—" he leaned for a look, "—boy like you a passport? We'll just have to fix that right now, won't we?"

Chunk, savage protector and fearless warrior that he was, grumbled in ecstasy and flopped onto his back to expose his formidable belly for rubbing.

The man stood, smiled at Abbie and Lydia in turn, then took the clipboard from the woman's grasp despite how she tried to hold on to it. He pretended not to notice, pulled a pen from his own pocket, and scribbled on a piece of paper before offering it to Abbie.

She took it, seeing something anyone could have forged, and offered her thanks.

"My pleasure. Now, sorry about the wait but we've had convoys from Southampton and Bristol arrive just before you. It isn't usually so chaotic!"

His white, straight teeth shone from his smile contrasting

against his brown skin. Abbie caught herself staring, locked into the smile like she was the teenager. Shaking herself out of it, she muttered something about it not being a problem.

"Well, I'll leave you to it then. My name's Ty. I'm the senior marshal and facilitator in charge of civilian management for sector three. Any problems, just ask one of the marshals to see me, Miss…" He looked at the clipboard again before flashing the smile back at her.

"Taylor."

"It's *Mrs*," Lydia said, popping the bubble and prompting a laugh from him.

"*Mrs* Taylor, my apologies."

"What's sector three?" Abbie asked, letting the line pass by and continuing the conversation for reasons she didn't fully comprehend. Clipboard huffed and held out a hand, receiving her talisman of power back from Ty and leaving to continue her important work with a last, derisive look in Abbie's direction.

"I promise all my marshals aren't like her," he said, diffusing the tension and making Abbie giggle in a way that she didn't even recognise. "Sector three is one of four areas responsible for housing and looking after the civilian population. Effectively, the camp is split up into separate areas that can operate individually. Too many people in one place and things get, ah, *missed*."

Abbie wasn't focusing enough to understand what that might mean, and Lydia's insistent tugging at her arm broke the spell.

"Mum, we've lost our spot," she grumbled, making Abbie look at the line and deflate at the thought of having to join the back again.

"Allow me," Ty offered, gesturing for them to follow him to the front of the line where he cut in so smoothly that nobody could justifiably challenge him. He placed them next in line, smiling at his two marshals manning the admissions gate as though they had just been granted VIP access into a music festival.

"All the information you'll need is on the main bulletin board, just over there," Ty said, gesturing at a vertical expanse of chipboard ahead of them. "We'd have handouts, only…" He shrugged, as if the loss of electrical equipment was as inconvenient as the photocopier going down.

"Can you tell us what's going on?"

"Ah, sadly no. Believe me, I would if I knew."

"So, what? You're military? Police? Government?"

"None of those," Ty said with a soft laugh. "We're just civilian facilitators here. There are military teams here, of course, but I'm sure they have other things to be concentrating on."

"Like evacuating people from the cities?" she asked, hitting him with a hard question and watching for his response, but he barely faltered. There was a tiny flicker of something – annoyance or shock that she might be on the right lines maybe – but it was gone before she could hope to read it.

"They're doing what they need to, I'm sure. Just sit tight here and we'll all get to go home at some point soon."

Checking their bed allocation as a way to change the subject and avoid an awkward silence, Abbie asked for directions.

"Down that way, fourth left, and follow the line," Ty told her, but she had missed the direction he had pointed in. He smiled, flashing that smooth brilliance at her again.

"There's a map on the bulletin board if you get turned around. Mealtimes are rotated among the sector for who goes first… you're in… B block, which means you go last today. Sorry about that."

"It's fine," Abbie said with a smile.

"No, it's not," Lydia muttered loudly enough for Ty to hear but quietly enough for him to pretend he hadn't and save Abbie the embarrassment.

"Well, as soon as you're ready, just go to that man there and tell him where you need to be," he said, pointing at a marshal wearing his orange vest unfastened as he leaned against a concrete block like the kind people used to shut off roads.

"Ty, can I grab you for a minute?" someone shouted from behind them. He smiled at them in turn, giving Chunk a bonus head scratch, and disappeared with mock salute and a heroically cheesy line.

"Duty calls! Any problems, get a marshal to come find me."

"Mum, I don't like it here," Lydia said quietly, leaning a little closer to her so their heavy backpacks bumped together.

Abbie looked around, seeing far too many people wearing sullen expressions sitting around with nothing to do. She didn't like the feel of the place either, as if she could smell the trouble brewing, but knew it wouldn't help either of them for her to voice that now. Forcing a false but happy singsong tone into her voice, she got them moving.

"Bulletin board! Let's see what's on there, shall we?" She squeezed her hand a little tighter and set off, jerking Chunk's lead to get his attention and make him follow.

They were jostled getting to the front so they could see the board, finding a map drawn in marker pen showing where the residential blocks, toilet facilities, and cafeteria were.

There was a convenient red arrow drawn on it, with the ominous words 'You're here now' scrawled beneath.

Abbie didn't know if a comma would change the way those words made her feel or not, but she got the distinct impression that leaving wasn't an easy option.

She saw the times for food written on paper shielded from the elements behind a clear, plastic document wallet and checked her watch to find out they had missed the lunch session. That left them another five hours and fifty minutes until their allocated food slot.

She pulled them back from the board where people were pinning scribbled notes on scraps of paper to the wood. Each of them told a person they hoped would make it there to meet them at a given place. She considered leaving one for Shaun, for Lydia's sake if anything, but he was hundreds of miles away and no doubt being herded into a camp just like this one somewhere.

She looked at the marshal Ty had pointed out, watching him until she could place the tingle in the back of her neck, and only when she saw him look over both shoulders and slip a hand into his pocket did she figure it out.

He took something out, small and reflective, but she only saw a flash of it before it was in another man's hand and hidden behind a weird kind of handshake like the two men were arm wrestling, but decided to hug instead. Backs were slapped and the marshal walked away with an exaggerated gangster lean to his step.

Abbie decided they could find their own way to their accommodation just fine without him.

The walk took them a few minutes, weighed down by unfamiliarity and heavy bags, but eventually they located what looked like a tightly packed row of single-storey buildings that looked more like a storage lock-up than actual living quarters.

Locating B-4-43, seeing the symbols painted in white with what had probably been a stencil and a rattle can, she tried the handle.

It swung open, revealing a windowless room more akin to a prison cell in size and fittings than anything else she'd ever seen. There were two old, musty smelling camp cots much the same as the ones they had been sleeping on near home, only these were a much older variant of the design and smelled like they had been in storage as long as the damp, uncomfortable trucks.

There was nothing else in there, and Abbie tried to hide her disappointment from Lydia, who had no such misgivings and dumped her bag before she dropped down on the nearest cot to lie flat and let out an exasperated groan.

Chunk climbed up beside her, trying to squeeze his bulk along the length of her body as if taking her lead on their next mission.

"Well, it ain't much…" Abbie said, trying to spin a positive.

"That's really true," Lydia agreed, still with her eyes closed as if trying to assimilate and file everything she had already experienced that day. Abbie felt awful for her having to go through all of this at her age. She felt awful for herself too, as she considered that just a few days ago, all she'd had to worry about were normal problems, like being annoyed with work deadlines and colleagues. Like wishing her husband would snap out of it and be the man he used to be. That he would want to come back to them.

Abbie slipped off her own pack and settled down carefully onto the other cot, finding it far less comfortable than the newer iterations. Before she could relax, the hollow, tinny sound of someone knocking at their door startled both of them.

"Who is it?" she snapped, holding out a hand to keep Lydia where she was after the girl had shot up in panic.

"Hello?"

Abbie stood, opening the door a crack and wondering what fresh hell they were about to be subjected to. Peering outside, she saw a woman – rich, hazel skin and shiny, black hair – smiling from a safe, respectable distance. She had both hands on the shoulders of a boy maybe ten years old. He was thin and seemed suspicious, as if he disapproved of the newcomers.

"Hello. I'm Gita, and this is my son Amal," she said in English edged with an Indian accent. Abbie wasn't worldly enough to be able to place it with any more accuracy than that – not that it mattered to her, but she liked to know things.

"Abbie," she replied flatly, leaving daughter and dog out of the equation for now.

"We saw you arrive. We live just over there…" Abbie followed her pointing finger to see an identical unit on the opposite side of their alley and three doors down. "Most people living on here are working during the daytime. My husband, Amal's father, he moves supplies for the marshals. Where have you come from?"

Abbie frowned, unsure how to take in everything she was saying and gauge how much she should give away about themselves. Then something in how Gita spoke fought through her stress and exhaustion, and Abbie recognised a frightened woman who had nobody to talk to but her son.

She understood that instantly, wanting so badly to be able to unload to another adult and still shield Lydia from the full truth of what was happening. She relaxed, opening the door wider.

"This is my daughter, Lydia," she said, turning to see the girl propped up on her elbows in bed and giving a happy wave. "And this is Chunk."

On hearing his name, the dog took it as a summons, bounding off the bed and trampling Lydia in his desperation to already be at the next place. Amal cried out, burying his face in his mother's stomach.

"Sorry, he is afraid of dogs," Gita said apologetically as Abbie called the excited dog back to her.

"Get back inside," she said, shoving the animal in and shutting the door with her on the outside.

"Not your fault. He still thinks he's a puppy and won't believe anyone who says otherwise," she said with a smile as she delivered the well-used line to excuse their boisterous companion.

"You say your husband works here? As a marshal?"

"Yes, also no. He is not a marshal, but he does work here." Abbie wanted to ask more, wanted to grill the woman for everything she knew about the place that was making her feel very uneasy, but a loud blast of a truck horn stopped their conversation.

They all turned, seeing a convoy of military trucks crawling through the road littered with refugees aimlessly waiting to be told what to do and where to go. Abbie set off towards them, in the mood to demand answers.

"Mum?"

"Stay there," she shot back over her shoulder at Lydia.

What was it Jez said? You can't just speak to the manager?

That was exactly what she intended to do. She was

prepared to go what Lydia called "Full Karen" if needs be, but luck swung in her favour for once.

She didn't know what the truck was, but it wasn't one of the stinking, mothballed transports she had ridden in for hours ignoring the pins and needles in her backside. It was more modern, which made her ask herself why it wasn't as useless as her car had been.

She stopped in the road, hands on hips like she was fully prepared to kick off, and stared as the front seat passenger opened the door and leaned out into the gap it made.

"Abbie? What the—"

"I'd like some answers please, Corporal Hallam," she barked, unaware that her voice could sound as it had, so filled with steel.

Jez glanced back inside at the driver, looking slightly embarrassed, before dropping down and running the few yards to her.

"Look, we need to get gone, but I'll explain later—"

"You'll explain now. We're here because *you* said we'd be safe at the docks. What the fuck is this shit?" she asked, raising her voice and gesturing around them with both hands.

He tried to hush her, even going so far as lifting his gloved, left hand to lower her arm but withdrew when she shook him off her.

"Look, I… I only thought as far as the dockyard, okay? I told everyone I knew around there to get to safety. I've had my balls almost chewed off for my name coming up too many times already."

"So I should be grateful? This place does *not* feel exactly safe, Jez. My *daughter* is here, and there's people dealing drugs openly in public. Marshals, Jez, *marshals*. Dealing drugs. And you lot are the first military I've seen since we got here. Where are the police?"

"You guess is as good as mine. We've been told that we're pulling out of these camps to keep military and civvies isolated. Don't know why. Didn't even know we were coming here if I'm honest."

"If you're *honest*? What—"

"Oi! Hallam, get a fuckin' move on would—"

"*Do* you mind?!" Abbie erupted, silencing the marine who had interrupted her to berate Jez.

"You can have him back when I've finished talking to him or you can leave without him, but either way I'm finishing my fucking conversation, got it?"

She hardly recognised her own voice, but she knew she'd taken just about enough shit for one lifetime and the lack of information was testing her already thin patience.

The marine backed off a few paces and said nothing.

"The quick version," she demanded in a lowered voice.

Jez Hallam looked hard at her for a few seconds before an exaggerated outward breath signified his surrender.

"Western Europe has been blinded. Shut down by what the bosses believe was a series of thermonuclear detonations high up in the atmosphere—"

"*Nuclear!*"

He cut her off with a raised hand that spoke more than words could. It politely told her to shut up and listen, that she wanted answers and he was trying to give them.

"China, North Korea or Russia… it doesn't matter. War isn't against us, we're just collateral. Like we aren't worth fighting. All the action's going on across the Pacific and not the Atlantic, and we're likely to be hit again."

"Hit? Hit how? With what? More… more EMPs? More nukes?"

Hearing the words come out of her mouth felt surreal,

adding to the list of things she never thought she'd have to say.

"Doubtful. Cities and key military installations are most probable."

"And places like this," Abbie added sternly, having added up the factors and reached a logical conclusion, but Jez was shaking his head.

"Buzz is that civvies aren't legit targets to them. Reckon it's just about stopping us getting in the scrap."

Abbie took a second to translate what he was saying, rearranging the obvious and unnecessary jargon.

"So, we're safe here but you aren't? And you're going away so, what? We're all safer?"

Jez shrugged, showing some annoyance at the continued interrogation.

"We're still about. Got more people on the list to fetch back here, only you won't see much of us—"

He flinched as the horn was sounded again directly behind him. Abbie had seen the silent discussion behind the glass and seen the driver lean on the controls, but she had still jumped at the volume of it.

"I've gotta go, but here…"

Jez fumbled in a pouch and took out a heavy folding knife. Abbie stared at it in her hand as if about to ask what she was supposed to do with it, but good sense kicked in and she stuffed it into her back pocket.

"B-four-forty-three," she said, watching his eyes glaze over for a split second as his brain secured that piece of intelligence away safely to be retrieved when he needed it. Nodding once, he climbed back up into the truck and Abbie stepped aside to let it roll past.

She had to wait for two identical trucks to go past before

the road was clear, save for the small cloud of dust the massive tyres had kicked up.

Returning to their shed – there was no other word for it – she smiled and continued her conversation with their neighbour before braving the communal shower facilities.

Chunk was left behind, secured inside their tiny accommodation and no doubt taking full advantage of the facilities, but Abbie was careful to keep the folding knife close to her while she took a hurried shower and stood guard to defend the cubicle her daughter used.

CHAPTER TWENTY-FOUR

Rolling Solo

S haun felt the rush of excitement as he drove down the road, weaving his cumbersome new vehicle between abandoned, useless cars and vans.

Three heavy lorries had all piled up ahead, forcing him halfway into a ditch and relying on the power of the off-road capability to get him through. The golf buggies would have fit through narrower gaps, but they couldn't climb in and out of wet ditches like the military surplus vehicle did.

It was a payoff, however, and not all plain sailing. Much as the golf carts were better than pedalling an uncomfortable bike, the Wolf was better than riding in an open electric cart. The downsides were that he barely fit behind the wheel, his knee kept hitting something sharp that seemed to have been designed purposely to cause injury. It was noisy even at low speeds, and somehow the cab seemed to fill with a whiff of exhaust fumes that forced him to keep the window rolled down; only that admitted even more white noise if he pushed the needle past twenty-five.

He regained flat ground on the far side of the crumpled trucks, imagining their air brakes failing in perfect, horrifying synchronicity to block the road with a finality of such destruction he couldn't even consider seeing what cargo they held.

Selecting second gear and pressing on, urging the throttle pedal down a little more, he glanced beside him at his literal shotgun passenger, wondering if he could even point it at someone if the need arose. He'd shot before many times, even joined a clay pigeon club some years ago during one of his hobby phases, and the ethos behind it all was gun safety. The thought of using it as a weapon and not a tool made his chest feel cold.

Each abandoned vehicle forced his blood pressure higher. Each carefully negotiated collision wreckage upped his nervousness to the point where he gave up on the main road and turned off to follow a more circuitous route south on lesser roads with less evidence of human activity.

He blasted through villages and skirted the edges of towns, eager to stay moving and not get bogged down with the guilt of owning a working vehicle.

Each place he passed would have those in need of help, and each of those would have a compelling reason why he should be the one to provide it.

He made two hundred miles in that first day, rolling steadily to conserve fuel and only stopping twice to take a short rest and stretch his tired body.

Not wanting to risk finding a building and separate himself from his vehicle, he pulled off the road into a field through a rotting, wooden gateway, and parked up under a tree with the truck's nose pointed at the road.

He ate, he drank, and eventually he lay down in his sleeping bag fully clothed with his right hand resting on the shotgun as he fell into an exhausted sleep.

———

Dawn brought with it the fear of confusion. Movement outside the truck startled him awake as it was jostled on its suspension, making him cry out in alarm and sit up with the shotgun ready in both hands.

Part of his brain told him that if he pulled the trigger inside the truck he would likely never hear properly again. At the least he would be deafened by the confined explosion and the overpressure a shot would cause, but as his brain shouted this warning to the rest of him, he relaxed, seeing what his intruder truly was.

The familiar patchwork of black and white, not often seen but always representing the species, passed by as a tail swished to bang against the flat panels of the bodywork.

Shaun slumped, feeling his heart hammering in his chest like the kind of music he heard coming from cars belonging to boys who thought a Friday night spent loitering at a drive-through was socialising.

He fought his way out of the sleeping bag, and pulled the stiff handle upwards before muttering abuse at himself and unlocking it first. The door popped, swinging outwards to admit the fresh air of early morning and the muted, sonorous moo sound coming from the animal.

"Huh. Real cows," Shaun said in absent amusement, as if

those not mottled with the familiar black and white pattern were somehow inferior.

The nearest animal turned its head to face him, eyeing his presence with disinterest and issuing a louder protest.

The sound filled him with an empathetic sense of discomfort, which made him think he was losing it if he was suddenly becoming the cow whisperer, but the swollen, hanging udder told him why the cow was unhappy.

"Sorry, girl. Nothing I can do about that," he said, struggling free of the truck and leaning the shotgun against it to relieve himself against the base of the tree. The cow watched for a while, turning away and ponderously walking back to join the others of her kind, as if she had been elected as the one to go and talk to him.

The uncomfortable, exhilarating, terrifying, lonely journey continued. He went through phases of emotion much as he had with hobbies in the past, only these phases lasted a couple of minutes at a time and swung his emotions around inside his head like a wrecking ball.

His head hurt from the speed of his tumbling thoughts, forcing him to act before he had to admit defeat. He pulled over to dig out a water bottle, then popped four, small ibuprofen tablets from a blister pack and washed them down with half the bottle. Then he froze.

Movement ahead. At least he had thought it was movement. Water dribbled from the hairs on his chin, but he dared not move, not even to swallow the mouthful of water, lest the imaginary threat went away without first revealing itself.

Right there, beside the road in some infant parody of the innumerable vehicles now abandoned, a pram sat forlornly.

It brooded, as much as an inanimate object could brood. It accused him of being criminally uncaring.

Shaun broke a little, unable to harden his heart in time to be selfish and press on to fulfil his own mission and get home. He knew it would slow him down, but the look on her young face tugged at his heartstrings.

Would Lydia be proud of him for not helping anyone along the way? Anyone else, that was, because he'd already saved Libby from unpleasantness more than once.

He decided she wouldn't, and with practised hands he slipped the truck back into gear and rolled forwards just as some hint of movement again tickled his vision ahead.

He spoke to himself as he drove, warming up his voice that hadn't been used since his brief, one-sided conversation with the cow first thing that morning.

He saw the movement again, his eyeballs flicking to snap on to the target he had located as his body remained locked in the driving position. A person: messy hair piled atop her head, seen in a glimpse before it ducked out of sight.

His first instinct was to flee, to get away from the other people in this deserted stretch of nowhere, but the head popped back up and looked in his direction wearing an expression of pure relief mixed with fear.

She seemed simultaneously relieved and heartbroken, and nothing Shaun could do would allow him to drive on after seeing that expression.

He pulled up twenty paces away, handbrake ratcheting noisily into the locked position as the only sound to fill their little patch of nowhere.

She stood, emerging from the weak cover she had taken refuge behind, and in her arms was a bundle wrapped in blankets that made him almost shudder with nervous anxiety.

"Please," she said, almost sobbing.

Shaun didn't know what she was asking for, only that she needed help in any form it could come.

He unclipped his seatbelt and slid from the truck in a single, fluid movement, running towards her as soon as he had cleared the reach of the door.

"What's happened? Is she okay?"

The blankets were a mess of colours, but the topmost was pink and made of tattered crocheted wool. Dirt stained it in places, and his chest went tight at the thought that the bundle inside the blankets was beyond any help he or anyone else could provide.

"She's…" the woman – girl really, now that he was close enough to see she could barely be long out of her teens – sobbed as if the words were too painful to get out. She offered the wrapped bundle up hopefully, desperately, and as soon as Shaun reached out with both hands to take it from her, he knew he'd fucked up.

It weighed nothing. Not the featherlike, hollow lack of weight of a small baby, but literally the absence of anything wrapped up. Nothing was inside the burden. There was no form to it. He straightened and pulled open the blankets to reveal more rags rolled together. Even though he knew the answer, even though he understood it all on an instinctive level, he still looked her straight in the eye and asked the question.

"Why would you?"

Her expression answered without words. Gone was the lost, desperate hopelessness of a young girl. In its place was the cold, hard look of an addict prepared to do whatever it took to achieve whatever utterly selfish personal goal had fuelled her immediate need.

The scrape of shoes on tarmac over his right shoulder signalled his second mistake in not checking the area first, which hit him in self-hating obviousness at the same time he realised he had left the truck running.

And the loaded shotgun resting on the passenger seat.

The sight of such a weapon, so innocuous to someone accustomed to the handling of them, was utterly alien. Seeing the twin barrels of the 12-bore from the perspective of the dangerous end was so foreign, so disconcerting, that Shaun felt an involuntary loosening in his bladder.

He mentally clamped down on that unbidden urge before he could humiliate himself further, and tried to force a calmness on himself because panic would only drive these unskilled creatures deeper into dangerous territory.

Perhaps the biggest surprise, beyond facing the gaping maws of shotgun barrels, was that he didn't have to try very hard to keep his cool. He should be panicking. He should be falling to his knees and blubbering for his life. He should be scared.

But he was more annoyed than frightened. Angrier with himself than these opportunists.

"What else you got?" the girl behind asked, rounding his unmoving body while keeping out of his reach. A kitchen knife had appeared in her right hand, and that frightened him more than the shotgun did. It would be harder to avoid than the two shots the gun held if this went any more wrong than it already had.

"No luck, that's for bloody sure," Shaun answered drily. The shotgun lowered from the firing position it had been held tightly in to reveal a boy no older than the girl. He was an adult, of that there was no doubt, but Shaun didn't think he'd reached that status long ago. He placed them both at nineteen or twenty, not that age made them any more or less dangerous.

"Yeah? You look pretty lucky to me. Car and a gun? You're living the fuckin' dream, mate."

His gaunt, angular face and fake voice annoyed Shaun. Nobody spoke like that unless they were trying to. Yet another thing to blame on the social media pop culture generation.

"I'll be on my way then," Shaun said, but he didn't move a muscle.

Shotgun boy still held the weapon pointed at his chest. Shaun reckoned that if he tried, if he threw everything he had into an explosive start or somehow distracted him, he could close the gap between them and knock the barrels aside. Knife girl bothered him, though, because she was totally unaware of what a shotgun did and stood too close to the firing line between them.

Both ambushers fidgeted anxiously, neither able to stand still, as if the nervous tension of their crime was almost too exciting to contain, while in contrast Shaun remained statuesque.

He had no idea where the calm came from. It was more than the confidence he had felt on both occasions when Anton had led a small gang against him. It was more than the confidence he felt when sparring in the gym, either on the mats or in the ring.

This calm confidence came from the sudden realisation that he knew more about what was happening than they did. He knew more about what *would* happen than they did. He was in control of the situation, and only he knew that.

The thought sounded ludicrous even to him, but as he watched them vibrate with nervousness he felt more and more at peace. It was as though he had somehow levelled up. Like he'd unlocked an achievement won by the build-up of the experiences of the last week and which tipped him over some unseen ledge to fall into a pool of rejuvenating liquid.

He felt warm. No, he felt *hot*. All his muscles throbbed like a drag car holding revs to launch when the lights went out. He was physically ready to end the confrontation, but power and rage alone were useless without a plan. Without thought. He was ready to reverse the power in the situation, but they weren't.

They laughed at what he said, as though the very idea of them letting him go was the best joke they had ever heard. The laughter bordered on uncontrollable as the tension in their bodies sought any avenue of escape. It was maniacal, and it betrayed just how scared they were.

"You done this much before?" he asked conversationally, stopping the laughter dead and earning a renewed aiming of the shotgun in his face.

"Shut the fuck up," knife girl snarled. Shaun frowned, exuding disquiet at her language and tone. He realised belatedly that he still held the bundle of blankets and turned his body slightly to drop them on the floor, save for the dirty, crocheted one that had sparked some deeply buried memory of his own daughter when she was tiny.

He held it up, inspecting it for damage and dirt before deciding it could be saved. He began to fold it neatly, speaking as he made precise movements with his hands.

"I mean, did you check the back of the truck when you took the gun?"

He held the blanket up to be sure the corners matched before his hands met and he turned the whole thing ninety degrees and let it drop down.

Knife and shotgun exchanged a brief look, the gist of

which was that shotgun had not, in fact, checked the back of the truck.

"And did you check if I had any other weapons?" he asked knife girl, eyes still fixed on his task as the blanket became a neat square one quarter of its original size.

Shotgun glanced at knife, eager to throw blame back in her direction to cover his own mistake.

"Well, I don't. And there's nobody in the back of the truck. But you wouldn't know that, would you?"

He united them in their anger which was directed back at him like a nervous body language demonstration.

"Two options here," he said conversationally as he paused before deciding that the blanket needed another fold. "Either you let me go on my way, or one of you has to use the thing you're carrying. Now, I'd prefer option A, but—"

"Shut the fuck up!" knife girl snarled, but Shaun could already hear the fear in her voice. Her confidence was meting away like ice in the sun, and after the elation of their sick trap working, he could feel the tears threatening to come.

Tears of frustrated anger, like the ones he should be experiencing, only he wasn't. He was almost enjoying himself.

"Okay, I'll be quiet. You two take a minute and decide—"

"She said to shut the fuck up, dickhead!" shotgun boy yelled, only his voice cracked to betray that he wasn't large and in charge like he expected to be with a gun in his hands.

Shaun burned inwardly, mentally running through every scenario he could envisage to resolve the standoff with maximum violence. He burned with a controlled rage but didn't feel angry. He didn't feel uncontrollably emotional about it, and that realisation was almost euphoric.

"Shutting up," he said apologetically, folding the blanket a final time and holding it patiently in both hands at his waist, noticing for the first time some small, almost insignificant detail about shotgun that made all the difference.

Knife and shotgun moved closer, turned to face one another as if about to engage in a rapid conflab about what to do, as if he wasn't standing right there, and when their eyes left him, his body acted before he consciously realised.

The blanket flew from his hands and spread like a rudimentary fishing net, enveloping both of them weakly as it failed to fully expand. The shotgun barrel twitched but didn't go off, just as Shaun knew it wouldn't because the safety catch was still on, failing to show the little mark of red paint signifying danger.

Even if it had, Shaun was already two long strides to his right where no deadly projectiles could touch him at such short range.

He changed direction just as suddenly, advancing on them from the side so that when the ratty blanket was pulled down from their faces, he wasn't there.

Terror widened their eyes as movement in their peripheral vision snatched their attention to where he was now, only he was no longer standing patiently with an infuriating calmness but was coming for them.

Unarmed, he was *coming for them*.

Shaun wound up his right hand in some rapid, odd parody of an anime fight scene. His brain even threw images of himself flying with explosions and lightning behind him, but the reality was far less flamboyant, and far more devastating.

The right overhand punch landed with brutal power,

glancing off shotgun's left shoulder to slightly lessen the impact, but not enough to disrupt the biological response.

The fist landed squarely on the left side of his skinny neck, impacting directly on a faded, scrolling tattoo of some name Shaun's brain didn't register at the time.

He fell like he'd been shot, and the crumpled bag of meat hit the roadway with a sound and sight that would have turned Shaun's stomach had he not been so enraged that he was capable of delivering a blow like that.

It was different from when he had been set upon in the alleyway. Different again from when he was defending Libby, Amanda, and Harper.

Shotgun boy's feet left the ground like he was some obscene crash test dummy, knocking knife girl spinning to the roadway as if he'd successfully scored a lucky shot bowling and knocked down split pins.

He stooped, retrieved his gun, and casually turned it to point the dangerous end in their direction.

The young man was out of the game; sleeping uncomfortably in a heap of limbs that looked about as natural as it did comfortable. Knife girl still held her weapon, but when the two dark circles of the shotgun looked her square in the face, her grip faltered, and the weapon fell to the ground with the smallest of sounds. He leaned into the gun, pulling the stock hard into his shoulder in anticipation of the kick, and his right index finger began to curl around the trigger and caress an increasing pressure onto it.

Her shaking hands came up to beg for her life, and the look of fear on her face broke whatever spell he had put himself under.

His hands suddenly shook as badly as hers did, and he lowered the barrel rapidly to try and convince himself that he hadn't been about to execute an unarmed girl on the road.

He straightened up, forcing himself to look away from the life he had been a breath away from taking, and regarded shotgun man.

He seemed even younger now that he slept. Amazing, he thought to himself, how the appearance of a person can change when they go from pointing a gun in your face to unconscious. Gone was the aggressive intimidation, and in its place was something almost child-like.

Ashamed and disgusted – disgusted with himself and humanity in general – he staggered a few paces backwards and spoke to no-longer knife girl.

"You know how to do the recovery position?"

She nodded rapidly, giving Shaun the impression that she'd agree that grass was purple if he suggested it.

"Do it now."

Slowly, awkwardly, and almost comically, she rolled onto her front and lifted her right knee up towards her chin. Shaun almost laughed, only he bit the noise back down because he knew it would come out like a crazy, yelping bark.

"Him, not you," he managed to say. She didn't even have the decency to look embarrassed, so terrified was she that their victim would show them the same level of kindness they had evidently intended showing him.

"If he vomits, clear his airway," Shaun instructed, unsure why he was parroting a first-aid instructor's words at her.

"Clear his… what?"

"His airway… oh, for fuck—" Shaun took his left hand off the gun and rubbed aggressively at his scrunched brow as if he could keep the angry thoughts locked inside through sheer will.

"If he pukes," he went on in a voice that had lost all patience and treated her like the idiot he suspected she was, "put your fingers in his mouth and hook it out."

The girl looked repulsed, but Shaun decided he'd done far more than his civic duty to provide care for an injured person, even if he had injured that person for good reason.

He backed away, watching the girl watching him with frightened suspicion that bordered on hatred, but was too far gone into fear to make the look she gave menacing.

More afraid of himself – of what he had become inside of a week – Shaun climbed back behind the wheel and rolled away from the place, leaving the part of himself that was soft of heart behind.

CHAPTER TWENTY-FIVE

Etiquette

A bbie took a long, fortifying breath and tried to keep her shit together.

The great British standard of queue etiquette was being tested beyond the tutting and the foot tapping that she believed to be the acceptable forms of showing one's annoyance. People shouted, demanded the line move on, and did the pedestrian equivalent of honking their horns in traffic.

It created tension, it boiled her anxiety like a kettle, and she found the general mood vulgar.

Gita and her son had walked with them towards the canteen for their section of the camp, simultaneously eager to show them the way and grateful of the company. She talked constantly, jabbering on about the world and what needed changing as through the reality they were experiencing wasn't reality at all, but simply a distraction as inane as reality television.

"And you know something else?" she said, turning to face Abbie with a smile, only she didn't get to finish her next thought because the man behind her let out an exasperated breath so forcefully that his hot, tobacco-stinking breath wafted over Abbie's cheek.

"Fuck's sake, what's the bleedin' hold-up now?"

Suppressing a shudder, Abbie fought down the first five responses that presented themselves for immediate deployment in her brain, but luckily the line moved forwards amidst a collective groan of tutting and huffing noises.

It took a further ten minutes, according to the hands of her watch that was wound almost obsessively at every opportunity she got, to reach the head of the line where their disposable plates and cutlery were issued by an unsmiling woman who looked like she'd rather be anywhere but there.

Abbie couldn't blame her. She wanted to be at home with a fire crackling, a glass of merlot and Chunk asleep at her feet as she caught up on the week's TV recordings. But she also wanted a Lamborghini Huracan and a villa in Cyprus, both of which seemed about as achievable right at that moment.

If the food served by the navy at the docks was bad, this was the slightest of improvements. It was still bad, of that there was little doubt, but she clung on to the hope that clouds had silver linings, no matter how weak they were.

Something masquerading as a hotpot was served to them, only to Abbie it looked like gallons of instant gravy had been mixed up, to which had been added three sliced onions, two carrots, and a bucket of anaemic-looking sausages.

Ahead, Gita looked at her plate and cautiously attracted the attention of the server.

"Excuse me, is there a wegitarian option?"

The way she pronounced the word made the request, under the circumstances, seem even more like a joke.

Without skipping a beat, the server reached out with a pair of tongs and removed the sausages from the gravy as if that resolved the issue.

Abbie accepted her portion with gratitude, because she had been raised to be polite no matter what the circumstances and was pleased to hear her daughter echo that gratitude ahead of her as she took possession of two slices of dry, white bread that would not have looked less appetising had it sported mould spots on the crusts.

To Lydia's credit, or perhaps the girl's hunger was affecting her vision, she accepted the meagre offerings gratefully and moved on to where they were serving a small, prepackaged pot of fruit segments in a jelly that Abbie knew would cause her heartburn just by looking at the sealed tubs.

All the while she took her turn and waited politely, all the while she took the time to look at the person serving her and offer a smile along with her thanks, to try and make them feel like a person and not part of a machine, she felt the impatient presence of the man behind her.

He stood too close, breathed too loudly, and offered far too many opinions.

"Fuck is that? Come on, love. I'm a growing lad…"

Abbie's eyes involuntarily closed as she attempted to bite back the retort that wanted attention like a drunk heckler at a comedy club. To her horror, and if she was honest, a small amount of pride, Lydia's stage whisper was perfectly timed.

"Growing *out*wards, yeah."

"Fuck did you say?" he barked, loud and arrogant like the bully Abbie imagined him to be. He could call her all the names he wanted. He could scream and shout and she'd either walk away or give back as good as she got, but nobody, *nobody*, talked to her child that way.

"You ever seen someone circumcised with a plastic

spork?" she asked savagely, turning on him and looking up into his soft, jowly face, wearing a look that promised a painful encounter if his next words weren't carefully chosen. He had large hair, still styled to stick up like an advert for something she wouldn't buy, and his exposed arms were covered in scrawling tattoos that looked like a child had drawn on him in his sleep. She was instantly reminded of a pop star who had grown older and much fatter.

"She shouldn't body shame people like that," he muttered, acting hurt and coming across as more of a teenaged girl than Lydia did.

"And you shouldn't be rude to people, else they might be rude back," Abbie explained, talking down to him patronisingly like he was a child on the slower end of the uptake spectrum. She knew she was goading him, knew she was being argumentative, but her stress was hacking down that door like Jack Nicholson with a fire axe.

"Maybe, while you're at it, you could take half a step back, stop breathing on me, and show some respect to people," she finished, her voice rising higher than his to turn that attention he sought back on him like a poison.

Satisfying herself with a final look up and down his frame to accompany the unimpressed sneer, she turned her back and hoped he would just leave it there.

The line shuffled on, moving faster for a short time as their interaction had created a bubble they had to fill.

They received a bottle of water each – unlabelled and made of desperately thin plastic that would make its reuse seem more like a cylindrical bag than a bottle – and paused for Abbie to scan the room and find a space to eat.

Seeing a spot where the corner of one table was free, she hustled the two of them over to where Gita was waving for her attention and smiling, totally unaware of what had just happened in the queue.

They joined them, the stress showing on their faces as Gita's expression dropped.

"Something is wrong?" she asked with concern, but Abbie shrugged it off dismissively.

"Nothing, just an idiot with a big mouth," she said, smiling at Lydia as they sat and began poking at the dish before them. Abbie took a tentative mouthful and found that the taste of salt was so overpowering that it masked the rest of the meal into something almost acceptable.

"And you, missy," she said as she chewed. "Try to keep comments like that to yourself, oka—*oof.*"

She was prevented from finishing her gentle admonishment by hot flesh leaning into her back, and to her surprised horror, a pudgy hand reached over her head to snatch up the fruit pots from hers and Lydia's plates.

"Donate to the cause, fucking bitch," the man said, releasing the pressure of his gut from her back and turning away with his prize held in one free hand.

Abbie's face contorted where Lydia's registered only fear and shock. She stood, one hand reaching inside her jeans pocket for the folding knife Jez had given her, and before anyone could protest or try to stop her, she was standing and advancing on the man's back without a single clue what she was going to do besides retrieve their property.

She hadn't even intended on eating it, but the fact that it was destined for Lydia made the theft all the worse for the perpetrator.

Her right hand moved, snapping outwards for the blade to extend before she hid it behind her back and forced a smile onto her face the likes of which a snake's prey might see before the life was squeezed out of it.

Yard rules. Don't take any shit, establish dominance, be the one nobody wants to fuck with...

The words of her instructor at the gym came back to her, finally providing a voice for the feelings she was experiencing. Those words had been given to a woman in tears who was facing a short custodial sentence for what she had once referred to as creative accounting, but what the magistrate had called fraud. She didn't know why she recalled that overheard TED talk, but it was fit for her situation and she went with it.

If she took it once in this setting, where there were no police and nobody to protect her from these playground bullies, she'd continue to take it from more and more people until both she and Lydia were voluntarily giving up their food.

Her heart hammered in her chest and the adrenaline coursing through her body made her feel reckless.

Be the baddest bitch in there, the voice came to her from the depths of her memory. *Set your stall out, and let everyone know you are* not *the one to fuck with...*

"Oi, Justin Ballbag," she called out when she was a few metres away, still advancing like a missile and just as capable of diverting her course without external intervention.

"Excuse me? I believe those don't belong to you," said a smooth voice that Abbie recognised immediately.

Betraying how enraged and target-focused she had become, Ty and an entourage of two yellow-vest-wearers entered her dance space. He was smiling, his hands behind his back in a display that she was sure was meant to look intentionally *not* intimidating. The presence, however, of the two marshals either side of him had evidently been recruited for the simple fact that they looked like bouncers at the kind of club that didn't call the police threw that attempt clean out of the nearest window.

The queue bully turned, hostility already pouring off him, but he seemed to shrink and melt when he saw the three tall men looking at him.

One smiled cordially, while the other two looked like they would happily kill him and rape him. In that order.

"Sorry…" he muttered; eyes cast down as he extended a hand bearing two pathetic fruit jellies.

"They don't belong to me," Ty said, still smiling but extending the humiliation of the man by stepping aside to unveil Abbie as if he was the only one who knew she was there.

Abbie watched in confusion as the apology was muttered again and the proffered fruit pots were returned to her. Using her left hand awkwardly because her right still bore the knife, she took them and said nothing.

"Glad that's cleared up," Ty said, smiling at the man who stayed rooted to the spot as if expecting a dismissal.

"Well… off you fuck then," Ty said, still smiling, to send the big man scurrying away before he turned to regard Abbie. He smiled, looking her up and down appreciatively as she held the pots in her left hand with her right still hidden behind her back.

"If it's all the same to you, I'd rather you didn't castrate anyone with a plastic spork. Someone will have to clean up the mess and that would slow down the meal process."

Abbie's mouth closed with a muted clap, and she forced an embarrassed smile onto her face.

"I wasn't…"

Ty lifted both hands, still smiling, and laughed lightly. It was the laugh that came from someone totally in control of themselves and their environment. It had 'confidence' stamped on it in red.

"Don't worry about it. Good for you. People like that have been getting away with it for a couple days and we've just became aware of what was happening."

Abbie smiled nervously, turning away and moving her right arm so that the exposed knife blade never faced Ty or his two goons.

She sat back down, hiding the knife in her pocket and presenting Lydia with her desserts.

"Um… thanks…"

"You're welcome. Now, as I was saying, try to keep inside thoughts inside, and not let them out in the future, okay?"

Lydia nodded weakly and crackled the thin plastic of her bottle as she twisted the cap off to wash down the salt mixed with gravy and the things that looked like the ghosts of sausages.

"You know, it isn't only things like this that are happening," Gita said softly, as if keeping her voice down could protect her son from the harsh realities of life as they currently knew it.

Abbie glanced at Lydia sideways before responding, seeing the girl concentrating on her meal and totally failing to act like she was casually not listening to them.

"Oh?" Abbie asked, unsure where the conversation was headed. Her heartrate had returned to normal, which unsettled her almost as much as Ty's sudden appearance.

"Yes, people have gone missing already," Gita said in a tone that sounded more like gossip than a missing person's report.

"Missing how?"

Gita shrugged and scooped another watery mouthful of flaccid onion and gravy into her mouth.

"One day they are here, the next they are not," she said, as if the explanation made everything clear. "They go in the night, and they don't come back."

"Well, isn't that the cheeriest thing I've ever heard," she said, unable to stop herself before the hurt look descended on Gita's face.

She knew a frightened woman when she saw one. She'd been a frightened woman not long ago, but she had hardened herself to cope with the realities of the harsh world they were living in when she'd been left alone with her daughter.

She didn't push, mostly because she didn't want any further revelations coming to light in front of Lydia. Instead, she offered the olive branch of companionable motherhood.

"How about we talk later? After the kids go to bed?""

Gita smiled warmly, pleased at the prospect of having an adult conversation all by herself.

"Has your husband finished work?" Abbie asked. "Seems like a long shift…"

"Oh, no, he will be at work until wery late," she answered, smiling widely and nodding as if to reassure Abbie and simultaneously close the conversation.

———

The rest of the meal went without incident, which surprised Abbie considering how she'd been ready to threaten someone with a knife if he didn't return two fruit jellies.

She kicked herself at the memory of what she had done. She had acted without even considering a way out – backwards or forwards – and that bothered her.

She needed sleep. She needed answers. She needed Shaun.

As much as she hated to allow herself to feel that way, as much as she had hardened her heart to being a single parent until such time as he pulled his head out of his arse, all she wanted right then was for the idiot to walk up to her and give that crooked little grin he gave when he wanted to suggest something inappropriate.

Only he wasn't there. He was hundreds of miles north, doing God knows what, and she was there, stressed to the gills, with a stroppy teenager and a dog who thought they were on holiday.

Chunk stopped to sniff at something, giving it his undivided attention for all of three seconds before he tore off at maximum acceleration only to travel five yards to the next new smell to grab his attention.

"He is a happy dog," Gita said, producing a gaudy flask and unscrewing the top to take a long, bubbling gulp. She offered the flask to Abbie, who took it, sniffed the spout, and turned a shocked glance in Gita's direction.

"I thought you didn't drink," she said. "Isn't it against your religion?"

"And I thought all white women your age played tennis," Gita said back, one corner of her mouth curling up in a smile that Abbie could see clearly in the moonlight.

"Fair point," she answered, tipping the flask back and enjoying the burn of the fiery liquid it contained.

"We are Punjabi, and we are not baptised. You are thinking of Muslims, perhaps?"

"I... I don't know. Sorry," Abbie said dejectedly. She

wasn't an ignorant woman by any stretch of the imagination, but her world had always been fairly small.

"We are Sikh, but we are not very… devout? Is this the word you use? Are you religious, Abbie?"

"No. Yes. I mean… well, I believe in God, only…"

"Exactly. If God says you must not drink when you need it, is he really on your side?"

The two women smiled and Abbie bumped Gita's shoulder in a gesture that provided both of them with more companionship and reassurance than either realised they needed in that moment.

"Your husband—"

"He has not come home for two days. It is something I tell Amal. I tell him that his father comes home when he is asleep and leaves again. It is better this way."

Abbie said nothing. Her own husband was also absent, but at least she had a clue where he was. He was probably sitting in his father's house doing what the old bastard had done for all of Lydia's life; drinking himself into an angry stupor before passing out and sleeping just long enough to wake up angry and repeat the cycle.

She saw it long before Shaun had. She saw it years before when his father still held down a job, when the daily cycle hadn't become employment all of its own, and she feared he would go the same way, as if genetics could dictate such a lifestyle.

He'd fallen into the cliché at forty, only instead of wanting the sports car or a motorbike or banging the twenty-six-year-old secretary, he'd retreated into himself and become an angry, morose man who saw no way out of the hole he had dug for himself.

He was always annoyed that a neighbour had been able to afford a Tesla, or that someone he knew had taken their wife and two kids to Florida for a fortnight. Every time, she tried to explain that the cars were procured on crappy finance deals and the holidays were paid for on credit cards that would take eight years to whittle down until they finally consolidated that debt with a different debt and perpetuated the endless cycle of adults addicted to the illusion of wealth.

She believed that the best car she could drive was the one she owned outright. She believed that the holiday she enjoyed the most was the one she had saved up for, had worked extra for, and which didn't leave her unable to provide for her family year on year as a result.

Shaun had always looked out of the window and envied what others had, instead of looking inside at what was there for him all along.

"Gita… I'm sorry… I—"

"It is fine. He will come back when he has finished his work," she said, cutting off the conversation with words that she obviously didn't even believe. Abbie offered no counter argument, but she did accept another long swig of the flask.

She wished she had a cigarette in that moment, not that she had smoked in years, but the urge along with the illicit drink had stirred the desire in her and she said as much.

Surprising her again, Gita pulled a packet from inside the folds of her dress.

"I'm sorry, they are menthol."

"Sold," Abbie said, eagerly twitching finger and thumb at the packet before it was even opened.

She took one, allowing Gita to apply flame to the tip and inhaling deeply before letting out a cough as the harsh fumes hit her throat. She inhaled again, remembering the feeling again, and thinking "fuck it" with every fibre of her being.

"He will come back," Gita said again, only wistfully this

time. "And if he doesn't, we will wat for him. He is a good man."

"Yeah," Abbie said, wishing that Shaun Taylor stood up to the same level of scrutiny and still engendered that level of faith. She steeled herself that Lydia would likely not see her father again, not for years at least, and that she would just have to be both parents to Lydia until someone worthy came along.

"You know one of the soldiers?" Gita asked, snapping her back to their secret, illicit conversation.

"Royal Marine," she answered on reflex, echoing what Jez had said on their one and only date. "And yeah, but not very well…"

"Well enough, it seemed. I asked Lydia if the man was her father. She was not very happy with me for saying this…"

"It's… complicated…"

"Many things in life are this way," Gita said enigmatically. The two women finished their cigarettes in companionable silence, ending the night with another swig from the flask and a brief embrace that both of them wished could be longer and tighter. Then Abbie went back to her tin shack to find Lydia sound asleep through exhaustion and Chunk occupying her bed without shame.

"Oi, fat arse. Floor!" she hissed, sending a grumbling Chunk off her sleeping bag and onto the foot of Lydia's cot where there was barely enough space for him.

She slipped inside her sleeping bag, lying flat on her back to stare at the ceiling and wonder just where the fuck her husband was.

CHAPTER TWENTY-SIX

Alone Time

S haun drove hard until he could drive no further. Releasing the pressure on the throttle slowly with top gear still engaged, he rolled to a stop and let the engine stall with a violent judder, just sitting there with his foot on the brake to stop him rolling backwards.

For long seconds that movement, that slight shift in position of his right foot, was the only indication that any cognitive process occurred inside his mind.

He sat motionless, catatonic, until suddenly he gasped in a sharp breath and held it, silence echoing inside the truck for a second before he seemed to swell, to charge up, and expelled the breath in a scream.

The noise that left his mouth was alien. Animalistic. It didn't belong to him and felt more like an exorcism. He was expelling all the tension and anger and fear that should have been experienced a few miles back up the road.

The breath was expended and he sucked in more, filling the tank to roar again, rising in volume and half an octave. He accompanied the vocals with percussion, hammering the heel of his right fist into the wheel hard enough to rock the truck on its suspension.

He raged like that for almost a minute, gasping in more air to feed the screams and rid himself of the pent-up emotions festering since the situation.

Exhausted, he collapsed on the steering wheel and entered the final stage of the process by bursting into tears. He sobbed loudly, forcing the last of the feelings out of his body and mind, until just as abruptly as it had started, he stopped and sat up straight.

Knocking the gear lever out of position and giving it the requisite wiggle, he reached down with his other hand and cranked on the impossibly stiff handbrake before sliding out to shake off his limbs and walk a rapid but random pattern around the open door.

Cuffing at his eyes with the sleeve of his jumper, he checked around to find himself alone on the abandoned road. Pressing a finger into each nostril in turn, he cleared the build-up of mucus that had accompanied his tears.

Suitably reset and devoid of obvious demons, he climbed back behind the wheel and went through the process to restart the engine. To his horror it struggled, coughing and clanking over and over as if unable to reach the critical mass required to ignite the fuel and resume the journey.

"Oh no. No, no, no... come on, you bastard," Shaun muttered, stopping the process and starting it over again in the absence of a better plan. He tried again, receiving the same pained mechanical noises.

"Please start... ple—"

The struggling noises stretched out into longer ones,

giving Shaun some sense of positive indication that he was doing the right thing.

"*Come on.*"

With a bark and a cloud of dark, unburnt diesel spewing out of the exhaust, the engine clattered into life. He gave it a few tentative revs to make sure it didn't die immediately, and to his delight it held a steady tick over. Not wanting to waste time or push his luck any further, he dropped the clutch, engaged first gear, and jerked away to continue south.

Another hour spent driving more cautiously took him closer to evidence of people. Smoke rose in wispy pillars ahead and to his right, indicating a fire large enough to be seen at that distance. That meant either something bad or enough people to warrant the blaze. Both options were ones he wanted to steer clear of.

More aware of his surroundings now, having learned that lesson the hard way, he checked both wing mirrors for any signs of activity before grabbing the map from the dashboard and spending five long minutes figuring out where he was.

Eventually deciding on a backtrack for a few miles to take a road east. He wanted to avoid the larger towns, and the very thought of going near a city terrified him, but he still had to make progress and by his reckoning there was the better part of two hundred miles under normal circumstances before he would reach home.

He found the road easily enough, making good time as it was wider and allowed him to breeze past any abandoned cars, except for one that needed a little light assistance from the front bumper to create a large enough gap to pass through.

Driving on, focused on his task – his mission – he almost

didn't see the convoy of vehicles moving right to left towards the junction ahead of him.

The tops of trucks and the billows of exhaust smoke electrified his brain, sending a dozen instructions to his body at once and forcing him to stand on the brakes while aiming the front of the truck at a van sitting motionless ahead. He tucked up close behind it, hoping he hadn't been seen and wouldn't be spotted.

With his window halfway down, he heard the cacophony of raucous diesel engines roll by, making him think that the convoy was large. It had to be military, there was little doubt of that, given how unorganised the general population seemed to be. Everyone was still sitting at home, waiting for the lights to come back on, and those without the means or sense to do so were marauding for the necessary items to keep themselves going.

Others, like him, were on the road doing whatever it took to get to where they wanted to be. His methods were more honourable, at least he hoped history would see it that way, but his already distrusting attitude towards people in general was amplified now beyond all recognition.

He waited, giving the convoy another ten minutes before he dared to move again. Opting to head further east again, sticking to smaller roads, he adapted his planned route so that he wasn't inadvertently chasing the convoy.

He found himself asking difficult questions as he drove, alertness not impacted by the internal discussion he had with himself.

Why am I avoiding people who could help me?

The immediate answer was that he would lose the ability to make decisions for himself. His vehicle would likely be requisitioned for the greater good, and he would probably be forced into some refugee facility for his own protection.

Simply put, he didn't want any authority exercising control over him, because they probably wouldn't give a damn if he needed to get home or not.

It wouldn't be their problem; it would be his. He preferred to keep it that way and pushed on until he realised that the appearance of the convoy had forced him into trouble even though he hoped he had avoided it.

People moved up ahead. They looked like an adult version of a Duke of Edinburgh party, all decked out for walking with heavy bags on their shoulders. Some even sported those go-faster sticks that he hated for no justifiable reason. He killed the engine, hitting the electronic fuel cut-off as he had been taught to, but it was too late.

They had spotted him.

He didn't hear the words, but his brain invented them just the same as a man started pointing and waving the outstretched finger in his direction desperately.

"Hey, guys, look! A car! There's a car!"

Shaun annoyed himself by inventing the term 'car' when referring to what he drove, for it was many things and none of them fell into the category of 'car'. Perhaps he made the man intentionally annoying in his imagination because his presence was so damned intolerable.

Shaun groaned, fiddling with switches and controls to restart the Land Rover before they could get to him, but they were already running, packs bouncing awkwardly and stupid walking poles flapping about aimlessly.

"Come on, come on, come *oooon*," he grunted as the engine made the same reluctant coughing sound like the mechanical equivalent of a teenager refusing to leave their bed. A noise made him look up, forcing his eyes to snap up and see the leader of their group, or at least the tallest and fastest of them, slapping a hand on the front of his ride. He was way above average height, wearing one of those baggy beanie hats that gave his head the impression of being a foreskin, and sported a grey beard fashioned into a stylish point beneath his chin.

He blocked the road, standing resolute in front of Shaun, like someone had ordered a Gandalf from Wish, and he totally failed to understand that cars went in more than one direction.

The engine groaned in longer notes and burst into renewed life. Shaun wasted no time in crunching the gear lever into reverse and applying a faster version of swapping pressure between left foot and right foot on the pedals.

He rocketed backwards, hitting something metal with a glancing blow but barely slowing his progress as he reverse-steered around it. Wish Gandalf roared obscenities after him, but the chase was abandoned almost immediately. Shaun slowed, squeaking to a stop, and watched as the group milled about in the road. They seemed to be arguing over what to do next, gesturing wildly in his direction, as if their original plan had been so bad that just seeing another vehicle had prompted a rebellion, and Shaun was struck by the feeling that he was a bad person. That he had to atone for what he had done, even though he had acted in self-defence.

That's bullshit and you know it, he argued with himself. *You were about to go way beyond self-defence.*

Perhaps these people weren't like others he had already encountered. Perhaps they were decent and would just be grateful for a lift to the next town to take the pressure off their feet for a few miles. He could spare that fuel, right? He wouldn't go out of his way. What harm could it do to just find out where they were headed?

Before he could second guess the decision, his left hand engaged first gear and his foot moved as though the two were interconnected to dip the clutch. Rolling forwards he saw the shock and elation on their faces, all except one of the group, and at ten yards away he stopped to allow them to close the distance between them.

Since his last encounter he had made sure he was rolling with the rear door locked as well as those to the cab, so when one of them tried to open the passenger door they stopped to frown in angry confusion.

"Out… out of the car or…" Wish Gandalf started saying. Up close Shaun could tell that he was far younger than he had first imagined. He spoke uncertainly, his voice wavering, until he cleared his throat and mimicked something he thought sounded tough and intimidating.

"Out of the fucking car. Now."

"No," Shaun answered, feeling that same cold sensation washing through his body, only not as pronounced as before. None of these people was armed, save for their idiotic sticks, and being locked inside a tough truck removed the immediacy of any threat.

"Don't make me… don't make me beat you up…"

Shaun wasn't sure if the threat annoyed or amused him, but he wasn't stupid and wasn't going to test the theory that the threat was an idle one.

Another of the group banged on the metal, angrier than Gandalf, and tried to make his point.

"Let us in or I'll knock you the fuck out," he barked, again sounding as though he was copying a line he'd seen on television. Shaun wasn't certain either man had been in a fight since they had left school and he wanted to politely enquire how the young gentleman intended to do that when they were on opposite sides of metal and glass. He wanted to tell them not to be stupid, that he'd been prepared to offer help until they started threatening him. What actually came out of his mouth was far less eloquent.

"You couldn't knock out a wank, you little prick," he said, raising his voice so they could hear him through the closed window.

Shaun glanced away from the look of horrified indignation on his face to check the reactions of the others, once again finding himself greatly disappointed by people in general.

He was absolutely certain that if their phones still worked, they would be recording him for future use, either to report him to the authorities for not doing as their entitled little arses demanded, or else to vilify him on social media for the attention.

Everything that disappointed him about people was on display right in front of him, from their aggressive sense of entitlement to his own inability to offer aid to someone in need.

Opting for selfishness over servitude, Shaun engaged reverse gear again to give himself enough room to drive around and leave the group in the road.

History would recall that incident differently, because it was one word against six and the majority ruled. They would also shout louder, he knew, which they probably believed made them correct.

He didn't care. They'd had their chance to receive help, and their opening gambit was to demand it with the threat of violence, so as far as he was concerned, they could collectively go and fuck themselves.

He just hoped there weren't people among the rest of the

group who would suffer because others didn't know how to say please.

————

Shaun was stressing out about the night because he didn't want to risk turning the engine off and not being able to restart it from cold. He also didn't want to leave it running all night attracting attention like a sixty-watt bulb bringing moths, or milkshake summoning boys to his yard.

He settled on what he felt was an ingenious solution, searching far and wide on his circuitous route south for the perfect spot.

Parking the Land Rover atop a small hill with the nose facing down, he cranked on the handbrake with both arms until it could go no further, then climbed down to stretch his back and empty his bladder.

Already he had settled into a regime of when he ate, when he drank, and after a matter of days he felt lighter and moved faster, despite the physical and psychological stresses he was experiencing.

When he settled down to sleep, he finally arrived at the most obvious conclusion for the change.

He'd barely had a drink in over a week.

He didn't consider himself to be an alcoholic, not at all, but if he was brutally honest with himself, he was heading for the moniker of 'drink dependant' unless he changed his ways. Well, the world had changed his ways for him, and he suffered none of the pain or guilt that came with trying to give up an addiction. He suffered no shakes, no hallucinations as people worse off than him had, and to think that all it took was the removal of every electronic device he spent his life glued to and a mission of utmost importance to achieve.

Sleeping fitfully as he often did after such raw moments of self-awareness, he was up before the dawn broke to find that his clever plan had worked.

He didn't bother trying to start it, just deactivated the fuel cut-off, dropped it into second gear with his feet on the clutch and brake, then fought with all the strength in both hands to release the handbrake.

Finally freeing it, he let the truck roll away downhill by releasing the foot brake then banged his left foot up sharply to startle the engine into life.

It came alive just as he'd hoped, revving sweetly, and delivering the torque in buckets as he bumped back onto the road and clunked it into third before giving it a little more throttle.

He felt renewed, invigorated even, and wanted to push on at top speed but good sense prevailed and he continued cautiously. After another hour, he realised that caution alone wasn't enough; he had to be lucky too.

CHAPTER TWENTY-SEVEN

Shock to the System

C harlie Davidson woke feeling much better than when he had gone to sleep. It was relative, because he still felt like he'd been in a damn plane crash, but as far as the last week had gone it was, undoubtedly, an improvement.

The best part was that, even though he had to go slow, he was able to sit up on the side of his bed without having to wait for his morning dose of painkillers to kick in.

Had any part of his existence been normal, he would have staggered to the toilet and concentrated on aiming. As no part of his existence was in any way normal, he simply glanced forlornly at the bag hanging beside his bed that was filled with a dark urine stained darker still by the traces of blood in it.

He was assured that was to be expected, but pissing blood was one of those things he imagined was fairly serious.

"You're up," a friendly voice said. He glanced up with a

stiff neck to see the smiling visage of the woman who had first treated him. Jasminder Kaur – or Jaz as she preferred – was as tall as he was, standing a couple of inches shy of six feet, but there the similarities ended. He was fair of skin and the baby blonde had never darkened, only faded into grey in places. Her hair was long and dark, and seemed to be effortlessly silky when all around him people were beginning to show signs of living without the amenities of abundant power and hot, running water. Her pale brown skin and large eyes were genetic markers of her mixed heritage, and combined with her confident air of competence, he couldn't help but feel an inappropriate attraction to the woman.

The term 'woman' was accurate, but to Davidson she was more of a girl. First-year resident medical students got younger with each year he got older, which made more logical sense than he realised, but he couldn't fault her bedside manner or her skills as a trainee physician.

"I am," he told her, although the groggy croak in his voice said otherwise. He still sounded asleep.

She checked him out, taking his blood pressure with an ease that spoke of pure repetition.

"Any changes in vision? Any new pain anywhere?"

"I still hurt all over, but I don't have any spots in my eyes," he told her, having worried the previous day that he would suffer a brain aneurism after he experienced some dancing shapes behind his eyelids. She put it down to the cocktail of medication he was being given and went so far as to consult with her senior and the on-call pharmacist.

With the raft of minor injuries to keep his concussion company, he was in remarkably good shape, apparently. He didn't feel like it, but his doctorate was in a very different field.

"How are you feeling in yourself?" she asked, perching a

part of her anatomy on the side of his bed that he tried not to look at for long. She took an old-fashioned mercury thermometer and gestured for him to open up. Answering her question was awkward, but he tried to talk around it.

"Better," he managed.

"Good enough to talk to some people?"

He nodded, wondering who had finally taken notice of his repeated requests to be allowed to leave and get back to the office. In his waking hours he had asked for a telephone, email, hell, even a carrier pigeon. Anything that would allow him to communicate with his office and headquarters in London.

She took back the thermometer and studied it before giving him an appreciative nod and wiping it clean.

Davidson went to stand, but she held out a hand to stop him.

"Whoa, whoa, no. I'll get them to come to you."

"I'm fine, I can walk," he insisted. To her credit she allowed him to stand, although she didn't stray far and held her hands out ready to get him back on the bed if his legs gave out on him.

After three steps his right knee turned to tissue paper and he staggered, clattering his left hand against a metal side loud enough to draw the attention of everyone in the large room.

His doctor had seen enough, making a loud but polite request to a man in military uniform to fetch a wheelchair.

Davidson allowed himself to be wheeled out of the makeshift ward that smelled like bleach and stale water, finding a table set up in a nearby room with Styrofoam cups and the welcome aroma of coffee.

"Ah, Doctor. And Doctor," a young woman said with a wide smile. Davidson assessed her from head to toe rapidly.

Not overly tall and not overtly strong, she carried herself

with the easy grace of a gymnast or some other kind of athlete. Neat, dark brown hair tied back in a tight bun, no makeup – or at least makeup so minimal that only a woman could tell if she was wearing any or not – and an epaulette on the chest of her camouflage shirt with two crowns embroidered on it. There was a hue to her skin that spoke of either a recent stint in a sunny country, or some genetic influence.

Davidson was ignorant of military matters, but he guessed from her demeanour and accent that she was an officer.

She sat, not looking up as Jaz left the room, shuffled a few pieces of paper bearing handwritten notes before she fixed him with the smile again. It didn't seem genuine to Davidson, and he experienced the sudden sensation of being in the opening phases of an interrogation.

The thought made him glance to either side, expecting to see a large picture mirror to mask the onlookers, but the walls were bare. In one corner of the room sat a small dome camera, but the absence of any little LED lights, and the fact that nothing else electrical worked, told him that they were talking without being observed.

She offered him coffee, adding the sugar and powdered creamer on request, and stirred the drink with a plastic spoon to make the whole thing very eco unfriendly.

"I'll cut right to the point, Doctor. I'm Lieutenant Gina Addison with the Royal Military Police. You've made some significant comments regarding…" she looked down at her notes, giving off a hint of theatre as the words she came back with were not ones easily forgotten. "Marburg virus. Specifically, a weaponised version thereof." She stared impassively at him, not asking a question that he could deflect, but leaving the airways between them open for him to fill.

"Look, I work for PHE—"

"Yes, we found your ID. Go on."

Davidson hesitated. The interruption seemed deliberate, calculated somehow, as if she was flexing her verbal muscles to see how he responded.

"We were... I was flying back from Copenhagen before..." he swallowed, not enjoying the physical manifestation of the feelings the crash had brought back to him.

"And that's where you learned of this threat?"

"I didn't say it was a threat."

"Weaponised Marburg virus? How is that *not* a threat?" she asked, facial features deadpan. He didn't know how to respond. Counter CBRN methods weren't his forte. He was more attuned to infection demographics and the pure science of virology.

"Good point," he allowed, sitting back a little to take a sip of the coffee that was still too hot, trying to pretend he hadn't scalded his top lip on the drink. He was trying to stay cool and see what she knew about it, as though he could master someone else's skill set in seconds.

It failed because she seemed to enjoy the comfortable silence far more than he did.

"Look, there were isolated cases presented from studies in Egypt, Turkey, Norway, and Poland. If I had to guess I'd say there would have been a dozen more in the former Soviet states, but they aren't big on sharing. You'd be surprised how many countries aren't big on sharing, actually."

"Or I might not," she said flatly. She still smiled, but Davidson got the distinct impression he was pissing her off somehow.

"In all cases the subjects were successfully isolated and there was no public panic. There's only a duty to inform the public if the risk of infection is very high, actually. You know how it is; panic is more dangerous than the actual risk, you know?"

"I do. Why is it weaponised?"

"I never actually said it…"

He trailed off, watching as she lifted the sheet of paper from the bottom of the stack as if on cue in a theatre production in which he didn't even know he had a role.

"*Weaponised Marburg. Probably from the Stans. Russians or Norks… maybe the Chinese. Need to tell HQ,*" she recited woodenly, sounding almost bored. He said nothing and she looked up, fixing him with her gaze. "You talk in your sleep. Shout, actually, that's how you came to our attention."

"I've been trying to tell people for days," he said angrily.

"If you say so."

"All of the research material was on my laptop."

"Which conveniently burned up in the crash."

"I don't find that convenient at all," he snapped, regretting it instantly as pain lanced through the back of his skull before it tried to burst out of his eyes like Alien.

"So, assuming what you're saying is true, what is the likely effect if it's released on the UK?"

Davidson's eyes goggled at her. She remained impassive. Serious. He swallowed hard at the implication before he opened his mouth, but nothing came out.

"I'll level with you, Doctor Davidson. We have been attacked with thermonuclear ordnance detonated in the upper atmosphere causing an almost nationwide blackout. A permanent blackout, Doctor. Nothing that wasn't EMP safe is fried and given how we don't manufacture the batteries or circuit boards we rely on for everything, this leaves us in something of a sticky situation."

"Attacked?" Davidson said, clutching onto the worst word he took from what she told him.

"Yes. Attacked. And our Gen thinks it won't end there."

"Your what?"

"Gen. Our Int."

"Int?" he asked, even more confused.

"Intelligence. We believe the EMPs were the first phase, and given what you have said, we have to anticipate that a biological attack is, at the very least, likely to follow."

"But... *attacked?*" Davidson said again, his mind stuck on loop because he didn't want to accept any of what she was saying.

"Yes, attacked. Now, what is the likely effect of this being released against the UK population?"

"Now? With no power? Devastating... it'll be devastating."

"Elucidate, please," she said, unwavering in her interrogation.

"It'll... look, Marburg takes a week to incubate, right? Only this takes twenty-four to forty-eight hours for the symptoms to show. It's aggressive, but with proper healthcare the symptoms can be negated – dehydration mostly – but... but without hospitals, transport, real-time communications? It'll be devastating."

"Ballpark figures? What's the lethality?"

"Seventy? Maybe ninety percent? Without the proper care at the right time, people will—"

"What can be done? Is there a cure? A vaccine?"

Davidson looked at her like she'd just suggested something ridiculous, and the look wasn't lost on the lieutenant. She bristled slightly but remained in character.

"How fast can a vaccine be developed?"

"There is no vaccine. And even if one could be manufactured, it would take every major player in the world working in concert with thousands of lab hours dedicated to testing. Even then, no real results can be known for months, maybe *years* after successful rollout!"

Davidson was animated now, rocking in his wheelchair with the stress of the situation and pain assaulting him from every part of his body.

"So there's no cure. What about isolation and treatment?"

"Isolation, yes. Only without constant medical care you can take that percentage and make it three figures."

"And what about the infectivity rate?" she asked, skipping over the implications of what he had just said.

"Infectivity…? Ordinary Marburg is bad, but there's no way to know. If this truly is a designed virus, then there's no way to know for sure. If you were making something like that, would *you* make it as infectious as possible?"

She didn't answer the rhetorical question because the implications were clear as day.

"Doctor, we want you to travel with us to another installation and work on this problem," she said. Davidson didn't know how or where to start responding to that, but his brain threw a question out of his mouth anyway.

"Where? And where is here, for that matter?"

"Here is a temporary refugee processing and containment aid centre. As for where, I'm afraid I can't give you that information."

"So you want me to do something without knowing what it is I'm doing and where I'm being taken. Do I even have a choice in this?" he demanded. She looked hard at him before answering.

"You can choose to comply with a polite request for your assistance or you can choose not to," she said, not stating any consequences for a refusal. She was confident enough in herself not to have to threaten, that much was obvious to him, but he knew what his answer would be.

Viruses were his life, as pathetic and tragic as that sounded even in his own mind, and if he failed to answer the call now, then his life's work would see him watching from the sidelines when lesser players took starting positions.

"How far is it? I'm not sure I'm physically—"

"It should take us less than a day to get there. We could even make it by tonight if we leave soon."

Davidson opened his mouth to say that he wasn't capable of travelling. He needed to go back to sleep after the energy expended during their short conversation.

"You'll travel with appropriate medical care, of course, and I'll be leading a small unit to ensure you are protected—"

"Protected?" Davidson squawked. "Protected from what?"

For the first time she allowed some annoyance to show in her body language, letting out an exasperated breath along with a slump of her shoulders.

"Doctor, do I need to spell out the basics of human nature to you? What happens when there's an extended power cut? People start looting. What happens where there are no emergency services? No food deliveries? We're only ever three missed meals away from anarchy, and the majority of people are happy to spend their lives ignoring that. This isn't America, Doctor. People don't store food supplies in case hurricanes flood their towns and shut them off from outside help. Without the local Spar, half the people in this country would starve inside of a week."

"But… you're helping them, right?"

"RLC are gathering refugees from the larger towns and cities. Places like this are being set up all over Britain, but it won't last for long. We only have so much food stored up."

Davidson put down his coffee, his hands shaking as the reality of their situation began to truly set in and fought the urge to vomit. He rested his throbbing head in his hands while she listed off the wider situation, but he only took in a fraction of what she said.

Western Europe was in the same situation as they were, and their chances of fleeing east or west were severely limited. That was as things stood now, and not if any further attacks came.

The fact that World War Three had erupted in the time it had taken him to fly from Copenhagen to England was a mental block for him, and he struggled to climb him mind over the obstacle.

"This doesn't make sense. The Cold War ended years ago," he said weakly. This earned a bark of laughter from Addison.

"Ended? It never ended, Doctor. It just stopped being public knowledge. East versus West has always been a boiling kettle. Why do you think we've spent billions keeping a presence in Europe? Why do you think those massive auto-bahns exist? Which direction are they pointed in? It's so we can roll tanks east and meet a threat head-on, only they've attacked via the back door and we're the ones who have taken it right up the a—"

Someone knocked at the door and it opened without invitation. Davidson listened to the pregnant pause before a male voice rumbled behind him.

"Sorry to interrupt, ma'am," was all he said, but the lieutenant seemed to know what he meant.

"I need an answer, Doctor Davidson. Are you coming?"

He looked up at her, his concentration forcing the pain away for long enough to meet her intense gaze and nod once.

A blur of activity followed. He was wheeled around while men and women in uniformed shouted back and forth. They used words and acronyms he didn't understand, but the package dumped on his lap was one he recognised from pictures.

"Sir, I'm Lance Corporal Henry. Do you know what a noddy suit is?" a young man said in a Yorkshire accent.

Davidson smiled at him. He'd been wearing protective suits since the young man crouching in front of him was travelling around inside his father. He nodded, accepting the suit and the assistance in putting it on.

Instead of white or yellow as he was accustomed to, everything was drab olive green as was the way with the military. As the suit was pulled up from to his waist and he gratefully flopped back down into the wheelchair, a figure approached wearing a similar outfit.

With her hair tied up, Doctor Kaur looked like some kind of adventurer rather than a medical practitioner. She smiled at him as she closed the distance.

"You didn't think I was about to discharge you without the appropriate medical care, did you?" she said as she dumped a paramedic's heavy backpack beside his chair.

"You... you're coming?"

She nodded happily, but her eye was drawn to the catheter bag hanging from the back of the wheelchair. She turned back, grabbing a passing orderly and giving instructions for it to be emptied. The man came back with a cardboard container resembling a wine carafe, and Davidson waited in embarrassed silence as the stink of strong urine filled the air around them.

Bag empty, Kaur checked him over and shone a tiny penlight in his eyes before nodding in satisfaction that they were good to go.

Addison joined them, dressed in battle gear and helmet with the iconic British military rifle slung over her torso. She gave orders, sending men and women scattering to carry them out, and everywhere was a sense of urgent excitement.

"You good to go, Doctor Davidson?" she asked, turning her body towards him and unveiling the handgun strapped to her right thigh.

"Charlie," he said. "Probably saves time to call me Charlie." She nodded, not offering her first name as she had when they initially met, which put Davidson firmly in his place.

She was in charge, of that there was no doubt.

Davidson was wheeled out of the facility, blinded by the weak sun and in awe of the wispy streaks of green and purple visible through the gaps in the clouds.

His eyes lowered, facing the twin rear doors of a massive, six-wheeled vehicle that were open and ready. The thing was the size of a small truck and was covered in a heavy meshwork of metal.

"Reckon you can walk a bit?" Kaur asked, still smiling as if nothing phased her. Davidson nodded, seeming stunned in contrast to the people bustling with activity all around.

Addison was at the tail of the vehicle, face serious and all business, as Kaur and the lance corporal he had already met helped him awkwardly up the high steps to get inside.

Henry helped him into a seat, fixing the four points of a harness together and showing him how to unfasten it. Kaur strapped in opposite him, with Addison in the back and another soldier he didn't know.

The doors were shut, and the massive engine roared with some tentative revs from the driver.

"Henry, up top," Addison said. Davidson watched as the soldier stood on a raised platform in the centre of the truck and poked the upper part of his torso out into the outside air.

"That's Docker," Addison said, indicating the other soldier strapping in beside him. "And Nichols is driving with

Smith." She turned away, leaning around to yell into the front.

"Second vehicle ready?"

A raised thumb was shown back, and they set off.

"Do we really need a tank?" Davidson asked the man beside him. Docker smiled, like he was embarrassed for the man.

"It's a Mastiff, not a fakkin' tank," he answered glibly, ending the conversation as the engine picked up in noise and speed to send them onwards.

CHAPTER TWENTY-EIGHT

Adapting to Change

S haun was no engineer. He appeared under the engine bay, looking at the components with a critical eye. For all the good it did him, he might as well have been looking at the guts of an alien spaceship.

Bulbs and tyres, that was the extent of his engineering knowledge when it came to vehicles, and although he knew enough to jumpstart a car, he had no clue where to begin diagnosing the problem. He had driven fine for hours, but intermittently losing power combined with the tired sound it began to make when he pressed on the throttle was causing him concern.

Leaving it running for fear of being unable to start it again, he released the bonnet with a sigh for it to slam shut. Climbing back behind the wheel, he gave it plenty of revs for first gear to do its job, but the usually effortless torque struggled to give the engine power and he was forced to press his right foot down hard to get going.

When he got up to speed it behaved normally, but when slowing to negotiate the many obstacles like junctions and abandoned vehicles, he found himself yet again fearing a terminal fault in the truck.

It juddered threateningly, sending feedback through pedals and steering wheel, only this time instead of a rapid dip of the clutch and a stab of throttle to rescue the ailing revs, the engine sputtered to a clattering stop.

He rolled for a while, clutch still down and eyes fixed firmly on the country road snaking away ahead where it dropped down into a dip not far ahead. He urged it to keep rolling, to make it far enough that momentum and gravity met up so he could start the engine again.

He'd given up trying to start it conventionally, fearing that he was merely adding damage to a mechanical fault, so relied on the undulating countryside to give the truck life.

"Come on," he snarled, gripping the wheel tightly with both hands and almost humping his body weight forwards as though that miniscule amount of additional inertia could change the outcome.

As the truck rolled slower, he glanced at the needle, seeing his speed fall below five miles per hour. He feared he might not get it started again this time, but the needle fell no lower. He stared at it, willing it to creep back up the other way, but it stayed stubbornly where it was for tense, long seconds.

Five miles an hour is good, he told himself. *Not much faster than walking but at least I'm not walking...*

But the needle crept up. Six, then seven, then eight miles per hour and up and up until he felt the acceleration through his body as the rolling chassis gathered speed on the slight decline he had been hoping to reach.

Ten became fifteen, and he slipped the gear lever back into second and let up his left boot hard.

Coughing to life, the engine barked out another characteristic cloud of black smoke. Shaun dropped the clutch again and revved the engine hard before slipping it into third and powering away carefully along the road.

It was easy for him to enjoy that minor triumph, that miniscule window of good fortune, but it was hard for him to believe that the rest of the day would go the same.

As it happened, his luck ran for precisely four miles before he rounded a bend sedately and saw a makeshift barrier ahead. It was comprised of a single car with its nose in the ditch and one rear tyre lifted a few inches off the ground. He thought it strange that such an insignificant detail would be etched on his mind when so much other information was trying to break through, but eventually the observation was kicked out of the way while his brain screamed at him that there were people behind that barricade which was completed with a hand cart and other detritus. Those people, unless the flash of silhouette from too great a distance for him to make out details lied, were armed.

His body made the decision for him, and he yanked down on the wheel with his right hand to aim the angular nose at a break in the stone wall barred only by a wooden gate.

In the battle between moving vehicle and wooden obstacle, he had rarely seen the wooden obstacle win such an encounter.

Unless the wooden obstacle was a tree, that was. They had a long and significant history of killing motorists.

The gate splintered into pieces, but the shock of the impact was far harder than Shaun had anticipated. He expected to blast through it like a toy car tumbling matchsticks, only it didn't feel like that at all.

Fearing that he had caused yet more damage to his ride, Shaun floored the throttle to bump painfully away at an oblique angle, crossing the field that had recently been adorned with straight furrows so precise in their alignment that the hypnotic up and down movements of the truck would have lulled him into a trance had he not been impacting his head on the ceiling of the cab.

He feared shots following him, so he maintained the painful escape for as long as he could bear as a better alternative to being fired on, eventually turning the wheel left again to run his chunky tyres between the raised lines of packed dirt and proceed at double the speed and half of the discomfort.

He aimed for another gate barring an exit to the big field, slowing down to attack this one with more caution, but the post must have been rotten because the whole thing fell away without breaking into smaller pieces.

Re-joining the road, Shaun picked a direction heading away from the feared pursuit and floored it, pushing the revs all the way to the top of the power band for each gear until he was hammering along at over seventy. It was almost as uncomfortable as driving over the field, but he maintained that speed for as long as he dared to be sure nobody would chase him down, all the while switching his gaze feverishly between the road ahead and the two wing mirrors.

Rounding another bend and standing on the brakes to avoid hitting a tractor caught halfway out of a gateway when the lights went out, he narrowly avoided hitting it and felt the metallic scrape of something on the roof.

Slowing, he saw buildings ahead and knew he had

nowhere to go other than through the village, so he selected a lower gear and tried to keep his speed up until clear of the buildings on the other side.

Only the truck had other plans.

Whining loudly, the engine gave off another noise he hadn't heard it make before. It was not a good noise, he knew that much, and when the engine began its now-familiar coughing and spluttering, he knew his luck had finally run out.

Rolling to a juddering stop, Shaun sat panting for breath behind the wheel as the clicks and pops of the dead engine faded away to silence.

He released the wheel, ratcheting on the handbrake one click at a time as his eyes scanned the seemingly abandoned village.

Nobody moved. Nobody came out to investigate why a vehicle had screamed into their idyllic setting and stopped dead in the middle of the road.

And it was idyllic. Cottages lined the road on both sides, set back a way and stretching out until a manicured village green appeared at the foot of a church far too grand to serve just this knot of houses. Woodland lined the left side where open fields stretched out to the right, and Shaun imagined there to be a village shop along with the statutory old pub somewhere nearby.

Pale orange stone comprised the makeup of the buildings, and the obvious newer builds mimicked the classic style almost perfectly, only their deliberate preciseness stood them out as the same but also somehow alien.

Shaun leaned forwards, getting a better view of the street behind him in the mirrors, but still he saw nothing and nobody. He had no idea what he would do if he did see some-one, guessing that would depend on what *they* were doing.

His left hand gripping the shotgun, he climbed down from the cab cautiously and moved to the front of the truck where the problem was immediately apparent.

A piece of wood was embedded between the slats separating the headlight clusters, and the smell of oily steam spoke of something far more terminal than the problems he had already faced.

He tried to pull it out, as if removing a splinter from such a complex machine would somehow revive it, but when he tried, the thing was stuck fast.

"It's not a bloody vampire, you moron. It won't come back to life," he chided himself quietly.

"Problem?" someone called out, making Shaun spin and issue a noise he couldn't replicate if he tried.

He saw a man, dressed in the soft green and brown colours of someone so attuned to country life that they felt the need to camouflage, smiling at him from across the narrow road. His body language didn't seem threatening, but the smile he shone in Shaun's direction lacked... something. His eyes weren't carrying the smile, that much was obvious, but it was more what they were doing that bothered Shaun instead of what they weren't.

They weren't looking straight at him, but just over his shoulder.

He spun, shotgun coming up into a more readily usable position without aiming it, but there was no threat lurking unseen behind him. He spun back, inadvertently pointing the shotgun at the man's chest, which prompted him to act. He didn't throw up his arms in the universally accepted 'don't shoot' pose, instead he threw himself over a low, stone wall, yelling.

"Jesus bloody Christ!"

Shaun watched him disappear, heard the impact of his

body hitting the far side of the wall with a chesty thud, then the abuse started up again.

"What the bloody hell are you playing at, man?"

Shaun pointed the gun up in the air, immediately feeling horrified at his actions.

"Sorry! Sorry, I… I thought you were looking at someone behind me—"

"I've got a bloody squint, you twat!"

Shaun's first reaction was to laugh, which only sparked further yelling.

"Why's that funny? You could've fucking shot me!"

"I'm sorry," Shaun said again. "Look, people were chasing me and—"

He never got to finish his sentence, because the high-pitched shriek of a two-stroke engine cut the air. They weren't in the village, not yet, but from the warbling sounds of the revs it wouldn't be long before they were.

Shaun abandoned the conversation in a heartbeat, stomping to the passenger side of the truck to snatch his backpack up.

Something in the back of his mind had made him do that. Some half-remembered article read during his endless hours of scrolling through the Internet and falling for clickbait that only led him deeper and deeper into the hole.

Something had told him that he needed to be ready to move, that he had to sleep with his boots on and always have his belongings packed ready. Like living life on the run, never knowing when the authorities would ballistically knock on the front door at dawn.

He pulled at the door handle until his brain reminded him that the same sense of caution had led him to travel with all the doors locked, and with the time window shrinking rapidly, he acted fast to retrieve his equipment and supplies.

Stepping back and turning the shotgun in his hands, he stabbed the wooden butt into the window to shatter it, reaching in and retrieving the pack before the glass had even settled.

He turned, aimed himself between two picturesque stone cottages, and ran for the cover of the trees.

———

What stopped him, oddly, was his bladder. Not the breathless exhaustion of a cross country sprint, not a fall or pulled muscle, but a bladder screaming signals up to his brain demanding attention and threatening action if it was ignored.

He stopped, checking all around him among the thick trees, as he unzipped and prepared to water the base of the tree closest to him.

His bladder lied. It was not full to bursting point as it had insisted, for instead of the expected deluge of hot fluid there came a reluctant, almost pathetic trickle.

Is that it? Shaun thought angrily, wondering what was going on inside his body for this strange sequence of events to transpire, but then the rational, analytical part of him took over and provided educated guesses as to what had occurred.

Adrenaline was what he settled on. He had experienced more of the hormone in his bloodstream in the last week than he had in the six months before that, and something in his mind conjured an explanation about the body ridding itself of unnecessary weight or something. Fight or flight. Or run away and piss yourself.

. . .

He wandered on for a while longer, peering between the trees for sight of anything man-made that he could use to direct himself homeward.

The temperature was dropping fast, and through the gaps in the treetops Shaun could see the sky darkening. His stomach growled at him, now that the adrenaline had been purged from his system, and that was more accurate a time-piece than any watch. Giving up on getting out of the woods before sundown, he cast around for a good place to spend the night.

Shaun had never once slept a night under the stars. He had camped, obviously, but he had never been bitten by the bushcraft bug. He had been fine with that right up until that very moment when he wished he knew more about survival than what he had learned watching Bear and Ed on TV.

Settling on a large oak tree with roots so old and gnarled that they separated the ground at its base, he dropped his pack down and rested the shotgun against the trunk before fishing around in the top of his pack for the folding saw he had taken from a place where he'd slept the night either three or six days ago; everything rolled into one when it came to recent memory, and what felt like weeks ago was a matter of hours.

He had initially rested his eye on the hatchet, feeling manly and at one with nature at the thought of hacking down a tree, but when he used his brain, he fell back on the concept of economy of movement and selected the saw that folded to the length of his forearm.

With a few false starts until he discovered the best tech-nique, Shaun cut a series of low branches from nearby trees and dragged them back to his chosen spot.

He intended to create a simple lean-to shelter without the complex technical knowledge required to make something last through bad weather. All he wanted was something to keep him enclosed and a way to be insulated from the ground, which was the next thing he sought.

Ranging further from his home for the night, he found a small sea of large leaves growing in a patch of weak daylight where a tree had fallen. They looked like they belonged more in Jurassic Park than… than wherever the hell he was, but he cut a large armful of them and hauled his mattress back to the clearing.

"Water, shelter, food," he recited quietly, thinking out loud as if his subconscious needed the company. "Or is it shelter, water, food? I know food is the last one…"

He carried food and water, although not a great deal, so he concentrated on his shelter. On entering the clearing, he froze, standing stock still like a dog trained to point when it saw a bird or some other prey.

Standing not five paces away, directly between him and the shotgun, was the most unimpressed, unconcerned deer he'd ever laid eyes on.

It looked like a deer, only with shorter legs and an almost cuboid body under a small head. The lower jaw worked fast as it chewed something, mesmerising Shaun into continued immobility while he watched it.

He had broken the first rule he'd made after the failed ambush, in that he had been out of reach of the shotgun. Had it been in his hand at that moment, he wasn't sure if he could even bring himself to pull the trigger and destroy such a beautiful animal in cold blood.

While he came to that realisation, the deer bolted; bouncing happily off into the trees to disappear.

Shaun watched it go before his mind metaphorically tapped him on the shoulder and pointed out the obvious.

You're obviously not that hungry yet. But you will be.

.   .   .

Despite being impressed with his efforts, the lean-to shelter of cut branches let in precisely all the night-time wind, making him wish he had thought to build a fire.

He dropped that whimsical idiocy as soon as he had conjured it, because there wasn't the room to set a fire inside his tiny shelter. He would have set his sleeping bag alight and probably died if he had, so he decided that controlled suffering was the way forward.

Pulling on the drawstring of his sleeping bag, be buried his face into his chest to seal himself inside and allowed the compound effect of heating the trapped air to warm him up enough that he fell asleep.

Waking to find everything covered in a light sheen of cold water, he struggled out of the already half collapsed shelter to see the faint glimmer of orange light dead ahead of him.

Some people learned bushcraft and navigation without technology, but most of what Shaun knew had been learned through various forms of media. He did not know where the sun rose and fell because he had learned it, he knew he was facing east because he had watched and read many things about the empire of the rising sun.

Japan was to his east, where the sun came from in the morning, so he kept his eyes on the distant orb and held his left hand out.

"Never."

He turned a quarter circle and gestured at the sun.

"Eat."

Turning another half circle, he pointed dead ahead.

"Soggy."

Holding out his right hand with his eyes still glued to the trees, he finished the peculiar mantra.

"Waffles."

Still facing south, he paused for a while, basking in the

glory of being a wild man of the woods, able to navigate using only the sun. Then he turned to gather his small amount of belongings and took a minute to kick down the shelter.

He didn't know why, only that the TV explorers took theirs down, and the task seemed to signify that it was time to move.

He hadn't eaten enough to partake in his usual morning routine – that of emptying his full bladder, making coffee, taking three sips and returning to the bathroom only to find his coffee had gone old in the time it had taken him to check the overnight occurrences in the virtual world. He was more of a participant in that online existence than he was in real life, only now that world had ceased to exist.

Others would be experiencing huge anxieties about that, but for him it was almost a liberation. Like being sober from an addiction and happy about it.

Thoughts of addiction led him down a darker mental path, so he shook it off and drank a bottle of water as he walked, before chasing it with two protein bars.

Keeping the sun on his left he, walked, heading in the direction he hoped was directly south so at least he was going the right way, knowing that he would eventually link up with a trunk road and be able to get his bearings.

Being a man who had grown up and learned to drive before satellite navigation was readily available to the civilian market, he knew how to read a map and as a result, had developed a sense of geographical awareness in his own country.

Now that he knew where east and west were, he was able to mentally plot the directions of other places.

"Nachos earn sassy wives," he murmured, trying to spend the time creating a new mnemonic he could share with Lydia.

"Now earth smells weird… never extract stinky willies…" he broke off into a puerile giggle and cleared his throat before continuing.

"Nobheads eagerly slap women… narrow eagles swim weirdly…"

He lapsed into silence as he emerged from the trees. He looked up, readjusted his direction to correct for south, and set off. He maintained that silence after thoughts of Lydia, thoughts of Abbie, had lulled him into a sullen mood.

———

Even though the English countryside seemed vast, he was worried that he hadn't seen a single person or main road for almost two hours. There were buildings, agricultural or residential in every case, but they were always off his path and too far away to detour towards.

Besides, he doubted very much that he would find the same willing hand of friendship as he had when he had been gifted a gun and a truck to fulfil his journey.

The truck was lost now, but the gun was still in his left hand, still unfired, and he was still heading the right way. That determination failed him completely when he found a road and the resulting road sign that told him he was much further north than he hoped he was.

Resigned to long days spent walking, he climbed a fence into yet another field and stopped.

Because the answer to his problems was wandering straight towards him.

CHAPTER TWENTY-NINE

The Way Things Work

Abbie waited in line with Lydia in front of her. Breakfast was a vastly different affair from the previous night's evening meal, in that they lined up and were issued a small packet containing a breakfast cereal of some indiscernible type, a carton of UHT milk and a random piece of fruit from a bowl.

Abbie took hers, looking left to see Lydia hesitating over a proffered orange. The man in his yellow vest didn't look up, just held the piece of fruit out to her while he talked to the person next to him. Lydia hesitated, looking back at her mother with unsure eyes.

"Just take it," she told her in a hushed voice which still attracted the unwelcome attention of the man on fruit issuing duty.

He looked Lydia up and down, sneering and sucking his gums before looking away like he didn't appreciate what he had seen. As he struck up his conversation again, Abbie only just managed to resist the urge to smack him around the head with her free hand for the look he had given her little girl. The man could only be six or seven years older than her, and in Abbie's eyes he was still very much a child.

As if sensing the hate, he leaned back to look at her before smirking and searching through the bowl to find what he wanted. With another sneer, one of amusement this time, he produced a long, straight banana and curled the fingers of his right hand around it very deliberately while he made low, desperate sounds.

She glared at him, so unimpressed that it almost leaked out of her pores, but that only made him laugh as she reached in and took and apple. The man and his friend laughed harder, as if their best source of amusement was to make rude jokes like a pair of five-year-olds.

As an afterthought, she picked up a far smaller, misshapen example of the fruit he still held and tossed it onto his lap.

"That one's more like it," she told him patronisingly, moving on so fast that neither of them caught the shouted response.

Lydia began to laugh, blowing raspberry noises from her pursed lips as she tried to keep it contained. Abbie allowed herself a satisfied smile, knowing from experience how easy it was to upset any adult male by questioning the size of his appendage. Among the many insecurities she had as a woman of forty, luckily for her, dick size and testosterone regulation weren't listed.

They turned left, cutting between two long, single-storey buildings to get back to their temporary home, but their laughter was cut off as two people fell in step either side of them in an orchestrated fashion.

"Give us your fruit," one said.

"That one's got coco pops," said the other.

Both Abbie and Lydia instinctively tightened their grips on their meagre breakfast, like Chunk growling as he chomped down his food fast in the presence of a rival animal.

"Fuck off," Abbie snapped, shrugging her elbow away hard enough to dislodge the one on her side. He leapt back, scrawny hands coming up in mock defence.

"Alright, keep your knickers on. We were just looking!"

Commotion to Abbie's right turned her head back again where Lydia grunted in fear while trying to maintain possession of her breakfast.

She dropped her breakfast, reaching for the thief with both hands but he was too quick for her. Just as thin and lithe as the other, he twisted the plastic bag from Lydia's grip but not before the young girl had changed her footing so that he tripped over her planted leg when he turned to flee. He lay sprawling in the dirt face down, and Lydia moved for him like she was back on the mats with the redheaded girl who was heavier than she was but not as fast or flexible.

Abbie saw this unfolding, was already moving to intervene, when an arm locked around her neck from behind. Just as the air supply was restricted, she felt a sensation she hadn't experienced before. It was something between a red-hot fury and a cold calmness, both of which frightened her and combined to grant her previously unknown powers.

She spun, wrenching her body back towards her attacker so all he did was hug the back of her head tightly to him, and instead of throwing a punch or breaking free, she pressed her forehead into his and leaned her body weigh in, walking both of them forwards until they slammed into the wall of a building as one.

Her hand was in her pocket and back out before either of

them made a sound, and the knife's blade was extended with a sharp *snick*.

She held him there, frozen as her forehead kept his face in position and his body locked tight to avoid any accidental injury. The tip of the blade was caught in folds of clothing, but the general area was so vulnerable that his response told her she was right on the money.

He released her, taking his hands away slowly, but she held him locked in their awkward embrace with her head pressed firmly into his.

She breathed heavily, and anyone watching might be forgiven for believing that she was trying to maintain control when the opposite was true. She was willing herself to hurt him, wishing she could go through with it and cut the little bastard's balls off for even thinking about touching her, but that shot of adrenaline wired her so tight that she was incapable of losing control.

She shoved back, freeing him, and just as she had heard so many times in her life, she found out that there truly was no honour among thieves because he ran as fast as he could, abandoning his co-conspirator like he was already dead.

Abbie turned her attention back to Lydia just in time, because the girl was bringing her foot up to deliver a blow to the back of the other one's head. In a stark contrast to Abbie's shaolin monk style self-control, Lydia was crying and had lost it.

She yowled when he was pulled away, delivering the stomp faster and with little effect, but she bucked and squirmed to try and get back to hurt him as her sobs became louder.

Abbie almost let her go, save for the fact that when the girl came out the other end of the stress-induced rage she had been forced into, Abbie knew Lydia would feel remorse for what she was trying to do to another person, justified or not.

"Let him go," she told the girl, hugging her tightly and letting her cry out the fear and adrenaline rush that her young body wasn't accustomed to. She held her there, blocking the alleyway between the buildings, until the tears stopped flowing and the angry sniff indicated she needed to be released from the embrace.

Stooping to pick up her breakfast, the torn plastic released the last of the little, brown, chocolate puffs onto the dusty ground and she broke down again, crying in pathetic anger at the loss.

Of the previously unwanted orange and the carton of milk, there was no sign. Abbie tried her hardest to comfort her daughter as they gathered up all they had left and hurried back into the daylight.

As they emerged from between the buildings, they attracted nervous stares. Abbie initially thought it was because Lydia was crying, but she soon recalled that the unsheathed blade was flashing brightly, clutched in her right fist. She hurriedly folded it away and pocketed the blade amid some sideways looks.

"Are you okay?" someone asked, stepping close to their path and forcing Abbie to steer them around her. The woman moved, ducking down to try and make eye contact with Lydia, and her body language made it clear she was trying to intervene in a situation in which she clearly assumed Abbie to be the bad person.

"Leave me alone," Lydia blurted out, making the woman stand tall and front up to Abbie as if this granted her the authority to challenge her.

"No! You! *You* leave me alone," Lydia said, pushing the woman aside without Abbie having to say a word.

They carried on, making the turns left and right as Lydia's sobbing ebbed away into angry sniffs, and when they reached their door, it was unlocked and flung open to reveal Chunk struggling to get himself the right way up from one of the beds. Lydia threw herself face down on her sleeping bag and started crying again.

Abbie didn't know what to do. How had she condemned them to such a dangerous place? How were so many people up to no good without anyone stopping them?

Then other thoughts hit her.

Were those two boys just trying to snatch a little extra food? No, one of them attacked me… or did her? Did he think his friend was being attacked? Did he react to what I did? Oh my God, I pulled a knife on a kid! Am… am I the bad person here?

"Knock, knock!" came the cheery, singsong announcement from beyond the open door. Abbie looked up just in time to see Gita's wide smile and happy face rearrange itself to express concern.

"Goodness, is everything alright? What has happened?"

"Nothing, we just ran into a little trouble getting breakfast," Abbie said. She set her milk, her cereal and the apple she had managed to retrieve on the bed beside Lydia and stepped towards the door. Gita backed away, allowing her the space to exit and close the door behind her, but not before a brown nose barged its way through the narrowing gap.

In the opposite way a rat escapes a trap, Chunk's head fit through, but the rest of his body would not. The door bounced back, giving him that hurt expression that said he didn't understand what he had done for her to so cruelly bludgeon him with a door, and then it opened back up so he could bound outside.

Gita froze, closing her eyes slightly as the canine tank

brushed under her skirts, but regained her composure when he had passed. Her expression returned to one of deep concern.

"Someone tried to steal our breakfast on the way back," she explained. Gita frowned.

"Did you go back here the way you came? Did you walk back past the line of people waiting?"

"No, we cut down between two... wait, am I missing something here?"

"People who want to exchange their food for other things go between the buildings. It is perhaps my fault that you did not know this. I am sorry, Abbie. Truly I am—"

"It's not your fault," Abbie told her. "It's mine. And mine for... never mind." She smiled then, resetting her face as if agreeing between her mind and her body to forget what had just happened.

"Does a lot of that stuff happen around here?"

Gita's eyes twitched to the closed front door and Abbie took the hint. She stepped further away from their little shed to stand in the middle of the strip, folding her arms across her chest.

"It is not all this way, at least not as I have seen. But I have only been here for three days before you..."

Abbie lapsed into silence, thinking as she watched Chunk perform a systematic search of the nearest corners before staggering a little with one fat haunch raised up to irrigate a section.

"Gita, would you do me a favour?"

"Of course." The woman nodded eagerly, almost desperate to please another human.

"Could you just watch Lydia for a little while? I promise I won't be long."

Gita was nodding rapidly before she had even finished

speaking. Abbie placed a hand on the woman's shoulder and smiled, unsure who was getting the more reassurance from that small gesture. She turned back to the closed door and poked her head inside, telling Lydia that she would be back soon and not to go anywhere.

"What? Where are you going?"

Lydia was suddenly animated, afraid for either her mother or herself. Or possibly both.

"I have to go and report what happened," she said, knowing it wasn't the entire truth but feeling justified that she wasn't lying. "I promise I won't be long, but you stay here, okay?"

Lydia's only response was to thump her head back down into the sleeping bag splayed out on her folding cot. Chunk, as if sensing her tears, nuzzled his way under her left elbow and grumbled until she reasted that hand on his square head.

Leaving them to it, Abbie backed out of the room again and made another promise to Gita that she wouldn't be long.

———

It took conversations with three marshals, two of whom were intentionally obtuse, before she found out where the section's leader should be.

As she walked, she started to comprehend the layout of the camp. Cut up into different areas, she imagined the organisation was to prevent too many people from mingling or gathering in one spot.

High fences partitioned those areas, and the cynic in her guessed each section held just enough people to be subdued with minimal effort should there be any kind of uprising.

Roads, but more like twin tyre tracks in the dirt, ran through the entire camp and led to the outside fence which was double skinned like a kind of airlock. Or a prison. People congregated in places along that internal perimeter, and ten minutes of watching from an incongruous spot showed her an open-top military truck rolling slowly around the camp.

As was the eternal question with all secure perimeters, she wondered if the security was to keep people in or keep people out. The right and wrong of whatever answer depended on a person's perspective, she guessed.

She left her spot, not wanting to hang around and attract attention, but mostly because the short time she had been out of sight of Lydia was heightening her stress level.

She found Ty, looking smooth and a little smug as usual, behind a folding table erected under a kind of gazebo.

The table was covered in handwritten reports. Notes were strewn in loose piles where others were impaled upon a large nail pointing upwards from a rough-cut square of wood. In spite of the warmth of the day, a small brazier burned behind him, and as she approached, she learned its purpose as a piece of paper was crumpled and tossed inside, destroying the information forever.

So much for digital forensics, she thought. The concept of industrial era technology was one that had been playing on her mind. It was probably the biggest reason that petty crime among the interned population was on the rise.

"Mrs Taylor. How can I be of assistance to you today?" Ty said smoothly. He didn't shout, but he spoke loudly enough for his words to carry the distance to her.

She was shocked out of her thought process by it, not expecting him to have seen her from so far off. Speeding up her pace, she waited until she was closer to the makeshift desk so that she didn't have to shout herself.

"Just wanted to talk to someone about an incident this morning," she said lightly. At the word 'incident' Ty's eyebrows went up and he waved the two attending yellow vests away without taking his eyes off Abbie.

The two assistants complied – *obeyed*, more accurately – and he waited until they were relatively alone before he animated again.

"Incident?"

"Yeah…" She drew out the word, almost embarrassed. She put her head down, unconsciously using the fingers of her right hand to push an errant strand of hair back behind her right ear. Realising how the gesture looked, despite her greasy hair and desperate need for a long, hot shower, she straightened and tried to give off an entirely different vibe.

"Two people tried to rob us of our breakfast this morning. We managed to get away, but my daughter is very upset about it all."

Ty looked hurt and concerned. He began to nod slowly, reaching for a piece of paper among the many without looking too hard, which told her that he already knew where it was and had an inkling of what information it bore.

"I'm so terribly sorry to hear that," he told her with so much genuine, heartfelt emotion that she began to understand how good a liar the man was. He made a show of looking at the piece of paper for ten whole seconds before he spoke again.

"Seems you aren't the only one to experience unpleasantness this morning. Two boys reported being beaten up and threatened with a knife for their food also… this won't do at all… Carita?"

He turned to one side, not looking before he spoke as though he knew the woman would be there, hovering, waiting for a summons.

Glasses, short bob haircut, bearing a clipboard and wearing an orange vest of power, Carita appeared. Looking eager, giving off simultaneous airs of being awfully official and awfully officious, she stood still with pen poised, waiting for instructions.

"I want our marshal presence increased at mealtimes. Too many incidents being reported for my liking." He spoke to the woman, but his eyes and false smile stayed fixed on Abbie.

He waited for the woman to take down the note and scurry away, eager to fulfil her task like she was paying him to be submissive herself. Ty picked up a fresh piece of paper; a normal sheet of A4 now useless for the printers it was produced to feed. He folded it twice, neatly and precisely, then tore it into quarters to stretch out the life of a resource their world could no longer produce or procure.

Smiling up at Abbie, who kept her face impassive and devoid of emotion or reaction so she didn't betray her involvement; so she didn't confirm his obvious suspicion that the two incidents were one and the same.

"I'll tell you what," he said as he started writing on the selected rectangle of paper. "I'll even request a uniformed presence for tonight. How's that?"

He smiled at her, turning his head to search for another runner loyal to his operation and seeing none after he had sent Carita away.

"Let me," Abbie said with a smile.

He regarded her, giving off a sense of something mixed between amusement and suspicion.

"It's no trouble at all. Just… just tell me where to go. Honestly, I could do with the walk and something to do."

He smiled, suspicion giving way to amusement. He handed over the piece of paper before reaching behind his chair. While his eyes were off her, she had to fight the urge to read the note, knowing that she would do so just as soon as she was out of his sight anyway.

He turned back to face her, offering a brightly coloured bundle of breathable cloth.

She stared at the yellow vest – the obvious sign of authority no matter what state the world was in – and her hesitation prompted a laugh from him.

"Take it. You'll need it to get through the section gates. Head that way—" he pointed off to his right, her left, "and tell them you have a message for camp HQ. You can't miss it when you get through to the centre. Give that to anyone on duty."

She didn't answer straight away. She repeated his instructions in her head to clarify and consolidate them, then she nodded.

"Got it. You want me to bring the vest back afterwards?"

"You keep it for now. Maybe you can start working for me?"

Abbie returned his smile. His was, she was sure, designed to be smouldering and smooth. It came across as wolfish and predatory, but hers was fleeting and intentionally ignorant of his intentions.

She walked out of his field headquarters, disliking the man even more on instinct, and shrugged her shoulders into the vest. She expected a change, a feeling of power or authority, but she only felt dirty for wearing it. She had no idea why she distrusted the authority, other than the obvious corruption that infested every facet of human society, and wearing it brought out the young rebel in her that had been suppressed since her youth.

The gates to the section yielded to the vest and a wave of the paper, and true to Ty's word, the epicentre of the camp was so obvious as to be impossible to miss.

There she waited in a short line of other people upon whom had been bestowed the power of the hi-vis vest, handed her note to someone who seemed unsure whether they were under-stimulated by their role or overworked. They read it, handed it back and pointed to another desk behind which sat, to her surprise, a police officer in uniform.

She walked over, returning the tired smile with one of her own. He hadn't shaved in a few days by the look of it, and the grey stubble threatening to become a beard told her this man was likely closer to retirement than the other end of his career scale.

She handed him the note, waited as he read it, and smiled again when he let out a breath with obvious intent. She had heard that noise come from so many people before in her life. From her boss when she asked for time off. From those who worked for her when she made it clear she expected effort from them. From contractors who wanted to increase their quote.

Not one of them had got past her before.

"Not sure we can... got a lot of places to be and not a lot of us to be there. I'll have to kick this up the chain and see what they say."

"That's fine," Abbie said, reaching over the desk and plucking the note from his grasp. "Can you just tell me where the marines are? I'll ask my friend."

EPILOGUE

Worse

"Is that your 'orse?" the young boy asked. He had emerged from a gated farmyard to walk alongside Shaun. He had the bravery of youth on his side, but the fact that he stayed on his side of the road told Shaun that the boy was no fool.

"I think she's her own horse, if you know what I mean."

The boy did not.

The two separate parties walked along side by distant side for a few more beats before the boy spoke again.

"Are you going into town? My dad says we can't go into town. He says bad things are happening—"

"Shaun!"

Both rider and pedestrian spun towards the source of the screamed name, seeing a woman running down the country lane with no regard for her appearance. It was the run of a woman who wasn't accustomed to running, and she seemed to care not one bit what was bouncing around uncontrolled.

She reached the boy and snatched him up, backing away from Shaun on his horse with a terrified glare. He held up his right hand, palm facing her, with his left loosely holding the reigns.

"Just passing through," he said, shocking himself at how casual he sounded having such a conversation. She said nothing, just continued backing away until Shaun had moved far enough off.

He didn't blame her. Didn't try to appease her or tell her he meant no harm. Truth be told, he had hardened over the last few days. Hardened to people, to his own emotions, and the companionship with his newfound mode of transport had helped ease him into that chosen solitude.

Animals, apart from wasps, snakes, and crocodiles, could be trusted. They weren't bad like people, at least less often, and when they were it was usually as a direct result of a person mistreating them.

And sharks. Shaun had never seen one in real life, but he was fairly sure he wouldn't trust anything with that many teeth.

He had adapted his appearance to match his attitude. Gone were the bright clothes designed to breathe and keep him dry. Gone was the fancy backpack with its straps and toggles. In their place was a much-reduced loadout, and all of it was hidden, neatly disguised beneath a dark green poncho.

He travelled light, relying on being able to find the things he needed when he stopped each night, and only the shotgun resting diagonally across his back showed a casual observer anything of worth. That and the horse, but both things could inflict some harm, so very few people approached him.

The only new addition to his gear was the replacement

pickaxe handle. His newer version was older and smaller, but it rested in a bag hanging just ahead of his right knee where it could be employed with little effort from horseback.

Shaun had to learn how to ride and care for the horse, who he had greeted with a flat palm like memory told him he should, and the horse snuffled at him in search of something edible.

"What's the matter, boy? You want a sugar cube or something?" he had said. In response, the horse had made a noise like a fat man sneezing and pranced back a few steps, showing Shaun its profile and the absence of something where its presence would have been obvious.

"Girl. Sorry. You like sugar?"

He had taken his time gaining her trust, walking a short distance away and letting her follow cautiously before he rewarded her with a tender touch and soft words.

In the wooden stable block on the other side of the field he had found the required equine bondage equipment, and through the judicious application of treats and significant trial and error, he had figured out how to gear up his new friend to be able to carry him.

The first day spent in the saddle had been agony.

The second had been cut short because of that agony, but that had allowed Shaun the time to scavenge an abandoned shop for a pair of jeans that didn't rub the insides of his thighs. With that seemingly small detail accommodated for, he resumed his southerly journey with purpose and passion.

Now, five days after abandoning the precious gift of a working vehicle, he arrived on a bluff of high ground overlooking the bridge spanning the estuary beyond which lay his home.

He expected to be stressed. Expected to be excited or nervous or experience any other raft of emotions, but he was oddly pragmatic about it.

Either they were there, or they were not.

He tried not to imagine the consequences of either option, because he literally had a physical bridge to cross before he crossed theoretical ones.

Sugar clopped her hooves over the empty expanse of tarmac, with Shaun twitching the reins slightly to direct her nose at a raised barrier. He didn't comply with the direction, didn't go around the roundabout to drive over via the unrestricted access, but instead went against the one-way system and rode his horse straight through the open exit barrier where the recently installed contactless payment modules sat vacant and lifeless just as the bridge itself did.

He could have taken the lower section where brave pedestrians could walk below the level of the passing traffic. He could have stuck to one side of the road and moved slowly, but something in his mind provoked him to ride Sugar right down the damn middle.

The iconic scenes from television programmes taunted him, mocked him for a poor recreation, and he cared not one bit, as though he had just ticked off a bucket list item.

Nobody approached him. Nobody made themselves known or moved within his sight. It was as though the city that ran all day and all night had suddenly ceased to live as it had before.

There was no way it could be empty, he knew that, but it also didn't unnerve him that others would be as cautious as he was. Or was when he wasn't riding a horse down the middle of three lanes of road with only twenty or so abandoned cars littering his otherwise perfect cinematic moment.

The deeper he got into the residential part of the outskirts where he lived – where he *had* lived – with his family, the more signs he saw to tell him what had gone on.

Suitcases of clothes lay abandoned at the side of the roads. Cars, useless without their working electronics, sat dormant on driveways and roadside alike, with others left in more hap-hazardous positions to demonstrate which ones had been moving when the sky lit up.

Sugar stepped confidently, maintaining her solid walking pace, but she seemed as wary as Shaun was. Once the high sides of buildings and the enclosed nature of having houses on either side had been comforting to him, but now he felt confined. He felt borderline trapped.

Finding his own home happened almost automatically. He wasn't sure if he had nudged his heels or twitched the reins, but somehow Sugar had made the turns and brought him to the house with the empty driveway. That was his first let-down. Her Golf should have been there, at least he'd hoped it would be, but the way the rest of the world was trying its hardest to appear uninhabited meant that he was unlikely to find them there.

Evacuation, that had to be it, he told himself.

The larger towns and cities had to have been evacuated.

He slipped his right foot out of the stirrup and lifted it over Sugar's head, clearing the horse with room to spare. He had lost that extra padding around the middle, shred the skin of his old life in less than two weeks, and although alcohol was abundant and free, he hadn't touched a drop since the night before he'd set out alone.

The front door lay open; yale lock broken free from the wooden frame by force. Inside lay muddy footprints and pieces of bark, and the trail of detritus led him to the empty basket where logs were brought in from the store beside the house. He didn't need to check, because he guessed that store was already empty, otherwise there was no logic in breaking into the house in search of more.

The cupboards were empty, and those items not deemed to be valuable enough were strewn about the kitchen as though they had been burgled by starving people who were picky about what they ate.

His feet led him upstairs, images of suicides forcing their unwelcome way into his mind's eye, and he distracted himself with inanities like being admonished for wearing filthy boots inside the house.

He hesitated outside the door to his bedroom – *Abbie's* bedroom – before he pushed it open to find it empty. The duvet was stretched tight and neat over the bed, and the arrangement of cushions – new cushions that he hadn't seen before – told him that at least they hadn't been rousted in their sleep. Then his mind nudged him, reminding him that the car was missing, and that they might not have even made it home after making their beds that morning.

His feet propelling him quicker now, he practically stormed towards Lydia's door to fling it open. Only then did a gasp escape his mouth and turn into a sob as his knees threatened to abandon him. Staggering slightly, he knelt beside her bed and looked at the dressing table where a fittingly girlish shade of lipstick had been used to write a message. It was a message to him.

Dad. Gone to Devonport docks. Come and find us.

A heart, undersized and uneven on the left side, sat beneath the words.

Good sense took over with the renewed sense of purpose, and he walked into the spare room where the fitted wardrobes still held some of his old clothes. They had been put there, set aside some time ago in the hope that he would lose a little of the weight he was gaining, and now they were pulled out for him to change directly into, stripping down on the spot to leave his dirty clothes where they lay.

He dressed, smelling that mild mildew scent that clothes in storage always gave off, and on autopilot he scooped up the discarded garments to drop them into the washing basket on the landing before moving through the house fast to recover a few more items. Stopping by the front door, he relaxed to see that Chunk's lead was missing, telling him that the dog had not escaped alone. He didn't think the daft animal would last a day on the streets, as loyal and loveable as he was, and that thought gave him some pleasure because Abbie and Lydia could take comfort in his company.

Back out on the driveway he retrieved Sugar, who had been cropping the overgrown grass that clothed their front lawn, swung himself up into the saddle and leaned forward to treat the horse with the sweet crunch of its namesake before pulling on her reins and aiming her in the direction of the port.

————

Abbie ate her food without looking at it. Her eyes were glued to the three groups hovering with such undisguised intent that it was laughable. Or at least it would have been laughable if their presence didn't offer the chance of something truly unpleasant happening.

A knot of police officers dressed in odd overalls and

yellow vests adorned with various pieces of equipment stood warily with visored helmets clipped to their waists.

On another side of the large hall was a group of marshals, equally obvious in their yellow and orange vests, only over civilian clothing and without any overt sign of weaponry, they seemed somehow *more* intimidating than the police did.

The final group comprised raised hoods and furtive body language. Like a street rap gang filming a low-budget music video, they egged each other on, taking it in turns to show off among their friends, and with each passing minute the tension grew in intensity.

Lydia was talking to her, but she heard none of the words. When her daughter got annoyed and demanded her attention, she shushed her without making eye contact.

Lydia lapsed into a sullen silence, which suited Abbie just fine. She kept watching, almost wishing something would happen, when another group entered the building to shift the entire dynamic on its head.

Echoes of déjà vu hit her as Jez and his team or squad or whatever word they used for it walked in. She recognised him; recognised him from the way he carried himself initially, then the shape of his head complete with scruffy helmet hair.

"Come on," she said, not wanting to leave Lydia there. Gita and Amal rose too. The latter on his mother's insistence and clearly annoyed as he hadn't finished his stodgy cake and custard which, despite the inferior quality, had been something of an exciting addition to the evening meal.

Gita had forgone questioning Abbie, recognising in her a woman with drive and confidence where she lacked that same ability to stand up for herself.

Abbie led, angling her approach to cut Jez off, but he had seen her as soon as she rose and was matching his own course correction to hers.

"I have been looking for you for days," she said, barely able to keep her voice low and attracting some attention. If Jez cared about that, he didn't show it.

"Sorry, it's been getting harder to get in and out of places. We've been on the road a lot."

She was still angry with him, even if she didn't understand fully her feelings. She knew that she and Lydia were there as a result of following his insistence that they go to the dockyards, but he didn't know what kind of place they would be shepherded off to after that, just as much as she hadn't. Until now..

She still treated him as though he was responsible in some way for them being there, and neither could really say why.

"Well, I've been looking for you," she said sullenly.

"Why? What do you need?"

"What do I *need*? Are you fucking kidding me? I need you to get us out of here. You see what's going on, right? You see how this is going to go?"

She gestured at the inert gaggle of police, the restless group of marshals and the confident, larger group of people she didn't know how to describe.

Jez looked, assessed it, and nodded slowly.

"Dick measuring. Won't be any trouble unless one of them gets brave. Most likely the police'll have to deal with him because everyone's watching, then the others'll get all brave and it'll kick off from there."

Abbie could see how his guess would play out, and she didn't like the way it looked in her imagination.

"Listen, give me an hour and meet me near the local command post," he said. Something in his eyes told her he was serious, that he had lost the energy to mess anyone around days ago, so she just nodded and led her procession of four towards the place where they could dump their trays and escape the slowly boiling kettle that was the food hall.

She left Lydia inside their room, nodded to Gita who stood outside her own door, and looked down at the huffing, excited Labrador performing a slow dance on the spot.

"Come on, fat boy," she said kindly, tugging his lead and setting off in the dark to wait for Jez and the answers she hoped he would bring.

Waiting there, breathing in the contaminated air of so many people living in one place, she frowned, looking up as the quiet drone of an aircraft sounded high overhead, just before an odd, alien, rushing sound grew louder high above her.

———

Shaun stopped his horse beside a smiling man sitting on a wide storefront step. He returned the smile, showing far more teeth than the instigator of their conversation did.

"Got anything?" the man looking up at him asked. The question was so open as to be interpreted in any way, but he narrowed it down through experience to mean drugs or alcohol. He shook his head, resisting the urge to give a lecture on the merits of clean living.

"Ah well. Ne'er mind," the guy responded with a shrug, like he expected to be let down so often he was happy about it.

"What happened here?" Shaun asked, lifting his chin in the direction of the dockyards where the security gates lay torn down on the roadway.

"They left."

"Left when? How?"

Another shrug.

"While ago. Trucks. Big, green bastards."

"Which way did they go?"

The man pushed himself up off the step awkwardly, like the way Shaun imagined a reanimated corpse would articulate, and Sugar shied away sideways a couple of steps. Shaun leaned down to pat her neck with his right hand automatically.

His spirit guide made a great show of looking up and down the street, squinting as if trying to see and remember at the same time, before he eventually pointed to the far side of the city where the ground rose steeply away from sea level.

"When?" Shaun asked, hoping the recollection would come with a figure attached.

Another happy shrug disappointed him, so he turned his attention back to the ruined entrance to the military installation.

"Much left in there?"

"Nope. What is, people's already claimed, id'n'it."

Shaun, surprisingly, knew exactly what the wavering man meant.

He gave another nod of thanks and touched his heels to Sugar's sides. He didn't need to kick the mare, because she was happy to move when she knew which direction he wanted. The lightest of steers with the reins angled her away from the city, taking them both back the way they had come to avoid moving through the concrete jungle and all the dangerous animals that might lay within.

As he rode, he tried to imagine the scene inside the docks.

Groups of people crowded around a pile of scavenged

supplies, protecting them day and night, and all the while looking for an opportunity to steal from the hoard of another group.

He imagined people fighting over useful items they found, and how groups with better weapons or superior numbers would roll over those unable to adequately defend their spoils.

Then he recalled that he was, deep down, a miserable bastard with no faith in humanity. On the whole, he had met more good people than bad, and of those bad the majority were opportunistic as opposed to outright sadistic. The world had not devolved into a Mad Max cliché overnight, despite his fears, and his cynicism almost made him pull on Sugar's reins and take him back down the hill and into the city where he could find other people and see if they wanted to come with him.

He stopped when he had turned her head, looking down at the city in darkness like it was a sight he had never seen before. It *was* a sight he had never seen before, and something about it was both beautiful and terrible in perfect synchronicity.

He heard it then. Heard the low drone of something that penetrated his consciousness and threw a single word at him.

Plane.

His eyes shot up, searching for the tell-tale blink of green and red on wingtips, but all he could make out was a fleeting image of a darker black moving among the almost moonless night.

Then the droning noise lessened until he could no longer hear it, but the sprawling city ahead and below him was transformed. It was turned from darkness and angular shapes into something else; something horrifying.

The dark streets, devoid of light and life with the absence

of electricity, blossomed into terrible flowers of orange, white and red.

The bombs fell systematically, almost as though a machine had planned where they would meet the ground, and Shaun stared open-mouthed at the callous destruction of the place he had called home for years.

Sugar whinnied in fear and threatened to bolt as the sound waves followed the distant, silent explosions. He held her tight, stopping her from running by pulling her chin down to her chest, as he continued to stare at his home being laid to waste.

Something final snapped inside him then. Some switch tripped, because up until that point he held onto a hope that the world might return to the state he knew one day soon. The power might come back on. The cars could be fixed, the electronics replaced, and soon their normal existence – the existence that he had so hated – could resume.

He told himself that when that day came, he would live his life, not spend it sullenly looking at others and envying them their possessions. Instead, he would celebrate each day with what he had.

Only that would never happen now because the lights going out was just the beginning.

END

Follow the survivors in LIGHTS OUT 2: After The Noise

If you enjoyed this, be sure to rate and review. Every review helps readers find new books and helps authors like me create them.

Consider joining me on Facebook and Instagram, and sign up for my newsletter at www.devoncford.com
I won't spam you, but I'll let you know whenever anything new or discounted comes out.

ALSO BY DEVON C. FORD

After It Happened

Post-Apocalyptic (UK)

Wasteland

Post-Apocalyptic

Defiance

Dystopian

Rise (with Nathan Hystad)

Post-Apocalyptic Alien Invasion

Toy Soldiers

1980s UK zombie apocalypse

Tranquility (with Josh Hayes)

Military science fiction

Territory Wars

Military science fiction

The Expansion

Military science fiction

New Earth (with Chris Harris)

Post-apocalyptic/extinction-level-event

Coming soon:

Commune 5:

The Battle for DC (with Joshua Gayou)

Commune: season 2 trilogy

Printed in Great Britain
by Amazon

78029909R00222